D0057078

NO LONGER PROPERTY OF
THE SEATTLE PUBLIC LIBRARY

ALSO BY DAVID HAGBERG

*Kirk McGarvey adventure
+Kirk McGarvey ebook original novellas
‡Edgar Allan Poe Award nominee
§American Book Award nominee

GAMBIT

DAVID HAGBERG

A TOM DOHERTY ASSOCIATES BOOK
NEW YORK

This is a work of fiction. All of the characters, organizations, and events portrayed
in this novel are either products of the author's imagination
or are used fictitiously.

GAMBIT

Copyright © 2021 by Kevin Hagberg

All rights reserved.

A Forge Book
Published by Tom Doherty Associates
120 Broadway
New York, NY 10271

www.tor-forge.com

Forge® is a registered trademark of Macmillan Publishing Group, LLC.

The Library of Congress Cataloging-in-Publication Data is available upon request.

ISBN 978-0-7653-9423-1 (hardcover)
ISBN 978-0-7653-9424-8 (ebook)

Our books may be purchased in bulk for promotional, educational, or business use.
Please contact your local bookseller or the Macmillan Corporate and Premium
Sales Department at 1-800-221-7945, extension 5442, or by email at
MacmillanSpecialMarkets@macmillan.com.

First Edition: April 2021

Printed in the United States of America

0 9 8 7 6 5 4 3 2 1

FOR LORREL, AS ALWAYS
AND FOR MY BEST FRIENDS IN ALL THE WORLD:
MY LONGTIME PUBLISHER, TOM DOHERTY,
AND HIS WIFE, TANYA. MY EDITOR, BOB GLEASON,
AND MY AGENT, HIS WIFE, SUSAN GLEASON.
I LOVE YOU ALL!

My apologies to the city of Georgetown.
I switched a few details to suit the flow of my tale.
No disrespect was intended.

GAMBIT: A maneuver in which a player seeks to gain an advantage by sacrificing one or more pieces.

PART
ONE

Opening Moves

*Can one man, no matter how good,
stand up to unlimited resources
against him?*

□

Leonard Slatkin had never worked through an expediter in his three years in the business, nor had he ever been paid $500,000 for the assassination of a single individual.

Although the intelligence he'd been given was spot-on, it had taken him nearly two weeks to arrange for the second-floor apartment in Georgetown, and another ten days of nearly around-the-clock surveillance of the windows in the third-floor apartment slightly kitty-corner across the street and the front door to the brownstone before he was sure that he would have a clear shot.

He came and went at normal times, in a business suit, an attaché case in hand, walking to the end of the block, and taking a bus into Washington, where he spent most of his days in Union Station working on his iPhone to gather as much information on his subject as he could. He was of medium height and build, with a totally unremarkable face and outward attitude.

By the second day, he had begun to wonder if a half a million was too small a sum. Too little by a very substantial margin. But he had no idea of the name of his primary employer, nor did he have access to the expediter. He was on his own.

Sitting in the dark now at the window in his apartment, the ordinary .223-caliber M16 military assault rifle resting on a tripod well enough inside the living room to be invisible to anyone outside, he waited patiently, just as he had the past three days since his preparations had been completed for Kirk McGarvey to return from Florida at the start of spring break and show himself at his window, five hundred feet away as the bullet flies.

The late afternoon was as bittersweet for Kirk McGarvey as it was for his wife, Pete. They hadn't talked much on the flight to Dulles from Sarasota, where he taught Voltaire at New College for one dollar per year. His passion had always been philosophy, but his life had been the CIA since he'd been in his midtwenties right out of the air force.

"Hard to believe," Pete said as they headed toward the ground transportation exit.

She was much shorter that McGarvey's six feet, and slightly built next to him. But she was voluptuous with a movie star's physique, and pretty oval face, with wide eyes and a mouth like Julia Roberts's—a little too large—but her ready smile making her perfect.

"That Otto's happy?" McGarvey asked.

"That Louise is gone."

It was all about history. After the air force when McGarvey had worked as an investigator for the OSI, he had been recruited by the CIA, where, after an extensive series of psychological examinations, he had been placed in the Company's black ops division—a unit that never existed on paper.

And he was good, a natural-born killer—an *operator*, in the parlance. After a couple of field runs, mostly as a bagman bringing operational funds into a badland, he'd been assigned his first kill in Chile, where he took down a general who had been responsible for the deaths of hundreds of innocent men and women.

He'd been married by then, and his wife objected to his too-often unexplained absences. After the Chilean op, she had given him the ultimatum: her or the Company. Psychologically battered by what he had just gone through, he chose neither. Instead, he quit the CIA and his wife and went to ground in Switzerland until, a couple of years later, the Company came looking for him with a new assignment, a thing that had to be done extrajudicially. The CIA had to be held blameless if the operation went bad. At all costs, Washington had to be kept completely out of the mix. The only fall guy would be McGarvey.

And at the time, he had become so irascible in his self-imposed isolation that he had practically jumped at the chance.

So it had begun, one impossible assignment after another, stretching back more years than he wanted to remember. Now at fifty, he wanted to step off the merry-go-round at last. He'd endured too many losses over the years— every woman he'd ever loved, including his first wife and their daughter— had been killed because of who he was.

Friends dead, isolation for long stretches, a kidney lost, bullet wounds, skin grafts on his back from a car bomb meant to kill him that had taken his left leg from below the knee.

Yet he was still in superb physical condition, some of it because of the luck of the genetic draw, but in a large measure because he willed it. He ran and swam nearly every day. Several times a year, he spent a few days to a week at the Company's training facility—the Farm—south of Washington along the York River, where he pushed himself to the limits. And never did he let himself merely laze away a weekend, not even a day.

"Sometimes you're like a monk in a monastery," more than one woman had told him. "Ease up a little."

His stock answer had always been: "I don't know how." The real answer was that his life had very often depended upon keeping sharp.

And now there was Pete, and he was just as afraid for her safety has he had been for the other women in his life, although she was herself a highly trained and very capable field officer who had more than once fought at his side and had even saved his life. They had become partners in every sense of the word. Able to read each other, able to sense each other's moods, anticipate each other's moves.

They'd brought only carry-on bags with them, so they had no need to wait for the luggage carousel. Outside, they got into the taxi queue. Pete was going directly out to Otto's McLean house, where Mary Sullivan was waiting for her, and Mac was going to their Georgetown apartment.

It was Thursday, and Otto and Mary were getting married in a civil ceremony at the house tomorrow morning, with only Mac and Pete and Mac's three-year-old granddaughter, Audrey, who had been adopted by Otto and his late wife, Louise, after Mac's daughter and her husband—both CIA employees—had been assassinated.

"Memories," Pete said. "Sometimes I think that's all we'll ever be left with."

"All anyone's ever left with," McGarvey said a little too sharply. He'd been feeling on edge for the past couple of days, even a little morose at times. Yet he couldn't believe that it was because his only true friend in the world had fallen in love and was getting married so soon after his wife's murder.

Pete looked up in surprise. "Nothing stays the same, that it?"

"I don't know."

"But everyone's happy."

Out of old ingrained habits, Mac watched an airport cop talking to a driver who'd pulled up in a dark green Tahoe in a no-parking zone. A windowless van passed slowly, and one hundred feet away across the several lanes of traffic, a man carrying a duffel bag was waiting at a crosswalk. In the farther distance was the possible glint of sunlight on a lens of what could have been a sniper scope.

Pete touched his shoulder. "What is it, Kirk?"

"I don't know."

She followed his gaze. "Okay, you have my attention, sweetheart. Is this one of your premos?"

Mac's premonitions—premos, as Otto called them—were feelings almost at the subliminal level that he'd developed over the past years as a defense mechanism. Something he'd picked up in a daily report, something he'd read in a newspaper or heard on television or online, some disconnected bits and pieces here and there that somehow made patterns inside his head, brought his awareness almost to the preternatural level. Hunches, they were sometimes called. Feelings. Inklings. Notions. Intuitions. Premos.

He turned to her, smiled, and shook his head. "Just putting myself in Otto's shoes. He sounded nervous yesterday on the phone."

"This is me you're talking to," Pete said. "Something coming our way?"

"Otto's darlings have been clear all last week."

"That's not what I asked."

Otto Rencke was the CIA's ranking computer expert. His darlings were a set of advanced programs that mined billions of data sources looking for anomalies—bits and pieces that didn't seem to belong. Things that more often than not led to nothing. But every now and then, something buried deep rose a little above the background noise and fit with perhaps a half dozen or more other anomalies to mean something.

"I don't know," Mac said, because he didn't.

McGarvey had the cabby drop him off at the corner of Dumbarton Avenue NW where it dead-ended at Rock Creek Park a half block from his apartment. It was a Thursday, and Otto had said that he was going to work, leaving Mary and Pete to work out the last-minute arrangements for tomorrow's wedding.

"Cold feet?" Mac had asked him last night on the phone.

"You're damned right. But second thoughts? No way."

The late-afternoon traffic was light even on the parkway along the creek behind him, and standing alone with his bag in hand as the cab drove away, he listened to the sounds of a siren a long ways off back toward the city. Somewhere closer, a horn beeped once, and church bells rang from the university campus. Normal sounds. But nothing felt normal to him, and he didn't know why except that he was spooked.

Neither he nor Pete had brought firearms with them on the flight. They had weapons in the apartment, but there hadn't seemed to be the need just now to carry. They were coming for the weekend, a wedding, nothing more.

Nothing moved on his street. He stood for just a moment, then turned and went around the barrier and made his way down the shallow grassy slope toward the parkway, on the other side of which was the creek, holding up by a tree ten feet from the rail.

He phoned Otto, who answered on the first ring, out of breath as he often got when he was excited. The man was a genius with all the oddities and complexities that went with that level of intelligence.

"Oh, wow, Pete just called, worried about you."

"What'd she say?"

"Wanted to know what my darlings were up to. And I told her plenty, but nothing bearing down on us. Anyway, I'm the one who's supposed to be getting nervous, not you."

"How's Mary?"

"I don't know what I'd do without her," Otto said, stumbling just a little over the last two words. "I'll always love Lou; don't ever think I won't. But she's gone, and Mary's here."

Tall, gangly Louise Horn, all arms and legs akimbo, narrow, angular face, and a million-watt smile, had come over to the CIA from the National Security Agency, where she'd been a chief satellite product analyst. From the moment she and Otto had met and begun working together, it was as if they'd always been a couple; almost clones of each other.

As a long-term bachelor, Otto had been a slob; his clothes usually a mess, his long, red, out-of-control hair reminiscent of an Einstein, his sneakers unlaced, his sweatshirts and ball caps with the logos of the old KGB or CCCP, dirty. His only real vice—not alcohol—were Twinkies and heavy cream or half-and-half, which he never seemed to be without. As a result, he'd been overweight and out of shape for most of his life.

Lou had changed all of that. And the people in the intel community in and around Washington who'd always been afraid of his genius coming unglued and sending just about every mainframe inside and out of the beltway crashing down around their ears had breathed a collective sigh of relief.

When she had been shot to death during an assignment last year that had gone bad, Otto's world had come crashing down around him. Pete had been with her and had taken her death very hard, blaming herself for not preventing it. Not doing something.

"Not throwing yourself in front of the bullet?" Mac had asked her at one point.

"Something like that," she admitted, scarcely able to choke out the words.

And then Mary had come into their lives. She was an IT genius in her own right, in some ways even smarter than Otto with a higher IQ but without the oddities. She could have been a middle-grade schoolteacher in a small midwestern town; quiet, even meek. But when she spoke, softly, everyone listened, because what she had to say was always brilliant and spot-on.

For the past eight years, she had been considered the ranking genius in what had been the Company's Directorate of Science and Technology, so when she and Otto had found each other, no one was the least bit surprised. Lou had reined him in; now it was Mary's turn.

"What's got your dander?" Otto asked. "Someone on your six?"

"Probably not. Just a feeling."

"A premo?"

"Not that much," McGarvey said, glancing over his shoulder up Dumbarton as a cab turned the corner and passed his apartment building.

"But?"

McGarvey shook himself out of his funk. "Where you going on your honeymoon?"

"Honeymoon?" Otto asked after a brief hesitation, and Mac had to laugh.

Slatkin had been a loner all of his life, which had been a plus point when he had applied out of the South African Air Force Intelligence Division for a position with the Special Forces Brigade, known informally as the Recces.

The small, tightly knit counterinsurgency unit had seen combat in Rhodesia, Mozambique, and along their own border. Slatkin had been extensively trained in everything from weapons and explosives to infiltration, exfiltration, and especially hand-to-hand combat and was assigned to the Fifth Special Forces Regiment based at Phalaborwa in northern Limpopo. His specific assignment was as an assassin, a job at which he excelled, especially when he was given a target and was left to his own devices. All he'd ever required was intel. He took care of the rest.

His one weakness was money. He'd been born and raised poor in the white slums of Jo'burg, and within three years of joining the Recces and after four successful hits, he'd resigned and had gone freelance.

He'd never regretted the decision, because he was good and he knew it.

One of his burner phones buzzed, and he answered it. "Yes."

"Your subject is one hundred fifty meters away."

"What is he doing?"

"Watching traffic on the parkway. He may suspect something."

A specialty of Slatkin's had been reading people from their voices. Their inflections, the stress levels, the hesitations, the oftentimes outright lies or exaggerations. Most people in the hiring side of the murder-for-hire business were terrible actors. They were the moneymen accustomed to never being questioned.

But this man, an American, was a puzzle. He wasn't money, but he spoke for it. A lieutenant who had connections. Maybe an ex-cop. But he had good sources of information.

"Is he armed?"

"We don't think so."

"Is his woman with him?"

"He's alone."

"Is he aware that he is being watched?"

The man hesitated for just a fraction.

"Do not lie to me," Slatkin broke in.

"It's possible."

"Possible or likely?"

"Likely."

"Thank you."

"What will you do?"

Slatkin thought the question was odd. "Watch for him."

"And then?"

"What I was hired to do."

The man did not reply.

Slatkin switched off the phone and took out the battery and SIM card and laid them aside.

He checked the sight picture in the M16's scope, steady on the third-floor living room window across the street. Then, without taking his eyes off the street below, unholstered his Glock 23 compact pistol, checked the load and action against the possibility that the situation this afternoon would devolve into a close-quarters combat op, and laid it on a side table close at hand.

TWO

□

Otto's house in McLean was a two-story colonial near the end of a cul-de-sac in a neighborhood of similar single-family dwellings. He had mostly kept to himself, so he'd never gotten to know his neighbors, though they used to wave whenever he drove by.

Until last year when there had been a brief incident of gun violence that had been officially listed as a random shooting. Now the neighbors didn't wave so often.

Mary's blue Honda Civic was parked in the driveway when Pete's cab dropped her off. She paid the fare and walked up to the door.

"Good morning, Pete," Lou's AI-constructed voice from one of Otto's darlings came from midair about face level.

It was always startling. "Good morning," Pete said.

The door opened. "Otto and Mary are in the kitchen."

Pete wēnt inside, put her overnight bag down, and walked straight back to the kitchen, where Mary—all five feet two of her—was cooking something at the stove, and Otto was sitting at the counter speaking softly as if to himself, a bottle of Dom Pérignon in an ice bucket beside him, an empty flute next to it.

Mary turned around and smiled. "Just champers for now," she said. "Good flight?"

"Not bad."

"Linguine with white clam sauce, and some Dungeness crab legs. Okay?"

"Perfect," Pete said. She sat down and poured a glass of Dom.

Otto picked up his flute without missing a beat, and they clinked glasses.

"What's he working on?" Pete asked.

"Whenever your hubby gets a premo, Otto goes into high gear," Mary said over her shoulder. She gave a little deprecating shrug, which had become her signature gesture whenever she didn't have any real answer.

"Has he gotten anything?"

"Nada," Otto said. "Lots of crap going down all over the place, as usual, but nothing that would directly affect Mac."

It was good news. "Is he at the apartment?"

"He had the cab drop him off at the end of the street."

Pete knew exactly what he was thinking. It was one of the lessons the recruits at the Farm were given. "It's almost always better to be safe than sorry."

Almost always one of the trainees at the CIA's boot camp made some quip to the effect that they were in the wrong business to think about staying safe. And no one offered an argument.

Slatkin's hobby when he had been a kid in Jo'burg was magic. He'd begun when he was six by putting on shows for his parents, grandmother, and two cousins, who all lived in the one-bedroom shack of a house just down from the prison complex on Constitution Hill.

Later, when he'd perfected some of his sleight of hand illusions, he put on shows during assemblies at school. And he'd become quite good. Plus, the talent had stuck with him.

Let them see the truth but direct their attention to something else.

He checked the sight picture through the assault rifle scope again; it was never wrong to recheck everything as often as possible. Perfection was the difference between success and failure. The target reticle was centered on the window across the street at about the height of a man's chest.

McGarvey would approach his apartment building with caution because something had evidently spooked him. Or he would turn away and possibly alert the authorities. But alert them to what?

Slatkin got up and went to his attaché case lying on the table in front of the couch and took out a roll of plastic tape, three inches wide, along with a glass cutter and suction cup on a short handle.

These he took back to the window, where he laid the tape on the sill and, first checking to make sure that no one was out on the street, attached the suction cup to the window at the spot directly in line with the muzzle of the M16 and cut out a piece of glass two inches tall and as wide.

Quickly laying the glass aside, he pulled off a piece of clear tape and covered the opening.

From outside, especially at the distance from the street and from the front entrance to McGarvey's building, the plastic covering the hole in the window would be all but invisible. You looked up and saw a window, nothing more.

Settling down in the chair, he put his eye to the scope. He could not detect the plastic tape. But now, the bullet would not have to pass through glass, which could possibly—though not likely—deflect its path, making it necessary to fire a second shot.

A bit of sleight of hand to nudge up the accuracy.

Slatkin had considered all the options almost from the beginning of the assignment and especially when he had delved into McGarvey's background.

McGarvey's phone vibrated in his jacket pocket. It was Otto.

"Are you still in place?"

"There's nothing here. I'm getting set to go in. Has Pete showed up?"

"Yeah. You want to talk to her? She's sitting right next to me."

"No."

"My darlings are showing nothing. No tints."

Otto's programs, which displayed results on whatever monitor he was using, would change color depending on immediate threats. Lavender was the worst. No color meant nothing imminent was about to come down around them.

"Okay."

"Kirk," Pete broke in. "Make a one-eighty and take a cab back here. I'll call Housekeeping to make a sweep of the neighborhood."

Housekeeping was the general term for the CIA's off-campus security teams. Sometimes they were sent out to sanitize a shot-up or damaged scene of a battle, something at which they were especially good. At other times, they would consist of a team of three or four operators, who would go into a locale to check for threats. They might come as plumbers or air-conditioning specialists, or sometimes as deliverymen—FedEx, USPS, a florist.

The point of the teams was not only to ensure the safety of a principal operator if need be but to keep an incident or possible incident out of the hands of local law enforcement.

"Not yet," Mac said. "I'm going to drop my bag off and get a few things at the apartment and I'll come over. I thought you and Mary were working on the wedding details."

"They have it covered."

"Anyway, Otto's cooperating for a change," Mary said. "We're doing it here tomorrow. Our chaplain is coming over at nine."

"Audie?"

"We sent her down to the Farm for a day or two," Mary said.

The Farm was the CIA training facility outside of Williamsburg, where they sent her if trouble was brewing.

"So grab your things and get over here. I bought four bottles of champers, and we need some help dealing with it."

"And watch your ass," Pete added.

McGarvey walked back up to where Dumbarton dead-ended just past Twenty-Seventh Street NW, where he waited for a light gray Caddy SUV just passing his apartment to turn right, and then he went across.

It was a weekday, so most people who lived here were at work, and the street was almost empty of parked cars. By long-ingrained habit, he scanned the cars that were at the curbs out of the corner of his eye, looking for something, anything that seemed out of the ordinary—the rooftops and windows of all the buildings, especially those across the street from his apartment.

But there was nothing. And he felt as if he should settle down. Nothing at the airport. Nothing on the way in. Nothing here on the street.

Yet every one of his senses was jangling as if he had been connected to a sharp electrical current.

THREE

□

Slatkin instinctively sat back when he spotted McGarvey walking up the street as if he hadn't a care in the world, looking neither left nor right, just straight ahead. Yet he had gotten out of the cab at the end of the street and had waited for something, or someone.

The expediter had promised an eye in the sky, which Slatkin had taken to mean a directable surveillance camera on the roof of one of the buildings in the neighborhood. In the past several days, he had spotted three possibilities, but it had been more than sufficient that his contact had had real-time intel from the beginning.

Using a second burner phone, he called the contact number, which was answered on the first ring as usual. "Yes."

"He just showed up."

"Has he spotted you?"

"No."

"Wait for your shot."

"Of course. Otherwise, the police would arrive possibly too quickly for me to get clear. I will wait as planned for him to appear at his window. The shot will be silenced, and it will be thirty minutes or more before his wife or friends become concerned."

"There will be no second payment for failure."

"Naturally. Have you been able to crack the encryption algorithm on his phone?"

"Unfortunately not, but we're keeping clear for the time being."

"Why?" Slatkin demanded. "The intelligence could be extremely helpful."

"It would appear to be the work of the CIA," the expediter said. "Can you do this simple job for us?"

McGarvey had reached his building, and he was unlocking the lobby door.

The possibility that the man's telephone was equipped with an encryption program designed by the CIA came as no real surprise. At one time, he had been the director of the Company, and his best friend was the leading computer expert on the planet.

One good circumstance had come as a pleasant surprise. McGarvey and his wife had left Dulles in separate cabs. The assignment was to assassinate only McGarvey. The man's wife was a highly trained and well-experienced intelligence operator in her own right. Taking her out at the same time as her husband would have upped the difficulty by more than double.

"Of course I can," he said, and he hung up.

The lobby door was framed by two narrow strips of glass. McGarvey stood to one side and glanced out at the building across the street. As he had walked up the street, he had noticed something not right out of the corner of his eye. The reflections in the two windows of the third floor were not the same. One of them appeared to have a small flat spot about halfway up from the sill.

From this vantage point, however, he couldn't make out the difference. It had been noticeable only from the oblique angle down the street.

But he'd seen it, and he had a pretty fair idea what it might be.

His phone vibrated, and he answered it. "Yes."

"You're in," Otto said. "No one took a potshot at you?"

"Something's wrong with one of the windows in the third-floor apartment across the street. Might be nothing. But it could be something I've seen once before. I'm going to check it out."

"What something?" Pete asked.

"Could be a hole in the window with a piece of plastic covering it. Reflects the light differently than glass. Saw it in Mutoko when I was still in the air force. It was rumored that a Soviet military attack was going to take place during a meeting in one of the hotels. The Premier, maybe. Anyway, the shooter was stationed across the street. He cut a hole in his window and covered it with Saran Wrap so no one would notice it from the street. When he took the shot, the bullet's trajectory hadn't been degraded by going through glass."

"Got it," Otto said. "Colonel Vasili Didenko. He was there in secret to offer training to the South African Air Force. The rumor was that the shooter was a South African. Something internal."

"Someone didn't want Zimbabwe playing with the Russians," Mary said.

"The hit was a success, and the shooter was never found," Otto said. "But there's nothing here about a hole in the window."

"I was there with three other guys bird-dogging the meeting. It was one of those little odd bits that showed up as a one-liner in our after-action report. And it showed up again eight or nine years later in a training exercise at the Farm. It's the only reason I remember it now."

"So what the hell does some South African shooter want with you now?"

"I don't know, but I'm going to find out," McGarvey said.

"I had a feeling you were going to say that," Pete said. "I don't suppose you'd stay put until I get there?"

"It'll be over by then."

"I thought you'd say that, too. Keep your ass down, sweetheart."

The image of McGarvey's head at the narrow window beside the door appeared briefly in Slatkin's scope. His finger tightened on the trigger, but the American was gone.

After several moments, he re-aimed the rifle so that it was once again pointed at the left of the two third-story windows across the street, and he sat back.

Besides his magic, Slatkin was blessed with a much higher tolerance for conditions outside his control, which had always manifested itself in an extraordinary amount of patience. He could sit on point, waiting for a subject to appear in his sniper scope for hours without looking away.

He had no idea where that inner resolve had come from; it had been inside of him for as long as he could remember. In fact, he was often surprised when he learned that the subject he was facing wasn't also made of the same stuff.

But the question at hand now was McGarvey, no ordinary man by any account, and a highly competent and accomplished assassin in his own right. Why had the man looked through the lobby windows? If it was because he thought that an assassin had been waiting for him—and the record that Slatkin had dug up indicated that numerous attempts had been made on McGarvey's life—why had he walked up the street in plain view as if he hadn't a care in the world?

Everyone lived by a certain code or directive, which could be put down to mere habit. Each person did their unique thing.

What was McGarvey's? And what was the man up to?

Slatkin sat forward in his chair so that he could look through the scope. His thing now and always was perseverance.

McGarvey took the stairs up to the third floor two at a time, stopping at each landing to listen for anything out of the ordinary. But there was nothing. Everyone was at work or out of town.

He checked the lock at his door before he let himself in, but there was no evidence of tampering.

Just inside the living room, he moved toward the short corridor past the kitchenette, keeping well enough away from the two front windows so that he presented no clear shooting solution, only a very brief silhouette.

In the bedroom, he got his Walther PPK in the rare 9mm version, loaded a magazine in the handle, attached the suppressor onto the muzzle, and cycled a round into the firing chamber.

Stuffing the pistol into his belt at the small of his back beneath his jacket, he passed through the living room again, and downstairs, keeping well away from the door windows in the lobby, he went to the rear door into the narrow alley.

Maybe there was nothing to it. He thought there was, though he had no idea who would be gunning for him this time or why.

But he was going to find out.

FOUR

□

Pete, driving Mary's Honda, the Glock 24 pistol Otto had loaned her lying on the passenger seat, crossed the Key Bridge, weaving her way through traffic, not giving a damn if a cop got on her tail for speeding. She wouldn't mind leading the entire D.C. police force to Dumbarton. Someone was gunning for her husband, and she would take all the help she could get. Mac would be pissed, but she'd make it up to him.

Otto came on the phone. "He's not answering."

"Means he's busy," Pete said. "Leave him alone."

"Do you want me to pull the trigger?" Otto asked. Before Pete had stormed out of the house, he had composed an urgent all-stations message that a gun battle was about to go down in Georgetown. All that was needed was for him to hit the Send key.

"I want to see what the situation is. I'll let you know."

"Watch your own ass," Mary said.

"Will do," Pete said, making a very hard right onto busy M Street NW, just missing a brown UPS van.

Six blocks later, she headed north on Wisconsin Avenue, then right on Dumbarton a little more than four blocks to their apartment, traffic back here nonexistent for the moment.

She pulled over and parked in time to see Mac coming around the near corner from their place, crossing the street and keeping close to the buildings on the right side, head toward the middle of the block.

Keeping the pistol at her side, the muzzle pointed away from her leg, she started after him on foot.

Slatkin had caught only the brief glimpse of McGarvey in the lobby door window, and a fleeting shadow of the man in his apartment window, but then nothing else. And that had been nearly ten minutes ago. He was starting to worry.

He phoned his contact, but the number warbled, and a recorded announcement said that the number was no longer in service. He'd been cut loose for some reason.

How loose, though?

Using his iPhone, he brought up his Guernsey Island bank account and entered the ten-digit password. The last blind deposit of $250,000 that had been made twenty-five days ago was still in place, making his total available balance slightly more than $1.75 million. His expediter had not withdrawn the funds. The operation, despite the misgivings he'd shared with his contact, was still on. When it was finished and the second half of the payment was made he would be nearly halfway to the $5 million he figured he'd need to retire.

He looked up and leaned forward, his eye to the scope, but at that moment, a Mercedes passed, and he caught the reflection of a woman in the rear passenger window. She was on the sidewalk just below on this side of the street.

The woman was unknown to him, and yet she seemed familiar.

With the car gone, he could no longer see her. But her image nagged at him.

He pulled up the file stored on his laptop. Part of it had been sent to him from his expediter, but a large part of it he'd gleaned from his research over the past week or so. Scrolling through it, starting with McGarvey, then moving on to Otto Rencke and his now deceased wife, Louise Horn, he came to one of the later files, which showed two images of McGarvey's partner and his new wife, Pete Boylan.

Looking up from the two photographs—one of her coming out of the CIA's main gate in Langley—he was 100 percent certain that the woman whose reflection he'd seen in the window of the Mercedes was she.

And if she were here, downstairs, in front of the building, it could very easily mean that McGarvey was downstairs, too. Or perhaps even inside already.

Setting the computer aside, he detached the scope from the rifle, laid it on the table next to the phone and his pistol, then removed the rifle from its tripod and stepped into the relative shadows at the narrow hallway back to the bathroom and bedroom from where he had a perfect line of sight to anyone coming through the door.

He settled his nerves and reduced his thoughts from the past and the future into the here and now, willing to hold his position for however long it took.

McGarvey and his wife were coming, and he would kill them both.

McGarvey held up short on the second stair just below the third-floor landing and cocked his ear for a long moment to listen to the sounds of the building.

The lobby door had been opened and then immediately closed. He'd had heard the street noises, a horn somewhere off in the near distance, and maybe the slight breeze ruffling the trees in front.

He waited for one of the downstairs apartment doors to open, but someone started up the stairs, their footfalls very light as if they were trying for stealth.

The last thing he wanted was to involve an innocent civilian in a shoot-out, but he was caught between whoever was coming up the stairs and a possible shooter just down the hall on this floor.

He also didn't want to engage a shooter in a gun battle in which he didn't have the clear advantage. He had no real fear for himself, but if he were the target for an assassination, he wanted to take the hit man alive—wounded most likely, but still living—so that he could find out who the bastard was. Who had sent him.

His best guess right now would be the Russians for a couple of ops he'd done recently involving their people.

Whoever was coming up the stairs stopped on the second-floor landing, but then continued up.

Mac started down, keeping his pistol out of sight at his side.

The person below stopped.

Mac took one step more, and then he smelled a perfume that he recognized. Joy by Jean Patou. He had bought it for Pete when they were in Paris a couple of years ago just before they got married. It had become her favorite.

At the turn, he came face-to-face with Pete, who'd raised her pistol, and he put a finger to his lips.

He waited for a couple of beats for her to calm down, and then he went down the last steps to her. "What are you doing here?" he whispered.

"I wasn't going to let you have all the fun."

It was a typical Pete explanation, but it was too late now to send her away. "The front apartment, facing ours. Could be more than one, but I doubt it."

"What's the plan?"

"You're going to act as backstop. Anyone gets past me, take them down."

She started to object, but he held her off.

"I have no real idea who wants me or why, so I want to take whoever it is alive if possible."

"Not at the expense of your life, goddamnit."

Slatkin expected that it was the woman from outside—McGarvey's wife—who was on the stairs. He opened the door a crack. He thought he could hear her voice. It was possible that she was talking on the phone, because there was nothing to indicate that McGarvey himself knew something was wrong.

Evidently, his contact had been blown, which was why the man had not answered the last call. It could possibly mean that the cops were on the way here, or worse yet, a Housekeeping squad from Langley could be on the way.

But if he had to guess, he suspected that McGarvey himself was still across the street in his apartment.

Time to find out.

He eased the door open a little farther and slipped out into the corridor in sock feet, leading with the silenced M16 on full automatic.

FIVE

Otto had ignored the glass of champagne at his side for the past fifteen minutes, trying with no real results to come up with some new angles for his darlings to pursue. On the assumption that the shooter across from Mac's apartment was the South African who had, so far as they knew, used the trick of cutting a hole in a window and covering it with plastic, he'd gone looking for any other bits and pieces that would identify the man. That, of course, was assuming a shooter was in the apartment.

So far, his programs had come up with nearly half a dozen possibilities, three of them from the Special Forces Brigade, one of the others a cop, and the fifth a paratrooper who had been discharged for being intoxicated while on duty. In fact, he had been drunk doing a dangerous HALO—high altitude, low opening—parachute jump.

The cop was dead, the paratrooper was serving time in prison for statutory rape, but the three shooters from the Recces were still at large. The interesting part was that the three specialists were not wanted for any crime, though they were suspected of a number of assassinations—but none of them on South African soil. They were clean, because they were professionals.

Using those last-known identities, plus a broad list of assassinations anywhere in the world other than South Africa, he went looking at offshore bank accounts in Europe and the Caribbean, matching large deposits that bracketed dates before and after each hit. He couldn't come up with names, only the deposits.

One had come three weeks before the hit on the Russian in Zimbabwe, and the second half—if that's what it was—twenty-four hours after the Russian had been taken out.

Using the same bank account in Guernsey, he looked for other before-and-after payments that matched other assassinations. He came up with five that matched, plus one for $250,000 that had been made three weeks ago.

The date matched no assassination, because the hit had not been made yet. And Otto was convinced that the total of a half million was to take Mac down.

All he lacked now was the name of the South African shooter and from where the payment had originated.

Slatkin flattened himself against the wall a few feet from the stairs and held his breath to listen for voices or any other sounds from below. But the building was deathly still.

He held the M16 loosely in both hands, the muzzle of the suppressor pointed up toward the ceiling. Breathing deeply to calm himself, he was about to swivel on his heel while bringing the assault rifle to bear on anything that moved below, when he smelled a woman's perfume and held up.

Mary came around the counter and refreshed Otto's glass as she looked over his shoulder at the laptop screen. "What are you into?"

"I'm trying to match the dates of assassinations worldwide with before-and-after payments made to a dozen different Swiss and offshore accounts. I came up with one set of payments to a bank in Guernsey, the last one made three weeks ago, but it's still open."

"No second payment?"

"Right," Otto said.

"Who's the shooter? Mac's South African?"

"It's possible, but I'm not sure yet."

"No name yet?"

"No."

"Because you can't gain access to the account details, only the raw income stream," Mary said. "And in the meantime, Pete and Mac are in harm's way right now, or on the verge of it."

Otto looked up. "What are you thinking?"

"This guy's got to be on someone's radar."

"Yeah?"

"You've been concentrating on income to that account. How about expenditures? What's he spending his money on?"

"And how much does he have?" Otto said.

"My guess is that he's building himself a nest egg so that he can retire. The question is where."

"He already knows where," Otto said, excited now.

"Right, and he's made a down payment on his little beach hut in the sun," Mary said. "But Mac and Pete might be able to use some help right now."

"I'm on it."

Pete stood next to Mac and one stair tread down, her pistol pointed past him toward the head of the stairs.

Mac leaned down to her so that he could whisper in her ear. "Start downstairs when I nod, and make some noise."

She looked skeptically at him.

"I want to draw him out."

Pete's phone vibrated, and Mary came on the speakerphone.

"Your shooter is South African. The Recces. He's the one who took out the

Russian military attaché in Mutoko. The same window glass trick Mac spotted. Thing is, we have his Guernsey account, which he's stocking to finance his retirement. And he's already paid a hundred thousand down on a beachfront condo in Saint Martin—the Dutch side."

McGarvey pointed a finger at his chest and shook his head, then crouched down and raised his pistol in a two-hand grip aimed at the head of the stairs.

"Do you have a name?" Pete asked.

"We're working on it. Otto's into the Fifth Special Forces Regiment database now. We have him narrowed down to one of three Recces operators."

"Okay, no need for a shoot-out at the O.K. Corral. Mac's watching from our apartment, I'm going over there now to let him know what we've got. Maybe we can talk this guy down. Find out who financed him this time. We might be able to make some sort of a deal."

"Watch your back," Otto came on. "This guy probably has no stomach for a face-to-face match. He'll want to shoot you from behind. He's a fucking coward. All of his stripe are."

Slatkin was doing his best to control his rage. The bloody bastards knew! And at this point, he no longer had the backup of his contact. Everything he had worked for: the risks he had taken; the isolation from the few comrades-in-arms whom he had considered his friends; the one girl he had fallen in love with, and who he had planned on looking up once he was settled on Saint Martin, were gone. All of it.

He no longer had patience.

His only option now was to kill the woman and hunt down the man so that he could get his final payment and go to ground somewhere else.

But if they had somehow gotten to his Guernsey account, it was possible they could seize it, and everything would be gone.

He heard the woman on the stairs, and he swiveled around, bringing the assault rifle to bear when McGarvey was there.

Before he could pull the trigger, McGarvey fired and kept firing.

The first two shots hit Slatkin in his right knee and hip, sending him backward off-balance. By reflex alone, he fired a long burst, but the muzzle was pointed upward, the bullets plowing into the plaster ceiling.

The next shot hit his groin, spiraling upward into his abdomen with an incredible burst of pain, and his lights went out, his last conscious thought about Elena.

SIX

☐

Thomas Bell, who was Slatkin's contact for the entire project, called the Hay-Adams room service and had a bottle of Dom Pérignon and four ounces of beluga caviar delivered to his room, posthaste. He was in a mood to celebrate.

If all had gone as expected, he would be flying to Athens this evening, top shelf, of course, on his mysterious employer's nickel to set up the second stage of THE OP, as he had come to think of it, in all-capital letters.

Until two months ago, he had been the number-two manager of the Palais d'Amour, the newest, most luxurious of all the casinos in Las Vegas. His specialty was making things happen for the high rollers. Women, of course, but also accommodations, transportation day or night to or from anyplace on the planet, private parties, food, drink, anything, even the outrageous—such as a trained female llama to room 2127 last year.

He'd never known his father, but his doting mother had been the madame of an upscale bordello in the Hamptons, and from her, he had learned the art of immediate and unquestioning service.

His champagne and caviar came. After he'd tipped the waiter, he phoned his contact, a woman with a sexy French accent. It sounded as if a party were in full swing in the background.

"Oui?"

"It's done."

"The outcome was as we'd hoped?"

"McGarvey entered the building first, and his wife came a few minutes later. Her being there was an unexpected bonus. Two for one. Considering the firepower Leonard had and the fact he was on high ground, they never had a chance."

"It's not exactly how we wanted it, but it'll do," the woman said.

Something about her voice was familiar, but Bell had nailed her attitude from the first time they'd talked. She was ultrarich and accustomed to getting exactly what she wanted, when she wanted it. He knew the type. But he also expected that she was just an intermediary like him.

"I'll play it closer to the scenario that you ordered the next time," he said.

"Yes, you will," she said, and she rang off.

Bell sat back and considered if he should turn on his monitor to see if the police had arrived on scene yet, but he decided against it.

. . .

McGarvey had looked through the unconscious man's pockets, finding only a hundred dollars in American bills, a wallet with a New York driver's license in the name of Leonard Sampson, and nothing else.

Inside the apartment, he was examining the piece of clear plastic covering the opening in the window when the four men got out of the van.

"Incoming," Pete called from the corridor.

He went to the doorway. "Housekeeping?" he called down as the four started up.

"Blakely and my crew, Mr. Director," a man replied.

"Come."

Pete holstered her pistol as Blakely appeared.

McGarvey remembered him. "Bill, you guys got the jump on this situation."

"Yes, sir, Mr. Rencke gave us the heads-up, told us what to expect." Blakely bent over the body and placed two fingers on the right-side carotid artery for a couple of moments, then spoke into a lapel mic. "Unit one. Need an ambulance stat, this location."

"I thought he was dead," McGarvey said.

Blakely looked up. "Almost, but not quite. I think you'll have a couple of questions for him if we can bring him around."

The other three came up the stairs and assessed the situation.

"Is there anything else, Mr. Director?" Blakely asked.

"No."

"Then we'll get to it. Have this place right as rain in thirty minutes. Easier that no one was in the building."

McGarvey and Pete went across the street to their apartment, and as she got a couple of beers from the fridge, Mac stood at the windows, staring across at the other building.

He had no idea why he had expected someone was coming after him, but now that the man had been taken out, he felt no relief. In fact, he was beginning to get the notion that today had been just the opening move.

"Penny," Pete said, bringing his beer.

"It's not over."

"He's dead, or damned near. It's over."

"Just the start."

"Okay, you have my attention, Mac. What's eating you?"

"Otto's darlings have come up with nothing, yet here the bastard was. He knew where we lived, he knew we were out of town and when we were coming back."

"That's a stretch."

"He wasn't camped out. No food in the fridge. No dirty dishes. The bed hadn't been slept in. Towels in the bathroom clean, none in the hamper. He got there this morning and waited for me to show up. He had eyes on our place."

"One of the rooftop surveillance cameras. His, or an assistant's?"

"I got his iPhone. Otto will probably find at least some of the answers."

"But?" Pete asked.

"Takes money. If he turns out to be the South African contractor Otto thinks he is, whoever hired him has deep pockets."

"So who hired him? The Russians?"

"Right now, I'm more interested in the why," McGarvey said.

Otto plugged Slatkin's iPhone into his laptop. It had shut down automatically at some point, but one of his programs got past that switch and into the phone's memory.

"We're in," he said when the phone's screen died. "Shit."

"What?" Mary asked at his side.

A couple of line fragments, bits of code, appeared briefly on the laptop and then disappeared. Otto sat back and after a moment looked up at his wife-to-be. "The damned thing's been erased. And it wasn't a civilian program."

"No," Mary said. "But it doesn't necessarily mean this was a government assassination operation."

"What then?" Pete asked.

"Either someone with connections or with a lot of money," McGarvey said. They were gathered back in McLean at Otto's safe house.

"Or both," Mary said.

"Lou, let's start a search following the parameters just now discussed."

"The obvious start point would be the SVR or GRU," Lou's AI voice said out of thin air just across the counter from them.

Mary started to say something, but McGarvey interrupted.

"Maybe not the Russians," he said.

Everyone turned to him. "Who, then?" Mary asked.

"The Pentagon first, and then the White House."

□

SEVEN

Slatkin had been taken to All Saints, the small, state-of-the-art-equipped private hospital that catered exclusively to wounded intelligence agents and in some cases high-value individuals.

It was two in the morning when Dr. Alan Franklin, the chief medico for the three-story unit located in Georgetown just a few blocks from the Mc-Garveys' apartment, came out of the newly remodeled operating room on the third floor and down the hall to the waiting room where Mac and Pete were waiting.

"He needs a new kidney and liver."

"How long does he have without?" McGarvey asked.

"I've stopped the bleeding, but I'd give him only hours, unless you tell me you need more time."

"Is he awake?"

"Quite frankly, he'll probably die before the anesthetic fully wears off."

"Can you give him something?"

"For the pain?" Franklin asked. "He's not feeling anything."

"I meant to wake him up. He came here to assassinate me. I want to know who hired him and why."

Franklin looked away. "When I raised my hand and recited the oath, it was to save lives, not take them."

"Mine was the same," McGarvey said. "Only it was to protect innocent lives, American lives."

"Yes, I know. But that very often has entailed taking lives," Franklin said. He nodded toward the doors to the operating room down the hall. "Like that poor bastard's, who I could save given the go-ahead."

"Then what?" Pete asked, a bleak note in her eyes and voice.

"Put him and whoever hired him on trial for attempted murder. It's the way we're supposed to do things in this country."

"He wasn't going to give Mac a trial."

"I'm not an idiot. I know how things work. And I've patched up your husband more than once."

"And me," Pete said. "But what if it was the Russian government who hired him?"

"Then we turn it over to the diplomats."

McGarvey shook his head. "We need to talk to him, Doc. Wake him up."

Franklin nodded, a heavy look in his eyes. "This guy was just the start, is that what you're telling me?"

"It's one of the things we want to ask him," McGarvey said.

"Ten minutes," Franklin said. He turned to go, but Pete stopped him.

"What will you use?" she asked.

"Midazolam."

"Try flunitrazepam."

"Could cause a heart arrhythmia. Possibly fatal."

Pete said nothing.

"Ten minutes," McGarvey said.

Slatkin had been wheeled into the adjacent recovery room where he lay on a gurney, a blanket up to his chest. He was hooked to several monitors, including one for his heart that showed a steady but weak rhythm, plus oxygen and an IV bottle.

Helen Berliner, one of the nurses who had taken care of both Mac and Pete on more than one occasion, was there when they came in. "Doctor says I can stay with you if you need me."

"No reason for you to get your hands dirty," McGarvey said.

She glanced at the patient. "It was another close call for you, wasn't it, Mr. Director?"

"He's lying there this time, not one of us, Helen."

"Just as well. I'll be right outside if you need me."

"When will he come around?" Pete asked.

Helen looked at Slatkin. "He's awake now," she said, and she left.

"I'll go first," Pete said. She went to the bed and gently caressed the South African's pale cheek with her fingertips.

Slatkin's eyes opened.

"You've been shot, and you're in a hospital now. Do you understand me?"

The lights in the room were not so bright that he couldn't see McGarvey just behind Pete. His eyes widened slightly, but then focused again on Pete. "Yes," he croaked, his voice very weak and ragged.

"We found your account in Guernsey; we know about the payment of $250,000. What we don't know yet is who made the payment. Will you tell me?"

Slatkin said nothing.

"You need a new kidney, and your liver has been damaged. But the doctor believes that he can save your life."

"Why?"

"Because that's what doctors do."

"I mean, why bother," Slatkin said. He looked past her at McGarvey. "I missed. And if I walked out of here, your husband would find me and kill me. It's the way he's always worked."

"You read the wrong files, or you didn't pay attention to what you were looking at. When he's shot at, he shoots back."

"Everyone who's come up against him has died."

"He's a very good shot. Maybe you'll be the exception. Help us and we'll help you. You have my word."

"Why should I believe you?"

"No reason, except you'll die without us."

Slatkin managed a weak smile. "I'd die anyway. My expediter would make sure of it. We only talked once, but I could hear it in her voice. She has more money than God, and she's always gotten what she wants."

McGarvey held his silence. It was the first decent clue they'd come up with.

"That what they taught you at the Recces?" Pete asked.

"Bitch," Slatkin said, and he turned his head away.

"We can protect you if you'll help us. Whoever your expediter is, she doesn't have more money than we do."

"When's the last time you met her?" McGarvey asked.

"Never did."

"Then how do you know she's a woman? And rich?"

"My contact made a mistake."

"Tell me about it," Pete said.

"That's all I know."

"What's your name?"

"Leonard."

"Sampson?" Pete asked.

"Slatkin."

"Why did you leave the Recces?"

"I fucked an officer's daughter."

"Why didn't they put you in jail?"

"It wasn't rape," Slatkin said. "She was twenty. A bitch, like all of you." He suddenly tore at the oxygen tube and IV and managed to raise himself up to a sitting position and reached for Pete.

She pushed his hand away and tried to ease him back on the gurney, but he fought her.

Blood suddenly began to spread on the blanket at waist level, and he began coughing up a lot of blood. He swung his fists wildly, his eyes nearly bulging out of their sockets.

"Fuck you all," he whispered, and he fell back, his mouth open as if he were trying to take a deep breath, but his chest fell still.

EIGHT

☐

Thomas Bell was aboard the British Airways 747–400 to Athens thirty minutes before its departure time, a glass of Krug in hand. Eighty-two C on the upper deck was a flatbed configuration. His partner in the window seat was a vaguely familiar middle-aged American woman by the name of Carol Grace who was flying to Athens to star in an English version of the stage play *Cabaret*.

The thought of sleeping so close to her on the long flight across the pond was enticing, though nothing could possibly happen, but the thought was there nevertheless, and it pushed his good mood even higher.

"Thing is, I hate to fly," she told him as the aircraft was closed up and they pushed away from the gate. "Always have."

"You'll sleep through most of it," Bell said. At a bit over six feet with a movie star's face and physique to match, he turned heads wherever he went. It's one of the reasons he'd been hired at the Palais.

She smiled nervously. "Oh no," she said. "I never sleep on these things. What if it crashes? They do sometimes."

"Well, you'll be a hell of a lot safer on this flight than you were in the cab out from the city. Pardon the language."

She laughed, the sound music to Bell's ears.

It seemed like ages since he'd been with a woman. The past three months had been nothing but business since the German Dottie Hauskelter had shown up at the high roller baccarat room and had bedded him that night and offered him a job that would pay one hundred times his salary, commissions, and tips.

He'd taken the job as the contact man for an assassin. He'd been taken aback at first by the nature of his job, but he had shrugged it off. The money was fabulous, and there was the promise that Dottie would return from Berlin from time to time to renew their acquaintances, as she'd put it.

Sex and money, not necessarily in that order, had always been Bell's main preoccupation. And here he was now flying top shelf after a successful mission and sitting next to a beautiful woman.

"Where are you staying in Athens?" he asked.

"The Electra. I always stay there. My treat to myself whenever I have to fly."

"The Metropolis?"

"Yes, you know it?" she asked.

"As it turns out, I'll be staying there for a few days. Maybe we could have drinks and dinner?"

"I'd love to. I have two days off before rehearsals start."

"Won't you be missed?"

"By the other actors?" she laughed. "Most of this crowd are more interested in looking at themselves in the mirror and reading their fabulous reviews."

"Can't be all that bad."

"Worse," she said. "You'll be a breath of fresh air. Believe me."

They turned onto the active runway, and in moments, the big jet accelerated.

"Jesus, Mary, and Joseph," Carol said, and she reached over and clutched Bell's hand in a death grip.

He had to smile.

"Sure, you can laugh because you're not crapping in your pants," she said.

"Like I said, I have a couple of days before rehearsals start," Carol told Bell at a late lunch the next day in the dining room looking toward the Parthenon.

"Lots to see in the city. I've only ever been here twice before, so I'm sure I've missed a lot."

"In that case, I'll be the girl guide. We can start on foot, but we'll have to rent a car at some point to catch some neat places outside the city."

"A lot of history here."

"Yeah, and it's still being made," Carol said. "Game?"

"I'm all yours."

They had adjoining suites, which Bell had thought was a fantastic stroke of luck. They'd touched down just before seven last night, and by the time they'd cabbed it to the hotel in the city and unpacked, Bell had figured she would go straight to bed. But she'd knocked on his door just before ten.

"Care for some company?" she asked. She was wearing only a white hotel robe.

"I'm all yours."

"I'd hoped you'd say that."

Actually, as far as the woman who was playing the part of Carol Grace was concerned, all of life was in reality an unreality. Everyone was an actor onstage, playing whatever part they'd learned as children. The face—or, more accurately, the persona—that we presented to the world was only one half of the truth. The remainder was buried sometimes so deeply in a person's head that they often could never tell the difference between truth and fiction. Not that it mattered, if you managed to keep your stories straight.

Carol was a well-preserved forty-eight instead of the thirty-five she played, because of a few hundred thousand dollars in face-lifts, dental work, tummy tucks, liposuction, breast enhancements, and leg and thigh shaping.

The only bits and pieces that hadn't been worked on were those involved in lovemaking, which was an art that, along with others, she had perfected years ago. She looked good, she spoke well, and she was dynamite in bed. Plus, she knew how to make money. Which was the point.

Only one man in her entire life had ever gotten the best of her, along with a very close friend, financially. And the two of them were going to even the score.

Revenge was petty, she'd read somewhere. But sweet nonetheless. And no one would get in their way.

The Acropolis was first on their list, but the tourists were so thick it was hard to see or do anything, and in less than an hour, Carol took Bell aside.

"I love people and all that, but this is nuts. Do you want to get off the beaten path?"

"I'm game as long as it's with you."

She smiled and took his arm. Downtown just off Syntagma Square, they found an Avis rental place, leased a Peugeot Allure SUV for the day, and headed east out of the center of the city through a working-class neighborhood.

"Mount Ymittos," Carol said. "One of Athens's more closely guarded secrets."

They parked near the ruins of what she said was an ancient Byzantine monastery and got out of the car.

They were above the city, the thickly forested mountain sloping up and away.

"I'm not much for churches," Bell said, but she took his arm, and they headed toward a walking path.

"Neither am I, but if you're game for a twenty-minute walk, I'll show you the best view of Athens from above, and a little spot in the trees off the path, where we can be alone."

"As I said earlier, I'm all yours."

"I'd hoped you'd say that."

About fifteen minutes later, they found the narrow track off the path that she'd been looking for and followed it down about one hundred meters to a very small glen, no more than a dozen paces in length and half that in width.

From here, they had a lovely view of the city below, and closer at hand, a grassy depression about the size of a pair of king-size beds.

Bell smiled. "Perfect," he said.

"Actually, you fucked up, and we can't tolerate mistakes," Carol said behind and above him.

Bell started to turn as she took a pistol out of her purse and fired into the side of his head.

He never heard nor felt the shot that killed him.

NINE

Ever since Mary Sullivan and Otto had gotten together, Mary had become point man for him and for Mac and Pete whenever something came up. Like Louise Horn, she was not only bright, she was an organizer.

She had called Housekeeping into action as soon as she and Otto understood what was going down at the Georgetown apartment, and it was she who arranged the meeting with the top brass at Langley for the following morning.

She met McGarvey and Pete with their temporary security badges at the elevator in the VIP garage below the Old Headquarters Building a few minutes before ten. Neither of them were CIA employees any longer, and even though he had been the director, he still needed a badge.

"Sorry about your wedding," Pete told her.

"It's just a piece of paper," Mary said on the way up in the elevator. "We'll take care of it when this blows over. In the meantime, we have a half hour before Taft wants to see us in his office, and Otto wants to talk to you guys first."

They got off on the busy third floor and walked down the corridor to Otto's suite of offices that had originally been meant for a team of six people who had at one time coordinated cover stories and arrangements for operators going overseas on missions. Now the three rooms belonged solely to Otto and his machines, including a pool table–size horizontal monitor that could show a dozen files, photos, and videos simultaneously.

But not every piece of information was digitized, even in this day and age. Strewn around his office were stacks of older books—a lot of them biographies of obscure people whom Otto had found interesting at one time or another, old newspapers and magazines, maps and ocean charts, drawings—some of them as old as the 1500s—in a dozen languages.

"Good morning, Mary," Lou's voice greeted them at the door, which clicked open. "Otto is expecting you."

"Thank you," Mary said, the expression on her face unchanged.

Pete had asked her a month or so ago if she minded having the voice of Otto's deceased wife as the voice of his darlings, but she had smiled and shook her head. "We're friends."

Otto was in the back office, his inner sanctum, standing over the horizontal monitor that was alive with charts, diagrams, and lists of people.

"According to what I'm looking at, no government agency on the planet is gunning for you," he said, looking up. "And that includes us inside and outside the beltway."

"Doesn't exactly narrow it down," Pete said.

"He wasn't a lone wolf," McGarvey said. He'd thought about it all night after he and Pete had gone back to their apartment to get a few hours' sleep. "He said he worked for an expediter. And he had some pretty good intel. He knew where we lived and that we were coming up from Florida."

"And he had plenty of advance notice," Mary said. "Housekeeping's preliminary after-action report said that he'd probably been living in the apartment for a week, maybe longer."

"Fingerprints? DNA?"

"Both. We have rock-solid confirmation that he's Leonard Slatkin. But he was kicked out of the service six years ago. Whoever he was freelancing for, it wasn't them."

"His spotter was good," Otto said. "Our guys found a surveillance camera on the roof of the building across the street from yours. It was feeding to a burner phone that's since been disconnected."

"Housekeeping looked at it," Mary added. "No forensic evidence. And apparently, no one in the building knew when it was installed or by whom."

"Whoever it was, they knew what they were doing," McGarvey said. "And their only mistake I can see was the piece of plastic on the window."

"But that's just the point, Mac," Mary said. "Against impossible odds—only the angle you were at to the window as you walked up the street allowed you to spot it. But why? What were you looking for? What got your hackles up? There was no reason for it."

McGarvey had asked himself the same question yesterday before they'd even gotten off the flight from Florida, and outside baggage claim when he had scanned the vehicles and the faces. And again on the way into the city, and when he'd had the cabbie drop him off at the end of the block.

Something had been tickling at him maybe for a few days, even a week. Maybe something he'd seen on a TV news show, or in one of the half-dozen newspapers he read every morning, especially *The Wall Street Journal* and *The New York Times*, or the magazines he subscribed to, among them *Jane's Defense Weekly*.

But nothing specific came to mind, except that he was on edge, and respecting that feeling—even though he didn't always know the why of it—had saved his life on more than one occasion.

"I don't know," he told them.

Upstairs on the seventh floor, they were shown into the director's office, where Harold Taft, the DCI, and his deputy director of operations, formerly known as the CIA's Clandestine Service, Thomas Waksberg, were waiting for them.

"I'm not sure if it's a good thing seeing you again," Taft said, "but I understand that you were in a spot of trouble again yesterday."

He was a short, slender man with the military bearing of the navy four-star he'd been until President Weaver had tapped him to head the CIA. In everyone's estimation, including McGarvey's, he was one of the better DCIs in a long time, because he was not only a no-nonsense man, he had experience. During his tenure in the navy, he had revamped all five military intelligence operations, including those of the Coast Guard, plus the DoD's Central Security Service.

Waksberg, on the other hand, was an obese civilian who'd been a chief of police in a medium-size Texas city, had worked as a district attorney in Dallas–Fort Worth, and moved to Washington during the Weaver campaign to work as the new president's legal consul. He had no intel background, but he was a bright man, and not so prejudiced as his predecessor, Marty Bambridge, who'd in the end turned out to be a traitor.

They all sat down, and Taft nodded to McGarvey. "Ball's in your court, but I understand there was one casualty."

"Yes," Otto answered. "We identified him as a former South African Special Forces operator who evidently turned freelance. He was paid $250,000, probably as a down payment, to assassinate Mac."

Taft turned to his DDO. "Do you have anything?"

"He was in our files as someone of minimal interest."

Taft waited.

"As far as we know, he's never operated on U.S. soil until now."

"Do you have any beef with South Africa?" Taft asked McGarvey.

"No."

The DCI almost smiled. "At least there's one nation's intelligence service you haven't crossed swords with at one time or another. So why was this guy after you? Or who hired him?"

"I don't think it was anything personal, but at this point, I don't know who hired him, though, as you understand, I have crossed swords with any number of people."

"We can rule out the usuals," Otto said. "Russia, China, North Korea, Pakistan, Turkey, Chile. My guess is that no government is gunning for him."

"Which leaves us what?" Taft asked. "Or who?"

"Otto missed one country," Pete said.

McGarvey reached over and touched her hand, but she ignored him.

Taft caught the gesture, and his mouth tightened. "Who?"

"Us."

The word hung there for a longish moment. "Us?" Taft asked. "As in the United States?"

Pete nodded.

"But not the government," Otto said. "Not even the White House."

"Christ," Taft said half under his breath. "Where does this leave us?" he asked.

"Unknown at this point," McGarvey said.

"Which means?"

"Someone is hunting me, which means I'm going to hunt back."

TEN

□

Villa Larius Lacus, overlooking Italy's Lake Como, had been built in the early 1700s on twenty acres of prime property next door to the famous Villa Carlotta, by a Milanese marquis. Only Lacus, which simply meant *lake* in Latin, had been purchased and completely renovated four years ago by the American multibillionaire Thomas Hammond, who'd made his fortune the old-fashioned way—by screwing people out of their money.

The afternoon was soft as Hammond sat drinking champagne on his grand veranda overlooking the corniche road as Susan Patterson's soft gray Bentley GTC Continental convertible, the top down, glided as if on the wings of angels in a romantic movie, and he had to smile.

Actress that she'd always been, she wanted to make a grand entrance wherever she could. At forty-eight, she still had the stunning body and good looks of a beauty half that age, unless you looked closely.

Where Hammond, who'd been one of the California dot-com boy geniuses, was worth in the neighborhood of $30 billion, give or take, Susan, who'd parlayed most of her early acting money into producing movies of her own, and then buying every movie theater she could get her hands on, plus a movie-only television pay-per-view network, was worth only a third of that.

But they were both players in every sense of the word. Cannes for the movie festival and Monaco for the Grand Prix race, Davos for the economic summit where the superrich mingled with governmental finance ministers, art and music festivals and the yacht run.

They'd both been guests at the White House, and she almost always dressed to the nines, her hair and makeup perfection. He, on the other hand, favored tattered jeans, black T-shirts, and boat shoes, his short, blond hair mussed, though he did look presentable in a French-tailored tuxedo.

Susan's car disappeared below as she turned onto the driveway up to the wrought iron gates, and moments later, Peter, the houseman who'd been one of the Queen's guards from the Scots Guards Regiments at Buckingham Palace, came to the french doors.

"Pardon, sir, but Ms. Patterson has arrived. Shall I show her up?"

"Yes, and we'll need another bottle of wine, and a glass; she'll want to celebrate," Hammond said.

Where'd he'd always been satisfied to drink a common Dom Pérignon, Susan was a snob and wanted a Krug—especially the '95 Clos du Mesnil Blanc de Blancs—if she was feeling good.

"Of course," Peter said, withdrawing.

A minute later, even before Susan had parked her car and come up, Clarice, the house sommelier, came with the Krug, her assistant a young man from right here in Lombardy carrying two flutes and an ice bucket. She presented the bottle, Hammond nodded, and as soon as they set it up, they withdrew.

Hammond was opening the bottle when Susan breezed in, her high cheekbones slightly red and puffy and her Botoxed lips tight. She gave him an almost chaste kiss on the cheek and plopped down across the table from him.

She was tired and frustrated. "That might be a bit premature," she said. "But I could use a decent drink."

Hammond poured for her. At the best of times, she tended to be histrionic, but this afternoon, she wasn't herself, and considering what they had put in play last month, he was concerned.

"How was Athens?"

She drained her glass and held it out. He refilled it.

"Closure," she said.

Hammond was vexed. "Don't be cryptic. What happened?"

"A fucking cock-up, that's what. I took the bastard up into the hills and put a bullet into his fucking moronic brain. End of story."

"Except for McGarvey, I'm assuming."

She looked away. "I don't know, Tom. According to Bell, it was a done deal. McGarvey and his broad somehow figured out what was going down, and they both went into the building."

"And then?"

"Nothing. Bell assured me that with Slatkin's firepower and the fact he held the high ground, he couldn't have missed."

"Reasonable—" Hammond said, but Susan cut him off.

"Are you fucking nuts?" she screeched. "The former director of the CIA is gunned down across the street from his apartment in Georgetown and it didn't hit the news?"

Hammond poured himself a glass of the Krug and smiled. It was good. "About what we expected, no?"

"We've gone up against this son of a bitch before and lost."

"We didn't lose; we just didn't win," Hammond corrected. "But Slatkin was just the opening shot. I didn't expect him to kill McGarvey. And if he had, I would have been disappointed." He shook his head. "No, sweetheart, this is just the beginning."

Susan looked away for a moment, the flute raised to her mouth, but she didn't drink. "Where's the profit in it, Tom?" she asked absently. "We lost an opportunity with the bitcoin deal he offered us. But so what?"

"I don't like losing."

She looked at him. "I like adventure as well as the next girl, but I don't like losing either. Especially not my life."

"Whatever the South African accomplished or didn't, you took care of it."

Her eyes widened a little, and she sipped the wine. "Actually, that part was pretty good."

"Better than acting on a sound set?"

She smiled. "Oh yeah."

"Then we're ahead of the game."

"A quarter million short."

"But not a half million."

They were silent for a while. Out on the lake, a speedboat towing a skier made brutally tight figure eights to the east, and farther up the lake, a pair of sailboats were apparently in a race. All life was a competition, Hammond thought. And he loved it. At this moment, he felt as if he were Sherlock Holmes in reverse; he knew the ending, just not the details of getting there. "The game's afoot," he said.

She was watching him. "It's just a game to you?"

"Why not?"

She put down her glass. "Oh, for Christ's sake, Tom, wake up and smell the roses or something. This game, as you want to call it, could end up costing some serious money. And if we fuck up, we could become the game. Have you considered that possibility?"

"Yes, and that's the entire point. You had a good time in Athens."

"I wouldn't go that far."

Hammond made no reply, and after a moment, Susan cracked a narrow smile and nodded.

"It was real," she said. "But there could have been witnesses. I could have ended up in jail for the rest of my life, a prospect I don't relish." She held out her glass, and Hammond filled it.

"*The Most Dangerous Game*," he said. "Ring a bell?"

"Sure, back in the early thirties. Joel McCrea, a big-game hunter, falls off a ship and ends up on an island with another big-game hunter—Leslie Banks, I think—who wants to hunt McCrea. A man hunting a man. The ultimate sport." It suddenly struck her. "Son of a bitch, is this what we're up to?"

"Why not?"

"Because we're not talking about a movie here. Revenge I understand. Or maybe there's something else going on—something you haven't told me about—maybe getting back in the bitcoin game. But this isn't a fucking movie."

"No."

"McGarvey's a CIA-trained assassin with a whole hell of a lot more experience than the guy we hired to take him out. He finds out that we hired Slatkin, he could come after us."

"That's the point."

"What point? Are you out of your mind?"

"He's being hunted, and if he hasn't figured it out yet, he will. And when he does, he'll hunt back. The game's afoot."

Susan shook her head, but her breath quickened a little, and some color came to her cheeks.

Hammond sat forward. "For all practical purposes, between us, we have unlimited resources. Just about all the money in the world. More than we could possibly spend in ten lifetimes. How many yachts, how many airplanes, or cars or houses, can we buy?"

"Boring sometimes."

"Boring almost all the time lately. But my question stands: Can one man, no matter how good, stand up to unlimited resources against him?"

ELEVEN

Dr. Stephen Held, the CIA's justice of the peace, came out to the McLean house to perform the ceremony at eight in the morning. Mary had originally wanted to use the chapel on campus and invite some of their friends and coworkers, but under the present circumstances, she'd made the unilateral decision that it would be better if they circled the wagons.

"We need a plan of action," she said, and no one argued with her.

This morning, Otto wore boat shoes, starched and pressed jeans, a crisp white shirt, and a European-cut blue blazer Mary had bought for him. His hair was brushed, the ponytail that just reached his collar tied neatly.

Mary wore a knee-length white dress with a modern art slash of red from bodice to hip as if she were a painting. She'd done her hair with Pete's help and was even wearing makeup, something she seldom did.

Mac and Pete remained standing behind them in the lanai all through the service, and when Held said, "You may kiss the bride," Otto took Mary in his arms, enveloping her much smaller body, and they kissed for a very long time.

When they parted, she was grinning ear to ear. "Wow, that's the best one ever," she gushed.

"Champagne," McGarvey said.

Mary laughed. "It's first thing in the morning and we have work to do?"

"That's why we got the Cristal, same brew we had when we got married," Pete told her.

McGarvey opened the bottle and poured five glasses for the toast.

"Live long and prosper," Held said, grinning.

"That's *Star Trek*," Mary said.

"The ten-to-one consensus on campus among everyone who knows you two thought it would be the most appropriate blessing," the minister said, finishing his drink. He put his glass down. "Now, if you don't mind, I have to get out to Arlington."

"Honeymoon?" Pete asked after Held had left.

"Later," Mary said. "Right now, we have work to do—finding out who's gunning for Mac and why."

"And making sure they don't succeed," Pete said.

McGarvey had been trying to work out some of the details from the moment he and Slatkin had shot it out on the third-floor landing, and the only decent clue they had for now. The shooter had said that his contact had made a mistake about the expediter, who was a woman and who was rich.

The problem he was running into was that the profiles of assassins and their handlers were almost always men.

"If he was telling the truth, the list of people we're looking for is a hell of a lot smaller than it could be," Otto suggested. "Our advantage."

They were sitting on the lanai off the kitchen, drinking the last of the champagne.

"So where do we start?" Mary asked.

"Female staffers at the White House, and ladybirds up at the Pentagon," McGarvey said, though the niggling at the back of his head was telling him that it wouldn't be so simple.

Otto read something of that from his expression. "But what? Talk to me."

"We need the why of it first."

"Lou," Otto said.

"Yes, dear. And congratulations to you and Mary."

"Thank you. Have you been listening to our conversation?"

"Of course."

"Crossmatch all the current White House and Pentagon females who have had any connection, however slight, with Mac."

"Do we have a time frame?"

"No, simply among the current personnel roster."

Lou was back almost immediately. "Seven at the White House, including the deputy press officer, Deborah Cass, who is a personal friend of President Weaver's oldest daughter. And fourteen at the Pentagon, the highest rank being navy two-star Grace Metal, assistant to the Joint Chiefs on deployments."

"Do you know who she's talking about?" Mary asked.

"Only vaguely," McGarvey said. "But neither of them would want me dead, and I doubt that either of them have the kind of money Slatkin was talking about."

"Maybe he was wrong," Mary suggested.

"I don't think so. He was dying and he knew it, so he had nothing else to lose."

"Any of those women ever fall in love with you?"

"Not that I know of," McGarvey said. And he caught the humor of it. "But I suppose I could ask."

"That's not the point," Otto said. "Access their personnel records, especially their security clearances, and crossmatch with all of Mac's operations going back to his tenure as DCI."

This time, it took Lou almost forty seconds before she responded, "I have three hundred twenty-five matches. How would you like me to sort them?"

"Ranked by the level of adversarial contacts."

"Three. Ms. Cass, whose profile suggests that she is in love with the president and could hold a grudge against Mac for his less-than-cordial relationship with POTUS. Admiral Metal because she'd openly considered it a gross misallocation of naval resources on the fruitless search for Mac in the Black Sea two years ago. And army colonel Dorothy Burroughs, whose assignment three years ago was with INSCOM. Her boss was Brigadier General Morton Hollis." INSCOM was the army's Intelligence and Security Command.

McGarvey knew the man's name. "He was one of the generals who said they would never follow Weaver's command if he were elected president."

"The same group of mid-level intel people who came up against you," Pete said.

"Her boss, not her."

"What's Colonel Burroughs's present billet?" Otto asked.

"She's a procurement officer for special aerospace projects."

"Practically unlimited money if she knows her business," Mary said.

"Any hint of impropriety in her file?" Otto asked. "Any inquiries?"

"Several," Lou replied. "Shall I sort them by date?"

"No," McGarvey broke in. "Are there any current inquiries into the files of other Pentagon procurement officers?"

"Yes. The issue is very common."

"Comes with the territory?" Pete asked.

"Indeed," Lou replied.

Otto spread his hands. "Doesn't mean she or any one of the others isn't guilty. But there's no smoking gun here."

No one said anything for a moment or two, until Pete broke the silence. "What's our next step?"

"On the assumption that Slatkin wasn't just a one-off, and that whoever wanted me gone will try again, let's make whoever his expediter was think that we have him alive. And he might talk."

"There's been no mention in the media about the shoot-out," Otto said. "The building was empty at the time, and Housekeeping did a good job sanitizing the place."

"And whoever hired him has good connections. They knew that Pete and I would be coming to D.C."

"Okay?"

"How?" McGarvey asked.

"They were probably watching us in Florida and spotted our move," Pete said.

"Why not kill me there?"

"Unknown."

"Let it leak that a so-far unidentified male was found seriously wounded in the vicinity of your apartment," said Otto.

"How?" Pete asked.

"An FBI site," Otto said. "He's being treated at GW University Hospital."

"Make it All Saints," Mac said. "That's where he was taken and where his body is still on ice. We'll give the staff the heads-up, and I'll be waiting."

TWELVE

□

Hammond's twin-engine Bombardier Global 7000 touched down at Washington's Reagan National Airport just before nine, and as soon as they'd reached the private aviation terminal, the hatch opened, and the stairs lowered, he left the plane.

The crew had been instructed to refuel and stand by for a departure sometime tomorrow. His bags would be sent over to the Hay-Adams immediately, arriving even before he did.

A Mercedes Maybach had been sent for him, and the uniformed driver held the door open for him. "Good morning, Mr. Hammond."

Hammond nodded and slipped inside.

Mikhail Tarasov, who until recently had been the major player in the Russian energy giant Gazprom, was seated on the opposite side. "Good morning, Thomas. I trust you had a good flight as usual." He was a slender man in his late forties, with light brown hair, and a nearly constant serious mien. He looked more like an American than a Russian.

"I'm surprised to see you here," Hammond said, and yet he really wasn't. Russians, especially the new oligarchs, did not take failure lightly. Hammond was wealthy, but Tarasov was wealthier and more connected with some internationally powerful people.

"Your call for a replacement has disturbed some mutual friends, who would like to know what game you're playing at."

The glass partition separating the front from the back was up, ensuring that whatever they said would not be heard by the driver.

"You know exactly what's going on."

"Nyet. It was not a part of the original deal. You wanted a favor, and we agreed if you would provide us with an untraceable favor. You have failed, and we want to know why."

"Our operator is dead."

"We have learned that may not be the case. In fact, he is apparently recovering at the small private hospital that the CIA uses to treat its wounded agents in Georgetown."

Hammond was stunned. "How do you know this?"

"We have resources. But the fact is the man you selected was not up to the job. You thought he was dead, and you asked for another man not much better than your South African. The question stands, Thomas, what are you and your movie star playing at?"

Hammond was angry. "Don't try to manage me, because if our arrangement were to go public, you would have more to lose than I would."

Tarasov laughed. "You underestimate us and overestimate yourself."

"I don't need you."

"Yes, you do, because we have a mutual goal. You help us and we help you. We just want to know what game you are playing. A very simple question for which a very simple answer would suffice."

They had left the airport and were on the Williams Memorial Bridge leading across the river into the city center. Hammond looked out the window for a longish moment or two, weighing his options. The gas-and-oil deal he had with the Russians had the real potential of making him something in the vicinity of $5 billion. It was more than the bitcoin deal McGarvey had offered them, and in the long term a hell of a lot less volatile.

The Russians had been skeptical at first that they even needed a front man in Western Europe until Hammond had convinced them of his connections. At the moment, most Europeans, especially the French, were mistrustful of the new American president but even warier of the Russians, especially since Putin had been reelected. He was being called the New Stalin, and it made a lot of people nervous.

Hammond was selling his personal connections. Along the way in the dot-com boom, he had made a fortune, but he had been smart enough to include a lot of hungry people in government—especially in places like the Netherlands and Belgium, and even France, where Russian oil and gas only accounted for small percentages of their energy needs.

"Talk to me, Thomas, as a friend and a business partner. Please."

Hammond held his silence as he considered his options. Either trust Tarasov and whoever the man was connected with in Moscow or back away from the deal.

The South African shooter who'd been hired through Susan's expediter—who was now dead—only knew the expediter. Even if he were given drugs to make him talk, he could never produce any link beyond Bell.

In the long run, it didn't matter if Slatkin was dead or alive. Hammond turned back to Tarasov.

"It is a game," he said. "One that will end up where we want to end up."

"Tell me."

"Actually, I wanted the South African to fail. I was almost 100 percent certain that he was no match for McGarvey."

"Then what's the point? We want Mr. McGarvey dead, and we don't want it traced back to Moscow. There are no other considerations."

"Including how I conduct my business?"

"Yes, but be careful you don't make a fatal mistake."

"Are you threatening me, Mikhail?"

Tarasov pursed his lips. "There are certain people in Moscow who feel that we should let this go. Just turn our backs on the entire deal and perhaps sweep up whatever debris is left behind."

"But there are others who think differently."

"Yes, and these men do not take mistakes lightly. Too much is at stake here, even beyond our deals in Greece and Spain."

"McGarvey will die, there's no doubt of it."

"But?"

"It's the how of it."

Tarasov turned away. *"Yeb vas."* It was a common, very vulgar Russian expression that roughly meant *fuck your mother.*

"I want to have some fun."

"Explain to me your fun."

"Big-game hunting."

"I don't understand."

"I'm hunting Mr. McGarvey for sport. The South African was my first shot, which I was almost certain would miss. Cost me only two hundred and fifty thousand. I'll double that offer for the next try. Four times that for the third, if needed. Eight times, ten times, whatever."

"Don't you think that he'll come to realize what's going on and hunt you back?"

"I hope so."

"He's good. Maybe the best."

"He'll make a mistake sooner or later."

"He has his own resources; supposedly, he's a millionaire."

"I'm richer," Hammond said.

"It's your life on the line."

"My shooters will never meet me face-to-face."

"I have a specialist waiting for you at the hotel."

"Does he know you?"

"Yes," Tarasov said.

"I'll videoconference with him, my voice electronically altered. It's actually very simple. The device isn't bigger than a cell phone, and in fact, I own the half-dozen patents. And I'll have an expediter for now who he will work with but never meet unless they fail."

Tarasov sat back. "It appears that you think of everything."

"Not really. But I can buy just about anything or anyone."

"But not me."

"No, which is why we're friends."

Tarasov nodded. "His name is Donald Hicks, and he was a Canadian Special Operations sniper."

"What's he doing on your side?"

Tarasov smiled. "You're not the only man on the planet with money, Thomas. And Hicks is very hungry since they put him out to pasture."

THIRTEEN

All Saints, set back from the street not far from Georgetown University, was guarded in front by an electrically controlled iron gate and from behind by a tall spike-topped fence, beyond which was a broad line of trees.

It was dark when Pete, driving her green BMW, dropped McGarvey off in front. "How long are you going to wait for someone to show up?" she asked. She was nervous.

"Overnight, at least," McGarvey said. "Maybe twenty-four hours. If they're sending someone, it won't be long."

"Whoever's gunning for you wants to get it over with in a hurry, is that what you're saying?"

"Something like that."

"We could put up a chopper, or at least drones to watch the place. Anyone comes within a hundred yards, we'll know about it."

McGarvey had known she would object to what he was doing. Just as Mary had tried to talk him out of it. Only Otto saw the logic, and the why, of it. "Our people would swoop in and arrest him?"

"Yes."

"Take him down to Belvoir for interrogation, which you would be a part of, but not in charge since you're not with the Company any longer. You're a freelancer, just like me."

"What's your point, Mac?"

"He would have rights. Constitutional rights that wouldn't let us do much more than waterboarding and maybe drugs—and even that would be pushing it. But in the end, if we couldn't prove anything other than trespassing, we'd have to release him."

Pete saw it. "But not you."

"If someone shows up here wanting to take a shot at me—or anyone else, for that matter—he's lost his rights as far as I'm concerned."

"You want that to happen."

"No. But if someone is gunning for me—"

"Which you think is the case."

"If it's true, then I don't want to screw around sitting on my thumbs waiting for it to happen. Either someone comes here tonight or tomorrow at the latest, or I'm going to start pushing back."

"Start where?"

"The White House and the Pentagon."

"If you start poking around, you're bound to find a hornet's nest."

"I'm counting on it," McGarvey said.

"I want to come in with you."

"Go back to McLean. If they can't get to me directly, they might try an end run. Otto and Mary are vulnerable."

Pete's mouth tightened, and she looked away for a moment. "I didn't do such a hot job last time."

She had been with Otto's wife, Louise, at an interview in Laurel, Maryland, when a shooter had killed Lou, who'd been standing less than ten feet from Pete.

McGarvey reached over for her hand. "You weren't expecting it."

"I should have been."

Gary Starrs, the brother-in-law of one of the SEALs who had taken out Osama bin Laden in May 2011, was chief of night security at the hospital, and he was waiting at the rear door as the gate buzzed open and McGarvey walked around from the front.

Starrs was an unremarkable man in all respects, standing just under six feet with a medium build, except for his eyes, which held the thousand-yard stare of a man who has seen close-quarters battles.

The green Bimmer drove off, and Starrs glanced over at the monitors at Security Post One, which showed a wide-angle view of the entire perimeter three hundred meters out. Nothing was showing. And nothing was eating at his gut, an instinct he had honed in four separate deployments to Afghanistan.

But when Mr. McGarvey asked for a favor, it was time to jump to, feelings or not.

Helen Berliner, the chief of nurses, came around the corner. "Has Mac called to say when he's going to be here?"

Starrs turned. "He's coming up the driveway."

Berliner had volunteered to pull a double shift when she'd been told that Mac was camping out here at least tonight for a possible confrontation with a bad guy or guys. In fact, the entire staff wanted to be on board, and she had to turn away most of them.

"Life goes on, and I'll need staffers who aren't asleep on their feet around the clock," she'd told her people.

This night, it was just Berliner and one other nurse, plus Gary and two others on the security team.

Mac had insisted on a minimal staff on the real chance that someone had eyes on the place. And he'd even asked that Dr. Franklin go home, leaving only Phil Geyer, the usual on-duty physician.

"Are your people set?"

"Yes, ma'am. Front and rear third floor."

"They're going to get damned tired staring out the windows without a break."

"They're just covering the two shooting positions," Starrs said. He nodded to the perimeter monitor. "Someone shows up and they'll get the word. In the meantime, they're mostly kicking back, staggered interior patrols every twenty minutes."

"We're covered?"

"Pretty much."

Berliner was looking at the monitors. "I thought you said that Mac was coming up the driveway."

Starrs looked up. McGarvey had disappeared from view. "Shit, shit," he said.

McGarvey held up to the left of the door, his back to the brick wall. He had ducked below the angle of the surveillance camera, and for the first few seconds, he'd hoped that whoever was pulling security was on the ball and would have come outside, guns drawn.

But it was nearly a full minute before Starrs burst out the door, his Heckler & Koch room broom in his right hand pointed low and right.

McGarvey waited until he'd cleared the doorway, and he rose and placed the muzzle of his pistol on the back of the man's head.

"You're dead," McGarvey said. "And the castle is wide open."

"Sorry, sir," Starrs said. He slowly raised his right hand. He was holding a small block of Semtex. "If I went down, my grip would have let go, and boom, one dead intruder."

McGarvey lowered his weapon. "Not bad. But the advice most field commanders give their people is that you don't win wars by dying for your country—you make the other poor bastard die for his."

Starrs nodded. "Anyway, it was just in case, sir."

"Just in case I missed," Berliner said from the doorway. She was holding a Beretta 9mm in her right hand, pointed directly at McGarvey.

Mac had to smile. "Okay, you guys win. But nurses aren't supposed to carry weapons."

"Not in a civilian hospital, they don't, Mr. Director, but this place is different."

McGarvey holstered his gun. "If someone is coming, it'll be in the night, probably just before dawn. But it's a long shot. I'm just clutching at straws here."

"What else can you tell us?" Starrs asked.

"It'll almost certainly be a lone shooter. A professional who won't make easy mistakes and won't discriminate when it comes to his targets. I'm number one, but get in his way and you're dead."

"Piss someone off?" Berliner asked.

Again, Mac had to smile. "Happens all the time. Maybe it's my personality or something."

FOURTEEN

At the Hay-Adams, Hammond and Tarasov went up to a Lafayette Park View suite and let themselves in without a bellman accompanying them. Hammond's bag had already arrived and his things laid out in the wardrobe and bathroom. A bottle of Dom Pérignon was chilling in an ice bucket.

"I'm flying back to New York tonight," the Russian said. "And then Moscow on Tuesday."

"You're staying for the interview?"

"Of course, unless you'd rather I not. It's up to you if you hire him, but he's a hell of a lot more competent than Slatkin."

"If I don't think so, do you have someone else in mind?"

"There are plenty more where this one came from. Believe me, you can't imagine how many crazies with guns are out there just looking for a chance to make a dollar or whatever currency you're offering."

"Is he here in the hotel now?" Hammond asked. He opened the champagne and poured a glass, but Tarasov waved it off.

"He put himself up at the Rosewood."

"I'm not familiar with it."

"It's in Georgetown, actually not far from the hospital."

Hammond was surprised. "Has he already been told about his target?"

"Only in the most general terms."

"Then how the hell did he know to book a room so close?"

"I don't know."

"What the hell else don't you know, Mikhail?" Hammond demanded. The assassin was too close for comfort; any number of things could go wrong—things that his money might not be able to insulate him from.

He had told Susan that he admired what she had done in Athens and admitted that he would have hired someone to take Bell down rather than take the chance himself.

She had smiled and shrugged it off. "Just another bit part in an action movie. 'Lights, cameras, sound, action.' Bang!"

Hammond took his iPad from his shoulder bag and set it up on the dining table, then got the champagne and his flute and brought them over. "Do we know his room number?"

"Yes, and he's waiting for our call."

"Does he know that he won't be able to see us or hear our actual voices?"

"His type very seldom meets their principals," Tarasov said. "It's considered bad form."

"You've not had a face-to-face?"

"No," Tarasov said. He came over, sat down, and gave Hammond the number.

Once, when Hammond was a shy, skinny little boy of five, his parents took him to the aquarium exhibit at the San Diego Zoo. He remembered standing in front of a floor-to-ceiling glass window looking into one of the exhibits. He'd just stepped forward and put a hand out to touch the glass when a gigantic polar bear appeared out of nowhere, a massive paw hitting the glass with a thump directly in front of the boy's face.

He'd stepped back, his heart nearly stopping, never so afraid for his safety until this moment as he stared at the image of Donald Hicks, the former Canadian Special Ops sniper who never missed and had also never learned to take orders from a superior, all of whom he thought were idiots.

The man stood in front of what might have been a laptop set up on top of a chest of drawers or desk. His massive, round head was completely free of hair, and that—combined with a narrow nose, high, delicate cheekbones, and wide, dark eyes—made him look exotic, almost movie-star handsome.

Hammond instantly had the thought that if Susan were here, she would insist they go over to the Rosewood to meet him in person. She would definitely want to fuck him.

"Mr. Hicks, can you hear me?" Hammond asked.

"Yes," he said. "You have a job for me that I'm told is urgent, heh? Let's get on with it." His voice was soft, his Canadian accent strong.

Hammond figured him for a man who'd been born and raised out in the sticks. An inbred bumpkin. "I want you to kill someone."

Hicks laughed. "Well, that's what I do. Who is it?"

"I'll send you his file when we're finished here. But I'll warn you that he is a well-experienced former CIA officer with a lot of field time."

"Name?"

"Kirk McGarvey."

Hicks's expression suddenly became animated. "Finally," he muttered.

"What?" Hammond asked, not quite sure he'd caught what the man had said.

"Finally someone worth the effort. I know this man."

Hammond was alarmed. "Personally?"

"By reputation. He was the director of the CIA at one time. I'd say you aim high; he's a hell of a lot more than just well experienced. He's considered to be one of the very best shooters anywhere in the world. Christ on a cross."

"I'll send you his dossier."

"Don't bother."

"Will you take the job?"

"Of course I will."

"One million dollars," Hammond said.

"Five million," Hicks responded. "Half now, and if I'm not taken away in a body bag, the remainder within twenty-four hours after the kill."

"No."

Hicks shrugged. "I could just as well hunt you for free."

Tarasov leaned forward. "You don't know who we are."

"I know you, Comrade Tarasov. I'm sure I could find your friend."

Hammond's heart skipped a beat. Looking into the Canadian's eyes, he could see the same expression—or lack of—that he'd seen in McGarvey's eyes on the boat at Monaco.

He reached forward to hit the Escape key, but Tarasov stayed his hand. "We agree to your terms, Mr. Hicks. But only if the mission is accomplished within the next twenty-four hours."

"That could be a problem depending on the man's location and his situation."

"He's at a small hospital just a few blocks from your present position," Tarasov said. "The real problem, however, which is the reason you will get your five million if you succeed, is that he knows that you, or someone like you, is coming."

"I accept," Hicks said. "Send me what intel you have on this place. The moment I'm notified of the deposit, I will go to work." He reached forward, and the screen went blank.

Hammond sat back, and for what seemed like a very long time to him, he gathered his thoughts. He looked up at length. "You're free with my money."

Tarasov shrugged.

"Can he do it?"

"Pay him and you'll find out. But in the end, it's nothing more than a rich man's game."

"Plus our deal."

"The ball is in your court, as they say at Wimbledon."

Hammond brought up one of his slush fund accounts in a small bank in Bahrain. Tarasov gave him the Canadian's account information from memory, and Hammond looked up.

"You've worked with him before?"

"Twice."

"He's good?"

"The best."

Hammond entered the information for the bank on Grand Cayman and hit the Send key, transferring the funds.

FIFTEEN

McGarvey left Starrs at his post at the rear entrance to the hospital and made the rounds of the entire building, starting downstairs and working his way up to the third floor and then the roof.

Besides the security detail, plus the doctor and the nurses, only two intelligence officers were in adjoining rooms on the second floor. One of them had returned from an op in Afghanistan with severe burns to his legs and back after a mortar round had gone off five feet from where he stood. By all accounts, he was a very lucky man.

The other patient was Dottie Valdez, who'd been the assistant chief of the CIA's station in Havana, who'd been arrested on her way home and charged with prostitution. In jail, she'd been beaten and gang-raped over a thirty-six-hour period until she'd been dumped back on the streets.

She'd somehow managed to make it back to the embassy where she'd been hustled under cover to the airport for a diplomatic transport back to the States.

Franklin said that physically she would recover fully, but it was her mental state that he was not so sure about. "The bastards had at her."

The only piece of luck—if it could have been called that—was that the cops who arrested her thought she was an American tourist. They had no idea she was CIA or that she worked out of the U.S. embassy. If they had, it would have turned into a major diplomatic incident.

Mac had looked in on her, but she'd been sound asleep, and he'd backed away and continued with his rounds.

Standing now on the roof, dressed in jeans and a dark pullover, his pistol in a quick-draw holster at his back, he kept far enough back from the edge that he was in the shadows and could not be spotted from the street or by anyone in the buildings opposite.

A taxi cruised past and turned left down toward Canal Road NW, a car horn honked in the direction of the university, and, very far in the distance toward the city, one or two fire engine sirens drifted across on a momentary breeze.

Ordinary night city sounds, the same as he'd heard dozens of times on operations in many places over the years. Lonely sounds against the backdrop of imminent danger.

Most often, he had been the hunter, and he knew how it felt. Now, however, he was the prey, and he didn't know who was hunting him or why, though if he was wrong about someone in the White House or Pentagon, it could have been the intel services of more than a dozen countries who would consider it a job well done if he were to be eliminated.

And yet that made no real sense to him, because gunning down a former director of the CIA was filled with some serious political blowback.

He turned and silently made his way to the rear of the building, again standing well enough back from the edge that he couldn't be spotted from below.

Five cars were parked next to the maintenance building that, among other things, housed the hospital's emergency generator. Beyond the garage was a tall iron fence with electrified spikes placed almost invisibly at the top. Beyond the fence was a dense stand of trees.

The hospital grounds had been breached only once a number of years ago, the killer approaching the fence through the woods and making it across and into the building. Since then, infrared and motion detectors had been installed, so that anything man-size coming within ten meters of the fence would set off an alarm, and the building would go into lockdown, FBI SWAT teams immediately dispatched.

Mac phoned Otto. "Anything on your board?"

"One figure, under what looks like cardboard about twenty-five mikes out, ten degrees left. He showed up about two hours ago, hasn't moved since. Lou's keeping an eye on him."

"Homeless?"

"Street's full of them," Otto said. "Even in Georgetown. And someone has apparently been camping here before."

"Too obvious," Mac wondered aloud.

"I can have the cops check it out."

"If he's after me and a cop shows up, it could go bad. I'll check it out myself."

"Could be just what he wants. Get you out of the castle keep into the open."

"Let's hope it's that easy," McGarvey said.

From his position behind the bole of a large oak, Hicks had a good sight line on the street bum passed out under the cardboard refrigerator box about thirty meters away.

Finding the stupid bastard on the street was a piece of luck, but if not that bit of good fortune, he would have found something else to use as cover. Disappear. Blend in. Improvise. Make use of whatever natural cover is available.

The bum had already been half-drunk, and when Hicks had given him a quart of Jack, the guy had been more than happy to roost for the night.

"Got a spot I use now and again," the guy said. "In the woods." He looked sixty but was probably in his thirties—long, scraggly white hair, a helter-skelter beard and filthy khakis, a moth-eaten sweater, and combat boots without laces. "Kinda private like."

Hicks had spotted the guy coming from there. "Are you ex-military?"

"Army Rangers. Hooah."

Hicks didn't believe the bum, but it didn't matter. He gave him a pack of Marlboros and twenty dollars. "Sweet dreams. Hooah."

McGarvey was inside the hospital, that much he was sure of. Just as he thought it likely that the man was there because he suspected that someone would be coming after him—though how the former DCI could know or suppose such a thing was a mystery.

The logic was thin. But it was what was at hand for the moment.

"If the easy way presents itself, check first to make sure that you're not walking into a trap, but then take advantage," one of the old hands had told the class. "You might not get another chance."

McGarvey left the hospital grounds by the front gate and hurried around the block past the Georgetown Recreation Center, traffic very light, nearly non-existent at this hour. Which was just as good. If there was going to be a gun battle, he didn't want any civilians to get into the line of fire.

If someone stumbled into the cross fire, he would have to back off. The problem would be distinguishing between an innocent bystander and an active shooter.

A low wrought iron fence separated the sidewalk from the wooded swatch. Pulling his gun, Mac eased over the fence and merged into the woods. Within ten feet, he was out of sight from anyone passing on the street.

He pulled up short and cocked an ear to listen.

Straight ahead, he could just make out bits of the hospital's roofline, but from here, the building looked deserted, or nearly so. Only one dim light shone from an upstairs corner window, which was a supply room. Someone must have left the door open, and the light he was seeing was from the corridor.

Possibly meant as a distraction.

The cardboard box camp was off to the right between here and the hospital's fence line. Mac couldn't see much of anything, but there was no need for it. The bum, or others, had apparently used the place before, because a narrow path had been worn in the grass.

Mac stepped to the left of the track and started through the woods, moving tree to tree, his pistol pointed down and to the right, away from his leg.

"Mac, hold up," Otto's voice came softly in his earbud.

About fifteen yards out, a man, with his back to McGarvey, leaned up against a tree.

"Looks like someone behind a tree," Otto said.

"I see him," McGarvey replied softly.

SIXTEEN

□

It was coming up on midnight, and Hammond stood at his window in the Hay-Adams, looking down toward Lafayette Park and what little traffic there was at this hour. Tarasov had left shortly after the deal had been made with Hicks, which left nothing but to wait.

In a measure, he was nervous—lives were on the line here, conceivably even his own. But he was also excited. He'd played games for most of his life, and certainly for all of his adult life. And he'd often think of some of his financial deals—especially during the dot-com boom when he'd made the bulk of his fortune—as killings.

Destroying another man or a woman—the gender didn't matter to him—was the name of the game. The homework, the pursuit, and the final deal in which his opponent was ruined financially were everything.

Twice in the last eleven years, two of the men who had considered themselves financial wizards had killed themselves after losing to Hammond. Those events had been sort of a rush for him.

But this game now that he was playing, for no other reason than boredom he admitted to Susan last month when he'd first come up with the plan, was the biggest high he'd ever been on.

It wasn't just McGarvey's life that was at stake; it was the assassins who would go up against him. Already one of them was dead, and tonight an even better killer was hunting the former CIA director.

Hammond wanted the Canadian sniper to win, and yet he didn't want the game to end so soon, so easily.

The house phone rang, and Hammond went over and picked it up. "Yes?"

"I need some company," Susan said.

Hammond was startled, but not displeased. "Are you here?"

"At the lobby bar."

He gave her his room number.

"I'll bring the champers," she said.

Otto, seated at the kitchen counter watching McGarvey approach the figure of a man leaning up against the tree, began to realize that something was wrong.

"Lou."

"Yes, dear."

"Give me a record of thermal scans of the man I'm currently looking at."

"The man's temperature is dropping."

"It's a dead body," Pete said from behind Otto.

"Scan the entire park for any heat signatures other than Mac's."

"I'm currently showing none."

"What about the man under the cardboard?"

"He is no longer there."

"No one else in the park?"

"Other than Mac, I'm seeing nothing," Lou said.

"What is your confidence?"

"Ninety percent."

"Why not one hundred?" Pete interjected.

"There are ways to defeat the imaging systems, such as a thermally opaque foil-lined jacket."

"Shit, shit," Otto said. "Give me low-lux eyes on the place."

Three cameras covering the rear perimeter of the hospital came on the monitor. One showed McGarvey and something else just behind him to the right.

Susan knocked once at the door, and Hammond let her into the suite. She was dressed in white silk trousers widely flared at the bottom and a sheer, almost transparent blouse with no bra. She was slightly tipsy, a big grin on her Botoxed lips. a slight flush on her cheeks.

It was hard to tell if she was acting or not, because she was almost always playing a role, but she smelled of alcohol.

"How's our new man doing?" she asked. "Has he made the kill yet? The lion to the prey, the gorilla down from the trees, the hawk on the downdraft, and all that crap?"

"I haven't heard."

"So, Tommy boy, are your nipples hard with anticipation? Mine sure the hell are."

The man propped up against the tree was a street bum, and he was dead. This close up, it was obvious to McGarvey that his neck had been broken.

Someone was at arm's length coming up fast behind him.

Otto's voice was in his earbud. "To your right, behind you."

McGarvey was already dropping low and reaching for his pistol as he swiveled sharply into the approaching man, catching him in the right hip with his shoulder and knocking him off his feet.

A large-caliber pistol went off just over Mac's head, the bullet plowing into the dead street bum's back, the sound muffled by a suppressor on the end of the barrel.

The much larger man grunted something and tried to kick his way free, but Mac was on him, batting his gun hand away.

The advantage was only momentary, and before McGarvey could bring his own pistol up and fire, the shooter managed to smash the butt of his pistol into the side of Mac's head, and he fuzzed out for just a moment.

"Son of a bitch," the man swore, his English flat and oddly accented.

He scrambled away on his butt and once again brought his gun around and fired a shot that went wide, and before he pulled off another, Mac brought his Walther up and fired two rounds, one missing, the second hitting the man somewhere on the left side.

The man kicked out with a booted foot, catching McGarvey squarely in the face, knocking him flat on his back.

Mac recovered groggily and fired two more shots, not knowing if they had hit, but the man scrambled away, disappearing into the darkness.

Otto, Pete, and Mary watched all of it, even the low-lux cameras, losing contact with the shooter.

"Are you okay?" Pete asked. She was beside herself with fear. If the shooter came back now, Mac would be vulnerable.

"Where is he?"

"Headed back toward Volta Place," Otto said.

"The bastard is big," McGarvey grunted, and he hauled himself to his feet and stood there for a long moment or two. "See if there are any surveillance cameras. I need to know which way he went and if he has a ride."

"Stay there. We're calling the Bureau," Otto said.

"No time," Mac said, and he started after the shooter.

Mary was on the phone with one of her contacts at the FBI. "We have a situation," she said.

McGarvey's image was finally lost on the low-lux cameras on the hospital's roof, and Otto was hurriedly scanning for surveillance cameras on Volta Place or anywhere else in the vicinity.

Lou picked up one on the rec center just as the shooter emerged from the woods and turned left toward the university.

"Left," Otto radioed to Mac.

SEVENTEEN

□

Keeping to the shadows as much as possible, Hicks made his way down Volta Place toward the university campus less than two blocks away. He had taken one shot to his left side, and although he wasn't losing too much blood, his rib cage hurt like hell. But he had to get off the street and under cover soon.

At the corner, he glanced over his shoulder, but McGarvey had not yet appeared from the woods. The son of a bitch had gone down, but he had managed to shoot back and was in the act of getting to his feet.

The bastard was tougher than Hicks thought any man could be, especially one who was fifty. He had definitely underestimated the former DCI, and it was a mistake he wasn't going to make again. If he had another chance.

Just before the corner, a cab cruised by, and Hicks almost hailed it but then shook his head.

"Goddamnit to hell," he swore softly, watching the cab turn left on Thirty-Fifth Street and disappear.

The fact of the matter was he'd screwed up his last hit, but the op had been contracted under a very strict blanket of secrecy so that his failure had not turned up on anyone's radar yet. And it was the only reason the Russian operator had recommended him for this assignment.

But sooner or later, the fact he had failed would come to light among the people who knew about these things, and his career would be over. He needed the money to go deep at least for the next few years, to give himself the time to sanitize his profile before he could get back in the game.

Which meant McGarvey had to die.

He turned around and hurried back fifty feet to where the line of trees ended next to an art gallery closed at this hour, and he ducked into the woods just as his quarry came into sight.

McGarvey was just in time to see the figure of a man duck back into the woods about seventy yards away in the direction of the university. He couldn't be certain that the shooter had spotted him and would be waiting in ambush. But he had to assume the worst.

Keeping his pistol pointed down in his left hand, hiding it from anyone passing on the street, he hurried down Volta, ready at an instant to jog left into the tree line.

"The Bureau is rolling," Pete said. "You copy?"

"Yes. He just went back into the woods, and it's possible he spotted me," McGarvey said.

"Could he be doubling back toward the hospital?"

"Anything's possible," McGarvey said. He spotted a small splatter of blood on the sidewalk. "He's wounded."

"Badly?"

"No," McGarvey said. He picked up the pace but moved left so that he was hugging the edge of the woods. To have a clear sight line, the man would have to step out into the open.

"Hold up there until the SWAT team arrives," Pete said. "Let them handle it."

"I want him alive."

"No one's going to risk their life on this guy. They'll be on-site in under ten minutes."

"Let them know I'm here in the mix; I don't want to get shot in the back," McGarvey said.

Switching his pistol to his right hand, he stepped off the sidewalk and made his way from tree to tree on a diagonal, which he thought might intercept the shooter if he was doubling back as Pete had suggested.

Hicks waited for a full two minutes before he poked his head out from behind a tree where he had a decent line of sight up the sidewalk to where he'd seen McGarvey come out of the woods. But the tenacious son of a bitch wasn't there.

From what he'd learned from the dossiers he'd been shown, he didn't think that the former DCI was the type to call for help. The man had built the rep of working on his own. He was a lone wolf except for his geeky friend who still worked for the Company and his new wife, who'd been a CIA interrogator. The geek wouldn't be coming out here, nor did he think that McGarvey would want his wife to get involved in a gun battle.

For now, then, it was just him and McGarvey. Exactly the way he liked it.

The former DCI was stalking him, so now it was time to turn the tables again.

McGarvey held up behind a tree and checked the load in his pistol, ejecting the magazine and making sure that when he'd fallen to the ground, the weapon hadn't been fouled by dirt. It was still clean, and he reinserted the mag into the gun's handle.

He didn't think the shooter would be the type to give himself over to the cops when the SWAT team showed up. And he had gone back into the woods because he hadn't given up on his assignment.

Who had hired the man, and why?

Turning his head to the left to partially mask the direction of his voice, he called out, "I'm ready to make a deal if you're willing to listen."

"Terms?" the shooter called. He was perhaps twenty-five yards out and slightly to the left.

"I'll give you a head start."

"What guarantees do I have?"

"A piece of free advice. A Bureau SWAT team is en route."

"What do you want in return?"

"Who hired you to kill me and why?"

"I don't have those answers."

It struck McGarvey that the man's accent was Canadian. "Nor would you give them to me if you did."

"Something like that," the shooter said. This time, he was farther to the left but definitely closer.

McGarvey eased to the right but still behind the tree, and he crouched down. "I don't think that you're working for any government, especially not Canada's. So it's not for your country, just money. Worth your life?"

"Who are you working for?"

"At this moment, myself."

"And your wife and Otto Rencke? Do you think they will mourn your passing?"

The shooter was to the left and very close.

McGarvey rose up and rolled left.

The shooter was right there and started to turn as Mac pointed his pistol directly at the man's head at a distance of less than five feet.

The man stopped. "Even you might miss at this range."

"No," Mac said. "Open your hand and drop your pistol. Any other move and I'll fire."

"Then what?"

"Give me the answers and you can leave. No real harm, no foul."

"What'll you tell the SWAT team when they show up?"

"You escaped."

"Noble of you."

"I'm just tired of being hunted. You're the second shooter someone's sent. I want to know who and why."

This seemed to surprise the man. "I didn't know."

"Who hired you?"

"I don't know that either, except that my initial contact was with a Russian. But he was merely a go-between."

"SVR? GRU?"

"He sounded like he might have worked as an intel officer at one time, but I don't think he was active."

"Do you have a name or a description?"

"Never met him face-to-face."

"How much were you promised?"

"Five million . . . ," the shooter said when a siren very close interrupted him. Without turning, he angled his pistol upward and fired.

At the last instant, McGarvey moved his head sharply to the left and fired his pistol, the shot catching the man in the side of his neck before he staggered a pace backward and then went down.

EIGHTEEN

Hicks was alive and conscious, but he was trying with everything in his being not to drown in his own blood that was pouring into his windpipe from the ragged wound in his neck. The bullet had hit his jaw and splintered, causing a major tear.

McGarvey was over him, kicking away the pistol that had fallen to the ground.

Hicks thought he was hearing a lot of sirens approaching from the east, though he was becoming more and more detached. The fact of the matter is he'd lost. McGarvey was good, a lot better than even his dossiers had suggested. Better than Tarasov had warned.

McGarvey grabbed Hicks's right shoulder and turned him on his side, and immediately, blood stopped pouring into his throat.

Hicks coughed several times, deeply, the pain raging in his neck all the way to the top of his head. But he could breathe if he kept it shallow.

The sirens were much closer now, maybe at the end of the block.

McGarvey clamped a hand over the wound, applying just enough pressure to slow the bleeding, but not so much as to impede breathing.

The man was saving his life, but Hicks could think of only one reason for it. Information.

"I would have kept my word," McGarvey said. His voice was a long ways off.

The sirens had stopped, and for a moment, Hicks thought he'd lost his hearing, but someone shouted from the street.

"Coming in!"

"Straight back, twenty yards," McGarvey called.

"Clear?"

"Shooter's down."

"No malice," Hicks managed to whisper. For some reason, he wanted to make that much clear.

"Just a job?"

"The biggest yet. I could have gone deep."

"Who was the Russian who hired you?"

"Deep pockets. But I think he was just an expediter working for an American."

"Do you have a name?"

"No."

"Description?"

"His face and voice were distorted," Hicks said, and he was drifting, the pain gone, McGarvey's face above him fading.

Four SWAT team officers, FBI stenciled on their vests, appeared behind and to the left and right of McGarvey and Hicks, their assault rifles at the ready.

"Mr. McGarvey?" one of them asked.

Mac nodded. "This guy's still alive, and I want to keep him that way."

"Medic!" the officer shouted, and within moments, another man in SWAT team incident dress appeared. He wasn't armed but was carrying a trauma bag.

The medic got down next to Hicks.

"One round hit his jaw, then an artery in the neck," McGarvey said.

The medic pulled a thick gauze pad from a packet and motioned for McGarvey to take his hand away from the wound, which immediately began spurting blood.

Mac backed off, picked up his pistol, holstered it, and turned to the officer who obviously was the incident commander. "You guys bring an ambulance?"

"Yes, sir. Have you been hit?"

"No. But I want to save this guy's life, if at all possible."

"His carotid artery has been nicked," the medic said without looking up.

"Take him to All Saints; it's just around the corner."

"That's for you guys," the incident commander said.

"I need this man," Mac said. "Otto?"

"Franklin's rolling," Otto said in his earbud.

"Send Pete over; I want her to run the interrogation if he can be stabilized and brought around."

"She and Mary just left," Otto said. "You okay?"

"He missed."

By the time Hicks was stabilized, loaded into the ambulance, and brought to All Saints, Franklin was there. After a short conference with the medic, the still-unconscious man was hustled immediately upstairs to the third-floor operating theater.

McGarvey went to the restroom at the end of the hall and cleaned up as best he could. When he came out, a suit from the FBI who identified himself as Special Agent Tom Duncan was there in the waiting room.

"How're you doing, Mr. Director?" he asked, getting to his feet. He was a tall, well-built man in his early forties, with light hair cropped short in the military fashion, a square jaw, and bright eyes. He looked like a recruiting poster for Special Forces.

"Fine," Mac said. "And thanks for the Bureau's quick response. You might have saved his life."

"Any idea who he is?"

"A Canadian, I think, and I wouldn't be surprised if he was special ops at one time."

"What'd he want with you?"

"He wanted me dead."

Duncan pursed his lips. He looked skeptical. "Any relationship to the dead man in the building across the street from your apartment?"

"They weren't brothers, if that's what you mean," Mac said sharply, and he immediately regretted it. "Sorry, but I don't care much for being hunted."

"Which is what both of these guys were doing, hunting you. But why? What's the connection between the two of them?"

"I don't know yet, but I'm assuming for right now that they were hired by the same people, possibly the Russians."

Duncan was startled. "The SVR or GRU?"

"It's a thought."

"From what I understand, they would have cause. But why not send one of their own? Why hire outsiders?"

"Lots going on right now between the White House and the Kremlin, and taking out a former DCI would carry with it some serious blowback."

"Do you think that there's a connection between President Weaver's and Putin's talks and taking you down?"

McGarvey nodded toward the operating theater. "It's one of the questions I want to ask him if he makes it."

"Keep us informed."

Pete and Mary showed up five minutes after Duncan left. Mac was still in the waiting room having a cup of coffee, and when they came in, Pete gave him a sharply appraising look.

"Are you okay?" she asked.

"I'll live."

Franklin, still in his operating scrubs, came down the corridor. He didn't look happy. "I lost him," he said. "Just too much damage to his carotid artery. And there were several bullet fragments in his right temporal lobe that we didn't catch until we had the bleeding under control."

"We'll get his fingerprints, dental records, and samples of his blood, saliva, and hair for a DNA analysis," Mary said. "Same as the South African. Something matching the two of them might turn up."

Franklin nodded. "Unless you're going to send me someone else this evening, I'm going home," he said, and he walked away.

NINETEEN

Hammond and Susan were having a late breakfast in the suite after an energetic night of lovemaking. She was nearly ten years younger than he was and had more stamina. Plus, she was almost always completely absorbed in herself, and there were times that he felt he was getting tired of her.

"Typical Hollywood," she'd once explained. "A leopard can't change its spots, and an actor sometimes doesn't know who the real person is."

They'd been on his yacht anchored off Cannes a few years ago. It was morning, and they were having breakfast like now.

"I don't want you to change," he'd told her, and he'd meant it.

"You'll get tired of me sooner or later. It's another Hollywood flaw, or plus, depending on your point of view. Jump in bed for a good fuck with someone new. Marry them eventually, and within a year, you decide someone else might be more interesting, and you drift apart to start it all over again."

"So let's be different and never get married to each other."

She'd smiled and nodded. "Freedom. I like that."

"Me, too," Hammond had said.

She took her coffee and went to the window looking toward the White House. "We should have heard something by now," she mused.

Hammond agreed. "He might have missed, or something may have come up."

"He'll want the second payment, and he'll want to keep you from getting nervous. Maybe you'll pull the first half from his account."

"Can't be done."

"My people tell me that anything can be done, if the incentive is there."

It was the first thing Hammond had thought of when he'd awakened this morning. But he'd decided to give it a little time.

He picked up his phone and called Tarasov's private number. It rang four times, but instead of rolling over to a voicemail option, the call was canceled. He hit the End button.

Susan had watched. "No one home?"

"No."

She came across, took the phone from him, entered a number, and put it on speaker mode. It rang twice before a woman answered. "Department of Justice, how may I direct your call?"

"Bob Perkins, please."

"Robert Perkins's office. Who is calling?" another woman answered.

"Susan Patterson. I just need a moment of Bobby's time, if he's fit company this morning."

"One moment."

Susan put her hand over the phone. "He's an assistant director of the DOJ's Domestic Intelligence Division. He's a fan, and we're old pals."

"Good morning, Susan. Surprised to hear from you," Perkins said. He sounded breathless as if he'd just run up a flight of stairs, or just excited that a movie star had called. "It's been a while. Are you in town?"

"I am. And I want to know what kind of an operation you guys are running here. A girl can't come to D.C. and feel safe on the streets?"

"My God, what happened? Are you okay?"

"I was at a party in Georgetown last night. And all of a sudden, it was like World War III was starting. I mean, sirens everywhere. And maybe even some shooting? I'm telling you, I was frightened out of my mind. I thought it was another Pulse incident."

"What time was this?"

"I don't know," she said, and she covered the phone again.

"After midnight?" Hammond said.

Susan took her hand away. "Sometime after midnight, maybe."

"Hold on," Perkins said.

Susan held out her coffee cup for a refill, and Hammond poured.

Perkins came back, and he sounded cautious. "There was a shooting up near the university, but I'm told it was a drunk with a gun threatening to kill his wife," Perkins said. "Where was the party?"

"I was just getting in a cab on M Street to come back to the hotel when we heard the gunfire. I'm not shitting you, Bobby, it scared the hell out of me."

"Not to worry."

"Did they kill the drunk?"

Perkins hesitated. "I don't know," he said.

"Okay, well, I feel safer. Maybe next time I'm in town, if you can keep the bad guys at bay, we'll get together."

"I'd like that," Perkins said, his tone not so light.

Susan broke the connection. "Your guy?"

"Could have been a coincidence," Hammond said.

"But you doubt it."

Hammond nodded.

"Let's get out of here."

"Okay."

"Where's the boat?"

The boat was *Glory*, a 380-foot motor yacht built a few years ago by the Italian shipyard Codecasa in Tuscany. She wasn't the largest vessel in the billionaires' circuit, but she'd made the Atlantic crossing three times now with absolutely no trouble. And last year, she had transited the Panama Canal.

"Seattle. We're having some work done on the engines."

"Jesus."

"I was thinking about spending a month or so on the inside passage up to Anchorage until it's time to take her back across the pond. Something different."

"The only ice I like is in my drink," Susan said, but then another thought occurred to her, and her expression and attitude changed. "You're not done."

"Not by a long shot."

"It doesn't bother you that the second guy probably failed?"

"I'd hoped he would," Hammond said. "I don't want it to end so quickly. I want the bastard to hang out in the wind for a while."

"Okay, so it's still a game. But we know what McGarvey is capable of if he finds out who's behind it. So it's a dangerous game. And I'll ask again: Where's the profit in it, Tom? It has to be worth something to you."

"It is. But for now, like you said, it's still just a game."

"Like the movie," Susan said. But she had another thought. "Which is why you want to get out of Dodge. Alaska until the dust settles on this move."

"I've never been up there. Have you?"

"You've already lost two shooters. How many more are you willing to lose?"

"In chess, it's called a *gambit*. Sacrifice a piece or two for a shot at the ultimate prize."

Susan shook her head in wonder. "You're nuts, do you know that?"

"Yes, but I'm rich, so I can afford to be."

Susan had a bellman bring up her bags, which she had parked in the lobby storage room, and when she had cleaned up and was dressed, she came out as Hammond was getting off the phone.

"Can't get in touch with your Russian friend?" she asked.

"Not yet," Hammond said. He'd opened a bottle of Krug, and he poured her a glass. "Do you have anything pressing in LA?"

"Nothing I can't duck out of."

"You're tagging along with me."

She took the champagne, drank it down, and offered her glass for a refill. "Wouldn't miss it for all the world," she said as he poured. "But it won't be just us aboard, will it?"

"No, we'll have a few friends up."

She grinned. "You're fun and all that, Tommy boy, but too much of the same thing can get boring. Maybe we can entice one of my exes to join us."

"Why not all four of them, and their current wives?" Hammond said.

She raised her glass. "The alibi heard round the world."

TWENTY

At Otto's house in McLean, Mary was making them breakfast, and Otto was helping. He went out to the screened porch in back with coffee for McGarvey and Pete. "Mary's Southern, so we're having grits with our bacon and eggs."

"I hope we're having more than coffee to wash it down," Pete said.

"I heard that," Mary called.

"Mimosas," Otto said, and he started back to the kitchen, but Lou's voice materialized.

"We have a fingerprint match on the shooter," she said.

"That was quick."

"They were in our own database. His name was Donald Hicks, thirty-seven, never married, though he was never evaluated as gay. Until four years ago, he was a highly decorated sniper for Canadian Special Operations."

"Then what?"

"He received an other-than-honorable discharge, and he dropped out of sight," Lou said.

McGarvey had an idea. "Lou, I'd like you to do a data search, starting four years ago."

"Of course, Mac."

"Can you access the records of passenger arrivals at all three airports in Moscow?"

"For Donald Hicks?"

"Yes."

"He may have traveled under false papers."

"Let's try Hicks first."

Lou uncharacteristically hesitated for a beat. "I'm searching now. But if his name does not come up, I can access the National Security Agency's facial recognition files."

"Unless he traveled under disguise," Otto said.

It almost sounded as if Lou laughed. "Of course, dear," she said.

"Make the same search for the South African shooter."

"Of course."

"In the meantime, get me a flight to Ottawa sometime this afternoon," McGarvey said. "And I need the name and private number of the current commander."

"The current commander is Lieutenant Colonel Horace Vickery. Shall I make the call on your phone now?"

"Please do."

"Who shall I say is calling, and the reason?"

"Tell him I'm calling and that I will explain," McGarvey said.

Mary came from the kitchen but didn't say a word. Neither did Otto or Pete.

By the time Mac had taken his phone out of his pocket and switched it to speaker mode, it was ringing. A man with a gruff voice answered.

"Mr. Director, your call comes as something of a surprise. How may I help, and with what?"

"One of your former operators, who was discharged four years ago, tried to kill me last night, and I'm trying to find out why."

"Sergeant Hicks," Vickery said.

"I'd like to fly up to talk to you and to anyone who knew him personally."

"Has he been taken into custody?"

"We had a gun battle, and he lost," McGarvey said.

"I see," Colonel Vickery said. "If you can snag a ride on a government or military aircraft, I can get you clearance to land on base."

"Mr. McGarvey will be arriving in a Navy Gulfstream C-20G," Lou broke in. "Direct from Andrews." She gave the tail number.

"I'll alert tower ops," Vickery said.

McGarvey hung up. "Anything on Hicks showing up in Moscow?"

"Nothing yet," Lou said. "Your ride is being preflighted, and your crew will be in place by the time you get to Andrews."

"Thank you."

"No sweat," Lou said.

"Do you want me to tag along?" Pete asked.

"Not necessary; I'll be back by this afternoon. If you or Lou think of any other means to trace either of the shooters, keep on it. As soon as I get back, I want to talk with Slatkin's old CO in the Recces."

"Will you want to fly over there?" Pete asked.

"Whatever it takes," McGarvey said.

"You don't think this is going away," Otto said.

"No."

Canada's Special Operations Regiment was based at Garrison Petawawa on the west bank of the Ottawa River in the Laurentian hills, 110 miles northwest of the capital. The sprawling base of more than five thousand military personnel, one thousand civilian employees, and nearly six thousand dependents had been in existence as a military training base since 1905.

McGarvey's ride touched down a few minutes before one in the afternoon, only puffy white summer clouds overhead, and a light breeze directly down runway 27. A jeep was waiting for him.

"I shouldn't be more than a couple of hours," he told the captain.

"Direct back to Andrews, Mr. Director?"

"I think so."

Colonel Vickery, in camouflage ODUs, was waiting in his office with another man also dressed in battle camos at base headquarters when McGarvey arrived.

They both got to their feet and shook hands. Vickery, who was a solidly built man in his midforties with a large head, square face, and a drooping jawline that made him look like a bulldog, introduced the other much shorter, more compactly built man as Captain Roger Confrey.

"Roger and Don went through training together and were deployed three times to Afghanistan," Vickery said when they were seated.

"You say that he tried to take you out, sir?" Confrey asked. He sounded and acted like a smart-ass.

"Yes."

"At what range?"

"Less than five feet."

Confrey shook his head. "Doesn't sound like the Don I knew. He was a long-range shooter. Nevertheless, I'm surprised he didn't succeed. No disrespect intended."

"None taken, Captain," McGarvey said. "Maybe he should have stuck with his sniper act."

Before Confrey could respond, Mac turned to Colonel Vickery. "We think he might have been working as a contractor for the SVR or GRU. Would that have fit with his profile? I understand he was given a OTH discharge."

Confrey started to say something, but Vickery held him off. "I was the exec here at the time. Don opted not to go through with a court-martial, taking his other than honorable instead. We had some pretty good evidence than he'd been a walk-in at the Russian embassy down in Ottawa. The RCMP gave us the heads-up, including some photographs."

"He didn't deny it?" McGarvey asked.

"No."

"Was he being accused of spying for the Russians?"

"No. He explained that he was applying for a visa. He wanted to go hunting in Siberia."

"Why was he threatened with a court-martial?"

"He held a top secret clearance, which meant he wasn't to have contact with any foreign government for any reason without authorization."

"So he quit, and you just let him walk out the door?"

"He actually had applied for and received a visa, and he'd signed up and paid for the guided hunting tour with a legitimate company."

"So he would have been given a disciplinary notice in his jacket and that would have been it?"

"Probably."

"Then why did he accept the OTH discharge?"

"Because he was hardheaded," Confrey said.

"But he did try to kill me, and now it seems more than likely he was working for the SVR, Captain. Makes him more than hardheaded. In fact, the price tag on me was $5 million, half of which had already been deposited in his offshore account."

TWENTY-ONE

□

The flight out to Seattle's Boeing Field went smoothly, though Susan complained most of the way that she was bored out of her skull. For all of her adult life, she'd surrounded herself with people.

On movie sets with camera operators, soundmen, makeup and costume people, set dressers, directors, and the occasional VIP fans and sometimes more than one boyfriend or husband at a time.

On-location shoots with the same numbers of moviemakers along with sometimes big crowds of extras, plus the onlookers at the fringes.

And although Hammond did enjoy her company in and out of bed, sometimes she was a royal pain in the ass, and he told her so.

An hour or so out of D.C., she had gone into the private sleeping compartment at the back of the plane and took a couple of lines of coke. To calm her nerves, she explained, and when she came forward again and sat down across from Hammond, she was animated but reasonably pleasant.

"I don't like being cooped up," she said.

Hammond poured her a glass of Krug. "I'm not going to put up with your bullshit much longer."

"I know that I can be a super bitch if I think shit's not going my way. But you're right about one thing." She looked out the window.

"What's that?"

When she turned back, she managed a weak smile. "We haven't heard from your number two, which means he's probably failed."

Hammond had realized the same thing last night. "It's one of the reasons I decided to back off for a bit."

"Why don't you just forget about it altogether?"

"It's too late. McGarvey won't let it go."

"I know. And that's what worries me the most. We're not going up against an amateur. This guy is good."

"It's me, not *we*."

She smiled. "That's very noble of you, Tom. But not normal. What gives, or is it that worriers want to hide under a porch alone so that they can lick their wounds in private?"

Hammond had thought about the advice Tarasov had given him at the beginning. "If you want the deal, there'll have to be a quid pro quo. But if you go ahead, don't change your outward lifestyle. Don't go into hiding somewhere. Stay out in the open with your circle of friends and lovers in full view.

Make it a game if you like, but understand that once you start, you won't be able to go back. You'll have to make sure that he dies."

And it had become a game in his mind before he'd hired Slatkin, a man he was sure would fail.

But now that they were in the middle of it, he was beginning to get a case of cold feet. And yet he had to keep telling himself that a man, even one as good as McGarvey, could not keep up against a constant stream of attackers, each one better than the last. Sooner or later, McGarvey would make a mistake. And in the meantime, the game was getting as interesting as climbing the north face of the Matterhorn without safety ropes except for his wealth, to which he wanted to add something significant.

He forced a smile. "Even I get to be noble every now and then," he said.

She raised her glass to him and took a drink.

Tarasov's advice was to continue as normal.

"Anyway, I have a surprise for you once we land."

She brightened. "Friends to meet us?"

"Something you like even more than that."

The landing went smoothly, but it wasn't until they had taxied across the field to Clay Lacy Aviation's private terminal and Susan spotted the KOMO television remote truck and the cameraman and woman reporter waiting out front that she became her old self—or at least her public self.

"You son of a bitch!" she shouted, laughing and unbuckling.

"I thought you'd like a little publicity," Hammond said.

"I do, but I look like the Wicked Witch of the West." She jumped up and headed to the rear. "Give me five."

Toni Hopkins, the pretty stew, came from the galley. "Looks like your call made a hit," she said, grinning.

"The lady does like to be in front of the camera. Any camera."

"Captain Bellows would like to know if we should take the plane back to LA."

"Yes. And you guys can have a couple of weeks off. We're taking the boat up to Anchorage."

"Supposed to be spectacular this time of year, if a little isolated."

"Something new," Hammond said, and he didn't know why.

Susan had done her face, fluffed up her blond hair, which she'd had colored last week, and put on a pair of skintight designer jeans with bangles up the seams, a very low-cut white blouse, and spike heels. "How do I look?" she asked, coming forward.

"Stunning as usual, Ms. Patterson," Toni said sincerely.

"Give that girl a raise."

"Consider it done," Hammond said.

The copilot, Joe Barnes, had opened the forward hatch and stood aside, and Eddie Bellows, the pilot, had turned in his seat.

"Good flight, guys," Hammond said.

"Thank you, sir," both men said.

Hammond took Susan's arm as they descended the steps to the tarmac.

"It would have been better if at least a handful of fans had shown up," she said.

"A handful would have been tacky, sweetheart, and it was too late to arrange for more."

They walked across to where the reporter and her cameraman were waiting, and Susan struck one of her hipshot poses.

"Susan Patterson, still as gorgeous as ever," the reporter said.

"Well, thank you, darlin'," Susan said. "It's lovely to be back in Seattle."

"A little bird told me that you might be here scouting out locations for an upcoming project. Any truth to the rumor?"

"You know I can't reveal too much about what might or might not be in the works, whoever the naughty boy was who let the cat out of the bag, but let's just say that Seattle has always been in my heart as one of the most photogenic cities on the entire planet."

"A beauty in the heart of beauty," the reporter said, and Susan lapped it up, practically purring.

Mac was due from Canada in two hours, and Mary and Pete were out back having a glass of wine and talking when Otto was coming downstairs.

"A possibly interesting development," Lou said.

Otto didn't stop. "The Moscow airport search?"

"No. I thought I might turn up something if I were to search backward to all of Mac's contacts over the past four years."

"Yes, go on, please."

"The business in Cannes after the attack on the AtEighth pencil tower on East Fifty-Seventh Street in Manhattan brought Mac in contact with a number of people."

"I know this. Please elaborate."

"Two of the principals who helped Mac gain access to the pencil tower across from the UN are being interviewed on television at this moment."

"Where?"

"An ABC affiliate in Seattle. You might want to watch the playback."

"What is your confidence that this may be of some significance?"

"Less than 20 percent."

Otto pulled up short on the last step. "How much less?"

"Two percent less, so eighteen percent total."

□

TWENTY-TWO

At Andrews, McGarvey thanked the navy crew for the quick flight to and from Petawawa before he got off the Gulfstream. "Interesting place," the pilot said.

"Out in the middle of nowhere."

"Maybe, but once we were out of Ottawa's TCA, we picked up a RCAF F/A-18 escort that landed just behind us and took off again a minute before you showed up."

"Making sure that we didn't stray?"

The pilot shook his head. "Making sure that the former CIA director got in and out safely. Somebody put out the word that you might be at risk."

"Did you talk to the crew?"

"No need, sir. It's SOP. We sometimes provide an escort for incoming noncommercial flights carrying VIPs who could be targets for assassination."

"I guess I must have stepped on someone's toes," McGarvey said.

"Yes, sir."

They had called ahead for a taxi, and as soon as they left Andrews's main gate, he gave the driver his Georgetown address, then phoned Pete, who was still with Otto and Mary.

"You're back?" she asked.

"I'm on my way to our apartment to pack a few things. Have Otto book me an overnight flight to Johannesburg."

"Okay, I'll wait until you get here to tell me what's up. But we have military stuff going over there all the time; we can probably get you a ride."

"Make it commercial this time."

"Okay, but that's two explanations you owe me. Do you want me to tag along?"

"No need. It's just going to be a quick in and out."

"In the meantime, Lou has come up with something interesting."

"She got a hit on the Moscow airport search?"

"It's something else," Pete said. "But you have to pass right by here from our place to get to Dulles, so we can go over in person what Lou came up with. Maybe you can come up with something we haven't thought of."

Otto got on. "I assume you're going out to talk to Slatkin's CO if he's still around. Do you want me to give them the heads-up?"

"No."

Otto hesitated for just a beat. "We'll talk when you get here."

"Might not be time; I want to be on a flight tonight."

"You have plenty of time. You're already booked. First-class Emirates leaves at five till eleven. So pick up your Thomas Blake passport."

"Rebook it under my own name," McGarvey said.

This time, Otto didn't miss a beat. "Bring your air marshal creds so you can travel armed. Just in case."

McGarvey had the cabbie wait for him as he went upstairs and packed a few things in an overnight bag, plus his passport and air marshal credentials, along with an extra magazine of ammunition for his Walther.

By long habit, he went to the front window but stood to one side as he looked out. The taxi was directly below, but so far as he could tell, nothing seemed threatening. No cars or vans parked that seemed out of place. Nothing on any of the rooftops within view. And nothing in any of the windows. Even the window on the third-floor apartment across the street had been replaced.

Nothing was out there, but he could practically feel the target painted on his back. Someone was gunning for him. They'd tried and failed twice, though Hicks had done a marginally better job of it than the South African.

But he didn't think it was over yet. And sooner or later, whoever was coming for him would be better still and maybe even luckier. His only recourse then was to go deep or continue hunting back.

And he'd only ever gone deep once, not to hide from an assassin but from his own life that had been shattered by an ultimatum that his wife had given him very early in his career.

His time in Lausanne had lasted only a couple of years until the CIA had sought him out to ask for help with a difficult assignment. He had reluctantly agreed to come back, which had begun a long string of operations, one of which had eventually led to the death of his wife after they had gotten back together, along with their daughter and her husband.

In fact, every woman since then had been murdered for who and what he was. And at this moment, he had terribly mixed feelings. He was frightened for Pete, and yet he was determined with everything in his soul not to let such a thing happen again.

This time, he was going on the hunt with a vengeance.

McGarvey's cab got to Otto's place in McLean that was only a couple of miles from the Dulles Airport Access Road off I-495 at a little before seven, leaving him plenty of time to make his flight.

Pete met him at the door, and when they were inside the front hall and he'd put his bag down, she took him in her arms and looked into his eyes. "Should I start worrying about you now?"

He smiled. "Save your worries for the other guy."

"Silly me. Somehow I thought you would say something like that."

They went back to the kitchen, where Mary had poured a cognac for Mc-Garvey. Otto was on the patio pulling steaks off the grill.

"Can't send you across the pond without something decent to eat and drink," he said, coming in.

Pete got the salad and Coronas from the fridge, and Mary got the baked potatoes from the oven, put them on a serving platter, and brought them to the table.

They all sat down, but no one reached for the food.

"Pete told me that Lou came up with something interesting," McGarvey said, breaking the silence.

Otto got his laptop from the counter and put it in front of Mac. "Hit Enter."

McGarvey did, and the brief interview with Susan Patterson, who was in Seattle with Hammond, came up.

"Susan Patterson, still as gorgeous as ever," a woman reporter said.

Mac looked up, but Otto gestured at the laptop. "Wait for it."

The interview only lasted a couple of minutes, but then Hammond, standing behind her and slightly to her left, said something out of place for the situation.

McGarvey backed it up and played it again.

"—let's just say that Seattle has always been in my heart as one of the most photogenic cities on the entire planet," said Susan.

"A beauty in the heart of beauty," the reporter said.

Hammond took Susan by the arm. "We have a boat to catch," he said in her car, but the mic was still hot, and the camera caught the expression on his face, then went blank.

McGarvey looked up. "Lou, what's the significance of this interview?"

"I'm at 18 percent, but I found it interesting that Ms. Patterson was lying; she is not in Seattle to scout for a movie location, and Mr. Hammond's posture and voice stress levels indicate that he may be under some pressure."

"Go on," McGarvey said, only the vaguest of ideas where Otto's AI program was heading.

"I was looking for connections to you that had gone poorly for the people you were dealing with. Mr. Hammond and Ms. Patterson may feel some animosity because of the failed bitcoin scheme you offered them."

"Thin," McGarvey said, but he was intrigued by how the AI program was dealing with human variables.

"Yes, Mac. My confidence is only 18 percent."

"Not high, but above statistical averages," Otto said.

TWENTY-THREE

At customs and immigration in Jo'burg's O. R. Tambo International Airport, McGarvey had to surrender his pistol and spare magazine of ammunition to the uniformed official, who also checked a database of all international air marshals to make sure McGarvey was on the list.

"Your weapon will be returned to you at the boarding gate when you leave tomorrow morning," the man said, his manner cool but officiously polite. "Do you have anything else to declare?"

"No."

"What is the purpose of your visit to South Africa?"

"I've come to speak with General Leon." Stanley Leon, a one-star, was the CO of South Africa's Special Forces.

"Yes, sir," the official said, and he handed McGarvey's passport over.

A short connecting corridor, guarded by a security guard and cameras plus notices that no one was to enter customs from this direction, led directly to automatic doors out to ground transportation. The multilane driveway was busy with people who'd just arrived on the Emirates flight queuing up for taxis, buses, and the outer lane for private cars and a couple of limos.

A man in his thirties, built like a star soccer player, obviously military by his bearing and buzz cut but dressed in a civilian suit, no tie, came over from his illegally parked Mercedes SUV.

"Good morning, Mr. Director. I've been sent to take you to your hotel."

"I'm here to speak with General Leon at Brigade Headquarters."

"Yes, sir, the general is expecting you. But unfortunately, non–South African civilians are currently not allowed on base."

"In that case, I'll find my own way to the hotel," McGarvey said, and he started to step around the man, who moved directly in his path.

"The general and his aide-de-camp will meet you at the hotel. A private conference room has been arranged, and I was told to assure you that any questions you may have concerning Sergeant Slatkin will be answered so far as national security concerns will allow."

It was about what McGarvey had expected, but he also knew that trying to speak to the general from Washington by phone or computer would have run into a brick wall. Now that he was here diplomatically, he couldn't be ignored.

"Then let's go."

"Yes, sir. I've also been instructed to inform you that you will not be allowed away from the hotel until it is time for you to leave on the return flight."

"May I ask why?"

"You brought a weapon into South Africa."

"I'm traveling as an air marshal."

"You're on the list, but you are not active."

"You've done your homework."

"Yes, sir."

General Leon, also dressed in civilian clothes, was seated at a small conference table at the hotel, two floors above the lobby. He was flanked by one man also in civvies, and like the driver who'd withdrawn, he was obviously military, his bearing and posture erect, his hair cut short, and his build athletic.

"Our meeting will of necessity be a short one, Mr. Director," Leon said, his South African accent so rounded he almost sounded Australian.

"I appreciate whatever help you can give me," McGarvey said, taking a seat across from him.

"Sergeant Slatkin has been a civilian for three years," the aide said, his manner clipped.

"I didn't think the Recces fielded assassins to take out former CIA directors," McGarvey said, his manner just as abrupt. "I'm here to find out why he came to kill me and who hired him."

"I can't answer either of those questions," Leon said.

"He maintained an offshore bank account that had been credited with a quarter of a million U.S. dollars. Was he worth it?"

"Evidently not," the aide said.

"The man's training was first class," Leon said. "He was good at his job."

"Was he tested?"

"If you meant by that did he draw blood? The answer is yes, but I cannot discuss any specific operation, you must understand."

"Did he ever travel to Russia for any reason?"

Leon glanced at the aide, who shook his head.

"No, sir, but . . ." He left it hanging.

"But?"

Leon nodded.

"He was involved briefly in a joint training mission outside of South Africa."

"Where?" McGarvey asked.

"I can't say, sir."

"When was the mission?"

The aide glanced at the general. "I don't have that information."

McGarvey turned to the general. "I meant how long after the mission with the Russians did Slatkin fuck your daughter?"

Leon's expression didn't change, but he got to his feet. "I want this man brought directly back to the airport, where he is to be put on the next airplane that is scheduled to fly anywhere as long as it's out of South Africa. If he resists, shoot the son of a bitch."

McGarvey sat back. "Evidently, Slatkin wasn't the only South African who wanted me dead."

McGarvey's driver from the airport brought him to the departures gates. The general's aide escorted him to an office overlooking the main concourse, where they picked up a sealed pouch. From there, they went to the Delta counter, where a first-class ticket to Rio de Janeiro was waiting for him.

The aide escorted him through security to a Delta boarding gate, where the last of the passengers were going through the door into the Jetway, and he handed the sealed pouch to the female gate agent.

"Take this to the pilot. It contains this gentleman's weapon and air marshal identification. He's not to have them back until you leave South African airspace. Do you understand?"

"Of course," the gate agent said. She disappeared down the Jetway and a minute or so later was back. "Done," she said.

"Don't come back to South Africa," the aide said.

"So long as you don't lose another of your operators," McGarvey said.

He followed the gate agent aboard the 747, and when he was seated alone in an aisle seat in the main deck third row and the hatch was sealed, one of the stews brought him a cognac.

"Glad to have you aboard, Mr. McGarvey," she said.

Another stew brought the sealed pouch back to him. "Captain's compliments, and welcome aboard, sir. He asks that if you need to make a phone call please wait until we reach ten thousand feet."

A few of the other passengers, realizing that he was a VIP by the way he was being treated by the crew, looked at him, and he raised his drink.

As the safety instructions came up on the seat-back monitors and the flight attendants were checking seat belts and shutting the overhead bin doors, he sat back and closed his eyes. He had found out exactly what he'd hoped to find out by coming here.

Slatkin was definitely working for the Russians, and General Leon had confirmed it.

TWENTY-FOUR

They were delayed overnight in Seattle to finish provisioning the MV *Glory* and had not gotten away until just after eight the next morning. The weather had been overcast and cool, and Susan was in one of her bitchy moods, which usually came on when she was without an audience.

That night, they were well up the Strait of Georgia, and on the second midmorning, Vancouver to their south, Captain Rupert Miller called Hammond in the saloon.

"We have a helicopter, Canadian registry, requesting to land on deck, sir."

Susan was watching a rerun of one of her older movies, even bitchier this morning than she had been yesterday. No one else would be joining them for at least four days, and she freely admitted that she had no idea how she would cope without going absolutely stir-crazy.

"Have we done something wrong? Is it a police or military helicopter?" Hammond asked, something clutching at his gut.

"No, sir. It's a civilian helicopter. The pilot says he's bringing a friend."

"Did he give you a name?"

Susan had turned down the sound of the television and was looking at him.

"No, sir."

Hammond didn't need something like this now. Especially not one of his financial advisers—or worse yet, one of Susan's hangers-on. He had purposely wanted isolation of his ship on the inside passage up to Alaska to think things out, consider his next move. Or even if there should be a next move.

The reality of the little game he was playing, engaging in a manhunt, especially a man of McGarvey's capabilities, had become troublesome, even daunting. He hadn't wanted it to be over with just the two attacks. He'd wanted it to continue, and yet now that both assassins had failed, he was having serious second thoughts.

"What shall I do, Mr. Hammond?"

"Reduce speed and let him land," Hammond said.

"Yes, sir."

Hammond put the phone down, and the yacht immediately began to slow. He went aft and watched out the sliders as a sleek blue helicopter with Canadian markings slowly approached. At the last moment, it flared and expertly touched down on the helipad.

The passenger-side door opened, and Mikhail Tarasov, wearing jeans, a dark pullover, and khaki jacket, jumped down and, keeping low beneath the slowly rotating blades, came forward to where Hammond was waiting.

"Who the hell is it?" Susan asked.

"Mikhail."

"Shit," she said, getting up. "I'm going below; call me when he's gone."

"You might want to stay and hear what he has to say."

"Push it, Tommy boy, and I'll jump ship and take my friends with me the instant we dock somewhere civil." She gave him a glaring look and took the stairs below.

A crewman had appeared and was chocking the helicopter's wheels as Hammond opened the slider for Tarasov. They shook hands.

"I'm a little surprised to see you," Hammond said. "How did you find us?"

"After that cheap stunt on the television in Seattle, it took just a few calls to the marinas to find out where you were and the fact you'd headed north."

"So what?"

"So your operator failed and you run for the hills. How obvious can you get?"

"How do you know he failed?"

"McGarvey showed up in person in Petawawa aboard one of the navy's Gulfstreams that the CIA uses."

It was the news Hammond was afraid Tarasov was bringing. "What the hell is Petawawa?"

"It's the Canadian Special Operations base where your shooter was trained."

Hammond's fear suddenly turned to anger. "Not to put too fine a point on it, but you supplied me with the contact info on both those guys. And they failed."

"You wanted them to fail, Thomas. You specifically wanted to give McGarvey a challenge that he would be likely to win. Well, it worked. Not only did he show up in Canada, he's just now on his way home from South Africa."

"So what?"

"He traced the shooters to their home bases."

"Again, what's your point?"

"Both of those guys had contact with Russia."

Hammond suddenly got it, all of it. "You recommended the shooters, so was it unfair for me to assume that they would be clean? No Russian connections? No SVR or GRU connections?"

Tarasov glanced out the slider at the helicopter. "Neither of them has a Russian intel file."

"Any Russian connections they may have had will carry no real weight with McGarvey. One of them was a Canadian, the other a South African. What are you worried about?"

"You."

Hammond spread his hands, actually relieved. "Life will go on."

"I meant what do you want to do next? Continue with the game, or quit?"

"Actually, I was thinking about ending it as is. But I don't like to lose."

"You may in the end, despite your money."

"You're in the same position."

"No, Thomas. You have wealthy friends and money managers. All of whom would drop you in an instant if they thought you were creating a risk."

"Again, you're in the same spot."

Tarasov shook his head. "You have movie stars on your side, hangers-on; I have a different class of friends."

"The ones who recruit killers for you."

"Da, and they don't give a damn who their targets are, as long as the money is right. So the question I came to ask you is still on the board. What do you want to do next?"

Hammond didn't have to think about it. "Continue the game, providing you can give me someone better qualified."

"As you wish," Tarasov said. He took a regular number 10 envelope from inside his jacket and held it out. "A man and a woman this time, and very capable. They're called the Chinese Scorpions."

Hammond laughed. "Theatrical."

"Do not underestimate these people. One of their conditions is that they meet you face-to-face."

Hammond had started to reach for the envelope but stayed his hand. "Why?"

"Their philosophy is a simple one. If they're hired to do a job in which they might lose their lives or their freedom, they want to know who hired them."

"If they're incompetent, they should fail."

"It's not a matter of incompetence. It's a matter of betrayal. If you are found out and give them up, they will hunt you instead of McGarvey."

Still Hammond hesitated.

"This isn't only about money now. So take care, Thomas."

"I was fucked over by the son of a bitch and his wife. And I didn't like it very much. Maybe they'll both die." He took the envelope.

Tarasov nodded. "Your call."

"Would you like to stay for lunch?"

"No," the Russian said. "I want to get as far away from you as I can, at least for now." He went to the slider, but then turned back. "I wish you luck. I sincerely mean it."

. . .

Susan joined him without a word, and they watched Tarasov board the helicopter and take off.

"Chinese Scorpions?" she asked. "I love it."

"You heard?"

"Most of it. Are you going to take the gig?"

"Of course," Hammond said. "But first, let's fill *Glory* with a lot of friends and have a party in the middle of nowhere."

"We don't have any friends, Tommy boy, but what the hell, it sounds like fun to me."

PART
TWO

Middle Game

When he realizes he is being hunted,
what will he do?
Hide or fight back?

TWENTY-FIVE

☐

Chan Taio, wearing only black silk pajama bottoms, walked out onto the open second-floor balcony of his and Li's duplex overlooking the beach and high-rises in Hong Kong's Repulse Bay and breathed deeply of the mild morning air.

At five ten, he was tall for a Chinese, and his muscles, especially those in his chest, were well defined. His facial features were almost Western mostly because he'd had his eyes altered when he was sixteen. A lot of his friends had done the same thing at the time. It was cool. And with the light brown wig he sometimes wore to cover his very short, intensely black hair, he could and had passed as a Westerner.

He was at Zen peace with himself, though one section of his brain—and his heart, if he were to be honest—yearned for another operation. At thirty-one, he and his partner, Li, who was twenty-seven, were at the height of their physical and mental abilities.

Their initial training days and nights for three grueling years had taken place at several mainland Chinese Special Operations Forces bases. Individual and small-team survival skills, camouflage, weapons, navigation, communications, infiltration and exfiltration, and close-combat scenarios, including sniper training and room-clearing in what were called *kill houses*.

Finally, they'd been recognized for their outstanding all-around abilities and had been sent to the Special Operations Academy for junior officers in Guangzhou, which had actually been the beginning of the end for them. They'd become too good and too independent for the strict SOF regimen that forever bowed to a civilian leadership that demanded total obedience. Included in their orders was the strict rule that officers did not closely fraternize with each other.

But he and Li fell in love at the academy after only three assignments— one of them when they were sent to London to kill a dissident who'd worked at a fairly high level for the Ministry of State Security in Beijing. The man had been responsible for recruiting, vetting, and assigning deep-cover agents around the world. At the time, he was working out of the Chinese embassy, and it was thought that he was making plans to defect to MI6 and had to be silenced.

They had carried out the op with what a colonel had reported was a terrible, silent efficiency. "They were scorpions," he'd supposedly said.

Afterward, they had asked permission through channels to marry, but their request had been denied. They got orders, her to remain at the academy, him to Hong Kong. They were at the end of their third two-year term of service, and they'd resigned their commissions within one month of each other.

Their discharges were honorable, so no one had come looking for them. Within a few weeks, Li had joined him in Hong Kong; they got married and began taking freelance operations, some ironically through the same SOF they'd been members of.

Li, wearing only the silk top of Tiao's pajamas, came to the open slider. "Enjoying the image of yourself in the glass, or is there another gaggle of Western girls in bikinis on the beach?" she asked, her voice musical.

"Both, actually," he said. He turned.

She had her iPhone, and she brought it out and handed it to him. "This came overnight," she said.

It was a text message addressed to COUNTER-T EXECUTIVE ACTION SOLUTIONS. It was their business. The Counter-T stood for counterterrorism, and twice, they'd actually taken the simple assignments, in both cases acting as glorified bodyguards for business executives working in war zones, once in Afghanistan, and the second time in Syria.

The real business of the business was assassination, such as the ones like the London op. They were fast, brutally efficient, obscenely expensive, and not once had they ever failed. In the trade, they had maintained the sobriquet as the Chinese Scorpions, nobody remembering where the moniker had originated.

"Is it from anyone we know?" Taio asked.

"The Russian."

They never knew the Russian's name, though they strongly suspected he worked for the GRU and that he handed out special assignments that couldn't be traced back to Moscow, and paid very well and very promptly.

"A special client needs an operation. Meet soonest aboard the MV *Glory* lying Skagway, Alaska. Legend as movie producers ex-Taiwan. Ten million U.S."

Taio texted back. "When?"

Li looked past his arm at the screen.

"Soonest."

"Who is the client?"

"Details to follow acceptance."

"Is he involved with movies in the U.S.?"

"Details to follow acceptance."

Li was a full four inches shorter than her husband and, at only a little over one hundred pounds, was tiny, her skin pale. People said that she looked like a porcelain doll. Her face was round, her lips full and her eyes wide and expressive. She smiled and looked up at him.

"What would you like to do?" she asked.

"We don't need the money." They'd paid ten million euros cash for their condo and owned a Mercedes convertible and matching Augusta motorcycles. Between assignments, they never took vacations, except locally. Their major source of recreation was planning, stalking, and killing individuals for hire. It was what they lived for.

"That's not what I asked, husband."

"I think we'd better dress warmly."

She raised an eyebrow.

"Alaska is bound to be cold, even at this time of the year." Taio smiled, and Li nodded.

"I'll make our travel arrangements and pack while you do our research on the *Glory*, on Taiwan's film industry, and our cover stories."

Taio went back to the spare bedroom, which they used as an office, and powered up the laptop, which was connected through a remailer in Amsterdam that couldn't be traced to Hong Kong. He pulled up Google and entered the ship's name, coming up with a half-dozen vessels, most of them general cargo or bulk carriers and one tanker, but the sixth was a yacht owned by Thomas Hammond.

Hammond's name came up with more than one million hits, most of them for the American billionaire who'd made the bulk of his fortune in the dot-com boom, especially in California among the start-up high-tech companies that he acquired through hostile takeovers and then sold when their values soared through the roof.

According to many of the news stories in *The Wall Street Journal, The New York Times, Barron's,* and other business and human interest outlets, the man was classified as a modern-era robber baron who didn't care who he ruined on his way to the top.

Now only in his forties, he was part of the elite jet set. A playboy according to the *LA Times,* who'd been born of simple working-class parents in Philadelphia, and had never attended college but had begun his career by working as a runner on the floor of the New York Stock Exchange, where he'd earned his first million by the age of sixteen.

The many photographs showed him with a variety of wealthy people from all over the world. But the most recent photographs from the last few years showed him almost always in the company of the American movie star and movie theater owner Susan Patterson, herself a multibillionaire. The woman was beautiful, and Hammond was handsome in the role as a laid-back California surfer.

Li came in and looked over Taio's shoulder. "Who's the woman?"

"A former American movie star. Her boyfriend is a billionaire named Tom Hammond. He owns the *Glory*."

Li laughed. "What the hell are they doing in Skagway?" she asked. "I looked it up. That's where half the world looking for fame and fortune showed up to get aboard the Klondike Gold Rush."

"A fitting place to meet a billionaire and his rich girlfriend."

"No question they can afford us, but I wonder who it is they want us to deal with."

"And why?" Taio asked.

McGarvey drove out to Langley with Pete, Otto, and Mary for an appointment with Taft and Thomas Waksberg, the DDO. The DCI's secretary had called earlier that morning and asked for the one-on-one meeting. Pete went with Otto to his third-floor office, while Mary escorted Mac upstairs.

"Don't try to rile the man too badly," she said when the elevator opened on the seventh floor.

"He won't like what I'm going to have to tell him," McGarvey said.

Mary smiled. "Mostly nobody does," she said. "But it drives everybody nuts when you start pointing fingers at the Pentagon and especially the White House."

"Then I suggest you guys stay out of it, especially you."

"You're on your own up here. I'm going back to my office next door and point my crew in the right direction to help out."

"And what direction is that?"

She shook her head. "I haven't a clue, but I'll figure out something by the time I get there."

Taft was waiting with the portly Waksberg in the DCI's small conference room. And Carleton Patterson, the Company's general counsel, showed up from the elevator at the far end of the corridor at the same time McGarvey came down the hall.

"Wait up," Patterson said. He was a tall, thin, patrician man with white hair, who'd been the CIA chief legal beagle for more years than anyone wanted to count. And he dressed the part of the venerable old lawyer in three-piece suits, the bottom button of his vest undone, his shoes always highly polished, his bow tie correctly knotted.

No DCI had seen fit to replace him, and it was said that he'd heard more gossip than even the walls in the OHB, or anywhere else on campus, had.

McGarvey always had a great deal of affection for the man, and the feeling was mutual.

"I haven't see you in forever, my boy," Patterson said as they shook hands. "And congratulations on your nuptials. Pete is well?"

"Thanks. Yes, she is. And you look good."

"I'm thinking about going to pasture one of these days."

"I'll believe it when I see it."

They were opposite the conference room door, and no one else was in the corridor.

"The general's a good man."

"Most everyone who sat in that office was," Mac said.

"But he's vexed. Some of his friends on this side of the river are starting to complain about you."

"Why?"

"News gets out, Mac. You're in town, someone has taken a couple of potshots at you, and already you're sniffing around the Pentagon and the White House again. Makes some of these people nervous."

"I get a little nervous myself when someone starts shooting at me."

"Trouble does have a habit of following you around," Patterson said. "Do you have any leads?"

"None. But both guys were ex–Special Forces—one from Canada the other from South Africa—which means they were hired guns."

"There are a lot of people who'd like to see you dead. The list isn't endless, but it's large."

"I understand that, but the money for the two guns who came after me was big."

"Governmentally big?"

"Yes. And curiously enough, the amount the second man was paid was twice as much as the first."

"Which means?"

"Whoever hired the first guy didn't think he would get the job done. So they hired someone better."

"Who also failed, and you think there'll be a third?"

"I'm betting on it."

Patterson nodded. "I thought you would say something like that," he said. He knocked on the door, and they went in.

"Here you are, then," Taft said. He was at the head of the table, Waksberg at his left. "Have a seat," he said, motioning to Mac and Patterson, who sat opposite.

"I assume that you've been brought up to date," McGarvey started.

"Yes. Any idea who's after you this time?"

"According to what we've figured out so far, no government I've clashed with in the past is behind it."

"We've come to the same conclusion," Waksberg said. "But your assumption that it's someone in the White House or Pentagon is an impossible leap."

"It's just a starting point. I've gone head-to-head with staffers in both places in the past year or two. You've read the after-action reports."

"Doesn't mean anyone left behind is holding a grudge," Taft said.

"Someone is."

"Whoever it is tried twice and failed twice. Don't you think they've had enough?"

"No," McGarvey said. "In any event, I'm striking back."

"How, exactly?" Waksberg asked. "Give me the operational details."

"To start with, I'm going to step on some toes and see what shakes out."

"By throwing out blanket accusations?"

"Yes, and I'd like your help."

"I don't think that you need anyone but Mr. Rencke's help," Taft said. "But in fact, I've ordered him and Mary Sullivan to step down."

"That may not be the best idea," Mac said.

"And I want you to peacefully surrender yourself to protective custody."

"No."

"It's not to protect you; it's to help protect innocent civilians who might get hit in the cross fire," Taft explained. "Van agrees." P. Van Gessel was head of security.

"That wouldn't work."

"Why?" Patterson asked.

"Whoever is after me would simply wait it out. Sooner or later, Pete and I would return to the real world, and it would start all over again."

Taft sat back, his lips pursed for a moment. "I've had two calls about this situation. The first was from General Leon in Pretoria. You came down hard on him."

"I meant to, and he did exactly what I'd thought he would do."

"And that was?"

"Protect one of his own."

"And what did that tell you?"

"That he wasn't involved in the attacks on me."

Taft nodded. "Good."

"The second call was from someone in the White House?" McGarvey said. "Who?"

"President Weaver, who has it out for you."

McGarvey shrugged. "That's too bad, because I have a lot of respect for anyone sitting in the Oval Office."

"But not Weaver."

"For anyone there," McGarvey said. "What did the president say?"

"He asked me to order you to back off," Taft said.

"And do what, exactly?"

"Voluntarily go into protective custody."

"Which I won't do," McGarvey said.

"I could have the FBI arrest you," Taft said.

"Yes, you could."

There was an awkward silence.

"What's next?" Patterson asked.

"I've pushed a little," McGarvey said. "General Leon responded, and so did the president. So now I'm going home."

"With a target on your back."

"Exactly."

□

TWENTY-SEVEN

Hammond left Susan with Ned Beetle, one of her ex-husbands who'd been the first to arrive with his wife, a Manhattan society girl, the ex-wife of a player in banking, and waited at the rail with his chief steward, Kathy Bliss, as one of the fishing charter boats he'd hired came out to where they were anchored.

At seventy-five with a light breeze, the weather for Skagway was almost balmy. Across the bay, two gigantic cruise ships were docked, and flash cameras had been popping off since the first helicopter had landed on Glory's foredeck a couple of hours ago.

He and Susan had put out the word that they were hosting a long week-end wilderness party aboard the yacht. But they didn't give the name of the place—only it's latitude and longitude: 59.27.30N 135.18.50W. It was to be a treasure hunt.

The charter boat pulled alongside with three couples, two of whom had flown a private jet to Juneau and then a twin-engine prop job up to Skagway, whose small airport was notoriously difficult, especially for small jets flown by pilots with no local knowledge.

First up the boarding ladder was Vitali Novikov, who owned a majority position in the Russian telecom giant MobileTele Systems with his twenty-three-year-old Italian movie-star wife, who was less than half his age.

"Vitali, surprised to see you and Gina here," Hammond said. He was certain that Tarasov had sent him to spy.

"When Tommy throws a party, one can't miss it," Novikov said.

Gina Bragga did not seem pleased. "You said it, wilderness. More like primitive."

"But here is like home. Russia used to own Alaska. Big mistake selling it."

"Where's Susan?"

"Inside," Hammond said, and Gina and Novikov left.

Next up were Toni Lama and her wife, Lisa, Broadway producers whose last seven plays were sold-out massive hits, four of which were still playing. Toni stood six foot three and was slender, almost the twin of Tommy Tune, while Lisa was just five feet and chubby. But she wrote the music and was a genius at it.

They air-kissed with Hammond.

"Glad we could get away," Lisa said, grinning. "If there could possibly be an opposite to New York City, this place is it," she said. "You and Susie always have the best parties."

"We try. Did anyone else come out with you?"

"The Taiwanese movie couple," Toni said. "First time we met them. Absolutely exotic."

"You guys have good taste," Lisa said.

For a brief moment, Hammond had no idea who they were talking about, but all of a sudden, it dawned on him who the Taiwanese couple were, and he managed a weak smile to hide his discomfiture.

"That's why we always want you and Toni with us," he said. "The others are inside. Drinks now and a surprise for late lunch."

The last up the boarding ladder were Taio and Li, beautiful people, both of them, dressed casually expensive in designer leather jeans, white shirts, and matching leather jackets, bright red silk scarves around their necks, and jaunty narrow-brimmed hats.

"Mr. Hammond, it was so nice of you to invite us," Taio said, offering his hand. "I'm Kuang Wei, and this is my wife, Kuang Fan."

They shook hands around, Hammond at a loss for words. If these were the Scorpions Tarasov had sent, then their appearance and personas were perfect disguises. They looked more like poets or perhaps small-school teachers than movie people or assassins.

"I'm very pleased to meet you. I'm sure my companion will have a million questions about the film business in Taiwan."

Li, who was so tiny and perfect in Hammond's eyes that she didn't look real, smiled diffidently and nodded. "Unfortunately, there isn't much to tell. Even though we're an independent nation, we still find that in some endeavors we bow to Beijing's style."

Hammond couldn't help but return her smile. "We must talk."

"Yes, please," Taio said. "Unfortunately, we cannot stay for your party. We are flying back yet today. Pressing business."

"Take over for me, Kathy," Hammond said. "I shouldn't be long."

Hammond brought the two Chinese contractors below to his office midships. In addition to a hand-carved teak desk and four flat-screen monitors on the walls, the room was equipped with an Italian leather couch, Lexan coffee table, and two leather chairs.

When they were seated, Taio and Li on the chairs and Hammond on the couch, Taio began.

"We have done our research on you. What we wish to know is your target and your reasons."

"First, I need to know your fee," Hammond said, trying to be the one in charge. It was his yacht, his money, and his project.

"Our fee will depend on your target and your motive," Li said.

"Tell me."

"You can afford us."

"I said, tell me your fee."

Taio and Li exchanged a glance, then got to their feet. "I'm sorry that we could not come to an accord, Mr. Hammond," Li said.

"We'll just see ourselves out," Taio added.

"Wait, goddamnit," Hammond said. "I have a right to know what I'll have to pay for your services." He'd been in charge just about all of his life, but right now, he felt that he had jumped into something way over his head.

Taio and Li just looked at him.

"His name is Kirk McGarvey. He used to work for the CIA."

Taio smiled. "A formidable man," he said, and he and Li sat down.

"Just a man," Hammond said, though he didn't know why.

"Why do you wish us to kill him?"

"Personal reasons."

"Our time is limited, Mr. Hammond."

"It was a business deal that went bad."

Taio said nothing.

"It involved a considerable position in bitcoins."

"How much did you lose?" Li asked. She was obviously the money manager in the partnership. Hammond couldn't imagine her as an assassin.

"Nothing."

"Then why go to the expense?"

"Because it's what I want."

The two just waited.

"No reason," Hammond said at length. "Look. Maybe you'd best go."

"Is it merely a game to you? A rich man's sport?"

"That's none of your business."

"But it's exactly our business, Mr. Hammond," Li said. "We will kill Mr. McGarvey, for sport as you wish."

"When?"

"Soon," Taio said.

"How much?"

"Twenty-five million euros in gold," Li said.

Hammond started to object, but Li continued.

"We will send you instructions for deposit at a location in Switzerland. Our work is guaranteed. That means if we fail, your gold will be returned to you within twenty-four hours."

"Is that satisfactory?" Taio asked.

Hammond had no idea what to say. But he nodded.

TWENTY-EIGHT

☐

McGarvey, sitting with Pete and Mary in Otto's office, telephoned army colonel Harry Ward at his office at the Defense Intelligence Agency around four in the afternoon and asked if they could have a chat. "No confrontation. I just need some information."

A few years ago, Ward was a major, still in the DIA, and had been on a periphery of a group of mid-level intelligence agents who had tried to sidetrack McGarvey from an investigation. The op had resulted in some deaths, nearly McGarvey's.

"Nothing more to say, Mr. Director," Ward replied.

"This has nothing to do with the other business. This is something else that I'd like some help with."

"Knowing you, I don't think I want to get involved. Sorry."

"I don't want this to turn into something ugly."

Ward was silent for a moment. "I won't meet you anywhere off base."

"Your office will be fine. And I only need a couple of minutes of your time."

"How about right now on the phone?"

"Face-to-face."

"0900. I'll leave word at the gate."

McGarvey hung up. "At least he agreed to see me."

"You shook him up, that's for sure," Pete said. "Do you want me to tag along?"

"If we gang up on him, he'll clam up."

"Do you think you'll get anything out of him?" Otto asked. "He isn't one of your biggest fans."

"More to the point, do you think he knows something?" Pete asked.

"I'm not sure, but he's in a position to know if something might be going down over at the Pentagon. He started chasing his first star when he made major, and he had the rep even then of keeping his head down."

"He may have the rep of keeping his head down, but if he wants a star badly enough, he'll fight back if he's pushed," Mary said. "You'll be poking a stick into a hornet's nest if he's somehow involved."

"That's the whole point," McGarvey said. "And I'm going to keep pushing until someone pushes back."

"Again," Pete said.

· · ·

The DIA's headquarters was one of more than a dozen different civilian and military units stationed at or adjacent to Joint Base Anacostia–Bolling in southeast D.C., across the Potomac from Reagan National. Among the others were the Department of Homeland Security Office of Inspector General, and several White House support units, including the White House Communications Agency.

A pass was waiting for him at the main gate, and he drove over to the sprawling six- and seven-story complex of buildings that housed more than ten thousand civilian and military personnel. Fully one-fourth of all the information that was included in the president's daily brief came from the DIA, which, unlike the CIA, concentrated on defense-military topics at the national level.

But the DIA also provided intel for the secretary of defense, the Joint Chiefs, and combat commanders. The agency was practically a wing of the Pentagon.

Ward's job was to oversee the Russian section of the Agency's watch center housed in the South Wing of the complex. Mac was met at the main entry by a young woman in civilian clothes, who escorted him up to the seventh floor and Ward's office.

"Someone will ring for me when you're ready to leave, sir," she said and left.

Ward's secretary, another civilian, but much older, looked up. "Good morning, Mr. Director. You may go right in." Neither she nor the aide had smiled.

The colonel in full uniform, his blouse buttoned, did not get up from behind his desk when McGarvey walked in, nor did he offer his hand, merely gesturing for Mac to take a seat. He was a nondescript man of medium build, balding on top with a gray fringe, narrow, pale blue eyes, and a mottled complexion that made him seem much older than his thirty-eight years. A West Pointer, he'd graduated in the middle of his class. According to the dossier Lou had provided, he'd worked in military intelligence his entire career, and his nickname was Don't Rock the Boat Ward.

"Thanks for agreeing to see me," McGarvey said. "I won't take much of your time."

"What do you want?"

"Someone has put a contract on me."

"I'm not surprised."

"In the past few days, two assassins have tried and failed. You may have heard something."

Ward pursed his lips and shook his head. "No."

Mac was sure the man was lying. "I'm pretty sure that there'll be more to come, and there's a possibility that the Russians, though maybe not officially, are somehow involved. It's why I came to you."

"Otto Rencke is your friend; I'm sure that he could help. Ask him."

"I did, and he mentioned you and your connections at the Pentagon. Past and present."

Ward visibly colored. "Look, you son of a bitch, I wasn't involved in the business you got yourself into the last time, and I'm sure as hell not in league with some Russian who might think the same as I do that it might be a better world without you."

Mac let it lie for a long moment or two. "What Russian might that be?" he asked at length.

"Any Russian, take your pick. There's an entire country of them who'd like to see you go down."

"Curious stance for a man in your position to take, wouldn't you say?"

Ward grabbed his phone and called his secretary. "Mr. McGarvey is leaving now," he said, and he was obviously careful not to crash the phone down.

"I'm sure there still are people across the river who feel the same as you," McGarvey said.

"Get the fuck out of here, or I'll call the SPs."

McGarvey got languidly to his feet. "Don't let me find out that you or some of your pals are involved in this thing."

Ward was barely in control. "Is that a threat?"

"Yes," McGarvey said, and he left Ward's office.

McGarvey crossed the river on the Douglass Bridge and made his way through town on Independence Avenue, traffic heavy as usual at this time of a weekday. He delayed calling Otto and Mary and especially Pete while he worked a few things out in his mind.

Ward had been lying, something he'd expected. But he didn't think that the man was involved. Nor did he now suspect that someone in the Pentagon was involved. If they had been, Ward would have known about it, and he wasn't a good enough liar to keep it off his face.

But the main point of this morning was to make sure that word did get back at least to the DIA's office in the Pentagon. And if someone over there was involved, they would make their move soon.

The other point was to wonder how he would deal with the situation if it was someone in the Pentagon gunning for him again. It made him think that maybe all these years inside and outside the CIA, everything he had done, was a colossal waste of time.

Back more years than he wanted to count, John Lyman Trotter, a man who he thought was his friend, told him once, "In this business, self-doubt is a cancer that will kill you as surely as the real thing."

But then John had turned out to be a traitor.

TWENTY-NINE

Hammond woke up a little after seven in the morning, and after a night of bad dreams, he was disoriented at first. He could not get the faces of the Chinese assassins, who in the night had morphed into scorpions and were coming after him, out of his head.

He reached over for Susan, but her side of the bed was empty, and then he heard the shower shut off.

Yesterday, after the man and woman had left, everything had become surreal for him. His guests seemed like they were never closer than arm's length, their talk and laughter out of focus, unreal. Yet he had gone through the motions of being an engaging host.

Susan had cornered him a couple of times demanding to know what was going on, but both times he'd held her off.

"Later. We need to talk about it, but not now."

They were out on the aft deck, and Susan had looked over her shoulder at the people in the crowded saloon. "They're here?" she asked.

"They were, but they're gone now."

"Did you hire them?"

He nodded.

"How much?"

"Twenty-five million. In gold."

"Jesus," Susan said softly. "Do you think they're worth it?"

He had asked himself the same thing all the rest of the day and through the night each time he'd awakened from his nightmare. But he hadn't come up with an answer that made any sense to him. For the first time in his life, he was truly frightened. Even more frightened than he had been of his stepfather who used to beat him just about every time the old man had come home drunk after working in the steel plant.

Susan hadn't pressed him for anything more when they finally came down to the master suite around two in the morning. Nor had they made love. She had just come to bed, rolled away with her back to him, and had gone to sleep. Which was just as well, he'd thought at the time, because he didn't think he would have been capable.

He started to drift off again, when he heard her briefly on the phone in the bathroom. She came in a minute later wearing a white robe, a towel wrapped around her head.

"I ordered coffee," she said. "And then we need to talk."

"Yes."

"Did you send the gold yet?"

"No."

"That's good, because we definitely need to talk, and it's not about the money."

Kathy Bliss knocked once at the door, then came in with a coffee service on a tray, which she put on the breakfast table across from the bed. "Good morning, guys. Shall I pour?"

"No, thanks, we'll manage," Susan said.

"Yes, ma'am."

"Are any of the others up yet?" Hammond asked.

"Only Mr. Novikov. He's been up for an hour now and went for a swim."

"In the Jacuzzi?"

"In the bay. It was a very short swim, and he went immediately into the Jacuzzi, where he's on his third vodka."

Susan laughed, and it sounded good to Hammond, like the old days, exciting and comforting at the same time. "All Russians are crazy bastards," she said.

Kathy inclined her head but said nothing as she left.

When she was gone, Susan poured them coffee and sat on the bed, pillows propped up at her back. "What were they like?" she asked.

"Dangerous," Hammond said without even thinking about it.

"Scorpions."

"Definitely."

"Then you need to think this out, Tom. We both do, but I'm just as much a part of it as you are. I got blood on my hands in Greece."

"I know, and it's only going to get worse," Hammond said. It was the other thing he thought about all evening before bed.

"This is not a movie. It's real. And if McGarvey ever gets even a hint who's after him, he'll come after us, and there's no power on earth that would be able to stop him. All our money combined wouldn't keep us safe."

Hammond held his silence.

"You're frightened, Tommy boy, I can see it in your eyes. So let's quit right now while we can."

"If we can," Hammond said, and for just an instant he had no idea why he'd said such a thing.

"This isn't one of your business deals where you screw somebody out of a few bucks, and they get pissed off and promise that they'll get even. We're dealing with real-life killers now."

"Who work for money."

Susan looked at him and shook her head. "What the fuck are you telling me?"

"This started out as a chess game. And we've sacrificed a couple of pieces."

"And money."

"Chump change," Hammond said, and one part of him couldn't believe what he was saying, and the fact that he meant it.

"This time, you're talking twenty-five mil, and that's not chump change."

"I can do one trade and make ten times that before lunch. But that's just a game now, too, and I'm getting tired of it. Bored."

"Making money's not enough?"

"No," Hammond said, though a hell of a lot more than ten times the Chinese killers' fee was at stake on the pipeline deal, something he'd not yet shared with Susan.

"You're out of your fucking mind, and I don't know if I want to be a part of it any longer."

Hammond forced a smile, even less sure of himself now than after he'd hired the first contract killer, and yet more determined. In for a penny, his mother used to say, in for a pound. "Not to put too fine a point on it, but it's you with blood on your hands. And you loved it."

Susan turned away. "It scared me. This whole thing scares me."

"After Athens when you got back to the lake house, we made love like never before," Hammond said. "Might sound trite, but for once in your life, you weren't acting."

She flared, a little color coming to her cheeks. "Fuck you."

"Look, if you want to back out, go ahead. As soon as I get rid of our guests, I'm going to the yard in Italy."

"Yard?"

"Codecasa."

"I'm not following you."

"Legend has it that when Rome burned, Nero fiddled. He played around, because he could. I'm going to do the same."

"Codecasa, where this ship was built," Susan said, suddenly getting it. "You've ordered a new yacht?"

"Not yet, but that's exactly what I'm going to do. Newer, bigger, faster, better. And I'm going to need your help with design, inside and out. And with a new name. Maybe the *Susan P.*"

"Don't be vulgar," Susan said, but she laughed.

"If you don't like it, I'll leave the naming to you," Hammond said, energized again. Alive. Aware. Happy.

He got his iPhone and opened his email. A sixteen-digit number had been sent to him from an anonymous source.

Susan watched him.

He phoned his chief financial officer Charles Flickenger's direct number in Los Angeles and got him on the second ring. They went back to the day Hammond had made his first half billion.

"Good morning, Tom. How's Alaska?"

"Full of ice."

Flickenger chuckled. "You've cooked up a new deal. What'll be this time?"

Hammond read the number on his iPhone. "Recognize it?"

"It's an account number at the International Bank of Geneva. Do you want to raid it?"

"I want you to send twelve point five million in gold."

"Dollars or euros?"

"Euros."

"When?"

"Immediately."

"Okay. So when do you think you'll get tired of the cold weather?"

"Susan and I are going back to Italy. We're designing a new yacht."

"Sounds like you're in another one of your spending moods," Flickenger said. "Well, you can afford it."

"I know."

Susan put down her coffee, got out of bed, took off her robe, and lay back down, her nipples hard.

"Gotta go," Hammond told his financial officer.

THIRTY

McGarvey got a one o'clock appointment at the White House with the president's chief of staff, Owen Sherman. He left Pete on campus with Otto and Mary and took a cab where he was admitted through the west gate and met by a staffer one minute early at the entrance to the West Wing.

"If you'll just come with me, Mr. Director," the young, earnest man said.

Mac followed him inside to a large corner office down the hall from the Oval Office, where Sherman was seated in front of an ornate coffee table. Harold Kallek, the director of the FBI, sat next to him, one empty chair across from the two men.

"Good afternoon, Mr. Director," Sherman said as Mac sat down.

Where Kallek was tall, all bony angles, with a long, narrow face and deep-set eyes, the president's chief of staff was a short man, everything about him round—his frame, his bald head, even his nose. His nickname since high school had been Charlie Brown, and if he'd ever resented it, he'd never let on. In fact, he was anything but wishy-washy. He was a sharp, decisive man, very hard around the edges, never soft and round.

"Considering your past service to the country and the recent happenings, the president is offering any help he can," Sherman started. "I thought it would be appropriate to ask Harold to join us, if you have no objections."

"None whatsoever," Mac said. "The more heads we can put together, the quicker we'll get this resolved."

Kallek nodded. "Two attempts have been made on your life. We have a pretty good idea why, but not who."

"I've made a few enemies," McGarvey said, not going any further for the moment. First he wanted to see how both men would handle his presence, because he was sure that Sherman as well as the president had an idea where Mac had already taken it.

"A host of them," Kallek said. "But this time, a South African and, of all people, a Canadian. Both men ex–Special Forces operators who apparently were working as contractors. But again, we come up against the same question—hired by whom?"

"The Russians?" Sherman suggested.

"It's possible. But I don't think it'll turn out to be an intelligence agency–directed business. There'd be too much blowback if it turned out that Putin ordered me killed."

Sherman spread his hands. "But you have some ideas."

"A couple that the president will not like."

"We've gathered as much."

"Not too long ago, I had a run-in with a number of people in the Pentagon who wanted to bring President Weaver down."

"Yes, and the president continues to be grateful for your help."

A group of mid-level military intelligence officers had worked out a plot to create a series of false but realistic reports of incidents around the world at places that were considered possible nuclear flash points. India-Pakistan the most critical. The idea was to dump so many major issues all at once on the president's lap that he couldn't possibly make the right decision.

Weaver would have come out looking so totally incompetent, such a danger to the U.S. that he would have to be removed from office.

"Are you thinking that someone still inside the Pentagon may be holding a grudge against you?" Kallek asked.

"It's possible."

"We don't agree," Sherman said. He got up, went to his desk, brought a thick file folder back, handed it to McGarvey, and sat down. "That's an outline of a classified after-action report of the incident. It was spearheaded by the Bureau with the cooperation of the DIA and every other intelligence organization within the military. The insane plot was broken up thanks to you, and everyone involved was dealt with."

McGarvey put the folder on the table. "I know."

The FBI chief started to object, but Sherman held him off. "Mr. McGarvey, as all current and former CIA directors, has his sources. So far as we're concerned, the business with anyone in the Pentagon holding grudges has been resolved."

"I thought that it might be, but there have been two attempts on my life, and I suspect that there will be more. I'm just checking all the boxes."

"Which is why you spoke with Colonel Ward," Kallek said.

"Yes."

"What are you doing here?" Kallek said.

"I'll answer that," Sherman said. "It's about Marty Bambridge and Bill Rodak. Marty was a traitor inside the CIA, and Bill worked here as a senior adviser to the president. They were both involved in another plot. And Mr. McGarvey might suspect that one of their friends might be behind the attempts on his life. Is that about right?"

"It's a start," Mac said, the meeting going exactly where he'd wanted it to go. Poke a stick into a hornet's nest, Pete had said.

"Are you sure that the CIA is clean?"

"We're working on it."

"And now the White House," Sherman said. "I suspect that you want to talk to the president, but I'd strongly advise against it. He's grateful for your help, but presidents when pushed have a nasty habit of sometimes pushing back."

"In any event, you're not here in any official capacity, Mr. McGarvey," the FBI director said. "You're here as a private citizen who is unfortunately—though not surprisingly—the target of two assassination attempts. It's a problem for the Bureau, not the White House."

"I agree," Mac said.

Sherman was surprised. "Then what are you doing here?"

"As I said, just covering my bases." McGarvey got up. "I'll take your advice and not bother the president this time."

"Trust me, Mr. Director, the Bureau is working the case," Kallek said.

"I know, and I appreciate your help."

"I've assigned people to cover your back."

"Thank you, I've spotted them, and so will the opposition if and when they show up again."

Sherman was skeptical. "What now?" he asked.

"My wife and I are getting out of Washington. For now, we're going back to Florida. Later, we might head to Serifos."

Sherman nodded. "It's a little hot here right now," he said. "In the meantime, you might want to take the after-action report with you. Though I'd like it back."

"Thanks," McGarvey said. "But I've already read it."

The aide escorted Mac out and asked if he needed a cab to take him back.

"It's a nice day, thanks. Think I'll walk."

Pete was waiting in her BMW around the corner on Madison Place next to Lafayette Park. He hurried across Pennsylvania Avenue and got in the passenger seat.

"How'd it go?" she asked, pulling away from the curb.

"The seeds have been planted."

"The DIA, which means the Pentagon, and now the White House," Pete said. "What about the Bureau?"

"Kallek was there in Sherman's office."

"Did you get to see the president?"

"I declined," McGarvey said.

Pete smiled. "Good thinking, but of course your meddling will get back to him as fast as Sherman's chubby little legs will carry him down the hall."

"Yeah. And it's about all we can do here in D.C. Time to go home."

"Casey Key or Serifos?"

"Florida for now."

"And wait for the next shoe to drop," Pete said, glancing at him. "Which it will."

THIRTY-ONE

By the time they got back to their duplex on Repulse Bay, the twelve and a half million euros in gold had been deposited in their Swiss account as Li had predicted it would be. They had talked about it in roundabout terms on the long flight from Dulles, and Taio had expressed his doubt.

Now in midafternoon, standing on the broad balcony, he turned as Li brought out a bottle of Cristal and two flutes. It was something they always did at the very beginning of each operation. After the wine this afternoon, neither of them would touch a drop of alcohol until they were finished and the final payment made.

"I could see it in his eyes," Li said, pouring for them. She handed Taio his. "All I could see was fear."

"He would be a fool not to be afraid. We know about Mr. McGarvey, and I'm sure that Hammond has his resources."

They touched glasses. The wine was very good and very cold, and Taio savored it. "That is one of my main concerns," he said.

"Hammond or his sources?"

"His sources. I'd like to know who they are."

"Because?"

"Because we may be forced to deal with them in the end," Taio said.

Li started to say something but then checked it for just a moment, until something suddenly dawned on her and she nodded. "Hammond may have used his sources to find us, and of course he'll report hiring us."

"Exactly."

"I see your point. We don't need to keep looking over our shoulders to see who is watching us. The question is, how do we find out, short of going back to Hammond?"

"We don't want to do that. He could withdraw his payment."

"What do you have in mind?"

"We start by sanitizing our appearance, as usual, and then going deep, but leaving a back door open just a crack. If his source is any good, they'll find us, and we'll be waiting. If not, it won't matter."

Li's highly modified iPhone lying on the table triple chimed, which meant the incoming call was encrypted. Only her friend Phenix Zhe, who worked in the Technical Surveillance Department of the People's Liberation Army general staff in Beijing, knew the number and had access to the sophisticated encryption algorithm. They'd known each other since childhood in primary school.

Li answered the call, switching to speaker mode. "Hello, friend."

"You two are off on another operation, and I just thought that you should be warned about your client Thomas Hammond."

It was no secret between them that Zhe had access to their Swiss account from which she was paid small sums from time to time for intel that was generally only available to agencies at the governmental level.

"Hello, Zhe, I'm listening as well," Taio said.

"Your target is a man by the name of Kirk McGarvey, who once served as the director of the American CIA."

"How do you know this?"

"We happen to have a friendly set of ears on his yacht in Alaska, who spotted you two coming aboard, but staying only briefly."

"Can we have his name, perhaps to reward him?" Taio asked.

"No need at this time. But I called to tell you that Hammond and his lady friend, Susan Patterson, who is a Hollywood celebrity, are not as they seem to be."

"*Shi de.*" *Yes.* "We've already gathered that from meeting him."

"Did he tell you that he wants Mr. McGarvey dead mostly for the sport of it?"

"And for money he didn't lose, but didn't gain having to do with a cryptocurrency."

"Did he also tell you that he hired two other assassins who both failed?"

"No," Li said, exchanging glances with her husband. "Were either of these operators known to us?"

"They were mostly local players in a very small pond—much smaller than your milieu. Both of them ex-military disgraced by minor infractions."

"Should we decline the operation?" Li asked.

"That's up to you two, but I would say that eliminating such a man as McGarvey would propel your reputations in the business to stellar levels."

"If we don't fail," Taio said.

"Do you have his file?" Zhe asked.

"We have a file."

"I'll send you ours. And if you decide to proceed, I wish you very much luck."

McGarvey's file was extensive, running to more than two hundred pages, covering his life as a boy on a ranch in western Kansas, through his service in the air force's Office of Special Investigation, then his recruitment and training by the CIA as a black ops player.

His first assignments had been merely as a financial bagman into places such as Moscow, and even once into Beijing, though Chinese intelligence never knew about it until several years after the fact.

His first wet assignment had been to take out a general in Chile who'd been responsible for the torture and executions of more than one thousand dissidents. In that assignment, McGarvey had also eliminated the general's wife.

Li had transferred the massive file to both their laptops, which they studied for the rest of the day, through dinner, and into the evening and bed, finally finishing around the same time just after three in the morning.

Taio made a pot of tea just as Li was stirring, then went out to the patio to watch the lights of the city and to think about what he had learned. The fact that McGarvey was a formidable opponent had come as no surprise, though what was striking was the man's apparent soft underbelly. He was a scholar of Voltaire, taught at a small, prestigious liberal arts college in Florida, and had even written a book about the French philosopher.

"What's not so common," Voltaire had written, "is common sense."

But apparently the quote most important to McGarvey, because it had turned up in so many places in his file, was the one about how it was better to free a guilty man than convict an innocent one.

Li came out with a cup of tea and joined him. For a longish time, neither of them spoke, staring across the bay at the lights and to sea as dozens of fishing boats headed out.

"He is a romantic, lost in a terrible destiny," Li said.

"Voltaire?"

"That, too. But his assignment to Chile where he was sent to kill a general and ended up killing the man and his wife has apparently haunted him for years."

"She was a monster as well."

"Yes, but he didn't know it at the time when he pulled the trigger. And even afterward when he'd learned the truth, he still made mention of it as a low point of his career."

"I read it, but what do you mean about his terrible destiny?"

Li looked at him, her pretty mouth downturned. "Since that time, his wife and daughter were killed by a car bomb meant for him."

"Yes, I saw that in the file."

"Then his girlfriend in Switzerland was killed, chasing after him. Another was killed at a restaurant in Georgetown. His best friend's wife was gunned down. And the woman he recently married was at least twice wounded, both times seriously."

"It's the business," Taio said.

"Yes, but don't you see my point? I'm certain that he looks on the deaths of every woman he's ever been involved with as retribution for his assassinating the general's wife in Chile."

Taio saw what his wife was getting at. "The key to McGarvey is his wife."

"Threaten her and he'll come running right into our arms," Li said.

THIRTY-TWO

Hammond and Susan arrived at the Pisa Airport aboard his Bombardier jet shortly before noon. They'd taken a twin-engine Otter from Skagway down to Juneau, where the crew brought the jet to pick them up. And then it was a grueling three-leg flight, first to LA to repack their bags, then cross country to Washington, where they stayed the night at the Hay-Adams, and then across the Atlantic.

Susan hadn't been happy about Washington. "Like pissing into the wind," she'd said at one point.

"McGarvey and his wife are in Florida," Hammond said.

"But the CIA is just upriver, and so far as we know, the computer geek and his wife are still there."

"Don't get your ass in a bundle, sweetheart. You're a movie star, and I'm an entrepreneur. We're players."

She'd managed a smile. "But this time we're playing in a different ball-park. McGarvey's."

"We've hired the best; now let's go spend some money."

The shipyard sent a Cadillac limousine to take them to the Principe di Piemonte Hotel with its views of the sea on one side and the Viareggio Promenade with its collection of art nouveau buildings on the other.

At Hammond's request, they were booked into the Seaview Suite, which was the best in the upscale but not fabulous hotel, where lunch settings for four had been laid out. A bottle of Krug was already chilling when they arrived.

"Your guests have been notified," the head bellman of the three who'd carried their bags up and unpacked said. "If there's anything else, please don't hesitate to call me personally."

Hammond pulled out three one-hundred-euro notes, but the bellman shook his head.

"Thank you, sir, but your stay with us has been taken care of by the Codecasas," the bellman said. He shooed the other two ahead of him and closed the door softly when he left.

"With what you're planning on spending, they could have done better than this," Susan said cattily.

"I don't think they're going to be very happy when I tell them what I want them to build for us," Hammond said.

"Us?"

"Like you said, in for a penny, in for a pound."

"Are you getting cold feet? Misery loves company, something like that?"

"On the contrary, I'm getting my second wind, and I'm starting to enjoy the hunt even more than I'd hoped I would."

Susan gave him an appraising look. "You're certifiable."

"And yet here you are."

"Along for the ride."

"Even if it takes us to hell?"

Susan nodded.

"Then to tell you the truth, I hope McGarvey kills the Scorpions."

"Jesus."

"I don't want it to end so quickly."

"Foreplay."

Hammond smiled. "Exactly. And I don't like losing, never have."

Ten minutes later, Antonio Codecasa—a distant relative of Giovanni Codecasa the shipwright, who'd founded the company in the early 1800s—showed up with a tall, slender, beautiful woman he introduced as Sophia Vargas, the company's chief interior designer.

Antonio had been the chief yacht coordinating designer when Hammond had ordered *Glory* built, and over the nearly two years it had taken from when the keel was laid down until the yacht was turned over as ready for sea in all respects, they had built a mutual respect.

"Antonio," Hammond said, the two men embracing.

"My old friend, I am very happy to see you again," Antonio said. He and Susan exchanged a kiss, and then he introduced Sophia, whose English was Oxford perfect.

"I did my apprentice at Seagrams," she explained. It was one of the major interior design studios in London.

"I can't imagine the Brits teaching an Italian anything about design," Hammond said.

"Sophia, who is a cousin to the family, taught them more than they taught her," Antonio said. "But then you're here because you want a retrofit so soon?"

"I want a new ship, and you're not going to like it."

"A smaller yacht?"

"Bigger."

Antonio was suddenly wary. "How big?"

"Five hundred feet."

"One hundred fifty meters," Antonio said. "Impossible. Our yard was strained beyond the limit when we built *Glory* at only one hundred fifteen meters."

"I don't want to take my business elsewhere," Hammond said. "Money is no object, you know this."

Antonio was shaking his head.

"I'll go into a partnership with you to build a new yard. Once the Susan P shows up on the circuit, especially Cannes and Monaco, our new yard will turn a fantastic profit."

Susan stepped back and almost dropped her flute. Hammond looked at her and grinned. "You don't mind, do you?"

"Jesus, you were serious," was all she could say, but she was impressed.

"I'll want it in two years."

"No," Antonio said.

"I'll write you a check this instant for whatever sum you name."

Antonio shook his head.

"Including a down payment on the yard."

Antonio shook his head again.

"You can't refuse," Hammond said.

"Three years."

"Thirty months, starting today. Give me a dollar figure, and I'll write the check. Then we'll have some lunch, and I'll show you some sketches I made."

"The Russian won't like it," Antonio said.

Viktor Sheplev's yacht Anna was larger than Glory but so over-the-top glitzy that most of the players on the circuit thought it was tacky.

"He won't know the difference. No other private yacht in the world will be classier."

"Yes, sir. And I will make sure of it," Sophia said. "Now, I would like a glass of champagne, and I would like to make a few sketches for you and your beautiful lady."

After a very long lunch, which included Hammond's check to Codecasa for $150,000,000, he and Susan went for a long walk on the beach, just beginning to empty out of the tourists going back to their hotels to clean up and get ready for the dinner hour.

"When did you come up with this idea?" she asked.

"When I decided that I'd had enough of Alaska, because up there in the wilderness, I was starting to get nervous."

"Fear is sometimes good," Susan said. "You were spending money, but you weren't really in charge. Here is different. Like you said, Nero fiddled while Rome burned. I get it. But why name what's going to be the grandest yacht on the circuit after me?" They stopped and she looked up at him. "Tommy, are you saying that you're in love with me?"

"If I was, would you tell me to go to hell?"

She pursed her lips, but then shook her head. "No one has ever said that they were in love with me and meant it."

"I am," Hammond said, and he meant it. But one distant part of him realized that he wanted Susan close to him just as a drowning man wants a life jacket. He was drowning over the McGarvey thing, and he didn't want to go under without company.

THIRTY-THREE

McGarvey walked down to the dock where his forty-two-foot Whitby ketch was secured and buttoned up against the weather. It was early afternoon, a light sea breeze making the summer heat and humidity bearable on the Gulf Coast island of Casey Key.

To his right on the expansive lawn that ran down from the two-story Florida-style house and uncaged pool behind it was the gazebo he'd had built for his wife Katy. It had also become Pete's refuge even before they'd gotten married. A place of peace and tranquility, both women had said at one point or another. Safety.

The island here was so narrow, bounded by the Gulf to the west and the Intracoastal Waterway to the east, that there was only one road, and the house lots took up the entire width.

Pete came from the house with a couple of frosty bottles of Corona with slices of lime in the necks. "Are we going for a boat ride?" she asked.

"I was thinking about it. Might not be a bad idea to head a few miles off-shore and putter around for a day or two. Maybe catch some fish, go for a swim if the days are calm enough."

"And have an unlimited view in every direction."

"Including up," McGarvey said.

Pete was a little startled. "I didn't think of that one."

"If I were gunning for me, I might consider using a lightplane."

"That would mean at least two of them. The pilot and a shooter."

"I would shoot back."

"*We* would shoot back," Pete said. "And forget about trying to send me back to D.C. It's more dangerous up there than here. Especially if you didn't announce where we were heading."

"But I did. I had Otto send emails to Ward over at the DIA and Sherman at the White House, in case either of them wanted to talk to me again."

Pete grinned. "I'm sure they both realized that you still didn't trust them and were setting them up in case something happened down here. Which couldn't have made them very happy."

"No."

"Something is going to happen here, isn't it?"

"I think so," McGarvey said.

Lou's voice came from a speaker in the gazebo. Otto had set it up about six months ago as part of the house security system and as a means of instant communications.

"You have visitors pulling into the driveway," she said.

"Are you carrying?" Pete asked, and McGarvey nodded.

"Can you identify them?"

"Two men, one of whom is James Forest, but the other is unknown to me."

Forest was chief of detectives for the Sarasota County Sheriff's Office, and an old local acquaintance of Mac's. He'd been involved in one way or another in several incidents that had happened here, including one at New College when a bomb went off in Mac's car, taking his left leg off just below the knee and nearly killing him.

"Tell them to come around back to the pool," McGarvey said.

"Of course," Lou said.

"Word gets around," Pete said as they headed up to the house.

Forest was a very young-looking, dark-haired man in his early forties who not long ago had worked as an undercover drug enforcement officer posing as a teenager. He was dressed in a sport coat and open-collar shirt, while the other, much larger man with thinning blond hair, a beak-like nose, and sour expression wore a shirt and tie despite the warmth. McGarvey immediately pegged him for a Bureau agent.

"That sounded like Otto's wife at the front door," Forest said.

"It's his new AI program," McGarvey said.

The other man nodded. "I'm Special Agent Owen Spader, SAC Tampa."

"Would you gentlemen like a beer?" Pete asked.

"Not on duty," Spader said, his tone abrupt enough to be irritating.

McGarvey motioned for them to have a seat at the poolside table. "What brings you guys out here?"

"We want to know why you're here," the Bureau SAC said.

"This is our home, and other than that, it's none of your business."

"You were involved in two shooting incidents in Washington."

"Georgetown, actually," Pete said.

"There were two fatalities."

McGarvey just looked at the man.

Forest was clearly embarrassed. "Do you think whoever is coming after you this time will try again? Down here?"

"It's a possibility, Jim."

"I've been instructed that if you were to admit to such a thing, I was to take you into protective custody," Spader said.

"No, thank you," McGarvey said.

"It wasn't a request."

"Lou," McGarvey said, not taking his eyes off the agent.

"Yes?"

"With my compliments, please telephone Mr. Kallek for me."

"He's not currently in his office."

"Find him."

Spader shook his head. "That won't be necessary, sir. My brief was to ask if you wished to be placed into protective custody but not to force the issue."

"Lou, cancel the call, please."

"Yes, dear."

"I'd like at least to station a couple of my people nearby."

"Whoever might be coming my way will be a professional shooter, almost certainly at the international level. No offense intended, but your guys would stand out like lighthouses."

"How about you, Mrs. M?" Forest asked.

"Run and hide?" Pete asked. "Not a chance in hell. And my friends call me Pete."

"What do you think?" Pete asked after the two men had left.

"A couple of guys just trying to do their jobs, especially Jim. It has to seem to him that just about every time I come down here, a shitstorm follows me."

Pete laughed out loud. "You do know how to show a girl a good time."

McGarvey studied her face. He was in love with her, but it wasn't the same as it had been with Katy. Just as intense, but different. "Sorry you married me?"

Pete gave him the same frank look. "If that were a serious question, I just might shoot you here and now and get it over with." She smiled a little sadly. "My only complaint is that it took you so long."

"I didn't want anything to happen to you, like the others."

"I'm a big girl."

Mac looked away. "And I didn't want you to think that I needed you to replace Katy."

"But you did, and I did replace her. Just in a different way, I hope."

"I wasn't looking for a clone or her twin sister."

Pete reached over and took his hand. "If you hadn't already guessed, Kirk, I'm head over heels in love with you. Have been for a long time. Whatever happens to you, happens to me. To us. You and me, babe, like the song."

"I'd hoped you would say something like that."

"Fair enough. We started with beers, so if you fire up the grill, I'll make burgers and beans. And afterward, we'll go over just how we're going to get ready for our guests."

THIRTY-FOUR

On the flight from Hong Kong to Geneva via Doha, Qatar, Taio read the long dossier on McGarvey again, and he picked out several troublesome bits and pieces he'd missed the first time. At one point, looking up, he caught Li's attention.

"What is it?" she asked, her little voice very soft. Even though they were flying first class and had no immediate seatmates, they'd kept their voices low.

"Perhaps we should have asked for a higher fee."

"He's a formidable man. Have you learned something new about him?"

"He has more kills to his credit than we do. Twice as many, actually, and that's just the ones generally credited to him."

"We knew this from the beginning. What is troubling you now?"

Li had picked out the fact that McGarvey was a romantic who had lost every woman who'd ever loved him, except of course for his current wife. And she had rightly assumed that a possible weakness would be the wife. If she were endangered, he would move heaven and earth to protect her. But therein lay the conundrum.

"His wife is his vulnerability."

"Yes, we know this. But what else?"

"Two attempts have been made on his life in recent days, but by amateurs who I believe were meant to fail."

"Our employer's little sport. He didn't want McGarvey to fall so easily. He wanted to play cat and mouse with the man."

"And McGarvey has almost certainly figured out by now what's happening, though he doesn't know who is behind it or why."

"He has to suspect the Russians, or maybe the Pakistanis. Their grudges run deep."

"That's not the point. What is relevant is that he suspects the attacks will keep coming until he is taken out," Taio said. "And if you were in his position, what would you do?"

"Go on the hunt myself," Li said, and she suddenly had it. "Do you think that he would set a trap, using his new wife as bait?"

"I think it's a possibility that we have to consider."

She shrugged. "His love must not run deep if he is willing to place his wife in front of an assassin's bullet."

"Unless he knows something that we don't."

"Which is?"

"I don't know yet, but I have an idea, and you're going to be my star player."

"I'm all ears."

They checked into the Grand Hotel Kempinski on the south shore of Lac Leman—Lake Geneva—under British passports that identified them as Austin and Claire Stilwell, husband and wife from London. Their accents were good, but not over the top.

In the many SOF schools they'd attended, they had been pegged almost immediately because of their looks for operations in English-speaking countries. They had been taught to speak in either an Oxford or upper-class Harvard accent. Even their French and German, though good but obviously not their native tongue, had a strong Oxford or Harvard accent depending on what passports they were carrying.

They had booked a suite overlooking the lake for their three-day stay and presented an American Express platinum card at check-in. He was dressed casually in a soft gray Armani suit, a white silk shirt open at the high collar, Gucci loafers, and a blond wig covering his dark hair, while Li wore a short off-white skirt, spike heels, and a sheer, nearly see-through soft yellow blouse, under which she wore a skin-tone bra. Her wig was short and red. Their appearances matched their passport photos.

They meant to call attention to themselves. In Hammond's parlance, they were just at the edges of the players circuit, a little too flashy, but nearly there. Heads turned when they walked into a lobby or bar.

Upstairs, they tipped the bellman well and ordered a bottle of Krug from room service. When it came, they each had a couple of sips, and then Li poured the remainder of the bottle down the bathroom sink.

Taio took a pair of matching shoulder bags from one of their suitcases, and they packed them with jeans, a light pullover sweater and boat shoes for him, a chambray shirt, spangly jeans, and pink Sketchers for her, plus two sets of American passports and driver's licenses for each of them in the names Frank and Judy Kane from Waltham, Massachusetts, and George and Carolyn Schilling from Minneapolis, Minnesota, that they'd hidden in the lining of the suitcase, along with a little over five thousand euros and ten thousand American dollars.

They had not brought firearms with them, nor would they attempt to take any through customs in the U.S. Almost everywhere they'd ever operated, they armed themselves with whatever weapons they needed from local sources.

"Time to go to work," he told Li, and they left the hotel with only the shoulder bags. Everything else would be left behind.

. . .

In just about every major city in the world, there were experts of one sort or another for clandestine hire. In Amsterdam and Paris, hackers were predominant. In London and Zurich, there were financial wizards who knew everything there was to know about money laundering. In Beijing and Seattle, the best internet device designers and plunderers had set up shop. Long rifles and handguns were easy to get in New York and Chicago despite tough gun laws. Man-launched missiles were for sale in Las Vegas. Surveillance equipment, a lot of it Russian designed but pirated from Cuba, was available in Miami. And in Billings, Montana, and Fargo, North Dakota, explosives were for sale in just about every back alley. If you knew where to look and who to call, you could get just about anything for a price.

Here in Geneva were a handful of the best plastic surgeons and disguise geniuses in the world, outside the CIA and the Chinese and Russian intelligence agencies.

Once they were clear of the hotel but still on foot, Taio phoned Dr. Wolfhardt Buerger, a man they'd worked with once several years ago. The doctor was a seventy-two-year-old coke addict, wife beater, and child molester. But he was the best in the business.

"Unless you have a lot of fucking money, leave me alone," the man said in English.

"More money than you can spend in the rest of your miserable life," Taio answered.

Buerger laughed. "I recognize that limey bastard accent anywhere. Whatever it's to be this time will cost you twice as much as last."

"Are you at the same place?"

"I moved last year to Vieille Ville." It was the historic district of the city, some buildings dating back to the fourteenth century. He gave them a number not far from the Bourg-de-Four, which was a large public square filled with elegant cafés.

"We'll be there in ten minutes."

"He's come up in the world," Li said when Taio hung up.

"In part because of us. But I think we'll also be his last."

Li was troubled. "What is it?"

"I think he is on the verge of becoming a serious problem."

"The cocaine?"

"His attitude. He sounded invincible."

"Do you think he's being watched?"

It was something Taio had considered. "We'll make sure before we go in. But when he's finished, we'll dispose of him."

Li put a hand on her husband's arm, stopping him. "There are others in the business who can help us."

"None as good."

"We don't need this job. Return the money, and let's walk away."

"I don't want to do that."

Understanding dawned in Li's eyes. "You want this assignment. You admire McGarvey."

"*Shi de.*"

"Careful you don't get us killed."

THIRTY-FIVE

McGarvey rented a Toyota SUV with deeply tinted windows from Hertz at the airport up in Sarasota using a set of ID creds under the name of Isaac Rogers from his go-to-hell kit.

Outside, he picked up Pete, who'd parked the restored Porsche Speedster in the short-term lot, and they headed up to MacDill Air Force Base in Tampa, fifty miles north.

Home to a number of units, MacDill also hosted the U.S. Central Command, USCENTCOM, that planned the wars in Iraq. Real-time intelligence was of vital importance to the unit; thus from the beginning, there'd been a very close bond with the CIA.

Yesterday, McGarvey had called Otto and outlined the plan for bunkering in on Casey Key, with the alternate of the Whitby out in the Gulf. Aside from a Glock 20 and two Walther PPKs in the rare 9mm version, plus Pete's subcompact Glock 29 Gen4 and the Very pistol aboard the boat, they had no other weapons.

"I know what you need, and I can get the hardware from MacDill," Otto had said. "But do you want anything heavy? Semtex, maybe, or even a man-held missile launcher?"

"No. First of all, I don't want to make a major splash, unless they come after us by air when we're out on the boat, in which case, a long gun will do. And if at all feasible, I want to take whoever they send us as undamaged as possible."

"You'll need pistols for several locations in the house, by the pool and in the gazebo, the standard Beretta 9mm, plus plenty of ammunition for each. Nothing fancy, but reliable with decent stopping power at short range."

"One for the boat as well."

"Hang on; I'm looking at the armory inventory," Otto said.

They were in the gazebo, Mac's phone on speaker mode, the volume down. Otto had beefed up security in and outside the house out to a radius of two hundred meters, which included out into the Gulf and across the Intracoastal Waterway.

Otto was back. "Okay, I'm getting you a couple of Heckler & Koch MP7A1 submachine guns, one for each of you to carry around. These will be the 4.6mm×30 iterations, with a lot more stopping power than the standard 9×19. Plus plenty of ammunition so that if it comes to a down-and-dirty gunfight, you'll have serious muscle on your side."

Pete nodded. "I've fired it on the Farm. I wouldn't want to face it."

"If you head out on the boat, whatever will be coming at you will either present a relatively slow-moving surface target or something faster in the air. One of you will be driving the boat while the other will be shooting back. We'll stick with Heckler & Koch. The HK323 assault rifle."

"We want the heavier round," McGarvey said.

"I'm seeing the model SG1 with the Trijicon optical sight. Is that what you want?" Otto asked. "It's chambered for the 7.62×51mm round."

"That'd damn near stop a tank," Pete said.

"Get us two plus plenty of ammunition," McGarvey said.

"Done. Flash-bang grenades?"

"They leave too much residue to clean up. But get us a couple of tactical lights, something bright enough to momentarily blind someone."

"Are you expecting more than one shooter?" Otto asked after a slight pause.

"It could be an entire assault team. But whoever it is will be better than the first two, I'm sure of at least that much."

"Whoever the expediter is will have to have access to a decent amount of untraceable money," Otto said. "I'll put Lou to work on it again."

"But don't rule out foreign sources," Pete said. "Maybe we've put too much emphasis on someone homegrown."

"Nothing domestic or foreign has shown up on my radar."

"Nothing with connections to a governmental agency," McGarvey interjected.

"Yeah," Otto said dejectedly. "But that leaves the rest of the eight billion plus people on the planet to check out."

"How about the movie star broad and her billionaire boyfriend?" Pete asked. "We crossed them last year in Cannes and Monaco; maybe they're holding a grudge."

"They're players—not someone likely to hire a killer. Anyway, to this point, they come up clean."

Otto had called ahead so that when they arrived at the gate, an escort wearing BDUs with captain's bars was waiting for them in a dark blue Ford Explorer with air force markings. He was well over six feet and very lean, with dark hair and narrow dark eyes. His name tag read MILLER, and he was all business.

Mac pulled over, and the captain came back. "May I see some IDs?"

They handed out their real driver's licenses, which the officer studied intently, checking their faces against the photos before he handed them back.

"Could you tell me the name of the gentleman who made the reservations?"

"Otto Rencke."

"Yes, sir," Miller said. "If you'll just follow me, we'll head over to pick up your package. Do not deviate from my tail, or you will be subject to arrest. Do you understand?"

"Yes," Mac said.

The captain got back in his SUV and was saluted through the gate by one of the APs on duty, who then turned away without acknowledging McGarvey.

The sprawling base that bordered on Tampa Bay was huge, and it took nearly ten minutes to reach an aircraft hangar just off the active runway as a KC-135 Stratotanker was lifting off.

Miller drove inside and pulled up in the far corner where a pair of airmen in work uniforms and hard hats were waiting next to a package about the size of a four-drawer file cabinet that was shrink-wrapped in dark brown opaque plastic and lying on its side on a pallet.

McGarvey pulled up next to it and popped the rear hatch, and he and Pete stowed the rear seats in their wells.

The airmen, both of them the size of football linebackers, hefted the package with some difficulty and loaded it into the back of the Toyota, which sank a little on its shocks. One of them closed the hatch, and both of them saluted the captain and left by a rear service door.

"Would you like me to sign something?" McGarvey asked.

"No, sir."

"I may need it for a few days."

"This afternoon, the items will be reported captured in action by Taliban forces. When you have no further need, have them destroyed."

"I think we can manage," McGarvey said.

The captain cracked the slightest of smiles. "I'm sure Housekeeping would be happy to accommodate you. And good hunting, Mr. Director."

They were escorted off the base and made the run to the airport in Sarasota, where Pete got into the Porsche and followed Mac down to Casey Key. He backed the Toyota into the garage and shut the door as soon as Pete parked the Speedster and joined him.

"It's a safe bet the two of us aren't going to lift that thing, let alone carry it into the house," Pete said.

She got a box cutter from the workbench as Mac opened the rear hatch and manhandled the weapons package to the tipping point, easing it onto the floor and then over on its side.

Pete used the cutter as Mac peeled the several layers of heavy plastic away, revealing the cache of weapons that were cushioned by a thick layer of foam rubber atop a half-dozen ammunition boxes.

Pete was impressed. "We could start World War III right here," she said. "But I'm glad this stuff is in our garage, not in the hands of some Taliban fighters out there."

The sheer firepower in front of them was impressive even to McGarvey.

He took Pete in his arms. "I want you to listen to me for once in your life."

She looked up at him. "Don't even say it, Kirk, because there's not one chance in hell I'm leaving here until we get this shit resolved."

"I could order you to go."

She laughed. "Do you suppose that would work, darling? Really?"

THIRTY-SIX

Dr. Buerger had changed radically since the last time Taio and Li had been to see him for some cosmetic work about three years ago. In that time, he had deteriorated; the pallor of his sagging skin almost made it look as if he had been dead for twenty-four hours or more. His eyes had become pale as well, and he had a bad body odor as if he hadn't bathed in a week or more. Even his hair had turned gray and had thinned. And although he'd never been a large man, now he was practically a skeleton.

Li was visibly shaken. "Maybe we'll come back next week," she said.

Taio wanted to agree with her, and he was about to say so when Buerger stuck out his hands at arm's length, both of them as steady as a rock.

"You're right, I do look like shit, but my hands still work, and so does my brain. So if you want something from me, I'll require your respect as well as your money, you Chink bastards."

Buerger had answered the bell and let them into the front stair hall of his three-story house, which was all dark wood and pale plaster walls, on which were hung fine paintings—many, if not all of them, Taio thought, were originals. And although the doctor looked like a wreck, the house was immaculate, especially the parlor on the second floor and even more so his work space on the third, looking down on a mews in the rear.

His laboratory, as he called it, using the British pronunciation, was a miniature but very well-equipped scientific station with a binocular microscope and other equipment, including a compact electron microscope in one corner. In another was a first-rate photo studio and worktable with the tools to produce perfect IDs, including driving licenses, social security cards, and passports for any country in the world. In another was a dentist's chair in which minor plastic surgeries could be performed, along with hair implants, various colors of contact lenses, and makeup that was so waterproof it could last for weeks even though the operator took showers daily.

The entire operation was state of the art, to match the man's expertise, which was rumored had been perfected in the Bundesnachrichtendienst—the BND—which was the German secret intelligence service, among the very best in the world.

"You have housekeepers," Li said.

"Of course I do."

"Will we be disturbed anytime soon?" Taio asked.

"Not for six days, and I could hold them off longer than that, depending on what you want me to do. In any event, they never come to this floor."

Li looked at her husband and shrugged. It was his call.

Taio took out his Frank Kane passport, Li gave him hers, and he handed both of them to the doctor, who took them over to his credentials workstation, flipped on a strong magnifying light, and examined them for just a few moments each.

"Nice work," he said, looking up.

"It's yours," Taio said.

"I know. But you've never used them, or the other set I made for you until now?"

"Once just after you altered our appearances."

"Then wouldn't you consider it dangerous to use the same identities again?"

"These identifications are on no database anywhere. We made sure of it before deciding to use them again."

The differences in their present appearances now and what they looked like in both sets of passports were small. Taio's head was bald then, he had a mustache and wore blue contacts, over which he wore glasses with thick dark frames. Li had long blond hair and green contacts. But the biggest change was the pigment of their skin. Taio was pale, while Li was tanned. And the changes had been made to their entire bodies, so if for some reason they were ever subjected to a strip search, the coloring would look perfectly natural.

The last time they'd gone through the changes, Buerger had lingered over the nipples of Li's small breasts and the area on either side of her pudenda. Taio hadn't liked it at all, and she had seen that he was on the verge of breaking the man's neck then and there. But she had signaled to him that it was okay, she would bear it.

They had discussed it on the way over, and Taio had promised that this time the doctor would die.

"Good, because if you don't kill the bastard when he's done with us, I'll do it myself. With a great deal of pleasure."

"Did you think to bring the glasses and contacts with you?" Buerger asked.

"We destroyed them when we finished our operation," Taio said.

"That's okay; I have replacements," the doctor said, glancing at the passports. "But you didn't get rid of these. Why not?"

"It would have been a shame to destroy such works of art."

"Bullshit, but of course I agree with you," Buerger said, and he looked up. "One million euros. Each."

"No," Taio said, and he held out his hand.

"Pay him," Li prompted.

"It's too much. We'll go elsewhere."

"No one is better."

"True, but where we're going, the officials don't look too closely."

"*Verdammt,* I'm not asking for the moon. And you came to me, which means you know the best and can afford the best."

"Two hundred thousand euros—one hundred for each of us."

Buerger didn't hesitate. "Let me see the money."

Taio pulled a wad of euros out of the bag and handed it to the doctor. "Here's five thousand."

"How do I know I can trust you?"

"Neither of us can trust the other. But I want the work done and believe you'll do another good job. And you need the money, and it's here in this bag, along with some other currencies."

"Let me see."

Taio pulled out a stack of American one hundreds. "Here's five thousand U.S."

"I'd take American dollars."

Taio put the money back in the bag and zipped it up. "When you're done."

Buerger pocketed the euros. "Who's first?"

"Li," Taio said.

The doctor practically licked his lips. He nodded toward the dentist's chair. "Disrobe, my dear, just like before, while I get my things."

"This time, you'll be professional about it," she said. "I'm not a piece of meat."

"*Naturlich.*"

Buerger kept his word. Starting with Li's back, including her neck, he sprayed on the tanning solution, which almost immediately colored her skin. Working down, he did her buttocks, without lingering, her dancer's legs, and even the soles of her feet and the backs of her toes.

It took less than ten minutes for the solution to sink into her skin and completely dry, before the doctor had her turn over.

"Close your eyes, please," he told her.

She looked at Taio, who nodded, and she closed her eyes.

He used a tiny aerosol sprayer to do her face, careful around her eyes and nostrils and completely avoiding her lips.

"You may open your eyes now, but do not touch your face," Buerger said when he was finished. "Now once I'm finished with your arms and hands, I'll have to touch certain parts of your body to make sure the spray gets to the natural folds and creases in your skin. You may be uncomfortable, but if you want a first-rate job that would stand up even to a gynecological examination, if it comes to that, you will pass."

She nodded and closed her eyes again. "Quickly," she said.

He was finished in fifteen minutes and had her lie there for another ten to allow the solution to completely dry before he let her up, and Taio took her place in the chair.

In the meantime, the doctor had laid out their contacts, Taio's glasses, and the wig for Li. He changed the solution in the sprayer to lighten Taio's already light skin a shade more, taking the same care to make certain the job was just as well done as it had been for Li.

"You'll need to shave your head every couple of days."

"I understand," Taio said.

The entire process took less than two hours. When it was done, and they had examined their bodies and especially their faces in the full-length well-lit mirror, Taio turned toward the doctor.

"Very well done, and I expected it would be," he said.

"Well enough for a bonus?" Buerger asked.

"I think so," Taio said, and he nodded to Li, who had come up behind the doctor.

Before Buerger could turn around, Li took his head in both hands, and with a knee jammed into the base of his spine, she made a quick, very sharp twist, and the man's neck broke.

He slumped to the floor, his eyes wide as he slowly died.

"He does nice work," Li said.

"And so do you, my dear," Taio told her.

THIRTY-SEVEN

Hammond and Susan flew back to Geneva, and once they had taxied across to his private hangar and the hatch had been opened to a warm early evening, he gave the flight crew the week off, transportation and all expenses anywhere in the world they wanted to go.

His pilot, John Davies, a relatively short, well-built man in his early forties with blond hair and blue eyes and the same good looks as Paul Newman had at that age, had been a fighter pilot for the air force before Hammond hired him. He was a no-nonsense man, married with two young children back in LA, and flying all over the world in just about every imaginable weather. He was a safety nut.

"I'll take the plane back to LA—she's ready for her annual—and spend the time with Meg and the kids, if you don't mind. I can have it done and be back here in seven days."

"That's fine, but I'd like you to do one thing for me when you get home."

"Sir?"

"Take your family somewhere exciting. Over the top, you know what I mean?"

"Maybe we'll just stay home and soak in the pool."

Hammond was slightly irritated, but he didn't let it show. "Whatever you want, it's on me. You're a hell of a good pilot. I wouldn't care to lose you."

"No chance of that, sir."

Once their bags were stowed in Susan's Bentley, which their driver, Tommy Doyle, a Londoner in his fifties who'd been a race car driver when he was younger, had brought down from the villa, they took off from the airport.

"Would you and the miss like the top down, sir?" Doyle asked.

"No, just get us home," Hammond said a little sharply. He was angry, but he didn't really know why, except that he was goddamned tired of arguing with people. Antonio, who wanted to talk him out of the new yacht; Sophia, the designer who overrode Susan on just about every choice of styles; Davies not wanting to do anything on the boss's nickel; and now Doyle, who didn't know how to leave someone in peace.

Susan squeezed his arm, but he ignored her, delving into his own thoughts. He wanted the Chinese assassins to kill McGarvey, and yet he didn't want it. He was afraid and yet flying high with the game he'd set in motion.

If McGarvey survived this round, it would be the next to the last. Two lone assassins had tried and failed, and if the Chinese Scorpions were taken down as well, Hammond knew he wouldn't be able to go deep enough to survive without finishing the business. His and Susan's public personas were just too large for either of them to hide. The only recourse, then, would be to send an overwhelming force to do the job.

Something like a SEAL Team 6 or Spetsnaz hit squad.

They wouldn't be cheap, but this had never been about money. In his mind, it simply came down to survival—his or McGarvey's.

Hammond's cell buzzed, and it was Tarasov. "I'm at your house having a drink of some very good vodka—Russian, of course. I assume that you've spent an appreciable amount of money ordering your new yacht."

"You're having us watched," Hammond said, even more irritated than just a couple of minutes ago.

"Of course I am, but I assure you that we're only interested in your whereabouts, not your love life, nor your drinking or eating habits."

"We?"

"Yes, my business partners in Moscow and Washington. We have a vested interest in you."

"I thought you worked alone."

"None of us ever do, though we like to make the world believe we do. Even you, Thomas, have your partnerships—me included."

"I've set everything in motion, so now what the fuck do you want?"

"I want you to listen to a couple of recordings, and then there is a letter of intent to be signed."

"Bullshit," Hammond said, but Tarasov was gone.

"What is it?" Susan asked.

"Mikhail is at the villa waiting for us."

"Goddamnit. Turn around and take me back to the airport. I want to get out of here."

"Sorry, but it's too late for that."

Susan flared. "I can go any fucking place I want to go, whenever I want. I'm not one of your fucking employees."

"No," Hammond said, almost sorry that he had dragged her into this mess. "You're not an employee, you're a partner. And a woman I happen to be in love with."

Her face sagged. "A woman with blood on her hands. And now that Russian wolfhound is at the house. His goons have to be following us."

"They are."

"Why?"

"I think that he wants to protect his investment."

"What investment? What else have you gotten yourself into?"

"Gazprom wants some natural gas pipelines into Western Europe, and they want to use my contacts in a blind deal. The government is to be at arm's length. It's supposed to be nothing more than an investment on my part."

"How many millions this time?"

"Not millions," Hammond said. "Five billion."

Susan sat back. "Jesus," she said softly.

They were on the corniche, only a couple of miles away from the villa now.

"I agreed to at least try to work the deal, but in return, I wanted a special favor from him and his friends in Moscow."

"To find assassins willing to take out McGarvey."

"Yeah."

"They want McGarvey dead, but they don't want Putin to be blamed. You've become their patsy because of some fucking game you want to play."

Hammond couldn't look away from her. He nodded.

"Let's just walk away while we still can."

"It's too late."

"If you're worried about the Chinese couple coming after us, just tell them to drop the assignment, but pay their entire fee. It'd be a win-win for them. They get the money but don't have to take the risk."

"Unfortunately, we're past that option."

Peter Wallace, their chef du villa, was waiting for them when they got off the elevator. "Welcome home, sir, miss," he said. "I've placed your guest on the veranda."

"You're fired, Mr. Wallace. I want you gone from this property within the hour."

"Sir?"

"Rule number one: loyalty. Never let someone into your employer's house without first asking for permission."

"But, Mr. Hammond, the gentleman has been here quite often over the past year. He spoke of you as an old friend. I only assumed that he was a favored guest."

Hammond was taken aback. But it explained one thing about Tarasov's knowledge. He'd installed bugs in the villa.

"I'm so sorry, sir. It definitely was my mistake. I'll just get my things and be gone."

"Wait," Hammond said. "I didn't realize who you let in, and you were absolutely right to do so. You made no mistake, I did. I can only offer you my apology and ask you to remain as chief of my house staff."

Peter nodded. "Your apology is accepted, Mr. Hammond, and I'll carry on, if I may."

"Please do."

"A bottle of Krug is on ice for you and the miss."

THIRTY-EIGHT

Tarasov was sitting at a table on the veranda sipping a small glass of iced vodka as he looked toward the lake, his back to the french doors from the house. He was dressed in his usual dark blue blazer, a white shirt, and khakis. All very American.

Hammond, Susan at his side, stopped at the doors for just a moment. He'd tried to keep Susan out of this meeting, but she'd insisted that since she had become a part of it—her hands bloodied—she would remain in 100 percent.

"Welcome home, you two," Tarasov said without turning. "This is a lovely spot."

"I'm a little surprised to see you here this morning," Hammond said. He and Susan walked out and sat at the table.

Tarasov smiled and poured champagne for both of them. "I took the liberty of ordering the wine. I thought you might want to celebrate."

"Celebrate what?" Susan asked.

"That you two have come so far with your little game and are still intact."

"What are you talking about, you son of a bitch?" Hammond demanded. He was angry and shaken because he was beginning to realize where the Russian was going.

"That Mr. McGarvey hasn't figured out yet who's gunning for him and come here to return the favor."

"It's not possible."

"Ah, but Ms. Patterson may have given up the clue that could help Mr. Rencke to unravel your plot."

"I didn't do anything of the sort," Susan flared.

"But you did, my dear hedonist, by opening your mouth on camera in Seattle."

"What the hell are you talking about?" she asked. "I'm a movie star; the interview was expected of me. Had I ducked out, it would have caused all sorts of fucking speculations."

"You've bugged this house," Hammond said.

"Da," Tarasov said.

"I'll hire people to dispose of them."

"They won't be found. Nor will the others we've placed here and there."

"I'll get someone who's good enough."

"But mine are the best. You can't imagine the people we listen to and the stories I could tell."

"Your friends are Russian spies?" Susan demanded.

Tarasov shrugged. "I have many friends, my dear lady, including you and Thomas."

"My jet is on its way back to LA for its annual maintenance inspection. Your bugs will be found."

Tarasov was unconcerned. "Not unless the mechanics are looking for them."

Hammond sat back, resigned. "You're here. What do you want?"

"We've gone this far with our dealmaking; I merely want to take the next step with you."

"You have transcripts from the bugs?"

"And from other sources. In fact, I have recordings of your hiring the two shooters who've failed, plus your conversations aboard the *Glory* with your new Chinese friends."

"Proves nothing, except that a Russian intelligence operation has been mounted against me."

"We have your banking activities as well. The gold you deposited into the Scorpions' account, and even the millions you laid down at Codecasa's for your new yacht. The *Susan P.* A beautiful name for a beautiful ship." Tarasov sipped his vodka and smiled, the gesture almost ironic. "That is, if you live long enough to accept her."

Hammond was shaken.

"Which is why I'm here, and why we've gone through all the trouble to help you with your little game," Tarasov said. "It's simply quid pro quo." He took a single folded sheet of paper and a pen out of his jacket pocket and handed them to Hammond. "Please sign it and press your right thumb anywhere on the page."

"What is this?"

"As I told you on the phone, it's nothing more than a letter showing your intent to act as Gazprom's agent in Western Europe."

"It'll never hold up in any court of law—in the States or internationally."

"No matter. It'll just point anyone interested in the direction of your collusion for financial gains to us."

"Something I've done all my life," Hammond said. "So what?"

"It links you with a Russian enterprise, something your President Weaver has banned under the penalty of your laws."

"It would also link Gazprom with a plot to kill McGarvey."

"No, it would simply link you to the plot—which in actuality is the truth. In fact, so far as anyone outside Moscow knows, Mr. Putin has a respectful if not warm relationship with Mr. McGarvey. It goes back a couple of years."

Hammond hesitated.

"Come on, Thomas, you started this. We merely helped—for a favor, of course."

Hammond signed the letter, adding his thumbprint. He had no other choice.

Mary called Otto's office and told him that she was pulling the pin early and getting out. "It's a Friday. How about taking a girl for a drink and early dinner?"

"Come on over. I'm working on a hunch, but I should have it settled by the time you get here."

"A premo?"

"Maybe," Otto said, and he hung up.

The problem he had been wrestling with for several days, ever since Lou had picked up the brief interview with Susan Patterson in Seattle, was Thomas Hammond. The man was a billionaire who'd made his fortune by stealing it, which meant he had connections just about everywhere in the world, and he was a man, who, by all reports Lou had been able to dig up, held a grudge.

Hammond had ruined any number of men, and three of them, during several wild market swings over the past ten or fifteen years, actually committed suicide because of it.

Barron's and The WSJ had at one time or another labeled him one of the world's great predators. A man who wants to win at all costs and who has earned a fortune because of it.

"Lou, I was just thinking."

"Yes, dear?"

"Can we find a connection between Hammond and any intelligence agency?"

"Foreign or domestic?"

"All of them."

"Of course the obvious connection has been the CIA between him and Mac and Pete during the Tower Down investigation. Plus, by extension, all of Mac's connections. The SVR during the face-off incident. The MSS in China, North Korea's State Security Department, Pakistan's ISI, France's DSGE, Germany's BND, and some years back Britain's MI6, and of course Chile's Agencia Nacional de Inteligencia."

"I was specifically asking about Hammond's connections."

"Hammond's relationship with Mac has put him on the radar of all those agencies whose files include his name."

"And Susan Patterson's?"

"Yes. May I ask in what direction you would like me to direct my inquiries?"

"Excluding the bitcoin deal Mac offered him, are there any other reasonable explanations why Hammond would have hired assassins?"

"Mary is here," Lou said.

A moment later, Mary came back to Otto's inner office. "Play that last inquiry, please."

"Excluding the bitcoin deal Mac offered him, are there any other reasonable explanations why Hammond would have hired assassins?"

"I can think of at least one," Mary said. "Hammond's in the middle of some business deal with a country that wants Mac eliminated, but not willing to take the blame. Quid pro quo."

"Or vice versa," Lou said.

THIRTY-NINE

It was nearly four in the afternoon when Mac decided it was time to take a break, and Pete agreed. They'd stashed the loaded Beretta pistols plus two spare magazines of ammunition in two guest rooms in the front, plus the master bedroom and study facing the rear of the house.

On the way downstairs, Pete had insisted on placing a loaded pistol on the first landing. "In case we're on the run with someone right on our tail," she'd explained.

They'd also placed pistols and magazines in the living room facing the front and in the dining room and kitchen in the rear.

"Starting now, we go nowhere without my Walther and your Glock," McGarvey told her. "If something starts to go down, we'll make a grab for the MP7s, one upstairs and one down here."

"Do you think it could happen as soon as tonight?"

"It's possible."

"If it were you coming up against a former CIA black ops officer with a hell of a track record, what would you do?"

"Defeat Otto's surveillance systems and come in soft and easy as quickly as possible in the middle of the night," McGarvey said. He had thought about it for the past couple of days. "But if I could manage, I would try to come during normal hours, posing as someone we knew, who'd been here from time to time."

Pete was a little surprised. "Someone from Langley?"

"Maybe, or possibly someone from New College."

"Means that people we know could be in real danger right now."

McGarvey had thought long and hard about that possibility as well. If he were the only target, it would be easier to handle than if the people he knew and loved were in the crosshairs.

He brought the last two pistols outside, one hidden by the pool and the other down in the gazebo, where he put it under one of the seats facing the water.

Pete came from the house with a decent bottle of pinot grigio from the wine cooler and a couple of glasses. She poured for them both.

"I was just thinking that if they come at us from the water, we'd best put only one of the assault rifles aboard the boat and the other right here."

"Okay, that's good thinking," Mac said.

"Except the part that we've made this place a fortress, McGarvey, and we could be stuck here indefinitely. And that's not like you. So what gives? Why all the hardware?"

"Because you refused to go someplace safe."

"Oh, for Christ's sake, Kirk, are we going to go through all that shit again?"

"I'm better off doing this alone, and you know it."

"You're saying that I'm a distraction?"

"Yes, you are."

Pete was getting steamed up. "I can shoot almost as well as you can, and you damn well know it. And in case you forgot, we're in this together, my dear. In sickness and in health, for richer or poorer."

Mac broke in. "Until death do us part?" he asked. He sat forward. "This is the real deal, Pete."

"I've been there before."

"And I've almost lost you more than once, when even once was way too many."

"I've almost lost you, too, lest you forget," Pete countered. She was genuinely angry, and it was their first real argument since they'd gotten married. "It's supposed to be you and me, babe, or have you forgotten that, too?"

Mac studied her pretty face, her cheeks slightly flushed now. She was stubborner than just about any woman he'd even known. But it was one of the many reasons he'd fallen in love with her, against his better judgment. From the start, he'd been a man who thought his only real option was to stay as independent as possible. He could and had accepted that he was on the firing line, the target for someone who wanted him dead. And there were plenty of those people, with a whole host of reasons.

And yet he had come to realize over the years, and especially right now at this moment, that he wasn't a loner, never had been. And that in a nutshell was his greatest problem—loving someone whose safety he could not guarantee.

Pete reached out and touched his hand. "If hiding here in plain sight is what you want, then well and good. I'm not going anywhere. But I'm just saying it's not only you, my darling. You may not know what direction they're coming from, you just know that someone is coming. And you want to overwhelm them with firepower, hoping for a shot that will put them down but not out, so we can find out who sent them and why. But you have to admit that two shooters are better than one."

"Whoever is coming next will be better than the first two. I don't think they'll stop until I'm dead."

"We're dead."

Looking into her eyes, hearing her voice just then, McGarvey never felt so cornered in his life. "We're dead," he said, though it just about choked in his throat. "Or we figure out who's behind it and target them instead."

"Mac," Lou said.

Pete's grip tightened on McGarvey's hand.

"Yes?"

"A blue Chevy Tahoe is approaching from the north."

"Can you identify the occupants?"

"The driver is the lone occupant, and I put it at 90 percent James Forest."

"Anyone else behind him?"

"No," Lou said. "One hundred percent Jim Forest. He's slowing down."

"If no one is following him, and if he turns in to our driveway, ask him to ring the bell," McGarvey said.

"I understand."

"And let Otto know."

"He already knows."

"Ask him to call us."

"Looks like Jim is paying you guys another visit," Otto's voice came from the same place as Lou's, which was just about at eye level and a couple of feet away as if he were there with them.

"Did you have any idea he was coming back?" Mac asked.

"Nothing I could find on his email accounts or on the police tactical lines or his cell phone," Otto said. "I assume you're talking about his connection with the Bureau. My guess is that he's coming as a friend."

Forest's interest went back a number of years since McGarvey had bought the Casey Key house. The local LE departments were often notified when sensitive people showed up as residents in the neighborhood. There were ex–intelligence officers, judges who'd served at the federal level, a couple of U.S. senators, any number of movie and television personalities, many retired high-ranking military officers, and dozens of multimillionaires, including Stephen King.

McGarvey's name was high up on the list of sensitives, not only because he'd once briefly served as director of the CIA but because more than one attempt had been made on his life. One in particular had been a bomb put in his car in the parking lot up at the college in Sarasota where he'd taught. A number of students had been hurt and/or traumatized, and the police, in the person of Forest, had begun to keep a close eye on him.

"More than a friend," Pete said.

"Someone is gunning for me, and he's come to ask me who and what we're doing about it," McGarvey said.

"He's just pulling into your driveway now," Otto said. "What're you going to tell him?"

"That depends on what he's going to ask me."

"Don't let him see the MP7s or the long rifles. They're military, and he could make a case for placing you and Pete under arrest. And to his way of thinking, he would not only be serving the best interest of the community, he would be helping a friend in trouble."

FORTY

The doorbell rang, and McGarvey picked up the gazebo phone. "We're around back, Jim. Join us."

"On my way."

A trawler chugged down the ICW, and as it passed, McGarvey reached for the Walther holstered at the small of his back, but the skipper tooted the boat horn for the Blackburn Point Bridge to open, and Mac stayed his hand.

Forest, in jeans, boat shoes, and a light-colored untucked fisherman's shirt, came around the corner of the house, by the pool, waved, and made his way down to the gazebo. "Hope you guys don't mind me dropping by unannounced."

"Are you on duty, or can I get you a drink?" Pete asked.

"Off duty, and I'd take a beer, please."

McGarvey motioned for him to sit down while Pete went up to the house to get a beer.

"I've always liked this house," Forest said. "Of course you know that Steve King has a place not too far down island."

"We've met," Mac said. "Are you here officially or just as a friend?"

"Both. It's just that the powers that be are getting a little nervous—hell, more than a little—and they know that you and I have history. They asked if I could come down and have a friendly chat."

"You already know that two attempts to take me out have been made by two different shooters."

"Professionals."

"Both of them former special ops people, one from Canada and the other South Africa. I talked to the COs of both units who claimed that once the guys left the service they disappeared."

"Did you believe them?" Forest asked.

"I didn't have any reason not to," McGarvey said.

Pete came down with the Corona.

"Anyway, I've never had a beef with either of those countries."

"Thanks," Forest told Pete, and he took a drink. "I've been following you for the past couple of years through the resources I have access to," he told McGarvey. "And from where I sit in the cheap seats, my guess would be that you're pretty high on the shit lists of at least Russia and probably Pakistan. I assume you've talked to people at Langley. What's their take?"

"No one thinks that it's a government-sanctioned contract," Pete said. "The political blowback for assassinating a former CIA director would be huge."

"There are ways of covering up stuff like that."

"It'd be harder than you think," McGarvey said.

"Well, someone's gunning for you and that takes money," Forest said. "Have you noticed someone following you? Bugging your phones, stuff like that?"

"No," McGarvey said, letting Forest try to work it out.

"Yet they evidently knew where you live and knew your routines. So someone was gathering intelligence on you."

"We found that the first guy had tapped into a neighborhood surveillance camera with a good view of our apartment building."

"What about the second one?"

"I was at a hospital in Georgetown."

"All Saints?" Forest asked.

"Yes."

"Have you found any connection between the two shooters?"

"No."

Forest was frustrated. "Look, I'm trying to help you as best I can. But I need something to go on. It sounds to me like the guys were working for the same paymaster, someone who had access to a decent intelligence agency."

"We've come to the same conclusion," McGarvey said. "And we also understand you and the Tampa SAC are worried that there'll be a third try right here."

"On the way from Sarasota, Spader told me again that he had been ordered to offer the Bureau's help, but if you didn't accept it, he was to stand down. Which leaves just us to watch out, because it seems like just about every time you show up, trouble follows you."

"Do you want us to pack up and leave?" Pete asked.

Forest looked at her. "In all honesty? It's exactly what I want." He turned back to McGarvey. "You have firearms here," he said as a statement not as a question. "And you have state-of-the-art surveillance equipment, something Otto Rencke has set up for you. So you've come here where it's easier to watch your three-sixty. You've been open about your movements, so in effect, you're expecting to be attacked. But you don't want any official help, which would keep the bad guy away, and you've bunkered in until it happens."

"Something like that," McGarvey admitted.

"Exactly like that," Forest said, resigned. "Have you thought about collateral damage like what happened at the college? Because that's sure as hell number one for me."

"The Alperts next door are in Europe, and the house to the south has been empty for almost a year."

"It's in what I've been told is a nasty probate fight in Atlanta."

"You've done your homework," Pete said.

"Self-defense; I've learned the hard way," Forest said. "But what about a car passing by out front or a pontoon boat filled with tourists coming down the ICW? If there's a gun battle, people could get hurt. Have you considered that possibility?"

"We're both excellent marksmen," Pete said. "And it's the off-season; only the locals here now. Even King is back in Maine."

"You've done your homework, too."

"Always do."

"How about if I get four of my SWAT team guys here? They could show up in plain clothes in an unmarked civilian vehicle. Two upstairs front and back and the same downstairs."

"You know why we're here," Pete said.

"What the hell is that supposed to mean?"

"If you know, then someone else in your department might know, too. And of course the Tampa SAC knows; in fact, the entire office is probably aware of what might go down. Can you guarantee that there are no leaks in your office or his?"

Forest started to object but then shook his head. "No. But my guess, if there is a leak somewhere, is that it would be in Tampa."

"Those guys get paid more than yours do," Pete said. "And your people are closer to the scene."

"What the hell am I supposed to say to that?"

McGarvey decided not to tell the cop about the Pentagon or the White House; it would add an unnecessary complication. "Nothing. Just go ahead and let things unfold as they may. Or may not."

"Trying to take you into custody wouldn't work."

"It didn't for the Bureau, and before that the Company."

"You don't want my SWAT guys either. So how about I camp out here for a few days? An extra gun wouldn't hurt."

"No, thanks."

"Not as a cop, just as a friend."

"No."

"Goddamnit, Mac."

"Let me tell you something else. The first shooter they sent after me was pretty decent. But just that, not fantastic. His experience was more along the line of taking up a sniper position a long ways from his target and then biding his time before taking the shot. The second operator was better. Much better by a large factor."

"But you managed to take both of them down."

"The third one will be someone at the very top of the game. An international assassin who knows his business," Mac said. "No offense, Jim, but you'd be way out of his league."

"Such a guy would have left footprints. Otto should be able to find him."

"We have some ideas, and we're still looking. But whoever this shooter is, he not only knows his business, he also knows how to hide his tracks. He's the invisible man."

"The only way we'll find him is when he comes here and takes his shot," Pete added.

FORTY-ONE

Li managed to sleep on and off during the long flight from Geneva to Atlanta's Hartsfield-Jackson Airport, but they were not traveling first class, and Taio was too uncomfortable even to doze off. He'd always been a self-assured man, but never to the point of arrogance. Yet he was seriously looking forward to going head-to-head with McGarvey, though Li had cautioned against it, and his better sense told him that she was probably right.

The American had to know or suspect that someone else would be coming after them. Just before they'd left the Geneva Holiday Inn Express for the airport, Tarasov had called on their encrypted cell phone to let them know that McGarvey and his wife had left Washington and were at their beach house on Florida's Gulf Coast.

"I have a pretty good idea that they're expecting company and have hunkered down till you show up," he'd said.

"Then we'll wait them out. Hammond gave us the job but with no timetable."

"I want this done as soon as possible."

"You may be our expediter, but you're not our paymaster," Taio said. "We're not going to rush; mistakes can be made."

"There are other considerations."

"No."

Tarasov was obviously angry, but he'd kept his tone even. "I'll pay you a $5 million bonus."

"Each," Taio said without thinking, and almost immediately he regretted it and was about to say so, but the Russian was first.

"Agreed."

"How soon?"

"Rent a car in Atlanta and drive to Florida. It should take you around six hours. I want it done and the two of you on the road back to Atlanta within twenty-four hours later."

"We'll need to sleep at some point."

"Sleep on the flight over. And then on the flight back to wherever you're headed next."

He had shared the sped-up timetable and the extra money with Li, and although she'd been skeptical, she'd bowed to his decision as she almost always did. She'd never been a pushover, but she was a good soldier and knew how to take orders if she trusted the lead officer.

The point of the matter, Taio thought as the plane began its long descent into Atlanta, was that he and Li had also discussed retiring at some point. When this operation had paid out, they would have plenty of money.

But the problem was twofold, something he'd not yet discussed with Li, although he had a fair idea which way she would lean. First, there'd always been the issue of failure—which, in their business, very often led to death or imprisonment. But secondly, he wondered if they would miss the thrill of the hunt and the sharp adrenaline rush at the time of the kill. So sharp sometimes that it was almost sexual.

The military psychiatrists at officers' school had discussed the issue with both of them—and at the time, they'd both thought that meant they would not be accepted for training. But the shrinks had assured them they were exactly the kind of people best suited for this line of work.

"Professional assassins don't do the job merely for love of country or even love of money when they go freelance, which I predict you will," their shrink said, "but for the thrill of it."

McGarvey would be their most formidable target to date, and Taio wondered whether they could retire or if they would be driven to find even tougher assignments.

What would they do with themselves, day after day?

But then he put his mind back to work on the operation at hand. Li's suggestion that McGarvey's wife would be a key to the kill was intriguing, except for the fact it might mean that he and Li would have to separate.

Thirty minutes later, Taio got online with his iPhone and booked them a room for three nights at the Marriott Courtyard near the Sarasota Airport, found the name and location of a gun shop in Bradenton, a city just north of the airport, and a boat rental place in Venice just south of Casey Key. When he was finished, he booked two round-trip first-class tickets to New York's LaGuardia from the Sarasota Airport for three days later.

They were on the hunt, and the old familiar feelings were starting to build inside him that made him think that when they were finished here, they would take a long vacation somewhere but never get out of the business.

Atlanta's Hartsfield-Jackson was like every other large airport in the world, a place of many corridors busy with scurrying people. It was nearly nine in the evening, local, when they made it through customs and immigration, some of the money divided between them, the remainder along with their Schilling passports hidden in the linings of the suitcases, and headed with their small carry-on bags to the car rental agencies, where they booked a nondescript Toyota Camry at the Hertz counter. And it was thirty minutes later before they were on the ring road that led to I-75 south, Li driving.

"You didn't get much sleep, did you?" she said.

"Enough."

"No, I can see it in your eyes. And tired people make mistakes."

"Amateurs make mistakes; we don't," Taio said a little too sharply. "You can drive while I tell you my plan, and then I'll get a couple of hours' sleep if you're good to drive all the way."

Li glanced at him. "Do you think that we can accomplish this in the twenty-four hours we were given?"

"I think so, but even if we miss the deadline, we'll still collect the second half of our fee, and we didn't have to pay Buerger."

"We would lose our expediter."

"If we remain in the business, there are others."

"That makes sense," Li said after a moment. "Our freedom means more than money."

"Or our lives, because let's not forget who we're going up against this time."

"Tell me again how," Li said.

He did, and when he was finished, Li nodded. "It's a way to get past their surveillance devices, if they have them."

"They're waiting for us, so I'm sure they're prepared."

"But they'll have to be gullible, especially the woman."

"They're Americans, and you pointed out that he's a romantic."

"We'll see," Li said.

McGarvey stood in the darkness next to the bedroom window looking across the road and down the sand dunes to the beach and the Gulf. It was after four in the morning. There was no moon or clouds, and the sea was so flat he could see the reflection of stars.

He'd been up and down most of the night, checking the front first, and then the back, even though it was unnecessary. Otto's surveillance system would alert them the moment anyone came within range. But it wasn't what you prepared for; that was almost never the problem. It was the unexpected circumstances that mattered. The attack from an unexpected direction, or an attack from where you thought it would come, but in a completely different form.

It wouldn't have surprised him to see an armed truck barreling up the road, guns blazing. But the last vehicle of any kind, a Mercedes convertible heading south, had passed by a couple of hours ago.

Since then, nothing had moved on the road, out in the Gulf, or along the ICW.

Pete came up behind him. "Just me," she said softly so as not to startle him.

"I thought you were sleeping," he said as she came into his arms.

"I was, and now it's your turn." She was wearing the same T-shirt and shorts she'd had on last night. She'd just lain on top of the blankets without even taking off her shoes.

Her subcompact Glock was stuffed in the waistband of her shorts, and one of the Beretta pistols was lying on the small table within arm's reach of where they stood.

"Nothing might happen for a day or two, maybe even longer," Pete said. "Both of us need to sleep and eat; otherwise, in a couple of days we'll be sitting ducks. Now, go lie down; Lou will warn us if someone shows up."

McGarvey looked toward the beach. "Someone's coming."

"You've known that for a couple of weeks now."

"But it'll be sooner than later. We won't have to hole up here for long."

Pete reached up and turned his face toward hers. "I heard an *and* in there," she said.

"It won't be over even then, unless they succeed this time."

"Which you think they eventually will if they keep sending their hit men."

McGarvey nodded, his worry for her safety spiking again. He felt like an old softy, but he'd been down this path too many times to feel any comfort or optimism.

"The list of the good ones is pretty small. Lou ought to be able to narrow it down."

"The best ones are on no one's list. What Lou will probably find is a list of assassinations over the past few years that have never been solved."

"She can look for methodologies."

"And find them, but if I were in the business, I wouldn't do the same thing the same way every time."

Pete smiled, the expression a little sad, her lips downturned at the corners. "But in a way, you are in the business, my darling. Both of us are."

FORTY-TWO

The Marriott was comfortable and inexpensive. After a few hours of sleep and breakfast downstairs, they drove over to the airport, where Li left the Camry in long-term parking while Taio went inside to the Avis counter and rented a Ford Edge SUV under the Schilling ID, which they would use until they left Sarasota.

When he'd picked it up, he drove back to the arrivals gate, where Li was waiting for him. She got in, and he handed her his iPhone.

"Find the Gun Barn in Bradenton," he said as he pulled away.

She retrieved it from the phone's memory where Taio had stored it on the flight over, and the map came up. "Turn right out of here onto University Parkway and then right again on Tamiami Trail," she said.

He followed her directions, and when they were heading north, past the west side of the airport, he glanced at her. She seemed tenser than usual for this stage of an op. "Are you okay?"

"A thousand things could go wrong. I'd rather be armed."

"We discussed it last night," Taio said. "If the woman gets even a hint that you're carrying a weapon, she'll take you down."

"I can handle myself."

"Yes, but McGarvey is the target."

"Yes, and while you'll be carrying an AR-15 with a bump stock, if you can still buy one, and coming up from the rear, I'll be the bait."

"This is America; just about any gun is for sale to just about anyone," Taio said. "And right now, you're the best chance we have for luring the woman out of their castle and McGarvey to come to the rescue of both of you."

"What if neither of them comes out? Maybe they'll call 911."

"Then you will be rescued. But in the meantime, their attention will be diverted to the front of the house. Which is the point."

"Let's not make this a gambit move," Li said, her voice suddenly soft.

"What do you mean?"

"Sacrifice me to capture the king."

Taio reached over and brushed a finger over her cheek. "This is not a game of chess. It's only one operation in a line of ops in which we've been partners." He smiled. "Unless you've forgotten, I'm in love with you."

She returned his smile. "You told me once, but I guess I forgot."

"Then let me tell you again."

. . .

McGarvey slept fitfully for only a few hours even though Pete had promised to alert him if she had the least doubt about anything. Since this business had begun last week in Georgetown, he'd been slowly wearing down. He was only fifty, but this morning, light streaming through the windows, he was beginning to feel his age.

He sat up and cocked an ear to listen. Pete wasn't here, and for the moment, the house seemed unnaturally quiet. He reached for his pistol at the same moment he heard her singing some country-and-western downstairs. It was something she only did when everything was right in her world, and he had to smile just a little.

No attack had come in the night, for which he was grateful, and yet he wanted it to be over with.

"Good morning, Mac," Lou said. "Did you sleep well?"

"No," McGarvey said. "Where's Otto?"

"Here," Otto said.

"How about running down the modus operandi for high-value hits over the past couple of years that are still unsolved?"

"Already on it, but other than Slatkin's trick with the clear tape over a hole in a window, nothing pops out from the background noise. The polonium poisoning of Litvinenko in London, a couple of long-range rifle shots, and one case in which a kilo of Semtex was put under the backseat of the Chinese ambassador to North Korea's limo—which was overkill—there's no set patterns that we can find."

"But if whoever is coming after you has upped their game and hired someone really good, it might be that the contractors are so good, they do it differently each time," Mary broke in.

"Or it's over and whoever's targeting you has called it a day," Otto suggested.

"I don't think so," McGarvey said.

Pete appeared at the door. "I don't either," she said. She'd brought a cup of coffee for Mac.

"It won't hurt to keep a tight watch for at least the next day or two, but after that, I don't know what to tell you two, except that keeping cooped up would drive anyone nuts," Mary said.

"If nothing happens today or tonight, we're going to take the boat out into the Gulf," McGarvey said.

"With a big target on your backs," Mary said.

"Same reason we're not surrounded by SWAT teams in full gear. I want to take the bastard alive."

"Making you even more vulnerable," Otto said.

"But this time, I have Pete covering my six," McGarvey said, finally accepting the inevitable.

Pete smiled but said nothing.

Purchasing the AR-15 had been ridiculously easy. After only a cursory check of Taio's Minnesota driver's license for any criminal activity, he and Li walked out the door with the assault rifle, three high-capacity magazines, and fifty rounds of ammunition, no questions asked.

Next, they stopped at a Walmart, where they got a bikini, a cover-up, sandals, and a floppy hat for her and a swimsuit, sandals, and a baseball cap for him. They also bought a compact beach umbrella in a small nylon bag, plus sunglasses for both of them.

Back at the hotel, Taio parked in the rear lot, well away from the front entrance with the trunk of the car facing the hotel. While Li leaned against the side of the car to act as lookout, Taio opened the trunk, pulled the umbrella out of its bag, loaded all three magazines for the AR-15, and stuffed the gun and the mags into the bag.

They entered the hotel through the back door and went up to their room, where they changed into the beachwear.

Watching his wife undress, Taio had the almost overwhelming urge to say the hell with the mission for the day and instead stay here where they could make love all afternoon. They could do the op tonight or even tomorrow.

Li caught his image in the mirror as she fixed the bra clasp, and she had to smile as she turned. "Actually, I would rather us stay here."

"Am I that obvious?"

"You always have been."

She went to him, and they embraced. "Let's make this our last operation," she said earnestly. "Go back to Hong Kong and do tai chi in the morning, and from time to time take a trip. On a cruise ship, or maybe a safari in Africa, or see Saigon, Tokyo, Australia. Be real people. Tourists."

"Starting tomorrow," Taio promised, and he meant it.

They left the hotel the same way they'd come in, and as soon as they were in the car and on the road, Li brought up directions to Sporty's Boat Rentals in Venice, about twenty miles to the south, and within easy striking distance to the McGarveys' Casey Key redoubt.

FORTY-THREE

Susan had gone into Geneva to do some shopping after a late lunch, leaving Hammond alone at the villa working his phone and computer. Life went on, and so did business.

Although he had more financial advisers and planners than he could shake a stick at—half of them at the TH Enterprises tower in Los Angeles and the other thousand or so spread over offices on Wall Street near the stock exchange and on Chicago's Loop—his most important business was his Strategic Liaison Group, what he referred to as his firemen.

Headed by A. Ramos Rodriguez, a Cuban-born whiz who'd received his M.D. Ph.D. in psychiatry with top honors from Harvard, along with his MBA on the side from the same university, ran the small office with only a handful of assistants just down the street from the UN.

Hammond's business interests literally spanned the globe, everything from media in Germany, mining in China and several other countries, perfume and wines in France, and of course a presence in a half dozen of the world's top stock exchanges. Rodriguez's specialty was meeting with and evaluating the financial advisers to the UN delegates from the countries he operated in and a few he wanted to do business with.

It was well after four in the afternoon, and Susan wasn't back yet when Rodriguez called from Washington. He sounded stressed, something unusual for him.

"I've been trying to get you all day. I thought you were aboard your yacht."

"Alaska was a bore. Is there a problem?"

"I don't know, but something is definitely in the wind."

"Don't be cryptic, Arturo."

"Last night, I had dinner and drinks with Viktor Kuprik at the Oyster Bar in Grand Central—one of his favorite eateries in New York, which he says is good for his libido. Afterward, we went to a male strip club over on Tenth, another one of his hangouts."

"He's gay?"

"Repressed, and I'm the only one he trusts to help with his fantasies."

"I'm not following you."

"Kuprik is the chief financial adviser to Feodor Morozov, who's Russia's UN ambassador, and your name came up last night."

"I'm listening," Hammond said, the first glimmerings of concern rising in his gut.

"Morozov wanted him to find out about you. Specifically your friends. Your Russian friends."

Hammond sat back in his chair and hesitated for a moment so that he could get himself under control. "Does he know that you work for me?"

"I didn't think so," Rodriguez said. "So I asked what made him think that I had any insider information on you."

"And?"

"He said that my name had come up as someone who knew a lot of people not only at the UN but just about everywhere else in the financial world and that I probably could get some information."

"What'd you tell him?"

"I said that I'd heard of you, of course, and I'd see what I could come up with if he'd give me something specific to work on. He told me just Russians who you had financial relations with."

"No names?" Hammond asked, the worry in his gut easing just a little. Tarasov had apparently gotten a little sloppy with someone he'd talked to.

"No."

"Give it a couple of days and tell him you couldn't find out much of anything beyond the Russians who show up at Monaco and Cannes and Davos and the other places on the circuit."

"That's the point; I can't, and that's why I called," Rodriguez said. "Kuprik was found in his bed just a few hours ago. Shot to death."

"Problem solved," Hammond said.

"No. The police are on their way now to find out if I know something."

"How'd they get your name?"

"I don't know; the stupid bastard may have written it down somewhere."

"You were seeing him professionally, and I assume that you have records to back it up."

"That's not the point."

"Confidential medical records."

"Of course, goddamnit, but what do I tell them if your name comes up? There's supposedly no connection between us."

"There is a connection. You briefly treated me for depression a couple of years ago when I lost friends in the pencil tower on West Fifty-Seventh that was brought down. Those records are confidential as well."

Rodriguez was silent for a beat. "Do you have a business deal with some Russian?"

"Of course I do," Hammond said. "Along with people in France, Germany, China, and a lot of other places."

"I don't know."

"Just do your job, Arturo, and let me worry about the details."

"I may decide to walk," Rodriguez said.

"Your choice," Hammond said, and he hung up.

The french doors in his office were open to the breeze off the lake. He got up and went out onto the balcony, where he leaned against the balustrade with both hands and stared at a small sailboat, its starboard rail awash as it tacked through the eye of the wind.

He wanted to escape, to run and hide, but out in the open. Among the players, his kind of people who spoke and understood the same language he did. The problem was there weren't that many Bill Gateses and Warren Buffetts in the world, and most of them were in competition with each other, though it didn't always show in public.

It was a serious game they all played, with money—intrinsically meaningless numbers in a bank's electronic ledger—as the means of keeping score, big yachts and airplanes and fancy houses the only outward signs of their wealth.

In a couple of years, when Codecasa delivered the *Susan P*, he would be the king of the hill at Monaco and Cannes, at least for a while until someone else showed up with an even bigger, fancier yacht.

He turned away. If he lived that long, the unbidden thought came to his mind. His biggest deal ever was the one he could never tell a soul. The only people who knew besides himself and Susan were the assassins and Tarasov. Hopefully, McGarvey and his wife would never find out the truth.

Back at his desk, he took the Chinese ZTE sat phone with the Russian encryption algorithm from a drawer and put in a six-digit alphanumeric code that unlocked it and speed-dialed Tarasov.

The Russian answered on the first ring. "Good afternoon, Thomas."

"We have a problem."

"If you mean Kuprik, he is no longer an issue."

"I just got off the phone with my financial adviser in New York who gave me the news."

"If you mean Rodriguez, what does he have to do with this?"

"He and Kuprik had drinks together last night, and the cops are going over to his office to interview him."

Tarasov was silent for a long beat. "I'll take care of it."

"You had Kuprik killed. Why?"

"Because he was indiscreet," Tarasov said. "What does your adviser know about your little game?"

"Apparently, not as much as the ambassador knows or suspects about what you're doing. He was the reason Kuprik was making inquiries."

"How reliable is your man? Will he keep his mouth shut to the cops?"

"I think so, but he threatened to quit working for me."

"You think or you *know*, Thomas? This is important for more reasons than just your little adventure."

"I can't guarantee him," Hammond said without giving it a thought.

"Can you live without him?"

"No one is indispensable."

"Me included?" Susan asked from behind him.

☐

FORTY-FOUR

McGarvey felt a lot better after a few hours' sleep and the breakfast of bacon and eggs Pete had fixed for them. He'd helped her clean up and then sat at the kitchen table overlooking the pool and beyond it the gazebo and the ICW as he unloaded and disassembled his Walther PPK with the well-worn handle, laying the parts and the bullets on a soft, lightly oiled rag.

Pete sat and watched him as he worked slowly and methodically. "It looks clean," she said.

McGarvey smiled. "It is," he said without looking up.

"I've seen you do this before other assignments. Are you just making sure of your equipment?"

"That, too, but it calms the nerves."

Pete almost laughed. "You of all people don't get nerves. It's about the only thing about you I don't understand."

This time, he looked up from cleaning the already immaculate barrel with a short ramrod and a small piece of oiled, lint-free cloth. "But I do get nervous," he said.

"Your hands are steady, never any sweat on your forehead, except for the time in Paris when you finally asked me to marry you." She reached over and put two fingers over the inside of his wrist. "Heart steady, less than one beat a second. Yet you're getting ready to defend your hearth and home—and me, from someone you think is damned good. Better than the first two."

McGarvey simply nodded, because there was no reason to explain something to Pete that she already knew since the first time they'd come under fire what seemed like a century ago.

Pete looked down toward the ICW. "Lou has us covered in all directions, and if whoever is coming has decent intel, they might be aware of that fact. And even if they have no direct evidence, they know about you and about Otto, and you're convinced that they're coming, which means they probably have a plan for getting through whatever defenses are in place."

"Which is why we're going to start making it easier for them."

Pete grinned again. "Why did I think you were going to say something like that?"

"Because we want this to be over with, and neither of us wants to sit around forever."

"What do you have in mind?"

"Soon as I'm finished here, I'm going to get the boat ready. You can bring one of the assault rifles and one MP7, plus some ammunition down and maybe some provisions. We'll head out to the Gulf nice and slow and easy and putter around a couple of miles offshore."

"For how long?"

"Overnight. If something hasn't happened by then, we'll come back here and get ready for Serifos."

"Whatever it takes, we're going to force the issue just like you did at the Pentagon and the White House, right?"

"I don't want to keep our lives on hold waiting for something to happen. And I need to know why, as well as who."

"We know why," Pete said. "I knew it from the first day I met you."

McGarvey said nothing, concentrating instead on finishing with his pistol.

"You've never been afraid of stepping on toes, anyone's toes; it doesn't matter to you. Weaver, Putin, Kim Jong-un. If something is wrong, you want to make it right."

"Tilting at windmills. Been doing it all my life."

"Not that at all, my darling. Don Quixote was a knight with rusted armor, something you're not. But maybe it's time to hang it up."

He knew where she was going, and he put up a hand to stop her, but she overrode him.

"Listen to me, Kirk. You're not a young man now."

"Only fifty."

"There are kids out there half your age with twice the reflexes."

McGarvey shrugged.

"Sooner or later, you'll be a millisecond too slow, your aim off by just a tenth of a centimeter, your sense of justice will blur your judgment at the wrong time."

"You're right, of course. But here we are," he said. This time, when she started to object, he overrode her. "And I don't want you in the firing line if . . . when that happens."

"Too bad," Pete said, rising. "Finish what you're doing, and I'll get our things together."

"Lou, what's on our perimeter?" McGarvey asked.

"Boat traffic is moderate on the ICW and light in the Gulf as normal for this time of year. Some noncommercial aircraft traffic from the Venice airport. My threat level assessment is at less than 5 percent."

"How about foot traffic on the beach and vehicles on the road?"

"Some beach activity around sunrise this morning and only some local road traffic, including several lawn care people and a Frontier Cable Systems maintenance van. I verified a work order."

"We're going sailing. Should be leaving within the hour."

"I'll keep you advised."

"Where's Otto?"

"Mary made him go home to sleep. They think it may be a busy evening."
Pete was just leaving the kitchen, but she stopped and turned back.

"What do you think?" McGarvey asked.

"Insufficient data. But a night attack would be optimal."

"Too optimal?"

McGarvey—barefoot, wearing swim trunks, no shirt, his prosthetic leg ob-
scene looking in his mind—went down to the Whitby ketch tied to the dock.
Unlocking the hatch, he went below, checked the status of the batteries on
the automatic charger—they were full—and by long habit powered up the
VHF radio and switched to the NOAA weather channel for this area of the
coast that included inland waters as well as those in the Gulf out twenty nau-
tical miles.

Topside again, he took the sail covers off, starting with the mizzen aft and
then the main. When he'd bought the thirty-year-old yacht several years ago,
he'd opted to stick with hand-raised and reefed sails rather than the electrically operated in the mast self-furling sails. Keeping systems simple meant that
at sea, out of the range of marinas, fixing something that broke was possible.

A pair of Jet Skis came up from the south, and standing at the main mast,
McGarvey watched as they approached. The drivers appeared to be boys,
possibly teenagers.

"Lou, evaluate the Jet Skis approaching."

"Rentals from Sporty's in Venice. Roger and Benjamin Kaplan, brothers
with Michigan driving licenses."

"Are there any other marinas with boat rentals either north or south of
my position?"

"Yes. Several dozen."

"Threat assessments?"

"All at less than 5 percent."

"Tell me when any assessment exceeds that number."

"Yes."

Pete came down with a small, two-wheeled pushcart of the type usually
found at marinas, filled with food and drinks, and handed the bags and
boxes across to Mac, who took them below. When they were finished, she
went back to the house for a second load as McGarvey stowed the steaks,
drinks, and other perishables in the galley's large cooler.

Topside again, he started the diesel and checked over the transom to make
sure that the cooling water was flowing before he went onto the dock and
released the spring lines, leaving only the bow and stern lines.

By two thirty, the rest of the provisions, plus the weapons and ammunition, had been loaded, and Pete stood holding the bowline. Dressed in short jean cutoffs and a light gauze shirt tied at the waist over her bikini, she seemed eager.

"Are you ready?" McGarvey asked.

"Let's get it done," she said.

FORTY-FIVE

□

Sporty's Marina was right on the Intracoastal Waterway, a short distance from the inlet that ran out into the Gulf. A dozen Jet Skis for rent were lined up in knee-deep water just off the narrow beach, and business was fairly brisk with a number of boats of all sizes and types under way.

A hundred meters or so south, just across from the inlet, a dozen or more small powerboats, including several Jet Skis, had pulled up at a small island. A small crowd of people had brought everything from barbecue grills, coolers, and beach umbrellas to even a boom box or two ashore and were partying.

"Looks like they're having fun," Li said as they parked and went down to the Jet Skis.

"Lanling gongren," Taio said dismissively.

"We've always been blue-collar workers, only now we have money."

"We have work to do, so keep your mind where it belongs. We'll play later."

A young salesman with sun-bleached blond hair, wearing flip-flops, board shorts, and a bright Hawaiian shirt mostly unbuttoned came down to them, a big grin on his face. "You guys want a couple of Doos, or do you want to ride tandem?"

"We'd like to rent two for the half day," Taio said. "Something fast."

"Sure thing. You've ridden before?"

"First time."

"Maybe you want to start at the bottom, not the top, if you know what I mean."

"We drive Augustas back in New York," Li said. "I think we can handle ourselves."

The salesman was impressed. "Go for it," he said. He pointed out a pair of Kawasaki machines at the end of the row. "You want speed, you can take the 310LX. They're total monsters. But even with three people, they still top out above seventy."

"Fine," Taio said.

"Cash or plastic?"

"Do you take American Express?" Taio asked.

"Is the pope Catholic?" the salesman asked.

They went up to the office, where they both had to show their Schilling driver's licenses and sign the rental contract, which included a waiver of liability for personal injury. The four-hour rental fee was high, plus a $500 damage deposit for each machine.

Li had wandered off, and as Taio's card was being run, she came back with a couple of bottles of water and two waterproof plastic pouches for their cell phones. "Add these," she told the salesman.

He grinned. "Included."

Taio signed the charge slip, and the salesman got a couple of keys attached to wristbands with eighteen inches or so of flexible tubing and walked them back to the machines.

"Actually, pretty basic to run these things," he said, climbing aboard one of them. He put the key into the ignition, and the machine kicked off with a husky snarl. "If you fall overboard, which can happen, the wristband will pull the key and put the machine in dead slow in a small circle so you can get back to it. Don't mess with the system. Okay?"

Taio and Li nodded.

"They're like bikes, except for steering. You don't have to lean into a turn as hard as you do with a bike, but you have to keep the engine running no matter what. Chop the power and you lose steering."

He cut the engine, got off the machine, and handed them the keys. "Take it easy at first until you get used to how they handle. But hey, this is Florida—have fun."

The Whitby, with a five-foot draft, which was a little deep for Florida and Bahamian waters, was a joy to handle even in stiff winds and fifteen-foot seas, which McGarvey had encountered twice on the way across the Gulf Stream from Florida's east coast to Freeport in the Bahamas.

When he had bought her, his wife was alive, so he'd named the boat *Kathleen*.

After her death, he'd toyed with the idea of renaming her, but when Pete came into his life, she had insisted that he not do it.

"It's bad luck," she'd said.

"It doesn't bother you?" he'd asked. He was still confused in those days about what he should be doing.

Pete had looked into his eyes and smiled. "Bother me that you named a boat after your wife? Of course not."

Mac, at the wheel in the center cockpit, got on the VHF radio and called the tender as they slowly approached the Blackburn Point Bridge. "Blackburn Point Bridge, this is the sailing vessel *Kathleen* approaching from the north for an opening."

Several other boats were already gathered and some circling on either side of the bridge, waiting for an opening.

Pete, who had sailed aboard only three times before but who was a fast learner, leaned against the coaming above the hatch, studying the small bridge through binoculars. "She's on the bridge."

This tender was a pleasant woman, unlike one a few years ago who'd thought that every boat driver who wanted the bridge opened—her bridge—was nothing but a pain in the ass.

The tide was running out, and Mac had to put the boat in reverse to hold his position as the bridge slowly swung open, and because of his size held there to let the smaller boats go first. When it was their turn, he barely nudged the throttle, and they were squirted through the narrow opening and out the other side, where he lined up between the red and green markers, putting him in the middle of the channel.

It was a little more than five miles to the Venice Inlet, which would take them out into the Gulf—which, at the slow speed they were making, would take at least an hour.

The afternoon was lovely, a light breeze from the west, a relatively low humidity, and eighty-four degrees under a perfectly clear sky. On days like this, things didn't go badly. Or weren't supposed to, and yet McGarvey had the gut feeling that whatever was going to happen would happen before the day was finished.

Pete put the binoculars back in their box just inside the open hatch and turned to face her husband. "It's close, isn't it?" she said.

"I think so."

Pete got her phone, put it on speaker mode, and called Otto, who answered as usual on the first ring.

"Are you guys on the water?" he asked.

"Just went through the Blackburn Point Bridge, and Mac's internal radar is humming. Do you have anything for us?"

"Nothing specific, but there is a lot of boat traffic; anyone passing you could take a shot, and at that range, they couldn't miss."

"Lots of witnesses," Pete said. "And the guy would have to make his getaway."

"Whoever it is has a plan. These kinds of guys never do anything without thinking about all the possibilities. Take care."

"Will do," Pete said.

"Keep a close watch on the house and perimeter," McGarvey said. "We're going to anchor just offshore."

"Daring him to shoot," Mary broke in.

"We'll be ready."

"Stay frosty," Otto said, and Pete hung up.

The navigable channel here was narrow, though the mostly shallow waterway itself was wide, in some places a couple of hundred yards. Big houses with expansive lawns and marked channels that the owners had paid to dredge and keep open led from the ICW to docks where their toys were up out of the water on lifts. There was a lot of money in this part of Florida.

"Do you want something to drink?" Pete asked.

"Go below if you would and open a couple of beers and empty the cans in the sink. Fill them with Coke or iced tea. From this point on, we're only going to make a show of drinking beer."

□

FORTY-SIX

They got their hats, sunglasses, and phones from the SUV and, Taio shouldering the umbrella bag that held the loaded AR-15 and two spare magazines, walked back to the pair of Jet Skis tethered to the beach.

The party on the island was getting into full swing now, and no one paid much attention to them as they untied the machines, turned them around so that they faced deeper water, and climbed aboard.

"I'll go out into the Gulf with you a little ways until we get the hang of these things," Taio said. "When we're ready, you'll head up the island, and I'll take the ICW."

"Call me," Li said, her voice tight in her throat as it usually was at the beginning of an operation.

Once they were into it, she always settled down beautifully, and Taio thought then as he had before, that she made not only the perfect wife but she was the perfect partner.

He reached across and touched her hand. "This will be done in an hour or two, and we'll be on our way home, where we can plan our vacation."

Li smiled. "And our retirement."

"That, too," Taio said. "Let's go."

They started their machines and Taio headed out first, careful with the touchy throttle. The machine was even more powerful than he'd thought it would be, but it was more or less like driving a motorcycle except that he couldn't do a wheelie.

He looked back as Li eased up along his left side, a big grin on her pretty face. She loved the Augustas, and it was obvious she was liking this ride.

A few of the people on the jetties waved as they headed out, and once in the Gulf, Taio hit the throttle, and the big machine responded like a rocket ship. About a hundred meters offshore, he turned hard to the right, and the Jet Ski heeled over almost like a motorcycle but raising a huge white wake.

Glancing over his shoulder, he was in time to see Li cutting a wider circle around him. He turned toward her, and she turned inward toward him. They both made a couple of more turns, then throttled down and approached each other, easing close enough so that they could talk.

"Fun?" he asked.

She nodded enthusiastically. "We're buying a pair of these when we get home."

"We'll be the terrors of Hong Kong's harbor," Taio said, and they laughed.

Incongruous just now, he thought. "I'm going inside. Once you reach the house, make a couple of passes, and let me know when you're ready."

She was suddenly serious. "Be careful, Taio. I want the vacation and especially our retirement."

"So do I," Taio said, and for the first time in their careers, he meant it. It was time to get out before the odds of being killed—or worse yet, being captured alive and sent separately to prison for the rest of their lives—reached 100 percent.

"*Zai jian, Taio.*" *See you later.*

"*Hao ba.*" *Okay.*

Hammond had a lousy night, scarcely able to get more than a couple of hours of sleep, and he'd spent most of the day working on projects, waiting for word that McGarvey had been taken care of, and now in the early evening, he was totally exhausted.

Sitting now on the patio picking at his dinner of lobster and truffled new potatoes, he was at sixes and sevens with himself over just about everything that had happened over the past month or so.

Susan had taken the shuttle down to see her European theater manager to work on a deal that would allow her to buy 350 screens, mostly in Italy but several in France and Germany. Her idea was to market showings of films made in places like Syria, Lebanon, and several other troubled Middle Eastern countries that would appeal mostly to the vast hordes of immigrants pouring in.

"A little touch of home," she'd explained cynically to Hammond.

"No money in it," he'd told her.

"If they can come up with five grand to have a smuggler take them here, then they'll have a few euros to see a flick. I want whatever they have left over, and in return, I'll give them a couple of hours of relief. Cheaper than seeing a shrink."

He'd been labeled as a raider without a heart for pretty much his entire career. But he'd merely taken money from people who were already rich and could afford to lose a few tens of millions. And it had been nothing more than a game to him.

But in his opinion, Susan had crossed over the line, and he'd told her so this morning before she'd left.

"You have to be kidding," she'd laughed.

"You're fleecing poor bastards who have nothing."

"This coming from a man who is willing to spend millions merely for a game? Of killing people for sport?"

"Hardly innocents."

"Come off it, Thomas, you got screwed over because of a bitcoin deal that was probably bogus to begin with. So you wanted to do something to

McGarvey and his wife, but you didn't want to get your hands dirty, so you asked your Russian pal to take care of it." The disdain in her wide eyes and the downturn of her pretty lips was palpable. "That's so fucking typical of you."

"The pot calling the kettle black?"

"I do my own dirty deals. And I don't have to sign away anything to do them."

"I would have backed the pipeline deal anyway."

"Something like that has never been on your radar, and you know it," Susan had said before she'd gone to the door. But then she'd turned back. "Be careful, Thomas, that this doesn't bite you in the ass. That could be a wound so deep you'd never be able to recover from it."

She was supposed to be back sometime this evening, but Hammond was beginning to wonder if he really gave a damn. She and her prima donna tantrums were beginning to wear thin for him.

He picked up his phone and called his Strategic Liaison Group office in Washington. One of the secretaries answered, but not until after five rings.

"SLG," she said, a touch of what sounded like hysteria in her voice.

Hammond knew what might have happened, and he realized that he really didn't give a damn about it either. "This is Tom Hammond. What's going on?"

"Oh, sir, it's Mr. Rodriguez."

"What about him?"

"He's dead," the woman blubbered.

"What the hell are you talking about? Dead, how?"

"He was getting out of a cab a couple of hours ago out front, and a truck or something ran into him. He never had a chance."

"Was the truck driver arrested?"

"We don't know."

"What the fuck do you know?" Hammond shouted.

"I don't know," the poor woman said.

Hammond broke the connection and slammed the phone down on the table, upsetting his wineglass.

The sommelier came out, but Susan was right there and sent him away. "I'll take care of it," she told him.

Hammond looked over his shoulder. "I'm in no mood for your shit."

She came out to him, pecked him on the cheek, then righted his glass, refilled it with the Marchesi Antinori Tignanello pinot grigio in the ice bucket, and used his napkin to sop up the spill.

"I'm here," she said. "Tell me everything so that we can figure out what to do."

FORTY-SEVEN

About twenty minutes north of the Venice Inlet, traffic had increased dramatically. Everything from small- and medium-size sailboats to small and large motor yachts, plus canoes and kayaks singly and in groups, and literally dozens of Jet Skis, most of them driven by young people, some McGarvey figured not even teenagers yet, crowded the waterway that in some places was less than fifty or sixty feet wide.

"Could be our guy in any of those boats," Pete said at one point.

McGarvey kept a sharp eye out ahead as well as behind to make sure they stayed in the channel. "A drive-by shooting?"

"Could be that simple."

"But not elegant."

"Could be if he's thought of an escape route. These kinds of people don't take a crap without figuring all the alternatives."

And that was the one thing he'd always kept at the front of his mind. What if the obvious wasn't so obvious? One bit or piece he hadn't thought of, but that the opposition had.

A bright green Jet Ski coming up from the south cruised past at a reasonable speed for the traffic and the narrowness of the channel. By habit Mac glanced at the registration number and then at the driver, who had what looked like a beach umbrella bag over his shoulder. The man wore a swimming suit, a light shirt, and a baseball cap.

Ordinary, McGarvey thought. *Too ordinary?*

He looked over his shoulder until the Jet Ski disappeared from view.

Pete had been watching. "Something?" she asked.

"I don't know," Mac said. He got his phone from the starboard-side cockpit locker and speed-dialed Otto.

"You have something?"

"A green Jet Ski just passed us headed north," McGarvey said. He gave Otto the Florida registration number.

"Just a mo," Otto said. He was back in a few seconds. "It's a rental from a place called Sporty's just above the Venice north jetty."

"Who rented it?"

"I'll check our records," Otto said.

"What'd you see that's bothering you?" Pete asked.

"He had what looked like a beach umbrella bag over his shoulder."

"So?"

"It wasn't full. The top half was flapping in the breeze. He wasn't carrying an umbrella."

"A long gun," Pete said. She grabbed the binoculars and looked aft.

Otto came back. "Probably not our guy. Name on the Amex card is George Schilling. An address in Minneapolis, Minnesota. Do you want me to do a background check?"

"Go ahead."

"Was he alone?"

"The only one on the machine."

"I mean was there another Jet Ski with him? He rented two of them; the second was to a woman named Carolyn Schilling, same address. Presumably, his wife."

"Only the one," McGarvey said. "But check them out anyway."

Taio went out of the navigable channel into knee-deep water and powered down to dead idle. The sailboat headed south that he'd passed was a Whitby center cockpit ketch, and the man at the wheel was McGarvey. The woman with the binoculars his wife. He recognized them from the file photos he'd dug up.

The problem was threefold: Where the hell were they going, why were they suddenly on the move, and what to do about it?

He had the answers almost immediately. It didn't matter where they were going or why they were on the move, because he was going to lure them back to their house, and they would have to pass him.

The boat was made of a lot of laminations of strong fiberglass that was designed to stand up to big waves out on the ocean, but not metal-jacketed bullets.

He got on his cell phone and called Li, who answered after three rings. *"Shi de."*

"I just passed the McGarveys headed south in their sailboat."

"Is there a lot of traffic?"

"Yes, but I have a change of plans."

"Wait, do you think that they paid you any special attention?"

"They watched me pass them, and the woman looked at me through binoculars."

Li took only a moment to respond. "They probably got our registration numbers."

"Almost certainly, but even if they checked at the marina, all they would get is our Schiller IDs."

"That's not the point, husband. They would have found out that Mr. and Mrs. Schiller rented separate machines. You passed them, but what about me?"

"But that's going to work to our advantage."

"How?"

"Get up to their house, pull up onto the beach, cross the road, and get inside as quickly as you can."

"They'll have an active surveillance system," Li said. "They'll know I'm there."

"Exactly what I want to happen. They'll have to turn around, and when they pass me again, I'll be ready."

"I'm not armed."

"You'll find something inside the house. A man like McGarvey would keep weapons in easily accessible places, especially if he believes someone is trying for him again."

"What about afterward?"

"I'll pick you up, and we'll get rid of the machines up north somewhere and find a car."

"Too much room for mistakes," Li said. "I'm sure the McGarveys' car is in their garage. We'll abandon it somewhere between here and the hotel, and from there, we'll get our things and take a cab to the airport and get the car we drove down from Atlanta."

"I'll move closer to the house to minimize the lag time before I can pick you up," Taio said. "What's your ETA?"

"I'm about ten minutes out, plus however long it takes for me to find a way in."

"With care."

"You, too. I want out of this as quickly as possible."

"*Shi de*," Taio said, and he meant it.

Nothing about this op was setting well with him. Their special ops brigade had adopted a number of Murphy's laws that the American SEAL Team 6 guys used. The one that came to mind now was: If everything seems to be going well, it probably means that you're running into an ambush.

Susan shared dinner with Hammond, and afterward, drinking the last of the pinot, she put a bare foot up on his knee. "When should we hear something?"

"They didn't say," Hammond said. Despite himself, his mood had brightened when Susan had arrived, and he was beginning to feel that he might almost be in love with her. She was a prima donna, but they had a history together, and she was his prima donna.

"Assuming they succeed, then what?"

Hammond had thought about that as well. "I pay them, and we move on."

"Move on as in what?"

"I'll have *Glory* loaded aboard a transport ship, taken through the Panama

Canal and dropped off in Gibraltar, and we can fly over and do Cannes and Monaco. Have some fun for a change."

Susan was silent for a moment or two, staring out at the lake. "What aren't you telling me, Thomas?"

Hammond was a very good liar, but he'd never been good at it with her. "There may have been a couple of complications in Washington."

□

FORTY-EIGHT

Still a quarter mile offshore, Li recognized the McGarveys' house because of the wide overhangs on the second story and the gently sloping brown and light brown slate roof. She debated calling Taio, but he'd given her the last-minute plan, and she would stick with it, but with a slight variation.

Making absolutely sure that no one was on the beach and that no vehicles were on the road, she turned sharply toward the shore as she gunned the Kawasaki's powerful engine, and the machine shot forward. Moments later, she jogged hard to the right, and then again to the right at high speed, but erratically as if she had lost control, all the while closing in on the beach.

A hundred yards out, she took the wristband off, made an extreme turn, and fell off the machine, which veered off to the left.

For several seconds, she floundered in the water but then straightened out and swam like an amateur afraid of drowning, her arms flailing. It took a full five minutes for her to reach water shallow enough for her to stand, and she staggered ashore.

Still no one was on the road as she made it up the path, then crossed over to the McGarveys' place, then down the wide driveway to the front door, which was locked.

She was 100 percent sure that she was showing up on the house's surveillance system, so she lurched as if she were on her last legs, or was drunk, around back to the pool area.

The sliding doors into the kitchen were locked, so she turned and went down to the gazebo, where she sat down, her elbows on her knees, her head lowered.

"I'm here," she said to herself when she spotted the handle of a pistol taped to the underside of the bench seat across from her. "Herd them to me, husband. I can help."

Taio found an ideal spot on the island side of the waterway. A house with a fairly short marked channel looked as if no one was at home. The pool furniture had been covered, as had the big barbecue grill on the patio. A small powerboat up on a lift and a pontoon boat tied to the dock had also been covered with bright blue canvas.

He powered slowly up the channel and tucked in behind the pontoon boat out of sight from anyone passing in the ICW.

Laying the umbrella bag on the dock, he untied one of the lines holding the pontoon boat in place and tied it around the handles of the Jet Ski, securing it from drifting away.

Next, he undid a corner of the canvas covering the boat and, taking the umbrella bag, climbed aboard. He pulled the AR-15 out of the bag, inserted one of the magazines, jacked a round into the firing chamber, and, making sure the weapon was ready in all respects to fire, he laid it aside.

He loosened a small section of the canvas enough that he had a clear sight line to anything out on the waterway, and then, mindless of the heat, settled down to wait.

The ICW passed behind an island where a lot of people had pulled up with their boats and were partying just within sight of the Venice Inlet when McGarvey's cell phone buzzed. He put it on speaker mode. It was Otto.

"I found the wife. She came up about a hundred yards offshore from your house, and it looked as if she lost control of her machine and went into the water."

"Are you sure it's the wife?" McGarvey asked, throttling way back.

"I couldn't catch the registration number, but it looked like the same model green Kawasaki as the husband was driving. Anyway, I thought she was going to drown, and I was going to call 911 when she got control of herself and swam to shore."

"Where is she now?"

"Sitting in your gazebo with her head in her hands."

"What's Lou's evaluation?"

"Not enough data; she's given it only a 28 percent probability that the woman and her husband are the ones gunning for you. Their creds check out as valid, and the screen grabs of her face we took from the surveillance cameras don't show up on any database we have access to."

"Did she try to contact anyone after she got to shore?" Pete asked.

"She was wearing a beach jacket of some sort, but she lost it in the water. All she's wearing now is a very skimpy bikini, no place to hide a phone or a weapon."

"Yes, there is, if she's determined enough," Pete said.

"And it's possible she'll find the Beretta I taped under a seat in the gazebo," McGarvey added.

"If they're the shooters," Otto said, "what do you want me to do? At least call Jim?"

"Does it look like she's in any physical trouble?"

"No."

"Then she won't need medical help," McGarvey said. "We're turning around and going back to the house."

"If they're the ones after you, the wife showed up to lure you back, and the husband who you passed on the ICW is waiting for you to do just that so he can take his shot."

"Any sign of him?" Pete asked.

"No, but he could be waiting just outside the perimeter."

"Which would make them smart."

Taio laid the rifle down and tried to phone Li, but after four rings, he gave up. Either she'd lost her phone, had her hands full driving the Jet Ski—which in any case would be too loud for her to hear the ring—or she had gone ashore and was in the house already.

If the latter were the case, the McGarveys would be turning around and heading back.

It could take as long as forty-five minutes or even an hour before they got to this point. But he was a patient man.

He crawled out from under the canvas on the shore side, got his bottle of water from the Jet Ski, and went back inside, where he took a drink. Easing the canvas cover up a few inches so he had a clear view of the boats passing on the waterway, he picked up the rifle, switched the safety off, and settled down to wait.

McGarvey slowed to just above idle as they approached the Crow's Nest restaurant and marina, the channel out into the Gulf a couple of hundred feet dead ahead. "I've changed my mind," he said.

"I'm all ears."

"If they're the ones gunning for us, the husband is waiting for us somewhere near the house, but we won't know which side of the channel he's hiding until he takes a shot. And if he's any good, he won't miss."

"One of us could go up the mast; he might be concentrating on the cockpit."

"Whoever's up top would be an easy target. And hunkering down below the coaming in the cockpit wouldn't do us any good either. If he brought a long rifle in the umbrella bag, the rounds could penetrate the hull."

"I could take the dinghy ashore once we get a little closer and come up from behind him," Pete suggested. "Catch him from behind."

"We still don't know which side of the channel he's on," McGarvey said.

He shoved the throttle forward, and the Whitby surged toward the jetties. Then he got on the phone and called Otto.

"We're going out into the Gulf, anchoring offshore from the house, and taking the dinghy in. Keep an eye on the woman, and let us know what she's doing."

☐

FORTY-NINE

The early evening was soft, a light breeze coming off the lake through the open sliders in the bedroom of the villa ruffling the gauze curtains. Susan and Hammond had made love and were lying in each other's arms.

"When will we know?" she murmured.

"When I get notice that the second half of the payment was made into their account," Hammond said.

He was still torn two ways. One part of him wanted it to be over, and the other wanted the game to continue. It was nuts, but he was also torn between excitement and being more frightened than he had been since his biggest deal in the middle of the dot-com that had netted him his first billion and ruined the poor bastard who'd gone up against him.

"I have a better idea," Susan said. She got up and padded out of the bedroom.

"Where the hell are you going?" he called after her.

"Just a sec," she said.

She came back with her iPad, and, sitting cross-legged beside him on the bed, she powered up the machine and then googled Sarasota area news outlets.

Almost immediately, a list of local television and radio stations and newspapers came up on the screen. She chose WWSB, the ABC affiliate in Sarasota.

"If the former director of the CIA and his wifey get into a gun battle, it'll hit the news almost immediately," she said. "We just have to sit back and wait."

Hammond had to smile despite himself and despite what he had put into motion. "In the meantime, we'll just have to amuse ourselves any way we can."

"I can think of a couple of things," Susan said, setting the iPad aside.

Taio checked his watch. Traffic on the ICW came in spurts. At times, the waterway was busy, almost crowded, but then for stretches of time, no boats passed. But if Li had made it to the house and the surveillance system had picked up her presence and the McGarveys had been notified, they should have turned around and come this far by now.

He tried her cell phone again, letting it ring ten times before he hung up.

The only thing left at this point was to salvage whatever he could to get them the hell out of harm's way.

Switching the AR-15's safety on and taking out the magazine so that the gun would fit into the umbrella bag, he got off the pontoon boat, untied his Jet Ski, and headed back out to the ICW, keeping his eye for the Whitby in case his timing was off.

They had lowered the dinghy into the water on the way up from Venice and, because the seas were mostly calm, towed it on a fairly short tether. The Kawasaki was barely moving on dead idle, and as they slowed down and approached it, McGarvey called Otto.

"We're just offshore. What's the situation at the house?"

"Nothing's changed. The woman is still sitting in the gazebo."

"Waiting for her husband?"

"That's what it looks like."

"Has she found the Beretta?"

"No," Otto said. "But it's within arm's reach, so when you go in, take care."

McGarvey rang off. "Get down in the dinghy, and I'll get you close to the Jet Ski," he told Pete. "See if she left anything behind."

Pete hung off the transom and pulled the little boat close aboard, and as soon as she was in, McGarvey maneuvered the Whitby over to the Jet Ski.

Pete reached over and pulled something from one of the compartments. "A cell phone in a plastic bag."

"Stand by. We're going in," McGarvey said.

He went forward and lowered the Danforth anchor. The water here was only twenty feet deep, so he let out one hundred feet of line, cleated it, then went back to the helm and put the ketch in reverse until the anchor bit. He shut down the engine and pocketed the key.

Pete was waiting in the dinghy. He handed her pistol down, shoved his in the waistband of his shorts at the small of his back, and climbed down into the dinghy, and they headed to the beach.

Taio maneuvered slowly past the boats waiting for the Blackburn Point Bridge and crossed beneath the low span and through the several boats waiting on that side, careful to make no wake, which would make people angry at him. Angry people remembered those who did something to them.

When he was clear, he sped up and came within sight of the McGarveys' house and the empty dock, and he throttled down again and made his way slowly ashore, all of his senses alert. The situation had gotten completely out of hand. All he wanted now was to collect Li and get the hell out.

Easing the Jet Ski behind the dock of the house two doors down from the McGarveys', he tied it off, got the AR-15 from the bag, loaded it, and headed off.

Li thought she'd heard the distinctive growl of the Jet Ski that Taio was driving, but then it stopped. It had been very close, perhaps less than a hundred meters to the south. Whoever was monitoring the house surveillance system knew that she was here, but it was unlikely that they were aware she'd spotted the pistol taped under the seat just in front of her.

It was a race now. Either Taio got here first or the McGarveys would.

Pete ran the bow of the dinghy up on the beach and cut the engine as Mac jumped out, his Walther in hand.

A car passed on the road above, and Pete was right behind him as he went across the low sand dune and held up.

He called Otto. "Has anything changed?"

"Yes. The other Kawasaki pulled up at the Parkers' house two doors down from you. A man carrying an AR-15 got off and is heading your way. ETA maybe three minutes tops."

McGarvey pocketed the phone. "Company's coming," he said to Pete over his shoulder and hurried across the road.

He didn't bother with the front door, but both of them went around back to the rear of the house, where they pulled up.

The woman was seated in the gazebo her back to them. She was bent over again, her head down as if she were frightened or in pain.

"Get to your feet with your hands up!" McGarvey shouted.

The woman rolled to the left onto a knee as if she were startled out of her mind and was collapsing. At the same time, her right arm came around.

She had the Beretta in hand and started firing, the rounds smacking into the side of the house inches from where McGarvey had been standing.

"Keep her busy, but try not to kill her," Mac told Pete, and he raced to the front of the house, and, rounding the corner, ran to the to the south side and toward the rear.

He could hear Pete firing back, her shots measured, but the Beretta was finally silent, the fifteen-round magazine dry—either that or the woman was down.

"Li!" a man shouted at the same time Mac reached the back of the house and cautiously peered around the corner.

The same one from the Kawasaki that had passed them on the ICW was rushing up the lawn from the next-door house, the AR-15 in hand.

"Stop!" McGarvey shouted.

Taio brought the rifle around and, without missing a step, sprayed the corner of the house at the same time Mac fired three shots, all of them catching the man in the side of his torso, sending him sprawling.

He twitched twice and then lay still.

"Pete?" McGarvey called.

"I'm good. You?"

"My guy is down. What about the woman?"

"She's down. Good to go."

"Clear here," McGarvey said, and keeping his pistol pointed ahead, he walked down to the assassin's body.

PART
THREE

Endgame

*In the end, the only real hope
was to send an overwhelming force
to finish the thing.*

FIFTY

□

Hammond was in the bathroom just finishing with a shower at eleven in the evening when Susan shouted something from the bedroom. He didn't quite catch it, but she'd sounded mad. Another one of her histrionic outbursts.

He tossed his towel toward the hamper and reached for a bathrobe when Susan, still naked, came to the door, her iPad in hand, an odd, almost frightened look on her face. He immediately knew what had happened in Florida.

"They're calling it a shoot-out on Casey Key," she said.

Hammond didn't know how he felt, except it wasn't good. "McGarvey?"

She was looking at the iPad's screen, the volume so low that Hammond couldn't make out the words. She came forward and held it out for him, but he shook his head.

"Is the son of a bitch dead?"

"No, and neither is his wife. Not a scratch between them."

Hammond turned away and looked at his image in the mirror. The Scorpions were supposed to be pros. They never missed. When Tarasov had suggested them, even he had seemed to be impressed. Their credentials were among the best in the business in the entire world. They'd never botched an assignment, nor had they ever been connected with any assassination. Their reputations and contact information were on no known database and came by word of mouth only to a very few people anywhere whose business was hiring talent such as that.

"Casualties?" he asked.

"A man and a woman."

Hammond's anger suddenly rose out of nowhere. "Killed, wounded, captured?" he shouted without turning away from the mirror.

"Presumed dead in a shoot-out with the former director of the CIA and his wife, also a former CIA employee," Susan said, her voice flat.

Hammond turned to her. She was frightened, and he realized just then that he was frightened, too.

"So what are we supposed to do now?" she said. "We couldn't run and hide if we wanted to; we're fucking personalities, especially me."

"We're not going to run."

"Then what?"

Hammond went to the wall phone and called downstairs for a bottle of Krug and two flutes to be brought up to the master bedroom balcony. When he hung up, he managed a slight smile. "Get dressed, sweetheart; we have some things to decide before I give Mikhail a call."

Susan shook her head. "Are you out of your fucking mind?"

"Probably, but it's too late for either of us to back out now. The Canadian and South African snipers are dead, and now so are the Chinese couple, and I'll recover everything I paid them, plus if we're lucky and they had substantial accounts, I'll raid them as well. Who knows? Maybe I'll turn a profit."

"You are nuts."

Hammond's fear faded a little as he began to accept what would have to be done to finish the game. He'd known that McGarvey was not only good, the son of a bitch was lucky, which was a hell of a combination in anyone's book, but he hadn't realized until just this moment how good the man was.

"You might be right, but as you said, we can't run and hide. We have to finish it once and for all."

"Without being killed ourselves—or worse yet, get arrested and sent to prison somewhere."

"McGarvey would have to find out who's after him, which won't happen, because we have Mikhail as our expediter," Hammond said. "Now get dressed."

He brushed past her, got his phone, and started for the balcony.

"You met with the Chinese couple aboard the yacht in Skagway," Susan said.

"They're dead."

"You'd better hope so."

The wine was cold, the night soft, and the lights from across the lake were pretty. Susan had put on a silk Versace kimono, and she sat across from Hammond. They hadn't talked for nearly ten minutes after the sommelier had come and gone, content for the time being to make some sense of what had happened in Florida and figure out what to do next.

For Hammond's part, he was torn as he had been from the moment he'd hatched the plan to have McGarvey killed, between wanting the thing to be done with or extending the game as long as possible. And now, it had come to the second option.

"We don't have much of a choice at this point," he said, breaking the silence.

"As long as the Chinese couple are dead, you can just quit."

"I don't want to."

She wasn't angry or surprised, as if she'd known what he'd say. "You want to play this stupid little boy's game out?"

"Yes, I do."

"Why?"

Hammond asked himself that same question from the beginning, and he never came up with an answer that would satisfy himself let alone her. "Because I can?"

"Because you're bored with just making money."

"That, too. And the circuit. New York, Davos, Cannes and Monaco, and Mallorca, and all the other little amusements and all the same faces." He looked at the lights across the lake. "Don't you get bored?"

She followed his gaze. "Almost always, if you want to know the God's honest truth."

"You'd rather be in front of the cameras."

She nodded. "It's a lot safer than shooting some poor dumb bastard in the side of the head."

"Then make films."

"I have a business to run."

"Sell it to me for a buck, and let my management team take over."

"Why the hell would I do something like that?"

"Happens all the time when people like us get married," Hammond said. "We can coproduce all your films and get the best writers adapting the best novels we can acquire. We can afford to hire the best costars for you and start snapping up every screen we can find anywhere in the world. Plus, we could afford to build state-of-the-art theaters just about everywhere."

Susan was looking at him, her lips parted.

"Even if you made a movie every year, the principal shooting would only take eight or ten weeks. The rest of the time, we could play. Wouldn't be a bad life for the two of us."

"I'm too old," Susan said.

"Bullshit. I can name a dozen actors a hell of a lot older than you still up there on the screen."

She smiled. "I meant to get married."

"Nothing could be further from the truth."

"People who marry are usually in love."

This time, Hammond smiled. "You are a gigantic pain in the ass sometimes, but I do love you, and I guess I have loved you for a very long time. Plus, you're better than most of the other girls I've been with."

She reached over with her foot and nudged his leg. "Would it scare you if I said yes?"

"Yes, it would."

"That's good," she said. "But I won't change my last name, at least for the screen."

"Fair enough," Hammond said, and he raised his glass. "To us."

She raised hers to his. "Matrimony, holy shit."

When they sipped the wine, her smile faded. "Back to square one," she said.

"I want to finish the game."

"Okay. So tell me how."

"Our only real shot at this is to hire an overwhelming force to finish the thing," Hammond said.

FIFTY-ONE

The woman in the gazebo whom Pete had shot and wounded had been flown up to Washington, where she'd been taken to All Saints Hospital for care by Dr. Franklin and his staff.

She'd been hit in her gallbladder, which had to be removed, and in her hip, less than an inch from her spine.

It was eight in the morning when Franklin, his mask off, came from the third-floor operating room to where McGarvey and Pete were standing by in the waiting room down the hall.

"She'll live, no problem at all, without her gallbladder," Franklin said. "But it's the wound in her hip that'll cause her difficulties for the rest of her life, I'm afraid."

"She and her husband were professionals," McGarvey said. "They were here to assassinate both of us."

"I know, and they failed. My job is to save lives, even hers."

"When can we talk to her?" Pete asked.

"She'll stay in recovery for an hour or so, then she'll be moved down to the second floor. You can have at her then," Franklin said. "Now I'm going home."

When Franklin was gone, McGarvey phoned Otto, who was already on campus. "What have you come up with?"

"She and her husband rented the Jet Skis from Sporty's in Venice under the names George and Carolyn Schilling and paid with an Amex card. Their creds checked out legitimate, but Mary walked them over to Ed Banes, who's taking a close look."

Banes was chief of Special Projects in the Science and Technology Directorate, whose job—among other things—was building paper, plastic, and online credentials for the CIA's field agents. He was the best man on campus for spotting fakes.

"What else?"

"Other than the total LE and media shitstorm going on down there, I did find out that the car parked at the marina was rented at the airport in Schilling's name, and they bought the AR-15 at a gun shop in Bradenton under the same driver's license."

"How about fingerprints and DNA?"

"No match in any database Lou has found for the prints, and the lab should have an answer on DNA later today. But don't count on much. These people were professionals, and right now, we're thinking they're Asian, maybe Chinese. Dental work, pubic hairs, and a couple of markers that seem to show they've had some good plastic surgery, making them look Western. And their skin had been lightened recently."

"The PLA's special operations brigades?"

"If these two follow the same background path as the Canadian and South African who came at you, then I'd say it's a good bet."

"Keep us in the loop," McGarvey said.

"We will, but don't get your hopes up. To this point, it looks as if these guys were at the top of their game," Otto said. "In the meantime, the Bureau wants to debrief you, the Sarasota County Mounties want to have a moment of your time, and television newspeople from every network, including a half dozen from overseas, along with *The New York Times*, *Washington Post*, AP, and a host of others, are demanding interviews."

"What about Taft?"

"He's asked that you stop by."

"Anything from the White House or Pentagon?" McGarvey asked.

"Nothing yet. But you and Pete—especially you, Mr. Director—are at the top of the news heap."

"It'll pass."

"Yeah, but not unless something bigger comes along—like maybe Russia declaring war on us."

Hammond called Tarasov's number on the encrypted phone—the only number on that phone—at two in the morning, and the Russian answered on the first ring as if he had been expecting the call. And he almost sounded amused.

"I take it that you've heard the news. Not unexpected to you, I trust."

"You promised me that they were the best."

"They were, but McGarvey is better," Tarasov said. "And frankly, Thomas, I suggest that you hope they were shot dead before they had a chance to mention your name. If you have that man on your trail, you will be—as the Americans are fond of saying—shit out of luck."

"I'm not giving this up until the bastard is dead."

"You'll have to kill his wife as well."

"That's my intention. But I'll need your help again."

"Certainly. But don't forget our pipeline deal. Germany is still under fire for dealing with us, and as Germany goes, so does the rest of Europe. Weaver, on his second term, has made it his mission to stay friends with Mr. Putin while at the same time rein him in. A complicated, unpredictable man, your president."

"I want this over with so I can get back to my life."

"What can I do this time?"

"I'm thinking about a team effort. Maybe ex-Spetsnaz shooters. If you can round up a half a dozen men to hit him all at once, he couldn't possibly survive."

"That's an intriguing thought. But the question is where would this have to happen? Not in the Washington area—way too sensitive. And Florida is out because McGarvey isn't likely to stay there either."

"Why not?" Hammond asked.

"Too much media attention, for one. And by now, he's rock-solid certain that someone is determined to see him go down and probably won't stop until the job is done."

"Should we wait until he settles down?"

"No. But he's his own worst enemy right now. He won't stay in Florida or Washington for the simple reason he knows another attack is coming, and he'll want it to be on a ground of his choosing, and someplace where the chance of collateral damage is at a comparative minimum."

"Where?" Hammond asked.

"I have a couple of ideas, but don't worry, he'll let us know."

Li woke slowly from the effects of the anesthesia, and as she did, her entire body seemed like it was on fire, especially her left side below her ribs and her right hip.

She became aware that she was in a hospital room and that she had been operated on to repair the bullet wounds she'd received at the McGarveys' property.

Taio was dead, she was certain of it. Before she'd gone down, she'd heard a lot of shooting from the south side of the house, some of it rapid fire from the AR-15 down by the water, but then it had stopped. And McGarvey had shouted something, his wife replying.

She and Taio had finally lost, and the more awake she became, the more resigned she felt. Without her husband, without the beautiful retirement they'd talked about, life for her was not worth living. Especially not if it resulted in a jail cell.

Sooner or later, someone would be coming to interrogate her. It would be simple at first, but even wounded, she was strong. The one thing she could not stand up to would be drugs.

She pushed the sheet covering her aside, and with an extreme effort to get beyond the pain, managed to sit up and get her legs over the side of the bed.

A wave of nausea washed over her, causing a cold sweat to break out all over her tiny body.

She pushed through that as well and got her feet onto the cool tile floor and stood up, falling back immediately, the pain in her hip threatening to blow the top of her skull away.

Again she stood up and this time managed to stay on her feet. Pulling the IV tube from her arm and wires attached to monitors, she went around the bed to a chair and somehow dragged it into the bathroom and closed the door.

Someone would be coming to find out why the monitors had gone blank.

She jammed the metal frame at the top of the chair's seat back under the door handle. They'd get past that fairly quickly, even if they had to remove the hinges, so she had to hurry.

Turning to the mirror over the sink, she doubled up a first and struck it with every gram of her strength. But nothing happened. The mirror didn't break.

People were at the door, a woman shouting something that Li couldn't make out, because now she was thinking in Mandarin.

She looked at herself in the mirror. She wanted Taio to be with her. She was lost without him. She would be lost for the rest of her life.

A man was at the door shouting something incomprehensible to her.

"Taio," Li whispered to her image, and she bit her tongue with all of her strength, blood immediately filling her mouth and the back of her throat.

She sank to the floor and laid her head back on the toilet seat, gushing blood making it impossible to breathe.

FIFTY-TWO

First thing in the morning, Taft's small conference room on the seventh floor of the OHB adjacent to his office was crowded. McGarvey and Pete along with Carleton Patterson sat at one end of the table, facing the DCI, while Thomas Waksberg, the Company's deputy director of clandestine services, sat to their right. Harold Kallek, the director of the FBI, and a whip-thin, stern-looking Clarke Bender, who headed the Bureau's Directorate of Intelligence, sat to their left.

No one was smiling, and Patterson had warned McGarvey that this incident teetered on the edge of criminal prosecution for needlessly endangering the lives of innocent civilians. They had gone over in detail all three attacks—the two in Georgetown and the one in Florida.

"The fact of the matter is you were aware that you and your wife were targets for assassination, and yet you refused to surrender to protective custody," Bender said. He was a Harvard lawyer, and he acted like one. Either Harvard or Yale or you were a blue collar. "Why?"

"I wasn't going to jail for something I didn't do," McGarvey shot back. "And even if I had—even if my wife and I had—how long would it have been for?"

"As long as it took to find who were your attackers and arrest them."

"The Bureau has been on this for a couple of weeks since the first attack. How close are you guys to finding out who they were?"

Bender started to say something, but Kallek held him off.

"Not close at all, mostly because you haven't cooperated with us. Perhaps if you let us help."

"Sorry, Mr. Kallek, your people are very good, just as Mr. Taft's people are, but whoever is directing the players coming after us are better."

"You arrogant son of a bitch," Bender said. "Are you saying that you're better than all of us combined?"

This time, Patterson held McGarvey off.

"Yes, and he's proven it on numerous occasions, evident even if you've only glanced at his redacted file. The issue on the table here is not to penalize Mr. McGarvey for merely protecting his own life as well as that of his wife's but to help him as best we can."

"By letting him run around shooting up neighborhoods and terrorizing the locals?"

"Not of his doing," Taft said. Everyone at the table turned to him. It was the first he'd spoken. "Mr. McGarvey was attacked at his apartment in Georgetown. When he went to All Saints, he was attacked there. When he and his wife went to their home in Florida, they were attacked there. Someone is tracking his movements. I think that we all should be finding out who and why."

"We can start with the woman brought up from Florida," Bender said. "I believe she's at your hospital. I'll send a team over to question her."

"It won't work," Pete said.

Bender smiled condescendingly. "My people are quite good, Mrs. McGarvey. I can assure you they will get results."

"She killed herself last night."

"Wasn't there security?"

"She went into the bathroom, blocked the door, and killed herself before we could get in."

"Where did she get the weapon?"

"She bit her tongue in two and drowned in her own blood," Pete said. She sat forward. "You have no idea how dedicated to the mission these people are. You put your agents between us and them, and your people will lose."

"Spare me," Bender said.

"She's right," McGarvey said. He motioned to Pete, and they got up. "Thank you, gentlemen, but we're out of here."

"Where to?" Taft asked.

"Do you really want me to tell you?" McGarvey asked.

"Why not?"

"The leak could be in this room."

"Christ," Bender said. "I'm going to get a warrant for your arrest."

"Don't try it," McGarvey said. He turned back to Taft. "I have a lighthouse in the hills on Serifos. We're going there." He looked again at Bender. "That's a Greek island in the Aegean."

McGarvey and Pete took the elevator down to the third floor and headed to Otto's office. "Do you think Bender will try to arrest us?" she asked.

"He might try, but Kallek is no fool; he'll put a stop to it, especially if Taft doesn't want it to happen."

"But they're not going to sit on their thumbs."

"No, and that's what worries me almost as much as the next attack. I think they'll send some people out to the island, maybe put up a drone or two, and some of the good guys will most likely get hurt."

"Then why did you tell them where we're going?" Pete asked.

"Testing the waters for a leak," McGarvey said.

Pete looked at him. "My God, you are a cynic, aren't you?"

"Is there any other way in this business?"

Lou let them in, and they walked back to the rear office in the three-room suite, where Otto, his eyes closed, his feet up on the desk, was listening to Tchaikovsky's Violin Concerto in D Major. His darlings were displaying a rapidly shifting series of alphanumeric codes above him on one of the eight wide-screen monitors on the walls. The background was lavender, which meant trouble.

"The two shooters were freelancers," Otto said. "Ex Chinese special ops. Chan Taio and Zhang Li. Married, but they didn't change their surnames, which is sometimes the Chinese custom. We got it from their DNA but through a back door."

Pete perched on the edge of an adjacent desk. "Back door?" she asked.

"Yeah. Banes came up with the name of a forger in Geneva by the name of Wolfhardt Buerger, who he figured did the Schilling passports and driver's licenses," Otto said. "He was about the best in the world, and he knew it and wanted to brag. He left behind a flaw in just about every document he ever made. The number six in the sixth position."

"Is someone on the way to talk to Buerger?" Pete asked.

But McGarvey knew what the answer would be. "No need. He was murdered."

"Broke his neck," Otto said. "But the thing is, the good doctor kept records on all of his clients. I have a friend in the NBD—the Swiss intel service—who promised me a copy. Anyway, your Chinese friends were on the list."

"How about bank account numbers?" McGarvey asked.

Otto opened his eyes and grinned. "They didn't pay him this time, but they did for their previous passports and several other IDs. A draft on the International Bank of Geneva. It's a numbered account with a very good encryption algorithm that Lou has been working on for a couple of hours now." He looked up. "Any luck yet, sweetheart?"

"I may be getting close, but I have found something else that probably has no bearing but might be of interest."

"Yes, go on."

"Mac has had a previous relationship with the billionaire Thomas Hammond. Mr. Hammond maintains bank accounts all over the world, but recently, he may have had a transaction, in gold at that bank, to a blind account. Plus, Mr. Hammond owns a villa on Lake Geneva."

FIFTY-THREE

The dacha in the Zvenigorod district, just northwest of Moscow, was a refurbished summer palace of some prince in the last days of the czars. Set in the middle of a birch forest, the fifty-acre property was bounded by a wide creek and was only accessible by a narrow, blacktopped road ten miles off the M10 or by helicopter.

It was owned by Lieutenant General Oleg Kanayev, who was the main directorate general staff officer in charge of Russia's Special Forces that was also known as the Spetsnaz.

Tarasov arrived shortly after six in the evening aboard his Sikorsky S-92 helicopter and was met by a junior lieutenant driving an old Gazik—the Russian jeep. "The general is expecting you in the kitchen, sir," the lieutenant said.

Kanayev, in civilian clothes, was a surprisingly young-looking man in his early sixties, with thick pitch-black hair, a curving walrus mustache, and a broad Russian peasant's face with a stocky frame to match. He was seated at a long wooden table, eating pickles, slices of frozen raw bacon, and drinking vodka.

He looked up when Tarasov came in and waved him to sit down. "Close the door when you leave, Sergei, and see that we are not disturbed," he told the lieutenant.

When they were alone, Kanayev gave Tarasov a searching look. "Care for something to eat?"

"Not that," Tarasov said. In his estimation, the general was a pig, scarcely one step above an ignorant muzhik—a Russian peasant. But the man ruled the Special Forces not only with an iron fist but with great imagination.

"Why has Putin's favorite oligarch come out to see an ignorant old soldier? Or did the president himself send you?"

"I came to ask for a favor, but no, I'm not here on the president's behalf. This is personal."

Kanayev poured another vodka and sat back. "Intriguing. Something your billions can't buy you on the open market, so here you are. But before we get started, what's in it for me?"

"The word is that you'll retire in the next year or two. And even for a man of your rank, retirement pay is not enough to live a proper life."

"I'm listening."

"I was thinking about a 1 percent stake in Gazprom."

"Five percent."

Tarasov smiled. It was about the counteroffer he'd expected. "Two," he said, and he held up a hand before the general could speak. "It's not that big a favor for a man in your position, and 2 percent will net you a very comfortable retirement."

"A seat on the board of directors?"

"Even I couldn't guarantee such a thing, but I give my word as a gentleman that I would try."

Kanayev only took a moment to consider before he nodded. "What do you want?"

"I need a man and his wife to be assassinated as soon as possible," Tarasov said. "Three different attempts have already been made by some of the top shooters on the planet and have failed."

"Who is this couple you want killed, and why?"

"The reasons don't matter. Nor does the woman. But the man is important."

"Who is he?"

"Kirk McGarvey."

Kanayev almost laughed out loud. "He is a man with a considerable reputation. But to send one of my people to assassinate him is impossible, and you should know this. The blowback for a Russian soldier to kill the former director of the Central Intelligence Agency would be catastrophic. Shake the Kremlin walls, and I would get my nine ounces."

"Not one of your men; I was thinking about a hit team of six operators. They would have to get to the Greek island of Serifos, where McGarvey and his wife have a home in a converted lighthouse, in secret, and get out again."

"You're insane."

"The operation would be conducted in civilian clothes. False passports."

"All the money in the world would do a dead man nothing."

"Those who survived would receive five million euros. Each man who survived. Enough for them to set themselves up somewhere outside of Russia."

"It would still come back to us."

"Before they left, they would be given dishonorable discharges, which would effectively wipe your hands clean. They were rogue operators who had no place in the modern Spetsnaz that you control. You did your duty, painful though it was."

"Intriguing," the general said. "Why do you want this done?"

"The reason isn't important," Tarasov said. "Will you do it?"

"If I don't, what then?"

"I'll find someone else."

"I could report this."

"*Da*, but the decision is yours."

Kanayev pursed his lips, but then took a cell phone from his pocket and entered a number.

"Put it on speakerphone," Tarasov said. "*Otkytost*," which was openness—or, since Gorbachev, transparency.

"Three Twenty-Ninth, operations," a man answered.

"I wish to speak with Lieutenant Colonel Nyunin."

"I'm sorry, General, the colonel is not on base at the moment."

"Where is he?"

"In Moscow."

"Have him call me at this number immediately," Kanayev said, and he hung up.

"Who is Nyunin?" Tarasov asked. "Someone to be trusted?"

"*Da*. He is the commanding officer of the 329th Spetsnaz Special Purpose Detachment in Pskov Oblast, and he will have to be paid as well."

"It's your operation, your money."

"I will get nothing immediate from Gazprom. I'll need operational money. Cash in any Western currency you choose."

"How much?"

"An operation of this scope will be expensive. They will need off-the-shelf civilian weapons, civilian clothing, plus a long-range aircraft and crew capable of operating above nine thousand meters, and of course hush money to soothe their nerves as well as those of the officers who'll have to participate in the court-martial."

"Why such an aircraft?"

"The operation will have to be at night in total secrecy, which means the operators will have to make a HALO jump to the surface."

"I don't know this term."

"They fly at such an altitude so that no one on the ground will hear them, and at the proper moment, the operators will jump out of the plane and go into free fall until they come within a few hundred meters of the ground before they open their chutes. High altitude, low opening."

"What if they return home?"

"They will have to be eliminated before they talk. Anyway, who would believe a traitor?"

"What about your Colonel Nyunin? Can he be trusted?"

"Yes."

"How can you be sure?"

"Because he's my son-in-law."

Tarasov liked it. "The question stands, General, how much?"

"In what currency?"

"Euros or Swiss francs, your choice."

"Euros. I'll need five million in cash for payoffs and another five million in an untraceable UAE account that I maintain for the aircraft and crew plus the equipment."

Tarasov smiled. "Scratch a Russian and larceny comes out."

"It's a tough old world," the general said. "Agreed?"

"The funds will be in place within twelve hours."

FIFTY-FOUR

McGarvey and Pete took a cab back to their apartment in Georgetown, where they were going to pack a few things for Serifos, though they had just about everything they needed at the lighthouse, and it was the same for the Casey Key house.

"Are we just going to wait around until the shoe drops?" Pete asked once they got upstairs. "Or do we have a plan that makes sense?"

"We're going to stay away from town, if that's what you mean," McGarvey said. Pete had been withdrawn ever since they had left Langley, and she was moody now. He was a little worried about her.

"You're thinking about collateral damage."

"Always have been. Before nightfall of our first day, we'll stock up with whatever perishables we need and then settle in at the house."

"We don't have any surveillance out there, except for the perimeter Otto set up a couple of years ago. And now that the real Lou's gone, we don't have any contacts or procedures to borrow satellite time from the NRO."

"All of it's stored in one of Otto's darlings, plus a couple of extra names and passwords Mary came up with."

"If whoever is coming after us has half a brain, they could get past all of that," Pete said. "We have on more than one occasion."

"I know," McGarvey said. "But we're not going over for some R&R, so it'll be watch on watch. You sleep at night, and I'll sleep during the day."

"For how long?"

"I think whatever's going to happen is in the works right now."

Pete shivered. "I wonder if the Chinese couple on Casey Key figured that taking us out would be their last op? Maybe they were planning on retiring, but they just took one last job, and it turned out to be the wrong one."

"And?"

She took a moment to answer, and when she did, she looked into Mac's eyes as if she wanted him to understand how serious she was. "What about us? Time to get out?"

He understood her pain and fear, things he'd felt for pretty much his entire career, and especially since the death of Katy. He took Pete in his arms and held her close for several moments. "Believe me, I've thought about it. Making a life for ourselves that would have some semblance of normalcy makes sense."

"Good," she said into his shoulder.

"But for now, we have to keep our eye on the mission."

"Saving our lives."

"Yes. And I have a feeling that you're right about the Chinese couple think-ing it was time to get out, and it's why they made some mistakes that cost them their lives."

"Let's not do the same," Pete said. "And then we'll go on a real vacation and figure out what's next."

McGarvey smiled. "Scout's honor," he said. It was one of Otto's boyish phrases.

"Looks like you have company just outside," Lou said.

McGarvey took his pistol out of its holster at the small of his back and went to the front window and looked across the street as a man was getting out of the driver's side of a Caddy SUV. "Anyone we know?"

"Clarke Bender."

The Cadillac's windows were deeply tinted. "Anyone with him?"

"No."

Bender locked the car door and looked up at McGarvey's window, nodded, then came around the front of the car and started across the street.

McGarvey holstered his pistol and buzzed the front door to let the man in.

"I wonder what that little prick wants now," Pete said. She was still keyed up.

"He may be a prick, but he's just trying to do his job," McGarvey said. "And he's probably come here to try to talk some sense into us. So play nice."

Bender took the elevator up, and McGarvey met him at the door. The CIA officer's tie was loose, his collar button undone, the effect theatrical. And he smiled a little. "May I come in for just a minute, Mr. Director?"

"One minute," McGarvey said. "We're a little busy at the moment."

"Packing. It's what I wanted to talk to both of you about. That and offer my apology for coming off a little strong this morning."

McGarvey stepped aside and let him in. "Apology accepted. What can we do for you?"

"The Bureau wants to offer you its help. We know that you're going to your place in the Aegean to make a stand, but we sincerely hope it's not Custer's. And we think we can make sure that doesn't happen."

"I explained to you and your boss that whoever's coming next will be good. If you guys send over a team, it'll just be more targets lined up in a row. But if it's just the two of us, they'll have to concentrate their forces, giving us a shooting gallery."

"What do you think is going on?" Bender asked. "Who do you think is coming after you and why?"

"I don't have an answer to either of your questions, except that whoever it is has deep pockets."

"At the government level?"

"I think that would be too risky."

"So do we. It's a rogue operation, but do you think it's someone here in Washington who wants you eliminated, maybe for something they may think of as past transgressions?"

"I don't know."

"You spread the word at the DIA and even the White House, for God's sake. You were being provocative at the very least."

There was no answer to that, and McGarvey didn't reply.

Bender was getting frustrated. "Look, I came here to offer the Bureau's help, and not necessarily in the form of a strike team, but information. We've traced money, and in one case gold payments, to three different banks around the world, just prior to the three attempts on your and Mrs. McGarvey's lives. The gold was sent to a bank in Geneva, we believe to finance the Casey Key team."

"Yes, we know."

Bender nodded. "Otto Rencke," he said. "But does he know that all three payments were made from blind accounts in three different banks, none of which we believe came from Russia, North Korea, or Pakistan, your three biggest enemy states? But we think it's a real possibility that they may have come from the same source."

"Otto?" Pete said.

"Good morning, Mr. Bender," Otto's voice came from out of the air.

Bender was startled, but he didn't miss a beat. "Have you come up with a source?"

"We've identified a little more than two thousand possible sources, a half dozen from a Russian GRU group based in Amsterdam."

"We discounted any with government connections."

"These hackers work independently, much like the hackers who meddled with our elections a while back."

"Ultimately, do you think the three attempts made on the McGarveys was an arm's-length, Russian-directed operation?"

"We're working on it," Otto said.

"What else can you share?"

"One name, though it's a remote possibility, so slim we're only giving it less than 4 percent probability."

"The name?" Bender asked.

"Thomas Hammond."

FIFTY-FIVE

Hammond and Susan were just walking out of the Piaget Boutique jewelry store on Geneva's ultraglamorous Rue du Rhône shortly after six in the evening when his Russian phone burred. It was Tarasov.

"You will have your team in place within forty-eight hours, but it's going to cost you plenty."

"How much is plenty?" Hammond asked.

"I want you to start the pipeline deal immediately."

"Not until it's done."

"I'm not going to fuck around with you, Thomas," Tarasov said. He was angry. "I'm out on a limb now, and if you don't deliver what you promised, I'll make sure that you regret it."

Susan was only hearing one side of the conversation, but she clutched his free arm with some urgency.

"And don't you fuck with me, Mikhail. We have a deal, and I'll stick to my part of it, if and when you finish up. I have friends, too, who could easily shift the blame for everything onto the Kremlin, just like the election hacking shit not so long ago. I'm sure that your pal Putin could just as easily cut you loose, as he has others in your sort of position."

The connection was silent for several beats, until Tarasov came back. "Are you someplace where you can talk?"

"On the Rue du Rhône, and the street is crowded, but no one is paying any attention to us."

"I don't need any money from you; I've taken care of it. I just want performance when it's done."

"Agreed. So who are you sending this time?"

"A team of ex-Spetsnaz operators. They'll make a parachute drop over Serifos tomorrow night."

"Why not tonight?" Hammond demanded. "Get it over with ASAP."

"Because the McGarveys won't be in place until that afternoon. They're aboard an overnight Emirates flight, which is scheduled to reach Athens in the morning. From there, they'll have to take a ferry out to the island and get up to the lighthouse. By the middle of the night, they'll be dead tired."

"*Dead* is the only word I want to hear."

"And that you're working the pipeline deal is all I want to hear."

"Then let's see what turns out in the next forty-eight hours," Hammond said. He broke the connection and pocketed the phone.

"Trouble?" Susan asked.

"The McGarveys are on the way to their island, and Mikhail is sending a team of six Russian special ops people to take them out. No screwing around this time."

"Jesus, if this doesn't work, are you going to have the Russians on our asses?"

Hammond looked at her. It was the first time in their relationship she had used the word *our*. "No, they need me just as much as we need them."

Lieutenant Colonel Nyunin arrived by helicopter at his father-in-law's dacha a couple of minutes after eight in a light but steady rain. He was a short man, athletically built with a pleasantly round face and a direct manner. Some said that he looked and acted like a young Putin, which wasn't a bad comparison.

He was in uniform because he was on his way back to the base by military transport. One of the general's aides met him at the helipad and drove him up to the dacha, where Kanayev was waiting. And they embraced warmly.

"It's good to see you, Viktor," Kanayev said.

"And you, *Nana*." Papa.

"Let's take a walk," Kanayev said.

Nyunin understood perfectly why his father-in-law wanted to go out even though it was raining. In Russia, even for a general, one had to assume that the walls had ears. And he was curious what the old man wanted.

Nyunin took an umbrella from the stand at the back door, but Kanayev only put on an old cap. The days had been warm for Moscow, and the rain had cooled things down and cleared the air of Moscow's smog that often-times reached this far out.

They didn't speak until they were on the path down toward the lake. Kanayev went first. "I have an urgent project for you that has to be put in place within twenty-four hours and completed within forty-eight."

"Yes, sir," Nyunin said. He was one of the youngest lieutenant colonels in the Russian army, but he was wise beyond his years and was well respected because he not only knew how to take orders but how to carry them out.

"An American couple who will be holed up at their home in a converted lighthouse on a Greek island in the Aegean have to be eliminated. But the operation must never be traced back as an official action by any unit of the Russian government, including mine."

"Who are these people?"

"Kirk McGarvey and his wife."

"*Yeb vas*," Nyunin said softly.

"Indeed," Kanayev said. "I'll give you the number for a man who has the operational details. He is to be completely trusted. And he will provide you the necessary untraceable funds in euros for you to run the operation up to ten million. If there is a surplus, which I'm almost sure there'll be, it will be yours."

They stopped. "If something like this had come from anyone else—any officer other than you—I would have immediately said no, even if he and I were related," Nyunin said. "And it would be the very first order in my entire career that I've ever refused."

"This is important."

"But the former director of the Central Intelligence Agency?"

"An enemy of Russia, but that's not the point."

"What is the point?"

"It needs to be done."

"How?"

"Pick six of your best men, ask them if they would like to be rich, and offer them five million euros each in cash plus a dishonorable discharge."

"Those who survived, you mean."

"*Da.*"

"They could never come home."

"*Nyet.*"

"How do they get to this island?"

"The operational details would be theirs to make, but your contact will provide everything they need—civilian clothes and documents, off-the-shelf non-Russian weapons, plus an aircraft capable of flight above ten thousand meters."

"You're talking about a nighttime HALO operation?"

"That's one way, but that would be up to the team," Kanayev said, and he left it there for several long moments as he watched his son-in-law work it out. "Do you have such a team in mind?"

Nyunin took several more long moments before he nodded. "I know exactly who would be willing to carry out something like that—actually, I think they'd jump at it."

"Are they capable?"

"They're my men."

"Will you do this for me?"

"Yes, I will, *Nana*," Nyunin said. "But when it is over, I will resign my commission."

☐

FIFTY-SIX

The Spetsnaz base Promezhitsa was not far from borders with Estonia and Latvia but well away from the administrative center of the Oblast, like a state or county, at the city of Pskov. Well wooded in some spots with many rivers but swampy and mosquito ridden in the north, except during the brutal Russian winters, it was a much tougher training venue than that of the American SEAL Team 6, and the troops here were proud of the fact.

First thing in the morning, Colonel Nyunin had a runner fetch Senior Lieutenant Boris Vetrov to his office, who showed up within five minutes in regulation battle dress uniform, his blue airborne beret tucked neatly in the epaulet on his left shoulder.

Vetrov was a compact man in his late twenties, all angles, made of muscle, with a narrow face and deep eyes that never seemed to smile. He came to attention and saluted. "Vetrov, Boris A., reporting as ordered, sir."

Nyunin, seated behind his desk, returned the salute and motioned for the senior lieutenant to take a chair.

"How would you like to be rich?"

"Like anyone, sir, but if I had my choice, I'd stay with the brigade."

"This life comes to an end for everyone sooner or later."

"Yes, sir."

"I have a proposition for you to consider, but I'll need your answer this morning before you leave this office. The op would be strictly off the grid and carry with it not only a considerable money reward in euros but a considerable risk and some very unusual conditions."

Vetrov obviously was at a loss, but he nodded.

"Have you ever heard the name *Kirk McGarvey?*"

"No, sir."

"He briefly served as the director of the American Central Intelligence Agency, and he and his wife have since became freelance operators, once just a couple of years ago even going up against President Putin."

Vetrov was impressed, but he held his silence.

"By tomorrow evening or the next at the latest, he and his wife will be at their home in a converted lighthouse in an isolated section of the Greek island of Serifos. I want you to pick a team of five operators, who will be flown to the island for a night HALO drop. On the ground, you will locate and eliminate both of them and then make your way off the island."

"I have the perfect five, but I can see a number of issues—among them, our exfiltration after the op."

"That will be the least of it," Nyunin said, and the way he said it as well as the words themselves caught Vetrov's complete attention, but again, the senior lieutenant said nothing.

"The conditions will be the toughest to bear in the entire operation, all of which will be classified most secret for the good of the state, and that comes directly from the general staff. No one outside of you and I and your team must ever hear a word of this op. The blowback could be devastating to the *Rodina*, the Motherland."

"I understand, sir."

"Not yet, but you will," Nyunin said. "How soon can you have your team briefed?"

"Within the hour of leaving this office, sir."

"You'll probably need to take most of the day for prep and equipment change-outs, most of which can be issued from special infiltration supplies. You'll be going in civilian clothes, with Ukrainian credentials, using German Heckler & Koch primary weapons, along with Glock subcompact pistols in the ten-millimeter caliber. Take the Chinese HALO chutes. Nothing must connect you with Russia if you're captured."

"Except for our language and unit tattoos, sir."

"We'll take care of that as well later this afternoon. As soon as you've briefed and outfitted your squad, I'll want the six of you back here in my office."

"I'll have to come up to speed on the island and the McGarveys' exact location, as well as whatever firepower they may have at their disposal, as well as some plan for getting out."

"If you are a go, a civilian jet will touch down here this evening, load you and your equipment, and take off for refueling in Sofia. Aboard will be your briefing kit, including maps and exfiltration plans, along with a contact number for updates or unforeseen issues."

"What about the aircrew?"

"You will kill them, dump most of the fuel, and set the autopilot for a route south, where the aircraft will crash into the sea."

Vetrov sat back in the chair, his shoulders slumped, an odd, almost wistful expression on his face. "There's no plan for getting us back, is there, sir?"

"No, but I've been assured that an untraceable bank account in the amount of thirty million euros will be set up, to be divided among anyone who survives."

"I'm sorry, sir, but that still doesn't answer the question of returning to base. Unless that will be included in the briefing package."

"You won't be coming back, not here or to anywhere in Russia, but you'll be given medals of highest honors for service to the Motherland in secret."

Vetrov was bitter. "A small amount for losing a home."

"If it's any consolation, I'll be retiring myself," Nyunin said. "But you're a highly trained, capable man. You and whoever is left of your team could set up as independent operators. There is a great deal of need for your talents. You would not get bored. And in between times, you wouldn't be stuck living and training in a godforsaken shithole like this."

Vetrov nodded and got heavily to his feet.

"As soon as you're ready, come back here with your team," Nyunin said, the worst of his briefing coming right now.

Vetrov saluted and headed to the door, but Nyunin stopped him.

"One last thing, Senior Lieutenant."

"Sir?"

"There will only be one official record of this mission. And it'll be the dishonorable discharges you and your men will receive. You'll be leaving this base as civilians."

Vetrov nodded again. "I understand, sir. Plausible deniability."

When the senior lieutenant was gone, Nyunin opened a desk drawer and pulled the old Makarov 9mm pistol that his father-in-law had given him as a present when he'd graduated from the Frunze Military Academy.

Its serial number identified it as the very first pistol made in the very first manufacturing run in 1949.

But its age did not diminish its ability to kill.

In a detached sort of way, he wondered how Vetrov and his men would handle the situation. The operation itself would be almost routine, but the dishonorable discharge would be like a kick in the balls to young men who had dedicated their lives thus far to their country, the Spetsnaz, and their unit.

Those who survived would be together as a unit, but they would be free of the chain of command. And for men used to taking orders, used to believing that the officers above them knew what they were doing, it would be a difficult, maybe even impossible transition.

It was going to be the same for him after he'd turned in his resignation and it was accepted, something he knew his father-in-law would expect.

What he couldn't understand was why the general would agree to such an insane plan that had every chance in the book to fail, and fail badly. McGarvey and his wife would die, that was inevitable. But there was a decent chance that one or more of his operators would be captured and made to talk.

There was money for them—not a lot of money, but a fabulous sum for men of their ranks who were earning on average a little more or less than fifteen hundred euros a month.

What was more important—money or honor?

He was more concerned about honor, and at this moment, his hands and more importantly his soul seemed dirtied.

His wife, Katya, had divorced him three years ago, because, as she'd told the judge, her husband, just like her father, valued the military more than their families.

Maybe he would end it, he thought.

But not now, and he put the Makarov back in the desk drawer.

FIFTY-SEVEN

At three in the morning, the Turkish Airlines 8 flight to Athens was four hours out into the Atlantic from Dulles, and McGarvey hadn't been able to get to sleep yet, though their first-class accommodations were decent. Pete had fallen asleep after a glass of wine once they were in the air, and looking at her now, he was of a mixed mind.

He was afraid for her, and yet he was glad she was at his side. It was a new feeling for him, accepting that he wasn't going on an assignment alone, and liking it. In fact, it was completely alien to just about everything he'd been taught and had learned by hard experience in the field.

It had to do with trust. Not loyalty, not a fear that a partner would turn out to be a traitor, but trust in that a partner was capable. He'd never wanted to find himself in a situation where he not only had to take care of himself but watch out for the misstep that would put whoever was next to him in a bullet's path.

He looked at the window, the shade up. The cabin lights had been dimmed, but he could still see his reflection, pale now, almost like how he felt inside. And yet he'd finally—for the first time in his life—learned to trust. And he was damned if he knew whether he liked it or was afraid.

"Such deep thoughts when you should be sleeping," Pete said.

"I was thinking about us," he said.

She smiled. "You better have, because I was dreaming about you." She paused. "And about our game plan. You haven't said anything about how we're going to play it, and I thought I'd hold my tongue for a change until you're ready to clue me in."

Besides the Glock 29 Gen 4 that Pete favored, and one of his Walthers in the 9mm version, plus plenty of ammunition at the lighthouse, Otto had packaged a pair of HK MP7A1 compact submachine guns along with ammunition, in a diplomatic pouch, that was placed in the cargo hold along with their bags. When it came down to a gunfight, he didn't think that sheer firepower would be the sole deciding factor; finding the right spot would be just as important, but the room brooms would help.

His major concern was that, this time, whoever had directed the attacks on him would be sending what they might consider an overwhelming force. Maybe a team of four operators. Ex–Special Forces types who knew stealth tactics and were well connected enough to bring some serious weaponry to bear—like the updated version of the Russian-made RPG anti-tank weapon or the British-made, more compact and disposable LAW 80 rocket-propelled anti-armor weapon.

"I was thinking that, had we stuck with my original idea of using the house as our defensive position, we might have been more vulnerable. I think they were going to use the woman in the Gulf as a diversion to lure one of us outside and then come in from the ICW."

"She would have been the bait, and I would have been the mouse out to the cheese, with you watching my back," Pete said.

"Something like that."

"What about this time?"

"For starters, I think there'll be more of them, and probably better armed."

"How many, and armed with what?"

"Four, maybe six operators. RPGs or LAW rockets to dig us out of the lighthouse."

"You were thinking that we'd have the high ground," Pete said. "But they'd have to get that stuff onto the island. Might not be so easy."

"By sea in the middle of the night. Or if they're as well funded as I expect the others were, they could come in by air high and slow and make a parachute drop."

"Sounds military."

"I think that's likely," McGarvey said.

"Otto should be able to come up with some ideas."

"Plenty of ideas, but ex–special operators are a dime a dozen in the business."

"It'll be a night attack, and we'll be outside in the bush or behind a rock somewhere with good firing lines on our house," Pete said. She reached out and touched his cheek. "You sure know how to show a girl a good time."

The Hotel du Paris, Monaco's finest, had always been one of Hammond's favorite spots anywhere on the planet. After he had made his first five million, he'd treated himself and his girlfriend at the time to the Princess Grace Diamond suite, which even then was more than twenty thousand euros per night, worth every cent in his estimation. And he'd been staying there at least once a year ever since.

He and Susan had gotten up around ten and had sauntered down to the private beach, where they sat on chaise longues drinking Krug under one of the striped cabanas. It was just past eleven, and Susan said she was getting hungry.

"Let's finish the wine and then go up," Hammond said. "Unless you want a picnic lunch brought down."

"Out here," she said. "It's nice."

Hammond picked up the phone that did not ring but was answered immediately by a woman speaking English with a French accent.

"May we be of service, Mr. Hammond?"

"We need another bottle of wine, and fix us something for lunch."

"Do you have a preference, monsieur?"

"I'll trust your good judgment."

Susan had watched, and when he hung up, she managed a slight smile. "How do you do it, Thomas?"

"Do what?"

"Sit on the beach, drink wine, and order lunch as if nothing were going on?"

"It's a nice day, I'm with a woman I love, and I'm hungry."

"But it's going to happen in Greece in the next thirty-six hours, and if it fails again, it's very possible that a virtual shitstorm could rain down on us. Aren't you worried?"

He'd thought about that from the point when the second attempt in Washington had been made and failed, and he had been frightened for a time, but then he'd relied on his pipeline deal with Tarasov to provide him with a shield. Shortly after that, he'd once again played the situation like the game he'd wanted it to be from the start.

"Actually, no," he said.

She laughed. "You're either the smartest man I know or the craziest."

He laughed, too. "Probably a little of both," he said. "But the game's afoot."

"Sherlock Holmes."

Senior Lieutenant Vetrov showed up with his team a few minutes after 1800 hours, assuring Nyunin that they fully understood what was needed of them and had agreed without reservation to the terms.

"We're doing it for the *Rodina*," the senior lieutenant said.

"And yourselves."

"If you say so, sir."

The six of them crowded into Nyunin's office, and Vetrov handed them their terms-of-enlistment papers. All of them in battle camos stood at attention.

They looked young, Nyunin thought, barely out of their teen years. But they also looked hard, their bodies for the most part smaller than the average Russian, but muscled without being muscle-bound. Supple, with an almost wild animal edge to their faces and postures.

"Do you understand what you have been asked to do, and the requirements of the mission?" Nyunin began.

All of them nodded.

"This will be handled as a captain's mast, the result of which will be dishonorable discharges and a debt to you men that your country will never be able to properly repay except by its lasting gratitude."

No one said a thing.

"Sound off."

One by one, they reported their names, ranks, and serial numbers, beginning with Vetrov, and from his left, the youngest looking of them all, Vasili Anosov, Aleksei Petrin and Eduard Nikolayev—who could have been twins—Ivan Orlov with his Siberian looks, and Ilich Silin, a man near thirty who had the attitude that he was ready to cut everyone's throat.

When it was over and they were gone, Nyunin took the Makarov out and laid it on the desktop.

The Gulfstream G500 leased from a Bulgarian service was incoming and due to land within forty minutes. Vetrov's team would have changed into civilian clothes by then, and within fifteen minutes of the aircraft touching down, they and their equipment would be aboard and the Gulfstream airborne.

☐

FIFTY-EIGHT

Clarke Bender flew up to New York on a private FBI jet and was met at LaGuardia by Alicia Sherman, the Bureau's special agent in charge of the UN desk, who'd been working on the case she'd been sent twelve hours ago. She was a businesslike woman in her midthirties, a Harvard graduate on her way up, but she looked athletic, even hard around the edges, with a sharply chiseled face and deep blue eyes.

They got into a Caddy SUV, Sherman driving, and headed into the city. "There definitely was a connection between Rodriguez and Viktor Kuprik other than one of a simple business relationship."

She took a file folder from between the center console and her seat and handed it to Bender. "What we've come up with so far."

"I'll look at it later; for now, give me the highlights, because I think that we're running out of time," Bender said.

"Sir, it would help if I had some idea in what direction you want us to take this investigation. I mean, if it's a possible collusion between the Russian delegation and someone in Washington, maybe the White House, we could put together a good case for wiretapping."

"Nothing like that. This time, it has to do with a private citizen who may be in physical danger because of possible business dealings with Russia."

Sherman glanced over. "Physical danger?"

"Imminent. And Hammond Enterprises Strategic Liaison Group, which Rodriguez headed, might have something to do with it. Or at least they might have information we can use."

"Do we have a search warrant for the offices, or subpoena for Wilfred Maslak, who's the acting COO? We have Rodriguez's murder as an open case because of his connection with Kuprik."

"I don't want to slow this thing down, tying it up with lawyers. I spoke with Maslak, and he agreed to meet informally with us this morning."

"I'm surprised Hammond didn't put a stop to it. The guy's got a rep as a shark."

"That might not happen for a lot of reasons, one of which I'm trying to prevent this morning. Or at least it's something I want to find out."

"Whoever this private citizen is, he must be important, sir."

"Kirk McGarvey."

"Jesus."

. . .

The Strategic Liaison Group's offices occupied a part of the third floor in a building directly across First Avenue from the Dag Hammarskjöld Library. Sherman parked on the street in front and put an FBI OFFICIAL BUSINESS placard on the dash.

She and Bender showed their IDs at the door and were buzzed in by the security officer inside the small lobby.

"May I help you?" the cop asked.

"We're here to see Mr. Wilfred Maslak. Hammond Enterprises Strategic Liaison Group."

"You're investigating the accident with Mr. Rodriguez, I assume."

"Yes."

"You guys are about eight hours late. The office was closed and everything moved out even before I got here this morning."

"Everything?" Bender demanded.

"I went up and took a look myself when I came in. Nothing's left. They even swept the floors."

The Turkish Airlines flight arrived in Athens on time at quarter to nine in the evening local, and after getting through customs and immigration—with no questions about the contents of their sealed diplomatic pouch—McGarvey and Pete took the shuttle over to the nearby Sofitel Hotel.

The next ferry to Serifos from Piraeus left at five after seven in the morning, which gave them a full night to get some rest, and then all day the next day to get settled in at the lighthouse. McGarvey was pretty sure that if there was to be an attack, it would come in the middle of the night. Pete had agreed, and so had Otto.

They got a room looking away from the airport toward the hills sparkling with house lights and streetlights.

"I'm going to jump in the shower and then try to get a few hours' sleep," McGarvey said.

"Do you want to have dinner downstairs or here in the room?" Pete asked.

"Here."

"Any preferences?"

"Something Greek," Mac said, and Pete laughed.

If this time a team was coming after them, their numbers would be a disadvantage as well as an advantage. More firepower would tip the scale for the opposition, but in the dark, on unfamiliar ground, they could become disoriented under the right circumstances.

McGarvey had thought about it on the flight over, and he'd finally come to the conclusion he'd experienced in the field on more than one occasion—the man whose life was being threatened had the advantage if he kept his head. The adrenaline released knowing you were being hunted was a powerful stimulus.

The optimum situation would be four operators coming after him and Pete. Enough firepower to give the team confidence and yet a large enough number that a strategy of hit-and-run could scatter them. But it would become a problem if there were more of them, enough to set up a firing line or, better yet, an attacking front that was meant to herd their prey toward a fixed position.

When he was finished and in a robe, the waiter had just brought up their dinner of avgolemono soup, dolmades, a plate of salted sardines and pita bread with olive oil, plus a bottle of ice-cold Retsina wine.

"Is this okay?" Pete asked.

"Perfect," McGarvey said, and they sat down to it, Pete pouring the wine.

"What's the plan?" she asked as they ate. "Still sleep by day and wander the hills at night like gypsies?"

"It'll be a night attack, I'm pretty sure of it. There's too many people out and about during the day."

"I don't think that these people would give a damn about collateral damage."

"No, but they don't want witnesses."

"Okay, a night op. Makes sense for them, especially if they think to bring along night vision optics. Do a SEAL Team 6 on us."

"Blind them with tactical flashlights," McGarvey said, but he was beginning to get uneasy. She had warmed to the operation, almost as if she were looking forward to it.

"Do we go our separate ways?" she asked. "A circle of two, or one of us as bait?"

"Together. Each of us can effectively cover a one-eighty arc."

She raised her glass. "You and me, babe, together," she said, making the toast.

He was about to remind her that this wouldn't be some exercise they'd played at the Farm, when Otto called.

"No definitive proof yet, but Lou has upped Hammond's probability to 17 percent."

McGarvey had put it on speaker mode. "What do you have?"

"Bender paid a call to Hammond's office that liaises with the UN."

"The one that Rodriguez headed?" McGarvey asked.

"Yeah, and the place was empty," Otto said. "Bender called me himself and said the office had been totally cleaned out, not so much as a scrap of paper. A forensic team is fine-tooth combing the place, looking for whatever they can find. Maybe Hammond's fingerprints."

"Seventeen percent isn't a gimme."

"No, but he gave me two other tidbits. They're trying to find out where Hammond is at the moment and send someone out to interview him."

"He wouldn't talk without an attorney."

"No, but if he's involved, it would put him on notice," Otto said. "But there's more. Bender is sending a team over to Serifos to help you out."

"Goddamnit. Talk to Taft and see if the son of a bitch can be delayed."

"I don't know."

"Thirty-six hours."

"You think it's going to happen tomorrow night?"

"I think so."

"A premo?"

"Something like that," McGarvey said.

FIFTY-NINE

The Gulfstream was held up on the tarmac at the international airport out-side Sofia, Bulgaria, for nearly three hours before Captain Bogdan Borisov called from the cockpit and Vetrov went forward.

"There's been a delay," the captain said in Russian. He was a stocky Bulgar-ian with dark features and almost Siberian looks. His copilot, Darina Petrov, was a slightly built blond woman with movie-star looks and a hard expression in her eyes as if she would take no crap from anyone, especially a man.

"What is it?" Vetrov asked.

"We're to hold up here until tomorrow. Your drop isn't to be until twenty-four hours from now."

"At 0100," Vetrov said. Delays in any op were never unusual. You simply went with the flow. "We'll need a place to bunk."

"On board, I'm afraid," Borisov said. "They want us undercover during the day, so we've been given an empty hangar at Gama Aviation Services."

"Will we be allowed to use the hangar for calisthenics? Being cooped up is bad for us."

"Yes, but as I said, you will have to sleep aboard. We have plenty of water and provisions, plus toilet capacity."

"Very well. When will we be moving inside?"

"Within the next twenty minutes."

"Should we be expecting customs officials?"

"No. Everything has been arranged. In the meantime, I want you to keep the window shades down until we're inside."

"Will you and your copilot be staying aboard for the night?"

Darina looked up, a slight smirk on her lips. "Of course not," she said, and she turned away.

Vetrov lowered his voice. "If this is a setup, neither of you will live out the week."

"Lieutenant, we don't shit in our own nests," the woman said. "We're getting paid too much for that."

"Senior Lieutenant," Vetrov said, and he went back to brief his men.

The Louis XV Alain Ducasse restaurant in the hotel had been almost empty by the time Hammond and Susan finished their meal and the last of the Krug Clos du Mesnil Blanc de Blancs champagne. But because of their wealth, the waitstaff and sommelier did not press, and near the end, the chef du cuisine himself came out and had shared a glass of wine with them.

Afterward, they had gone up to the suite where they had taken a long, sensuous shower and had gone to bed and made love slowly, deliberately, but with more passion than Hammond could ever recall.

When they were finished, lying in bed in each other's arms, looking up at the ceiling, Susan laughed, the sound soft and at the back of her throat.

"What?" Hammond asked.

"We're getting pretty good at this," she said.

"No movie set, this time, no body double."

It took a long minute before she answered. "I'm going to say something, and I don't want you to laugh. I'm serious."

"Okay."

"I'm getting off the merry-go-round."

"What do you mean?"

"No more in front of the camera. I'm done."

"Bullshit. You're a damned fine actor, and you photograph well."

"I don't need it anymore, Tom. I want out. I'll continue to produce, and maybe I'll even try directing."

Hammond turned over on his side and looked at her. "What are you saying?"

"You know goddamned well what I'm saying."

"Mrs. Thomas Hammond?"

"Something like that, but without the name change."

"And then what?"

"We live our lives," she said. "Get old and cranky, get cirrhosis of the liver, gray hair, shit that even a good plastic surgeon won't be able to do much about."

"But?" Hammond asked. He'd heard it coming.

"Let's stay here for a bit and drop the McGarvey thing. It's just a game, it's dangerous, and it's expensive. Let it go."

Hammond was silent for a bit. "Is that a precondition?"

"No, just a respectful request," Susan said, and she smiled. "It's a phrase I never thought I'd hear myself say. But I'm saying it now. Let's quit the bullshit and move on."

Hammond was trying to form an answer when the Russian phone rang. It was Tarasov.

"Why did you shut down your New York office?"

"What the hell are you talking about?" Hammond demanded.

"The office was closed overnight, which in itself wasn't so bad, except that the FBI showed up apparently as a follow-up to the murders of Rodriguez and Kuprik. The place was empty."

Hammond was stunned. "Where the hell are you getting all this information?"

"That doesn't matter. What does matter is your team is waiting on the ground in Sofia for the operation tomorrow night. McGarvey and his wife are staying the night in an Athens hotel, and presumably, they'll be taking a ferry out to the island first thing in the morning. In the meantime, the FBI has found out where you're staying."

"So what?" Hammond practically shouted. "I can hardly take a dump without everyone knowing about it. It's the same for Gates and Jeff and Elon and just about every player."

"They're sending someone to interview you."

Hammond's stomach tightened. "Why?"

"You're in a better position to answer that than I am," Tarasov said.

"I only know what I've read in the papers. I'll fly Morton over. He can be here by morning." Morton Fay was Hammond's chief attorney.

"Do nothing of the kind!" Tarasov shouted. "You have an attorney present and they'll smell blood. You've done nothing wrong, nothing illegal; just keep that in your head. And whatever you do, tell that bitch you're in bed with to keep her mouth shut."

Hammond had nothing to say.

"This will be over in less than thirty-six hours, and then you have some work to do for me."

"What if they miss?"

"It's not likely, but it doesn't matter, Thomas. In thirty-six hours, whatever the outcome, it's over and done with."

McGarvey and Pete got off the ferry at the port city of Livadi, but instead of walking into town with the dozen or so other passengers, they found a taxi to take them up to the lighthouse.

The old man behind the wheel was a familiar face.

"Welcome home, mister and missus," he said, his accent very heavy.

"It's good to be home," Pete said. "You are well?"

"Yes, of course," the old man said. "Will you be coming back to town for shopping? I can come back up?"

"Maybe this afternoon," McGarvey said. "How has the tourist business been the past few days?"

"Tolerable for this time of year. But the market, especially in America, has been down this last quarter, so people are watching their spending."

"Anyone interesting show up lately?"

The driver looked in the mirror. "No. Are we expecting Mr. Otto?"

"Maybe later," McGarvey said. "But we'd just as soon have no tourists stopping by to take a look at the old lighthouse."

"A man and woman need their privacy," the driver said.

☐

SIXTY

Bender had enough pull at FBI headquarters to commandeer the services of a C-27 jet, which was the government designation for a Gulfstream G550, and to have a crew meet him and Special Agent Sherman—whom he'd brought down from New York—at Joint Base Andrews across the Potomac from Washington and fly them to France.

They'd managed to get a few hours' decent sleep on the flight, and an hour outside of the Nice Côte d'Azur Airport, Bender cautioned the other agent that they would have to proceed with care lest Hammond put up a screen of defense lawyers.

"The man didn't get where he is without being shrewd, which is his weakness. He's sure of himself. He doesn't think he makes mistakes."

"How do you want to work this, sir?" Sherman asked. "We have no direct evidence that he was in any way involved with the attacks on Mr. McGarvey and not much more that he was involved with the deaths of his office manager or the Russian diplomat."

"You're absolutely right, except McGarvey had a brief and not very satisfactory relationship with him a couple of years ago."

"The attack on the pencil tower in New York. I glanced through the file last night."

"What I could gather from the CIA's after-action report that was distributed to our director as well as the White House through the National Director of Intelligence's office, McGarvey ingratiated himself with Hammond by offering a financial deal involving a scheme to corner the bitcoin market and make a killing. The point was McGarvey wanted an invitation to a party at the tower near the UN that he somehow knew was going to come under attack in exchange for the deal."

"And you think that Hammond might be seeking revenge?"

"He has the reputation for destroying anyone who tries to come up against him in a business deal."

Sherman was shaking her head. "I'm sorry, sir, but that's so thin it hardly warrants a phone call, let alone a face-to-face interview."

Bender did not like to be contradicted, and he was angry for just a moment. But just for a moment. "Pull a small thread in a sweater and the entire thing falls apart. And trying to assassinate a former CIA director is a very big deal, and I'm willing to try anything to prevent it."

"A career maker," Sherman said.

Bender glanced at her. "Or breaker," he said. "Are you with me?"

"Yes, sir. All the way."

It was just coming up on two in the afternoon when they rented a car and drove the fifteen miles up to the Hotel du Paris. Bender's directorate had traced Hammond and his girlfriend, the actress from Skagway, of all places, to Geneva, then Italy, and finally here, which had not been particularly difficult.

The two of them, especially Susan Patterson, were highly visible people. Gossip magazines and tabloids covered just about every move they made.

Pulling up in front, they surrendered the car to a valet parker and went inside to the front desk. "We'd like to have a word with Mr. Thomas Hammond," Bender said.

"May I ask who is calling?" the deskman, dressed in a morning coat and starched shirt, asked.

"We're old friends."

"Oui, monsieur," the man said. He picked up a phone, said something that Bender couldn't quite hear, and replaced the receiver. "You may go up now, sirs. Mr. Hammond is expecting you." The man gave them the suite number.

Halfway across the lobby, Sherman glanced back over her shoulder. "How the hell did Hammond know that we were coming?"

Bender was troubled. "I don't know, but I'm going to ask him."

"This is my play," Hammond told Susan.

"Do you want me to go down to the pool?" she asked.

"No, we've done nothing wrong. But if they ask you something, which I'm sure they will, just play the empty-headed girlfriend. It's a role you know pretty well."

Susan was amused. "Screw you," she said.

The bell rang, and Susan, wearing a bikini and gossamer wrap, let the two FBI agents into the suite. They were dressed almost identically in dark suits.

Hammond, in white linen slacks, a short-sleeved, brightly patterned silk shirt unbuttoned halfway down, and no shoes, joined them in the entry hall. "Welcome to Monaco, though I'm not all that surprised you're here. May I see some identification?"

Bender and Sherman showed their credentials. "May I ask how you knew we would be showing up?" Bender asked.

Hammond smiled. It was the first question he'd wanted to be asked. It would immediately establish the relationship. "It's my business to know who's coming after me and why," he said.

He led them to the dining area, where he and Susan sat across the small table from the two FBI agents. The view from the big windows to the Med was nothing short of magnificent.

"Would either of you care for coffee?" Susan asked.

"No, thanks," Bender said.

"Then be brief, if you would," Hammond said.

"We'd like to ask you a few questions about the death of Ramos Rodriguez, who was in charge of your offices in New York."

"It's actually a liaison unit that did most of its work with the financial advisers to the various UN delegates across the street. I'm sure you know that I have business interests on both sides of the Atlantic, including South America."

"Perhaps with Russia and China as well?" Sherman asked.

"Naturally," Hammond said. "But if you've come to ask me about poor Arturo's death, I'm afraid I can't help. In any event, I was told that it was an accident, and I sincerely hope you're not here to tell me otherwise."

"There is some evidence that it may have been the result of foul play," Sherman said. "Especially coming so soon after the death of a Russian diplomat your man met with earlier."

Hammond had to keep from laughing. The stupid bastards were so oblivious it was almost painful. "I read about it—Kuprik, I think. Arturo told me that they had been trying to put together some sort of a project."

"What sort of a project?" Bender asked.

"Something to do with cell phones, but I'm not sure of the specific details except that it had promise. Are you suggesting there may have been a connection?"

"It's too early to say."

Hammond looked away for a moment as if he were gathering his thoughts. Susan sat straight-faced.

"I have to say that Arturo's death came as a shock to us all."

"Is that why you closed your office in the middle of the night?" Sherman asked.

"The place was hemorrhaging money without producing anything concrete. Actually, I decided several months ago to move those liaison duties to my main office in LA."

"Why move out so abruptly?"

"It's the way that I do business."

Sherman started to say something else, but Bender held her off.

"Would you have any idea why Mr. Rodriguez may have been murdered?"

"If it was murder and not an accident, I can think of a dozen possible motives and suspects," Hammond said. "Starting with the Chile's ANI—that's their intelligence agency. And of course North Korea, Pakistan, and, believe it or not, Russia. Someone in Moscow might have thought we were stirring up a hornet's nest with the cell phone deal."

Again, Sherman started to say something, but again Bender held her off and stood up. "Thank you for your cooperation, sir," he said.

"Anytime," Hammond said.

The FBI officers went to the door, where they paused and Bender turned back. "Does the name Kirk McGarvey ring a bell?"

It was the one question Hammond had expected. "Yes. The son of a bitch screwed me out of a significant amount of money a couple of years ago. And it pissed me off."

On the way down in the elevator, Sherman was the first to speak. "What do you think?"

"He's involved, I'd bet my retirement account on it," Bender said. "Now let's go talk to Mr. McGarvey."

SIXTY-ONE

The afternoon was getting on, and Vetrov stood looking out the small window to the left of the aircraft access door at the comings and goings of the airport, normal for a capital city, though nothing had taken off or landed during the long night.

His people were well trained and patient, and he was proud of them. His worries that they might lose their edge over a twenty-four-hour delay, after the emotional upheaval on base, had been unfounded, and he was glad.

They'd thrown themselves into the calisthenics through the day and played poker almost straight through the last twelve hours, showing absolutely no signs of being keyed up for the coming op. If they had any remorse over agreeing to dishonorable discharges, none of them had showed any signs of it so far.

The provisions aboard were either microwave meals or reconstituted items of the same variety cosmonauts still took into space, including powdered eggs, but again, none of the men had complained.

Ilich Silin came across from the aircraft with a bottle in hand.

"Where'd you find that?" Vetrov asked.

"In one of the secured lockers," Selin said, grinning. "It's not vodka, but it's a credible French cognac."

He passed the half-empty bottle to Vetrov, who took a deep draft. It was good.

"How much have the men had to drink?"

"This was the only bottle."

"*Dawbruhy*"—Good—Vetrov said. He took another draft, then tossed the bottle end over end toward the corner, where it smashed on the concrete floor.

"*Yeb vas*," Silin said, but he shrugged. "Just as well if this American son of a bitch is as good as you say he is."

"His wife is also a trained CIA agent, and by all accounts, she's pretty good herself."

"Is our brief to take her out, too?" Silin asked, the dour look back on his face.

"No, but I think it will be inevitable."

"What are our orders concerning civilians who might get in the way?"

"We'll be jumping at 0200, so I suspect there won't be many out and about at that hour."

"I meant afterward, when we've changed clothes and show up in Livadi for our reservations on the morning ferry?"

"We're leaving without weapons," Vetrov said.

Silin started to object, but Vetrov held him off.

"If we have to kill the crew and passengers and hijack the ferry for whatever reason, we won't need force of arms."

"True," Silin said.

"I want a total equipment check in thirty minutes, after which we'll have something to eat and then hit the rack. The crew will be back around 2400 to prep, and we should be wheels up at 0100."

"Yes, sir," Silin said, saluting. He did an about-face and went back to the Gulfstream.

Vetrov turned inward. Not everyone would survive the mission if McGarvey actually lived up to his rep. The former DCI was fifty, about the age when a man began to lose his edge, but they couldn't count on him being slow.

Vetrov had given a lot of thought to having his wife join him wherever he ended up. Finland, he thought, or perhaps Norway or Sweden. Even Ukraine, where he could offer his services.

Pete had found some canned oysters in a lemon-and-olive-oil sauce, along with a Spanish potato salad, a package of pita bread in the freezer, and a jar of tzatziki sauce in the pantry. It was late afternoon, the day still warm, but with a pleasant breeze off the Aegean that reached all the way up the hill to them. And they sat outside by the saltwater pool enjoying their scratch supper with a bottle of Retsina wine.

"We'll need to restock the fridge and pantry pretty soon," Pete said. "I could take the Mini Cooper into town and be back in a jiffy."

McGarvey had been thinking about the next attack, which was why he had decamped here, where any collateral damage would be minimal. The islanders—and there were only around fifteen hundred of them, a lot of them spread out in hillside homes, with almost no one in the hot, dry interior—had no idea that anything bad was about to happen. Because nothing bad ever did happen since the Romans used it as an island for exiles.

The lighthouse was at the end of the peninsula that jutted out into the city and looked down over the deep, almost unreal blue water of the bay and back toward Livadi. Only a few buildings were between them and the base of the peninsula and road, the last section of which he had built, that led down into the town.

So far, whoever was directing the attacks had a good source of intelligence, so they knew where the lighthouse was located. If someone was coming, it would be at night.

"We're sticking together," he said.

"You think it's going to happen tonight?"

"Yes, before we get a chance to settle in."

Pete looked down at the bay, beautiful and peaceful just now, and she shook her head. "They've got some goddamned good intel and a lot of balls to come after us," she said. "But who and why?"

McGarvey phoned Otto, who answered as usual on the first ring. It was just before noon in Washington.

"How are you guys?"

"We're at the lighthouse having supper. But I think whatever's going to happen will be tonight. The question is, where the hell are they getting their intel? Has Lou come up with anything? Even a hint?"

"To this point, she has a fairly high confidence, near 60 percent, that whoever is behind this shit has access to a government-level intelligence source. She's actually lowered Hammond's probability because she doesn't think even someone with his money would have that kind of a connection."

"What does it smell like?"

"The GRU," Otto said without hesitation.

"Then let's take a look at Hammond's business connections with anyone in Russia. Especially business deals that have gone bad in the past—in which case, someone might owe him a favor—or business deals in the making that could make use of Hammond's connections anywhere in the world outside Russia's borders."

"That could take a while, but I'm on it," Otto said.

Pete held up a hand.

"Hang on," McGarvey told Otto.

"You're assuming that Hammond is behind this thing," Pete said. "But we don't have a shred of direct evidence. So you guys had better not narrow your vision so that you ignore something else that might be staring us in the face."

"Did you hear that?" McGarvey asked.

"Yes, and she's right," Otto said. "And it's my fault. I've given Lou too short a leash. She's not completely AI yet, which means she tends to interpret everything literally. I'm going to have to do a major tweak to her programming to let her think outside the box, but without getting swamped by minutiae like what's always bogged down the NSA's telephone intercept programs."

"My bet is still on Hammond," McGarvey said. "Just a gut feeling."

"I'm on it," Otto said. "In the meantime, what's your plan for tonight? Are you guys going to bunker in and let them come to you?"

"No. We're going out into the field after dark and set up our own ambush."

SIXTY-TWO

☐

Twenty minutes out from Athens International Airport, Bender got a phone call from his boss, Harold Kallek. It was around five in the afternoon local, which put it at eleven in the morning in D.C.

"Clarke, do you want to tell me what the hell you're doing?" the head of the FBI demanded. He did not sound happy.

"Good morning, Mr. Director," Bender said. "We're following up on a couple of leads that I felt had to be done in face-to-face interviews. Has Mr. Thalley complained that I commandeered one of his agents?" Morton Thalley was the New York SAC.

"No. But I just got off the phone with one of Thomas Hammond's attorneys, who wanted to know why the hell you were harassing his client."

"I asked him for information on the death of his employee who'd apparently been working with a Russian diplomatic aide who was murdered the night before."

"Not your case."

"No, sir. But my real reason for interviewing the man was to find out if he knew Mr. McGarvey."

"And?"

"He said—his words: 'The son of a bitch screwed me out of a significant amount of money a couple of years ago. And it pissed me off.'"

"We already knew that," Kallek said.

"Yes, sir. But I wanted to know if he still harbored any resentment. It's obvious he does."

"It doesn't rise to the level of a conspirator. From what I understand of the man, he's a ruthless bastard, but not a murderer."

"I don't know, sir. But I got the distinct impression that if he'd had a gun in his hand and McGarvey were standing in front of him, he wouldn't have hesitated to pull the trigger."

"Right now, it's a moot point. We have no chain of evidence linking Hammond to the attempts that were made on McGarvey's life."

"No, sir, but I have established a motive."

"A possible motive," Kallek said. "Where are you at this moment?"

"We'll be landing in Athens in a few minutes, and from there, we're going to take a helicopter out to Serifos."

"McGarvey will send you packing if he doesn't shoot you."

"I don't think the latter is a real possibility, sir."

"Of course not, but he's not likely to cooperate with you. So what do you hope to gain?"

"His reaction when I tell him about our interview with Hammond."

Kallek was silent for a beat or two, and when he came back, his tone was measured. "I want you to hear me, Mr. Bender. Are you and Mrs. Sherman armed?"

"Yes, sir."

"Under no circumstances will you remain on the island after your interview. As a matter of fact, I want you to have the helicopter service hold until you're finished, and return you immediately to Athens International, where you will come home."

"That was my intention. Just the interview to gauge Mr. McGarvey's reaction."

"After which, you will leave. Am I clear?"

"Perfectly, Mr. Director."

Hammond and Susan came up from the beach before six to change for an early dinner. He wanted to walk over to the casino and play some high-stakes baccarat. They had talked a little about the game and the players usually found around the tables these days—mostly Russian and Chinese megarich who had replaced Arabs after oil prices had dropped to drastically low levels.

They had avoided discussing the visit by the FBI agents at the hotel earlier until now. Hammond came out of the shower, a towel around his waist. Susan was in the sitting room in a bra and panties sipping champagne, her makeup already done.

"Do you think it'll happen tonight?" she asked.

He didn't have to ask what she meant. "I don't know, but I hope so. I want it to be over and done with."

"Me, too," Susan said, and she was a lot more subdued than she usually was.

Hammond thought that she was frightened. He went across to her and kissed the nape of her neck.

She leaned back against him. "Let's get the hell out of here and go home."

"When it's over."

"Now. Call the crew and have them prep the plane. We can pack up and leave. Hell, we can just get out of here with the clothes on our backs; the hotel will send our stuff to us, or burn it for all I give a shit."

Hammond sat down across from her. "I want this to be over with as much as you do, because our lives are on hold until it is."

"Walk away from it, Tom."

"I can't."

"Because of your deal with the Russians, or because you still want this fucking thing to happen?"

"Both."

"You're out of your mind. We don't need more money, and this is just a goddamned game. Stupid."

She was right, of course. He'd known it from the moment he'd learned that the first attempt to kill McGarvey had failed. And yet in a perverse way, he'd been glad that McGarvey had won that round and the next two. It was what he'd wanted from the beginning, though after each failure, he'd become truly afraid for his own life. As if he'd actually gone mano a mano with the man himself.

He'd read somewhere that after a man had done some ridiculously impossible feat—like scaling Mount Everest or crossing an ocean in a canoe—he would look back as the adrenaline faded and think about doing the next impossible thing. The rush was almost sexual.

It was almost the same with this thing, and he'd been willing to lose the first few rounds, lose a few pieces to gain the bigger prize. A gambit play.

And just now, he was close.

The Russian phone lying on the dresser in the bedroom chimed, and Hammond got up to answer it.

"The operation is in the works for tonight," Tarasov said. "I want you two to stay where you are, act normally."

"We're going to the casino and then dinner afterward."

"Perfect. I'll let you know when it's done."

"You won't have to make the call; it'll be all over the news."

"Yes, and then you'll have to get to work on our deal," Tarasov said. "I don't give a shit about McGarvey; I never have. He's your game. This is just quid pro quo."

"There'll have to be a delay. At least a month to let the hue and cry die down."

"We want you to start immediately."

"You're not listening. The goddamned FBI is already on my case. If all of a sudden I start working on a deal for Gazprom, the CIA is bound to pick up on it. McGarvey is no friend of Putin's, and the connection will be made."

"I don't care."

"What the fuck do you mean, you don't care? Killing a former CIA director is a big deal, bigger if it's traced to you guys. And it's a Spetsnaz team who'll be doing the shooting. How obvious can you get?"

"They have been dishonorably discharged and kicked out of Russia, their families arrested. It was a rogue operation."

"A Russian operation."

"No, a Hammond operation done out of some insane sense of spite for a deal gone wrong," Tarasov said.

SIXTY-THREE

Pete had dark jeans, but McGarvey had to give her one of his black polo shirts, which was so ridiculously large she had to tuck it in her waistband. "I'm not going to win any fashion parade looking like this," she said on the way out of the house and up to the peak of the hill.

The sun was low on the horizon toward the interior of the island, and McGarvey had wanted to take a look from the highest point on the peninsula before dark and pick the likely path their attackers would take, and from that figure out a defense that made sense.

The late-afternoon ferry from the mainland had come and gone an hour ago, and occasionally, a bit of music drifted across the bay from the town. That had been drowned out a couple of minutes ago by a helicopter coming in from the northwest.

"Tourists anxious for a head start," Pete said.

"I'm not sure," McGarvey said, half to himself.

The ground was rocky and in most places covered with a dense scrub brush while at other places almost bare. Here and there were larger boulders, some of them big enough to hide behind. Light brown rock outcroppings fell down the side of the hills in waves like broad stationary waterfalls.

"Not sure about what?"

"It hasn't headed back."

"Maybe the pilot needs a little R&R and decided to stay for the night."

"Maybe," McGarvey said, but he was skeptical. He'd learned from long experience that anomalies were often the things that rose up and bit you in the ass if you didn't pay attention.

"Call Otto," Pete suggested.

"Let's do our walk around first."

They stopped at the highest point. Off to the east, the big island of Paros with the smaller island of Antiparos in front of it were shrouded in a distant blue haze as if they were another universe away. Just at this moment, there were no boats under way in any direction and only a dozen or two anchored in the harbor.

Up here, they were totally alone, and Pete got something of that from him. "Okay, now I'm getting really spooked," she said. "Talk to me."

"There are only two ways for someone to get to us—from the sea or from the air. It'd be a tough climb up the side of the hill, even using the old mine buildings as a cover, and there'd be too many witnesses. Lots of things could go wrong."

"A HALO jump, and when they were done, ditch their weapons—assuming they were successful in taking us out. Then what?"

"Stay put up here until it was time to take the morning ferry back to Athens."

"A HALO jump means military. Or at least ex-military. They'd have to be in dark camos for the night operation, but carrying civilian clothes to change into so they could get to the ferry without attracting notice."

"Which is why we're going to make as much noise as possible," McGarvey said.

"No suppressors. Someone's bound to sit up and take notice. But I thought you wanted to avoid any collateral damage."

"By the time the local cops got up here, this business will have been finished."

"One way or the other," Pete said glumly. "But if they don't want to make noise, then why don't we just make our stand in the lighthouse rather than out here?"

"Because I might be wrong," McGarvey said.

"If they hit us out here, a lot could go wrong for all of us."

McGarvey took a knee, and Pete hunched down next to him. "I think that they might be counting on us tucked in bed, and they'll land as close to the lighthouse as possible and come in fast and silent. We don't have locks on our front door or the kitchen door to the pool because I never saw the need for it. Which means they won't have to blow the doors. If they know what they're doing and there are at least four of them, they can stack up at the doors and come in ready to shoot. They'll drive us up the stairs, and we'll have nowhere to go."

"They'll have to figure that we'll call for help."

"First they'll hit the cell tower."

"More noise."

"If they have access to government-level gear, they can do it electronically."

"Sat phones?"

"I suspect the same," McGarvey said. "It's something Otto's going to look out for. If our sat link goes bad, he'll know an attack has started."

"But he can't call anyone for help. The local coppers would be hopelessly outclassed, and by the time anyone got here from the mainland, it would be all over but the shouting."

"He could trace the source of the satellite failure."

"And?"

"If it's Russian, which I think it probably is, Taft could call the president, who could call Putin."

"You think of everything," Pete said.

"It's the one bit I haven't thought of that's the worst of it."

"Never happens."

McGarvey smiled. "More often than I'd care to remember," he said.

He got up, and Pete followed suit. "Now let's take a look at what we're going to be dealing with after it gets dark."

A pair of taxis had come over to the helicopter terminal, and Sherman went over to hire one of them while Bender stayed behind to talk the pilot into waiting for them.

"Two hours tops, and we'll be back," Bender said.

"I have a fare on Kythnos," the pilot said.

"Five hundred euros to wait for us."

"No."

"One thousand euros." Before the pilot could object, Bender said, "Each."

"One thousand now."

Bender handed him a credit card, and the pilot swiped it on a handheld machine and handed it back. "Ninety minutes."

"Don't leave us."

"Don't be late."

The lower limb of the sun was just touching the top of the hills below them, illuminating Livadi in gold streaks across the now deep blue of the water in the harbor, when McGarvey and Pete started back to the lighthouse.

He had spotted several promising sites, a couple of them behind decent-size boulders and another at the west edge of one of the cliffs.

"I want to stay hidden until they get between us and the lighthouse, and then come up behind them, but at different firing angles," he told Pete as they headed back.

"How wide apart do you want us?"

"Depends on how many of them they are and how widely they're dispersed."

"A lot can go wrong."

"And probably will. But we'll have three advantages," McGarvey said. "We'll take them by surprise, we'll be behind them, and we'll be making a lot of noise."

"If they come."

"When they come," McGarvey said.

They came down the hill in time to see a taxi headed on the road back to town, leaving two people standing in front of the lighthouse.

Even from a distance of a hundred yards or so, McGarvey knew who they were, and so did Pete.

"The FBI," she said.

At that moment, a helicopter lifted off in the distance and climbed over the harbor as it headed to the northwest back to Athens.

□

SIXTY-FOUR

Bender and Alicia had just walked up the three broad steps to the front door of the lighthouse when they heard the distant sound of the helicopter lifting off. They turned toward the sound in time to see it rising above the town across the bay and heading away.

"Son of a bitch," Bender swore. He pulled out his cell phone and dialed the number for the helicopter service. A woman answered in Greek on the second ring.

"English, please," Bender said.

"Yes, sir. You have reached Aegean Transport Services. How may I be of assistance?"

"This is Clarke Bender. I chartered a helicopter to take my partner and me to Serifos. The pilot agreed to wait for us, but he just now took off. We're stranded here. I want him to come back."

"I'm sorry, sir. Please give me a moment to contact him by radio."

"Do it."

"What'd they say?" Alicia asked.

"They're calling the pilot."

Two minutes later, the woman was back. "I'm terribly sorry, sir, but there seems to be some difficulty with radio communications. Our pilot does not respond."

"Never mind. Send us another helicopter."

"I'm sorry, sir, but that won't be possible this evening. I can have one for you no later than 0800."

"We need to get off this island tonight!" Bender shouted.

"Again, my apologies, sir. There are several excellent hotels on the island. May I make reservations for you and your wife?"

Bender broke the connection. "We're stuck here for the night."

Alicia shrugged. "We'll interview the McGarveys and then take a cab into town. I'm sure we can find a decent restaurant and a place to bunk. We won't even mention it to my husband or your wife."

"Christ," Bender said.

He knocked on the door, and after a pause when there was no answer, he knocked again.

"Maybe they're out back," Alicia suggested.

The door was unlocked. Bender opened it. "Hello," he called.

. . .

McGarvey and Pete came around the corner just as Bender shouted hello at the open door.

"Here we are," McGarvey said.

Startled, Bender and the woman turned around.

"The question is, what the hell are you doing here?" McGarvey demanded, but he knew damn well why they had come.

"We wanted to interview you and your wife," Bender said.

"You've already had your interview."

"But we have new information, and we want your reaction," Alicia said. "May we come in?"

"Who the hell are you?"

"Alicia Sherman, FBI," she said, taking out her ID wallet and holding it open. "I'm the assistant SAC in our New York office. I was handling the investigation into the recent deaths of the Russian UN diplomat and the director of Thomas Hammond's UN liaison office. We think that there may be a connection with those events and the attempts on your life."

"You should have telephoned me," McGarvey said.

"They want our face-to-face reaction," Pete said. "Standard interrogation tradecraft."

"May we come in?" Alicia asked.

"How did Hammond react when you talked to him?" Pete asked.

Alicia smiled a little. "We'll only take a few minutes of your time."

"You came in by helicopter and it took off, so you're stranded for the night, I suspect," McGarvey said.

"We'll spend the night in town," Bender said. "We've come a long way, not only to investigate the incidents in New York but maybe, if we pool our resources, we might be able to help save your lives."

"Or get yourselves killed."

"Part of our job description," Alicia said.

"And get in our way."

Bender's eyes widened a little, and he glanced beyond McGarvey and Pete in the direction from which they had come. "You were out scouting. You think the attack will be sometime tonight?"

"It's possible, and we don't want you two getting in the way."

Bender started to object, but McGarvey held him off. "You have no military background. I checked. And whatever happens, if it's tonight, it will almost certainly be run like a military operation. It will be very fast, and they'll want it to be as quiet as possible so they don't have to deal with the local cops. You two wouldn't have a chance."

"I'm a Marine combat veteran," Alicia said. "Two tours in Afghanistan as a cop. And if you think I was just a dumb grunt, you're wrong, Mr. Director.

I was Lieutenant Sherman. First Lieutenant Sherman. And I almost always hit what I shoot at."

McGarvey had to laugh, though without any real humor, only resignation. "Okay, Lieutenant Sherman, the two of you might as well come inside and ask your questions. When you're done, you can go back down the hill."

It was twilight and getting dark when McGarvey led them through the lighthouse and back to the pool. He did not turn on the lights even though he was sure that the attack would come in the early-morning hours, maybe two or three.

Pete got beers for them and brought them out.

Bender shook his head and held up a hand. "We're on duty," he said, trying to be sanctimonious.

"Not tonight," Pete said. "Glass?"

"No," Alicia said, and she took one of the beers and drank deeply. "Good."

"What did Hammond say to you?" McGarvey asked when they were settled.

"He called you a son of a bitch and said that you screwed him out of a lot of money," Bender said. "He told me that you pissed him off."

"Fair enough from his side of the fence."

"He's holding a grudge."

"Strong enough to pay to have me killed?"

"I think it's a real possibility," Bender said.

"I agree," Alicia said.

"We're looking into his recent financial transactions, but most of them are from blind accounts or third- and fourth-party signatories who are lawyers, and whose orders are almost certainly verbal, which would give them attorney-client protection."

"We've done the same thing," McGarvey said.

"Mr. Rencke?" Sherman asked.

McGarvey ignored the question. "Hammond's a person of interest, but just that."

"Then who do you think is coming after you, and why?" Alicia asked.

"In this case, what I think is irrelevant, because there'd be nothing the Bureau could do about it," McGarvey said.

"We're listening," she said.

"Some of the bits and pieces we've managed to come up with suggest to me that the Russians may be involved, but strictly on an unofficial level."

"Can you share some of the bits and pieces?"

"No."

"Have you shared any of it with the CIA?"

"Some," McGarvey said. "Finish your beer, and we'll call a cab for you."

"We're staying," Alicia said.

"No," McGarvey said.

"We're just doing our job, Mr. Director. Protecting witnesses in a murder-for-hire plot."

SIXTY—FIVE

Otto met Mary at the cafeteria in the covered walkway between the Old Headquarters Building and the New Headquarters Building, floor-to-ceiling glass windows looking out onto the courtyard. It was well after normal lunch hours, but the place was still fairly busy.

They got their trays—Mary a salad, and Otto a burger and fries—and found a table with a view of the *Kryptos* statue, with the coded inscription Otto had deciphered a couple of years ago for an operation that McGarvey had been involved with.

"It'll be getting dark over there pretty soon," Mary said. "Does Mac think it might happen tonight?"

"He thinks it's a possibility. He and Pete went out on a scouting trip to look for some decent defensive positions."

"Lord almighty. Just the two of them against what'll likely be a Russian op."

"What makes you so sure it's the Russians?" Otto asked.

"Most of the time, I don't have Lou, but I do have my sources. And it's a fairly sure bet that Mr. T. Hammond has got himself involved with a southern European pipeline deal for Gazprom."

"That'll be an uphill battle."

"At least that tough," Mary said. "But Hammond has a lot of very solid business connections in France and Belgium, places that the Russians aren't exactly welcome with open arms."

"Granted, he may have a Russian connection, but what does that have to do with the attacks on Mac?"

"Hammond's angry because of the bitcoin deal that you and Mac cooked up last year, and added to that are the murder of the Russian UN diplomat whom a Hammond moneyman was involved with. And then the supposedly accidental death of the Hammond guy. A lot of coincidences, don't you think?"

"Too many," Otto said. "After lunch, we can talk to Lou."

"Way ahead of you, sweetheart. She upped a Hammond connection to 48 percent after I gave her the new data. That's almost fifty-fifty, close to betting odds."

"Do we have a name, someone in Moscow we can prove Hammond is connected to?"

"I haven't gotten that far, but between us, I think we might be abl come up with something this afternoon. Maybe in time to give Mac and Pete at least a slight edge tonight."

"Whoever the Russian is would have to be connected with the SVR or GRU, so maybe we can reverse engineer the thing."

"My bet would be the GRU. They're the people who control the general staff."

"Who control the Spetsnaz."

It was just before nine when Hammond took a seat at the baccarat table with a one-million-euro marker he'd established with the pit boss. He was well known, and his credit was without limits. All he had to do is say the word.

Susan stood behind him wearing a stunning off-the-shoulder slinky yellow dress with a strip of fabric around her narrow neck like a choker. The dress was cut low and loose enough so that when she bent forward to say something in Hammond's ear, her nipples were momentarily exposed. All the men in the private salle loved her, the women despised her. It was exactly the effect she loved.

First out, Hammond took the banque for €200,000, winning it with a five and a four, and spilled his champagne. The win, the wine, and Susan's dress all made for an unforgettable alibi, something he thought they needed.

His only concern, which he hadn't shared with Susan, was the Russian seated at the far end of the table. The man was Ivan Metropov, a multibillionaire with a big stake in Gazprom, whom he was sure Tarasov had sent to keep an eye on things.

As far as he was concerned, his main objective this evening was to beat the son of a bitch into the ground and let the bastard report that back to Tarasov.

"Two hundred fifty thousand," he said.

"Banco," the Russian immediately responded.

The aircrew showed up at eleven, fully two hours before they'd been scheduled to take off, and immediately busied themselves in the cockpit.

Vetrov went forward. "You're early. Is something wrong?" he asked.

"We got word that the DANS has taken an interest in us," Captain Borisov said. DANS was the Bulgarian national counterintelligence service.

"What sort of interest?"

"I don't know, but I'm sure as hell not going to stick around to find out. I was given a warning that they would be here within the hour, so we're leaving now. Are your people ready?"

"Our drop is not until 0200."

"Are you ready?"

"Three hours from now, Captain," Vetrov said, his right hand on the butt of his pistol in its holster on his chest.

"And that's when your drop will be," the copilot said. "Go strap in, because we're number one for takeoff once we get out of this hangar. And we will take off, Senior Lieutenant, whether you are ready or not."

"Your drop will be as scheduled," Borisov said. "We have plenty of fuel to hold in international waters until it is time."

"Won't someone take notice?"

"No," the copilot said.

Vetrov went aft to brief his people as the hangar doors began to open. Darina came aft and closed and dogged the hatch, then went forward. Moments later, the engines began to spool up and a tow vehicle showed up, attached the bar to the front wheel strut, and pulled the aircraft out of the hangar and onto the tarmac.

The mission and the exfiltration from the island after the op were foremost in Vetrov's mind, but killing the crew, especially the bitch in the right seat, would give him pleasure.

At the lighthouse, Pete had fixed them a platter of canned meats, cheeses, bread from the freezer, and an herb-infused good olive oil. Afterward, McGarvey had gone over what he expected would happen and how he'd originally planned on dealing with it.

"I'm not particularly happy that you're here, and I'm sure that Mr. Kallek won't be very pleased when he finds out," McGarvey said.

"Only if we get shot," Alicia said.

"If I had my druthers, I'd drive you back into town myself, but I won't leave Pete here alone, nor do I want someone to show up while we're both gone and set up a trap for us. So here you are."

"Here we are," Alicia said. "If something's going to happen tonight, when do you think it'll go down?"

"Two or later," McGarvey said.

"When you're supposed to be sound asleep."

"The one clear advantage we have is they won't make any noise. Afterward, they'll want to be extracted without having to shoot their way off the island."

"When are you going out?" Alicia asked.

"One thirty."

"For how long?" Bender asked.

"Until dawn," McGarvey said. "We're going to get behind them, and if possible follow them here, where you two will be waiting, and we'll catch them in a cross fire."

"Why haven't you called the local cops?" Bender asked.

"I don't want innocents hurt."

Bender said nothing.

☐

SIXTY–SIX

The shade of lavender on all the monitors in Otto's office turned darker, which meant trouble, the moment he asked for a search of recent GRU activities in the U.S., especially within a fifty-mile radius of Washington, D.C., and the same for Manhattan from Midtown South.

Mary stood leaning against the tabletop monitor as Otto sat with his feet up on the desk, his favorite pose ever since he had done away with all but one of the keyboards.

"May we narrow the search?" Lou asked.

"Starting with Thomas Hammond, I would like connections with the recent death of the Russian adviser Viktor Kuprik and someone within the GRU," Otto said.

"Hammond's Strategic Liaison Services' chief operating officer, Arturo Ramos Rodriguez, made several contacts with Kuprik."

"Do we know the nature of those meetings?"

"No specific data, except there is a high likelihood that Hammond was involved in some financial arrangement with an unknown Russian person or persons."

"Search for a connection to someone inside the GRU," Mary said.

"Yes."

"I would like you to do several other simultaneous parallel searches," Otto said. "Can you do that?"

"Of course," Lou said, and the near AI program almost sounded insulted. It was a bit of Louise Horn's personality that Otto had injected into the system.

"First, give me a name of someone connected with the GRU as well as the Putin office."

"Can you tell me the possible nature of this relationship?"

"Yes, the common denominator for all of your searches will be of a financial nature, ultimately leading back to a connection between Thomas Hammond and Kirk McGarvey."

"The most transparent connections are McGarvey's bitcoin offering to Hammond two years ago, and before that, McGarvey's connection with President Putin himself."

"Expand the search to someone outside of the GRU or the Kremlin who carries influence."

"General Oleg Kanayev, who is the main directorate general staff officer in charge of Special Forces."

"Spetsnaz," Otto said.

"Yes."

"Why did his name come up?"

"Within the last twelve hours, he announced his retirement, which is coincidental with a visit he had from Mikhail Tarasov, who is a Russian billionaire with close connections not only to President Putin but to Gazprom, a name from your earlier search request."

"Is there a connection between this man and Hammond?" Mary asked.

"A curious coincidence, perhaps. But in another simultaneous search, I have found Thomas Hammond and Susan Patterson currently seated at a high-stakes baccarat table at the Casino de Monte-Carlo. Surveillance cameras also show a Russian multibillionaire, Ivan Metropov, seated at the same table."

"Is there another connection?" Mary pressed.

"Metropov was a GRU lieutenant colonel before he resigned his commission to work at Gazprom as an assistant for special affairs for Mikhail Tarasov."

"Are there other coincidences?"

"Yes, it is rumored that Gazprom intends to build another series of oil and gas pipelines to Europe, specifically the Netherlands and Belgium, plus France, where Russia is not looked upon favorably, but where Thomas Hammond has many successful business ventures."

"We know that. Is there anything else?"

"General Kanayev's son-in-law is Lieutenant Colonel Viktor Nyunin, who is the commander of the 329th Spetsnaz Special Purpose Detachment in Pskov Oblast."

"More?" Mary asked.

"Less than twenty-four hours ago, six of Colonel Nyunin's veteran Spetsnaz offices were given dishonorable discharges."

"Jesus Christ," Otto said softly.

"Have they been arrested and jailed?" Mary asked.

"No," Lou said.

"Where are they at this moment?"

"Their locations are unknown."

Otto dropped his feet to the floor and turned to his wife. "Too many co-incidences?" he asked, his heart hammering.

"We have to leave that up to Mac and Pete to decide, but we have to warn them what might be coming their way," Mary said.

"But if it is Hammond gunning for Mac because of that bitcoin deal, and a Spetsnaz team is on it now, why the hell did he screw around hiring the Canadian, South African, and the two Chinese Special Forces operators? It doesn't make any sense."

"Did you ever read the story 'The Most Dangerous Game' or see the movie?" Mary asked.

Otto shook his head. "No."

She explained it.

"He's playing a game?" Otto asked.

"Could be he's upping the stakes each time to see how Mac handles it. It's called a gambit play—or in this case, *plays*."

Otto almost laughed. "I don't think Mr. Hammond, if he's the one behind it, will like how the story turns out."

At the baccarat table, Hammond was already up three and a half million euros, most of it Metropov's at the other end of the table, and he was getting tired of the game, which was for relatively small stakes to this point.

A small crowd of well-dressed spectators had gathered, which was usual whenever big money was being wagered. They were behind velvet ropes, security officers in tuxedos keeping a close eye.

Of the original six players other than Metropov, only two other men remained at the table, whom Metropov had graciously allowed to take small pieces of each bank as it came up. Hammond had lost a couple of hands, but after each one, he'd upped the bank and had won.

"Let's make this interesting, shall we?" he said.

The Russian nodded, his expression completely neutral. The other two showed no reaction.

Hammond raised a hand for the chef de salle, who came over and leaned in close. "Monsieur?"

"I'm going to make a considerable raise."

"Your credit is unlimited here, Monsieur Hammond. The casino will accommodate you."

"Twenty million," he announced as the pit boss moved off.

No one made a sound, all eyes on the Russian.

The other two players indicated that they were out. They pushed back their chairs, picked up their plaques, and got up. But they did not leave the room.

"Monsieur?" the dealer asked politely.

"Banco," Metropov said without bothering to call the chef de salle over.

"Is the gentleman's credit good enough?" Hammond said, and this time, the crowd stirred.

Metropov nodded, his expression neutral.

The dealer dealt two cards each, Hammond drawing a five and three.

"Carte?" the dealer asked Hammond, who shook his head.

"Carte?" the dealer asked Metropov, who shook his head, the faintest of smiles at the corners of his lips.

Hammond turned over his eight. Only an eight to tie and it would be up to him to raise the bet and continue, or a nine for the loss.

Without turning over his cards, Metropov pushed back, got to his feet, and left the salle, the crowd parting for him.

"Jesus, I'd love to see the bastard's cards," Susan said as the dealer retrieved them without turning them over.

"He had a nine," Hammond said. "I was sure of it by the look on his face when he threw down his cards."

"Then why did he withdraw?"

"He sent me a message that Mikhail is waiting."

SIXTY-SEVEN

McGarvey had lain down for a couple of hours of sleep in the top-floor bedroom, the windows facing the Aegean open to a light breeze that ruffled the curtains. Pete had gone to bed with him, but she laid a hand on his shoulder and said, "Kirk."

He woke instantly and looked up at her. She was fully clothed in the dark jeans and black shirt. "What is it?"

"Otto and Mary are on the phone; they have something for us."

McGarvey sat up, and Pete handed him a cup of coffee first. He took a sip and set the cup aside, and Pete handed him the phone on speaker mode. "What have you come up with?" He looked at the clock. It was just past twelve thirty.

"There's a 72 percent connection with Hammond, just like you'd expected almost from the beginning," Otto said.

Pete sat down on the edge of the bed.

"Go ahead."

"It looks like Hammond is working for or with a Russian multibillionaire by the name of Mikhail Tarasov, who has some upper-echelon position with Gazprom, though exactly what he does for the company is not clear for now, except that he's also pals with Putin," Otto said. "Anyway, it's likely that the company wants to build a pipeline into Western Europe, France, and Belgium, for starters."

"Neither of them likely to welcome the Russians with open arms."

"Right. But Hammond has some solid financial connections in both countries, as well as with the Netherlands."

"Okay so far, but where's the connection between Hammond and the attacks on me?"

"This is the bad part. Tarasov apparently went out to visit with General Oleg Kanayev, who holds a position on the general staff that runs Russia's Special Forces."

"Spetsnaz," McGarvey said, and he knew what was coming next.

"Kanayev's son-in-law is the commanding officer of the 329th Spetsnaz Special Purpose Detachment. Six of their officers were given dishonorable discharges—we think thirty-six hours ago. Afterward, they disappeared."

"Jailed? Executed?"

"It's possible, but at this point unknown," Otto said. "They just dropped out of sight."

"They're on the way here."

"That's Lou's best guess, and I agree with her."

"So do I," Mary said. "We have a small naval support base at Souda Bay on Crete, which is home to a Greek air force base flying F-16 aircraft. If the Spetsnaz team is coming in high and slow to make a HALO drop on your position, a couple of F-16s might give them second thoughts."

"No," McGarvey said.

"For God's sake, Mac, think it out," Mary said. "We're talking six-to-one odds. And these guys will be younger than you, highly trained, and almost certainly better equipped than you are. How are you going to handle it? You have to have some strategy."

"They'll be dropping onto unknown terrain, they can't know that we'll be expecting them and that we'll be in a defensible position at their rear. And the odds are better now."

"Yes, you have your wife."

"Don't count me out; I'm not such a bad shot myself," Pete said.

"Six-to-two is still lousy," Otto said. "Mary's right."

"Clarke Bender and Alicia Sherman, the assistant SAC at the Bureau's New York office, showed up this afternoon and refused to leave."

"Bender's never even been a street cop. He's been an academic and adviser his entire career."

"But Alicia tells us that she's a Marine with two tours as a cop in Afghanistan," Pete said. "So don't count us women out."

"You're stubborn," Mary said. "I get that. But why run such a terrible risk of getting you and the others shot to death? What's the point?"

"I want to find out who's behind this and why."

"Hammond."

"Lou is a good program, but she's not given it 100 percent because everything you've come up with is circumstantial," McGarvey said. "Hammond is an asshole who holds a grudge, but he might not be a crazy asshole willing to hire people to kill me because of a deal gone bad. A deal he backed away from."

"Tell him, Otto," Mary said, frustration in her voice.

"Mac is right," Otto said. "Just don't let Bender get killed, *kemo sabe*. Kallek would be all over Taft in a New York minute."

"I tried to get rid of the man. He has a free will, and he and Sherman decided to stay."

"Nobody has a free will around you, Mac," Mary said. "Didn't you know that?"

"Including you?" McGarvey asked, and he was sorry he asked the moment it came out of his mouth.

"I married your best friend, didn't I?"

. . .

Their camos were off-the-rack black, all Spetsnaz markings removed. Their weapons were German-made Heckler & Koch and Austrian-made Glock pistols with silencers in holsters on their chests. The only papers they carried were in the standard-issue, behind-the-lines kit that identified them as Ukranian civilians and included a few thousand euros in various denominations.

Their drop bags, which they would release at less than one hundred meters, contained civilian clothes, as well as the submachine guns, suppressors, and a lot of ammunition.

Their parachutes and oxygen equipment they would need jumping around nine thousand meters were Chinese made. And the four-tube night vision goggles were from the same manufacturer that equipped the U.S. SEAL Team 6 units.

The only thing they'd not swapped out were their Spetsnaz tattoos, just below the shoulder showing an inflated parachute, beneath which was the head of a snarling tiger. They hadn't been mentioned by the colonel because the understanding was that the team had been dishonorably discharged, were working a rogue operation, and in any case, the only way the tattoos would be seen was if someone lifted the bare arms of their corpses.

Captain Borisov called Vetrov, who'd been lying back with his eyes closed like his men, forward.

"We're thirty minutes out. Are you and your people ready?"

Vetrov checked his watch; it was just one thirty local on the ground. "*Taip,*" he said in Lithuanian. *Yes.*

Darina glanced at him, her left eyebrow raising, a smirk on her lips.

"Ten minutes out, we'll all go on oxygen. Five minutes out, your team will stack up, we'll throttle back, and Darina will open the portside door. On her signal, you will jump, and make it quick. Clear?"

"Yes," Vetrov said in English. "Where will you go afterward?"

"None of your business," Darina told him.

"We're cleared direct for Cairo to refuel, then return to Sofia," Borisov said. He looked up. "Whatever it is that you mean to accomplish on the ground, I hope you are successful."

Vetrov nodded. The man was decent, unlike the bitch flying right seat. He didn't give a shit about her, he didn't think that he would even fuck her given the chance, but it was too bad that the pilot would also have to die in thirty minutes.

The men were stirring when Vetrov went aft.

"Time?" Silin asked.

"T minus thirty," Vetrov told them. "If you have to take a piss, do it now. No time for a shit. I want a final check of weapons, oxygen masks, and night vision optics, which we will wear on the way down."

No one said a thing. They knew the drill, their objective, and their orders.

Vetrov took a bottle of vodka from the locker Silin had opened, took a deep draft, and held it up in salute. "*Yeb vas. Udachi,*" he said. *Fuck your mother. Good luck.*

He handed the bottle to Silin, who took a drink and passed it to Orlov.

"This time tomorrow, each of us will be in Athens in bed with a whore," Vetrov said. "And we'll be rich bastards!"

□

SIXTY—EIGHT

In Monaco, Hammond got a bottle of Krug, and he and Susan went down to the beach, which was deserted at this hour of the morning. The chaise longues in all the cabanas had been covered. Susan held the wine and flutes as Hammond uncovered a couple of them and pulled the small table between them, and they sat down.

"It's to be tonight, then?" Susan asked. She'd been subdued ever since the baccarat salle.

"It should start around two," he said. He glanced at his watch. "In a half hour or so."

"Jesus," Susan said. "And then it'll be finally over with, right, Thomas? No matter the outcome?"

Hammond opened the bottle of wine and poured. They touched glasses and drank. "No matter what," he said.

Bender and Alicia watched from the top-floor windows facing the interior of the island as McGarvey and Pete disappeared into the darkness. The circular bedroom had floor-to-ceiling windows that opened in every direction. But the ceiling was very tall, and above them, the kerosene lantern, large Fresnel lens, and gear drive that rotated the system when the lighthouse was operational were still in place.

It seemed surreal to Bender. Everything about the situation here and now seemed odd to him. He was an FBI agent but a deskbound man. An academic. A thinker, not a field officer like Alicia. And he wondered how the hell he'd managed to talk himself into it.

"You're an ambitious man, Clarke," the director had told him the morning of his official welcoming to the Bureau.

"Yes, sir, I am," Bender told him.

"You passed Quantico, though not with any distinction. But you did pass."

"I joined the Bureau not to arrest the bad guys but to figure out what they did wrong and where to find them," Bender said. And thinking about that morning now, he realized just how cocky he must had sounded.

"Which is why we hired you," Kallek had said three years ago. "Be careful that your ambition doesn't take you in the wrong direction."

Prophetic words, he mused now. But he needed an operation like this to add to his résumé, which would look good a few years down the line when he figured he would become the assistant director of the Bureau. And then Congress.

"You okay, Mr. Bender?" Alicia asked. She was leaning against the frame of the open window, from where she could look out but still be in the shadows, all but invisible to anyone coming up the hill.

"I'm a little nervous," he said, surprised that he had made such an admission.

Alicia smiled. "You'd be a fool if you weren't," she said. "I figure my heart rate is topping a hundred."

"I guess I'm no fool."

"But you've got guts. Anyway, whoever is coming will have to get past McGarvey and his wife, and the two of them have quite a rep. I sure as hell wouldn't want to draw down against either of them."

"The man is fifty. And everybody loses their edge sooner or later, even the best of them."

"And he goes down to the Farm every four or five months to keep his edge, and from what I've been told, the kids and the instructors have a lot of respect for him."

"Has he done Quantico?"

"A couple of years ago, and he passed with flying colors. I had a talk with Ed Ames when I found out we were going to have a chat with McGarvey. He said he was willing to offer the man the job of running the place, but he was too intimidated to pop the question. Ed's a tough guy and isn't easily intimidated."

"Everyone makes a mistake sooner or later. The odds sometimes get too big."

"Not this time," Alicia said. "My money's on them." She nodded in the direction Mac and Pete had gone.

At his apartment in Moscow, it was coming up on four in the morning, and Tarasov was in bed with his mistress, Larissa Kiselnikova, the former Bolshoi prima ballerina whose feet were so ugly, he kidded her from time to time that it was a wonder he loved her.

"But it's your crooked nose, Mika, that makes me ashamed to introduce you to my friends."

They'd been out dancing at the Pravda Club, one of Moscow's top spots, until just an hour ago, when they'd returned here, dismissed the chief of the house staff, took a shower together, and made love.

Larissa was half-asleep lying next to him, one bare breast exposed, when his encrypted sat phone chimed. It was Yuri Sepelev, his computer geek contact in the GRU.

"The EUTELSAT bird covering block thirteen will go dark in T minus five once I get the signal from the ground."

EUTELSAT was the European Telecommunications Satellite Organization, which administered all the communications satellites used by the forty-nine member states. Thirteen was the main bird that serviced Greece and its Aegean Islands, including Serifos.

"Nothing must be traced back to us."

"I know my job, sir," Sepelev said.

He was just a kid barely out of his teens, but he was highly respected in the Russian intelligence community, and like most junior officers, his pay was terrible. Since he'd began doing favors for Tarasov, he'd been able to move to a nicer apartment and buy a BMW and all the computer toys he'd ever dreamed of.

"You should be getting the call within the next quarter hour at the latest. Let me know when it's done."

"Their techs will be all over it within minutes."

"How long will we have until they fix the problem or bring up another satellite?"

"That's just it. They won't be able to pinpoint the problem, let alone fix it, and when they try to switch to another bird, my program will follow them."

"Very good," Tarasov said.

"But you must understand that nothing lasts forever. I'll want word the moment I can withdraw."

"It shouldn't be long."

"How long?"

"An hour, tops," Tarasov said. "If it took longer than that, it would mean that the team had failed."

"I can manage that," Sepelev said. "The remainder of my fee will be paid into my account the moment the bird comes back online."

"Da," Tarasov said, but the phone was dead.

Vetrov and his team got up on signal at 0155 and stacked up in the aisle aft of the portside hatch.

He phoned the contact number stored in the sat phone he'd been given on base. It was answered by a man.

"Da."

"We're five minutes out from the drop site."

"Udachi," the man said, and the connection went dead.

SIXTY-NINE

It was just before two when McGarvey and Pete got to the bottom of the saddle three hundred yards from the dark lighthouse above their position, and about the same distance in the opposite direction to the nearest buildings, on which no lights were showing.

The scrub brush was thick here, but the rocks were mostly too small to offer any protection, though as long as they kept low, they wouldn't be visible even with night vision goggles.

"It's beautiful at this time of the night," Pete said softly.

The lights in town across the bay came mostly from the hotels and the commercial docks on the other side of the inlet. The moonless evening sky up here was dark enough to see the stars and even some of the pale Milky Way.

"Yes, it is," McGarvey said.

"Good for stargazing, but I wouldn't want to have a picnic here."

McGarvey's phone vibrated, but it had switched automatically from satellite to cell tower mode.

"EUTELSAT's thirteen just went off-line," Otto said.

"It's started," McGarvey said.

"Yes, and Lou's best guess is that it's the work of a hacker in the GRU. They've got some pretty good people over there, same unit that hacked into the presidential elections in '16 and again in '20."

Mac looked up at the sky, searching for a small star or strobe light that was moving. "How long will it stay down until the system is cleared?"

"Within twenty minutes, I'd suspect. But if the Russians are half as good as I think they are, they'll infect the backup bird when the techs try to bring it up. And there'll be no real urgency because the traffic is very light at this time of the morning. So I'd say that they've bought themselves an hour, tops."

"Can they take the cell tower down on this side of the island?"

"There's only the one west of you at nineteen hundred feet, the island's highest elevation," Otto said. "And yes, if they have the right equipment, they can block its signals indefinitely."

"We're ready," McGarvey said, and he thought he spotted something very high up and to the south. "Stand by."

"What is it?" Pete asked.

"South, about twenty degrees below overhead. A thin line moving across the stars."

After a couple of moments, Pete spotted it. "There," she said. "But what is it? A cloud?"

"In a manner of speaking," McGarvey said. "It's the contrail of a high-flying jet."

"Hold on a mo," Otto said.

"Is it them?" Pete asked.

"Otto's checking."

"Nothing is scheduled from that—" Otto said, but was cut off in mid-sentence.

"The cell tower just went down," McGarvey said.

"We can't warn Bender or Alicia."

"They'll figure it out," McGarvey said. He unslung the MP7 from his shoulder and fired a short burst into the sky.

"Jesus, it's started just like he predicted it would," Bender said, going over to where Alicia stood at the open window.

She held up a hand. "Wait."

"Maybe we should go out there; they might need help."

"Shut the fuck up, sir."

The night was deathly still—no other noise, no other gunshots.

"What is it?"

"That was the other room broom," Alicia said. "But there was no return fire. McGarvey just warned us that the fur ball is about to go down." She glanced at Bender. "Just take it easy, okay? I don't want you shooting your own foot, and I especially don't want to be shot in the back."

He was looking past her out the window toward the bottom of the depression. "But how the hell will we be able to tell who it is if someone comes up here? I mean, it could be McGarvey or his wife."

"When they're close enough for us to shoot, they'll be close enough for us to recognize them," Alicia said. "Stay cool, because it'll be a while before anyone gets this far. Try to reach them on your sat phone."

Bender holstered his Glock 19M and tried his sat phone. "No signal," he said, looking up.

Alicia laid the room broom McGarvey had given her aside and tried her cell phone, but she had no signal either. "Whoever is coming is well equipped enough to take out the satellite as well as the island's cell phone tower. It means they know what they're doing, and they'll be well armed."

"Better than we are," Bender said.

The one round in the chamber and the four standard-issue 15-round magazines they carried gave them sixty-one pistol shots each, plus the half-dozen 40-round mags for the room broom Mac had left for them, for an additional 240 rounds.

"But we have the high ground, and they won't know that we're here," Alicia told him. What she left unsaid was that if whoever was coming managed to get past McGarvey and Pete, then this could end up as another Little Bighorn.

Vetrov and his five operators checked each other's equipment, especially the parachutes, then they and the pilot and copilot went on oxygen.

"Drop in two minutes," Borisov called from the cockpit.

Darina came back. "Are you ready?" she asked.

Vetrov gave the thumbs-up.

"I'll be glad to get rid of you bastards," she said. She undogged the hatch, but before she could pull it in and to the right, Vetrov took out his pistol and shot her in the head at point-blank range.

The noise was soft but loud enough for the pilot to hear it and understand what was happening. He was reaching for a pistol in a compartment beside his left leg when Vetrov came forward and shot him in the back of the head.

"Hatch," he spoke into his lapel mic, and almost immediately, the inside of the aircraft was hit with near tornado-force swirling winds, the temperature dropping to nearly below zero almost immediately.

He found the fuel dump switch, guarded by a red cover, and switched it, and by the time he got back to the open hatch, the plane had already began to climb because of the decreasing weight.

"*Teper, teper, teper!*" he shouted. *Now, now, now!* He stepped out of the aircraft, the wind slamming into his body like he'd hit a brick wall.

He immediately stabilized his altitude, head down, body angled forward, arms to either side for steering, and he began the long drop from ninety-five hundred meters to less than four hundred before he would open his chute. At forty meters, he would release his equipment bag, letting it fall five meters on its lanyard.

He checked his helmet's small rearview mirror to make sure that his crew was stacked up directly on his six, everyone's chute in good order.

The island, laid out like something from a virtual reality game, was exactly like the images they had studied over the past thirty-six hours while they were in transit. The harbor town of Livadi well off to the southeast to the right of his glide path was where it was supposed to be.

He angled slightly left, which would bring him across the bay and put him on the ground at fifty meters below the lighthouse. His operators would assemble at his landing site, and within ninety seconds they would have stuffed their parachutes in one large plastic bag, taken out their submachine guns, switched on their night vision goggles, and started up the hill.

They knew the drill, and they had their orders, so none would have to be given verbally. They were stealth fighters, and Vetrov was proud of what they were capable of.

□

SEVENTY

"Pick a bush and curl up next to it with your eyes skyward, your pistol in hand," McGarvey said.

Pete was momentarily confused. "What?"

"Get down and roll up in a ball. If they jumped out around thirty thousand feet, it'll take them three minutes of free fall before they open their chutes, and the clock has already started. They'll be equipped with night vision goggles, but at any distance, the resolution won't be good enough to tell us from scrub brush."

"I got it, but I hope they haven't figured it out, too," Pete said.

"They'll be watching the lighthouse, and we should be behind them if they're accurate with their landing."

"If these guys are Spetsnaz, they'll be just about as good as our SEAL Team 6 operators, and they should nail it."

"I'm counting on it," McGarvey said. "Now get on the ground and make like a bush."

Pete pulled out her Glock, lay down on her left side next to a bush, and pulled her knees up to her chest, putting her in a position so that her gun hand was free and she could look up at the sky as well as see McGarvey curled up a few feet away.

"This okay?" she asked.

"Fine. But don't open fire until I do, and don't waste ammunition shooting blind. Pick your target, and make sure he goes down. There's bound to be six or more of them, and I want to even the odds as fast as possible before they turn around and start shooting back."

"By then, with any luck, Bender and Alicia should start, catching whoever's coming in a cross fire."

"With any luck," McGarvey said. "Keep frosty, wife."

"You, too, husband."

Alicia had found a pair of Steiner mil spec binoculars hanging on a peg just within the doorway to the bedroom, and she laid her room broom aside and got them. First, she scanned the ground that sloped gently down to a narrow little valley where McGarvey said he and Pete would position themselves.

But making several slow sweeps where she thought they might be, she couldn't make them out. Either they had moved somewhere else or they were damned good at finding hiding spots.

"What do you see?" Bender asked. He was nervous.

"Nothing yet," Alicia said, and she looked skyward toward the north in the direction McGarvey figured the jumpers would be coming from. But if they'd made a HALO jump and were already in the air, they would be moving above 150 miles per hour. They would be dressed in black and would be nearly impossible to spot.

She laid the binoculars aside and picked up the submachine gun.

"Still nothing?" Bender asked.

"Nothing," Alicia said. Earlier, her nerves had been jumping, but now that she knew an attack was imminent, she'd calmed down, her heart rate barely above sixty. It had been the same for her in the Marines. As soon as a firefight started, she'd gotten steady, almost completely forgetting any fears she would normally have, a slight smile on her lips.

She was ready now. Her only real concern was for Bender.

The unwinding altimeter on Vetrov's wrist showed they were coming up on the three-thousand-meter mark, at which point, it was time to discard their oxygen masks. So far, his face had been covered by the mask, a Kevlar helmet on his head, so he had no real sensation of falling through the air. It was more like floating.

"Stage one," he said into his lapel mic, which was the signal to discard the German-made masks. He took his off and let it fall free to his right; it tumbled end over end away from him. The nearly two-hundred-kilometer-per-hour hurricane directly on his face was strong enough to curl his lips back and send ripples across his cheeks.

He looked again at his altimeter as he passed the two-thousand-meter mark, and he began to smell things. The salt air, perhaps, a hint of wood smoke or perhaps charcoal, maybe a baker using a wood-fired oven, baking bread for his morning customers who would be up and about in a few hours.

All of it was almost unreal, but he'd done these sorts of night jumps so often this one seemed almost routine, except that in a few more minutes, he and his people would be going into battle. And he found that he was looking forward to it, because afterward, he would be able to send for his wife, and they could settle down somewhere with more money than they ever dreamed was possible.

On the ground, McGarvey checked his watch. Pete was about twenty feet to his right, still curled up in a ball, facing him, her eyes bright even in the darkness. "You okay?" he asked, keeping his voice low.

"Just peachy. How about you?"

"They should be opening their chutes in under a minute. Safety off."

"Are we going to shoot before they land?"

"No. They'll be pistols ready as soon as they release their equipment bags, and they'll have the high ground. But once they touch down, they'll be busy for the first sixty seconds or so getting free of their chutes and gearing up. We shoot then."

"In the back?"

"Yes."

"It's a tough world," Pete said.

"We didn't make it so," McGarvey said. "And if I'd had my way from the beginning, I would never have drawn my gun except on a firing range."

"Stage two," Vetrov said into his mic as his altimeter wound down past one thousand meters. He pulled his rip cord, the hang gliding chute deployed with a nearly noiseless burp, and his speed almost instantly dropped to less than thirty-five kilometers per hour.

He put on his night vision optics. Their objective showed up about two klicks almost due south. It showed no lights. McGarvey and his wife were sound asleep in their bed. And by the time they realized that they had come under attack, it would be far too late.

Using the parachute's toggles left and right, he adjusted his glide path to set down about fifty meters from the lighthouse.

When he was sure his angle was correct, he scoped the ground from directly below him and slowly on a broad path all the way to the top of the hill. But there was nothing to be seen except scrub brush.

At forty meters, he radioed, "Stage three," released his equipment bag, and took his pistol from its holster strapped to his chest.

"There," McGarvey said, and he counted six equipment bags dropping from the operators.

"I see them," Pete said.

"Wait until I open fire."

"Will do."

At the lighthouse, Alicia spotted the parachutes, and she grabbed the binoculars and watched as the equipment bags dropped.

"I count six," she said.

"Jesus," Bender said. "Let's just get this shit over with and go home."

"Amen," Alicia said.

□

SEVENTY-ONE

Vetrov hit hard, his left foot twisting on a rock, a sharp pain stabbing his ankle, but he went with the momentum, rolling to the right, his pistol out and ready to fire.

He was up in an instant, and keeping low, he brought his parachute in hand over hand while scanning for any opposition and looking to his troopers. There were only three of them about ten meters back—Silin, Orlov, and Petrin, also busy with their chutes.

"Vasili, Eduard, copy?" Vetrov radioed.

"We hit a gust and landed short," Vasili Anosov came back.

"What about Eduard?"

"Here," Nikolayev came back. "I'm about twenty meters behind Vasili."

"Get squared away and get your asses up here on the double. We're going in," Vetrov radioed. Spreads like this drop weren't uncommon, but just now, it was more bothersome to him for some reason.

Nikolayev had the big plastic bag, so Vetrov and the other three merely bundled their chutes, gathered the shrouds, and tied them around the nylon so the fabric wouldn't be blown around on the light wind. Anything that large moving around down here would be a dead giveaway of their positions.

By the numbers as if in a carefully choreographed dance, they opened their equipment bags, extracted the MP7s, pocketed five of the six magazines they'd brought, and loaded the sixth into the weapons, jacking a round into the firing chamber.

They wore their civilian clothes beneath their black ODUs, their fake passports and other creds, plus a few thousand euros, in flat packs strapped to their chests.

The pain from Vetrov's foot radiated all the way up to his hip now, and each step he took was agony. But he was still mobile, which meant nothing important was broken.

Alicia was looking through the binoculars. "I count four of them," she said. The laser range finder showed them fifty-one meters downslope. They'd bundled their parachutes and had taken things out of their drop bags that she couldn't quite recognize, but she was almost certain they were weapons, until one of them turned in profile and she made out the same room broom that was lying close at hand on the low table beside the window.

"I thought you counted six parachutes," Bender said.

"I did."

"Where the hell are the other two?"

Alicia panned downslope until she picked out the fifth man bent over what was probably his drop bag on the ground, but not the sixth.

McGarvey motioned for Pete to keep quiet and stay down. He was too far away and it was too dark for him to know the exact number of jumpers who had landed upslope from their positions, but he could clearly see one man clad in black less than ten feet away downslope.

He and Pete had been bracketed, which could mean that they had been spotted from the air. But by the way the lone operator had gathered his parachute, McGarvey didn't think that was the case.

McGarvey laid his room broom on the ground and took out his SOG SEAL Ka-Bar strapped on his chest outside his shirt.

Pete was watching him wide-eyed, and he motioned again for her to stay down and make no noise.

The operator was just loading his MP7 and jacking a round into the firing chamber when McGarvey got up. Keeping low, he raced down to him, making as little noise as possible.

At the last instant, the Russian, sensing something, turned around, bringing his weapon to bear, but McGarvey batted it aside with his left hand as he closed in.

Anosov fired a short burst into the air, and at the same moment, McGarvey thrust the knife into the man's left side beneath his ribs, cutting the man's heart nearly in two. The Russian opened his mouth, trying to say something, but then fired off another burst from the silenced weapon as his legs gave way and he started to collapse.

"Incoming!" Pete cried urgently from behind him.

McGarvey grabbed the Russian's body, the knife still in his chest, and held it up as a shield as the second Russian approached in a dead run while firing his MP7, the rounds slamming into his fellow operator's back.

Stepping to one side, Mac shoved the body forward, then ducked low as Nikolayev continued driving forward, his momentum making it impossible to pull up short.

"*Sukin syn!*"—*Son of a bitch!*—the Russian grunted, trying to bring his weapon around as he crashed into Anosov's body.

McGarvey grabbed the submachine gun out of the man's hands, stepped back, and jammed the muzzle of the silencer into the back of the Russian's head.

"*Ostanovites', i vy budete zhit',*" McGarvey said. *Stop and you'll live.*

Nikolayev's eyes widened as he moved his head to the left, pulled a pistol with a large silencer on the end of the barrel from his holster, and fired. At the same instant, McGarvey pulled off a short burst, taking almost the entire side of the man's head, two rounds spiraling out the back of his skull.

"You're hit," Pete said at McGarvey's side.

McGarvey hadn't felt a thing. He looked down and felt at the ragged hole in the left leg of his jeans several inches below his knee. The round had hit his prosthetic leg but had done no real damage.

"I'll be goddamned," Pete said.

"Get down now," McGarvey told her, and he dropped to the ground, pulling her with him.

"What the hell?"

"These two were mis-drops; there're more up toward the lighthouse," McGarvey said. "And right about now, their mission CO is wondering what the hell happened to his people unless one of these guys told him." He showed Pete the lapel mic on the Russian's night camos. "I want him to keep wondering how many of us there are. Hopefully, he'll do something stupid and come down here to find out what happened."

"Doesn't sound so stupid to me," Pete said.

Alicia had watched everything through the binoculars, and when McGarvey and Pete dropped to the ground, she switched to the four operators farther up the hill. They had dropped into defensive positions, their attention downslope.

"Mac took down both operators who'd dropped behind him and Pete," she said. "The other four have taken an interest."

"What are they doing?" Bender asked.

"I think they're trying to decide exactly what they should do."

"What do you mean?"

"They have to know or at least suspect that two of their people are down, and they might be thinking about taking care of the threat below them before coming up here. But I'll bet that they're surprised in a nasty way."

"Let me see," Bender said. He pushed her aside, took the binoculars, and stepped to the open window.

"I'd watch what you're doing; you're in plain sight," Alicia warned.

"Vasili, report," Vetrov radioed. There was no answer. "Eduard, report." Again, his earbud remained silent.

"Someone is in the top-floor window of the lighthouse," Silin said.

"Do you have a clear shot?" Vetrov asked without turning.

"Da."

"Take them down."

Silin fired two long bursts, bracketing the open window, and the figure disappeared. "Done," he said. His weapon was dry, and he switched mags. "What next?"

"Down the hill to deal with whoever took Vasili and Eduard out," Vetrov said.

"McGarvey?"

"I don't know."

"Then who was in the window?"

"We'll find out later. For now, we're splitting—two left, two right," Vetrov said. "Move."

SEVENTY-TWO

McGarvey was hunched over the Russian with the knife in his chest, taking the room broom and four spare mags from the body. "They know someone is down here, and they're going to try to flank us," McGarvey said.

Pete hunched low and, moving fast, came over to him. "What's our play?"

He gave her the submachine gun and mags. "We're going up the middle, and when we get in range, we're going to make a lot of noise, so get rid of the suppressor and make ready to fire at anything that moves."

Pete stuffed the Glock in the waistband of her jeans and unscrewed the suppressor as Mac took the radio unit from the body, placed the earbud in his right ear, clipped the mic to the lapel of his black polo shirt, and pocketed the cell phone–size unit.

He took the night vision goggles from the body and handed them to Pete, then moved to the other Russian, took the night vision goggles and put them on his head, and lowered the eyepiece. Instantly, the night lit up green.

"Incoming, maybe fifty or sixty yards off to the left," Pete said softly.

McGarvey turned in that direction, and after a moment's search, he picked out two figures about fifty yards out hunched over but coming fast. It took him only a second or two to see another pair off to the right, maybe five or ten yards farther up the hill, but keeping low and moving fast like the pair to the left.

"If we can see them, they can see us," McGarvey said. "So stay flat, and let them come to us."

"They'll flank us just like they want to."

"That's right, and they're going to learn a lesson in just a few minutes: Be careful what you wish for—it just might bite you in the ass."

"Jesus," Pete said softly, scrunching down on her stomach as low as she could get.

"Lay out your spare magazines where you can easily reach them," McGarvey said. "Take the nearest pair on the left, and no matter what happens, just keep shooting. I'll take right."

McGarvey laid out two of his spare mags, with two more in his waistband.

"When you change out mags, give the new one a sharp rap on the side of the handle before you reload in case it picked up some dirt," McGarvey told her. His only worry now was for Pete.

"I've been through the Farm three times, and I know how to shoot, you chauvinist pig."

McGarvey couldn't help but smile. "Yes, dear," he said.

Bender had taken three hits to the chest. Alicia had raced to the bathroom for a towel to try to stanch the bleeding although she'd known it would be futile, but she had to try. He was a pompous ass, but a good man who believed in the Bureau's mission.

He'd died while she was holding the towel, and she sat back. "Shit," she said softly.

She wiped the blood from her hands, got the binoculars from where he'd dropped them, and eased back to the open window for a quick look, presenting little or nothing of herself to shoot at.

At first, she couldn't find the four black-clad operators where she'd last seen them. She panned slowly up the hill, but finding nothing, panned back down the hill.

They were about thirty or forty yards down from their landing spot and moving fast. But they'd split up into two pairs, one left and the other right. They were trying to flank McGarvey and his wife.

She looked back at Bender's body. There was nothing she could do here now.

Tossing the binoculars on the bed, she took up the room broom, stuffed a couple of spare mags in the waistband of her slacks, and headed downstairs in a dead run.

She'd counted four operators who'd landed just minutes ago, and she had scoped the same four running down the hill. No one was left between them and the lighthouse. If she was fast enough before they took the McGarveys out, she might be able to help.

Downstairs, she burst out the door, took the broad steps to the driveway, and then started down the hill, her feet barely touching the ground.

Both pairs of oncoming Russians opened fire at the same time, about twenty yards out, kicking up dirt and rocks left and right, closing on Pete's position but farther away from where Mac was lying.

He brought his room broom around to the pair on the left, and firing measured bursts took one of them down. Before he could switch aim, he was bracketed by incoming rounds, and he had to keep his head down.

The firing stopped.

"Pete, are you okay?" Mac said.

"I'm hit."

"How bad?"

"In the shoulder, and it hurts like hell, but I'll live."

"Stand by," McGarvey said. He keyed the lapel mic. "Unit leader, do you copy?"

No one answered.

"Two of your people are dead. We have their weapons, and I'm speaking on one of your coms sets. In addition, we have backup at the lighthouse covering your six."

Still there was no answer.

McGarvey raised his head a couple of inches just high enough so that he could see up the hill. The operators had hit the ground and were no longer in sight. For a second, he thought they might be withdrawing, but then he saw a figure racing down the hill from the lighthouse and closing in on the Spetsnaz position.

Even at the distance, he knew that it was Alicia Sherman, and she was carrying a room broom at the ready.

"Retreat! Retreat!" he shouted.

The black-clad operators down the hill had disappeared, and Alicia was certain that it was McGarvey who'd shouted, "Retreat!" She pulled up short and started to hunch down when a figure rose up just a couple of feet to the left.

She started to bring the submachine gun to bear on him when he was on her, batting the muzzle of her weapon to the side while jamming the muzzle of his room broom against the side of her head with his other hand so hard it drew blood.

She let the gun fall from her hand and collapsed on the rocky ground on her right side as if she had been knocked out. Her right hand, beneath her, was on the handle of the pistol in her waistband.

McGarvey had watched it all. He raised his room broom up just high enough so that the operator who'd taken Alicia down was in his sights.

"Ilich!" a man to Mac's right shouted.

McGarvey fired a short burst, catching Ilich in the side, and the man went down hard.

One of the remaining Russians on the right opened fire, dirt and rocks flying up within inches of McGarvey's head as he buried himself facedown in the dirt.

"*Sesfir!*"—*Cease fire!*—one of the operators shouted, and the shooting stopped.

☐

SEVENTY-THREE

"Sherman, are you okay?" McGarvey shouted.

"I'm good," she called, but her voice sounded distorted.

"Leaves only yourself and one other operator," McGarvey said into the lapel mic. "The odds have changed."

The earbud was silent.

McGarvey raised his head a few inches and scoped the rise ahead, but nothing was visible. The Russians hadn't retreated; they were just keeping low. "Dawn will be in a couple of hours. We can wait until then."

Still there was no answer.

"The EUTELSAT won't be down forever. Maybe another half hour or so, and then you'll be screwed."

"What do you propose?" a man speaking broken English came back in Mac's earbud.

"You have an exfiltration plan; leave the field now and go home."

"How do I know you won't shoot when I retreat?"

"You don't," McGarvey said. But something about what the man said and his tone didn't sit right.

"Then what are my alternatives?"

McGarvey suddenly knew. The man had said: *When* I retreat. *Then what are my alternatives?* He was stalling for time.

"Sherman, incoming!"

Alicia rolled over, bringing her Glock up, when one of the black-clad operators rose up just a few inches directly behind her and pointed the room broom at her head.

"Nyet," he said softly.

Sherman tensed, ready to bring her gun hand around and take the shot anyway, but the Spetsnaz operator shook his head.

After a couple of seconds, she relaxed. Very carefully, she lowered the pistol to the ground and pulled her hand back. "Do you understand English?"

"A little," the Russian said.

"I have no other weapons," she said, and she spread her hands. "I am surrendering. Do you understand?"

"Yes."

"I'm going to get to my feet now," she said, and before he could do anything, she slowly got to her feet, careful to keep her outstretched hands in plain sight.

The Russian said something into his lapel mic.

"I'm giving up!" she shouted toward where she figured the other Russians were positioned. "My name is Alicia Sherman; I am the assistant special agent in charge of the Federal Bureau of Investigation's office in New York City. I want to speak with your squad leader."

No one answered.

Without glancing back at the Russian on the ground behind, and keeping her hands out, she started across the open ground.

Vetrov was in a position now that he'd never been in before. For the most part, gun battles were fairly easy affairs and usually only lasted a few minutes. But watching the woman approach, he had to admire her guts, and yet she was a part of the opposition force, and his inclination was to simply shoot her.

"Come no farther!" he shouted. The woman was fifteen yards out.

She kept coming, her pace slow but even.

"Stop, or we will be forced to shoot you!" Vetrov shouted.

"You should have had the man who's hiding back there in the dirt do it when he snuck up on me in the dark like a coward."

"Have you got a good sight line on where she was?" McGarvey asked, keeping his voice low.

"Yes," Pete said.

"Keep on it. Anyone shows his head, don't hesitate—just take the shot, and keep shooting even if he goes down."

"What about you?"

"I'm going to finish it," McGarvey said. Staying close to the ground, he scrambled up toward the operator he'd been talking to.

"Why'd I think he was going to say something like that?" Pete said to herself as Mac left.

Alicia stopped about halfway between where she'd been ambushed and where she thought the operator who'd given her orders had to be. Maybe twenty yards out.

"I'd say shit or get off the pot!" she shouted.

She could almost feel the laser gun sights on her back and chest.

It seemed like forever to her, the night silent except for her own breathing. The side of her head where she been hit with the buttstock was on fire and already swollen, and yet, although she was afraid for her life, she'd put that in a separate compartment. Now it was between the operator behind her and the one in front, and McGarvey and Pete down the hill.

Coming out to provide a distraction had been her only remaining option to help.

"Well, you sons of bitches!" she shouted. "What's it to be?"

"*Nyet!*" the Russian ahead of her shouted.

Alicia dropped to the ground and covered her head with both arms. "Your turn, guys," she said softly.

The Russian behind Alicia popped up, his figure perfectly showing in Pete's night vision optics.

He started to raise his weapon, and Pete fired, missing with the first rounds to the right, but walking them left and hitting him center mass with at least three rounds, sending him backward.

She continued firing until her room broom went dry. Ejecting the spent mag, she picked up a spare, knocked it against the weapons handle, rammed it home, cycled a round into the chamber, and brought it up.

There was nothing moving, nothing left to shoot at. And after the terrific noise of the unsilenced weapon in her hands, the night was suddenly silent again, except maybe for a police siren from down across the bay.

The Russian had raised up a few inches, his room broom pointed to where Alicia had dropped.

McGarvey rose up and touched the back of the man's head with his room broom's muzzle. "Nice and easy now," he said.

Vetrov lay perfectly still.

"Despite everything, I don't want to kill you. All I want are answers."

"Mr. McGarvey, I presume?"

"Yes. You?"

"Senior Lieutenant Boris Vetrov."

"Spetsnaz?"

"The 329th."

"I've heard of your unit," McGarvey said. "But frankly, I'm surprised that you and your operators chose a dishonorable discharge and some money to take on a job like this. Who hired you?"

"I won't say."

"Won't or can't?"

"I'm not going to sit out the rest of my life in an American prison somewhere," Vetrov said.

"And I'm not going to let you walk away," McGarvey said. "We're clear up here," he called.

"You okay?" Pete shouted back.

"Yes. Alicia, how about Bender?"

"He's dead," Alicia said.

"Did you bring any restraints?"

"Flex-cuffs."

"Bring them up," McGarvey told her.

"I'm not going to let myself be taken to jail," Vetrov said. "I'll kill anyone who tries. The chance will come somewhere in transit, and I'll take it. You must understand."

"You're well trained, and you'll be treated with respect, but it won't be local cops. Who knows? Maybe we'll even trade you for someone the GRU is holding."

"So my only real chance is right now," Vetrov said. He rolled over all of a sudden, a silenced Glock pistol in his left hand.

"I guess I can't blame you," McGarvey said, and he pulled the trigger, emptying the entire forty-round magazine of 4.6×30mm rounds into the man's chest, neck, and head.

"Too bad," he said half to himself as Pete and Alicia both came running. "But it's late, and I'm tired of people gunning for me and my people, and I just didn't feel like seeing what you could do in hand-to-hand. So, fuck you, comrade."

EPILOGUE

As Dr. Franklin explained it ten days later, McGarvey's below-the-knee plastic leg was headed for the trash bin, which would effectively put him out of commission for six to eight weeks.

"After what you've been through, you need some time off, though it won't be much of a vacation," the doctor said at a meeting at All Saints. "In any event, you should retire, go back to Sarasota, and take up teaching again."

McGarvey was seated across from Franklin in the third-floor waiting room, the only space in the hospital large enough to accommodate him, plus Pete, Otto, and Mary, who'd insisted they be present for the pre-op pep talk, as Pete called it.

"Good luck with that," Mary said.

"Amen," Otto agreed.

Pete was holding her husband's hand. "We got the gist of what you want to do, but why the long recovery period?" she asked.

"He's going to have to learn to walk all over again before he can get back to running around the world shooting at people."

"Only people who shoot at me first," McGarvey said.

"Don't be a curmudgeon," Pete said. "Go on, Doctor."

"We're making him a new leg—actually, with technology that Otto suggested. The bone structure, for want of a better term, will be made of titanium, over which we'll attach bundles of carbon fiber interlaced with near microscopic strands of a gold-carbon fiber material that conduct electricity. The bundles will be shaped to mimic the natural muscles of a leg, ankle, and foot and will be grafted to the nerve endings in the stump of Mac's real limb."

"What's the catch?" McGarvey asked.

"You'll think, bend your knee, but it'll take some practice—a lot of practice—before your new leg will understand what's being transmitted to it. When the carbon fiber bundles get educated, and the command comes down the pike, the bundles will contract, and your leg will bend. But that'll be the easy part. Learning to walk, to run, to crouch down and then jump, to climb a ladder, to swim, and do every other movement that we pretty much take for granted after the age of two will have to be relearned."

"When do we start?" McGarvey asked. He wanted to get it over with so he could finish what had been started in Georgetown.

"MIT is sending down your leg sometime next week, and we'll have to run a series of tests before the actual operation. Say ten days from now?"

"Good," McGarvey said.

Franklin got up, shook their hands, and left.

Pete got up, too, but McGarvey didn't move, and she sat back down. "What?" she asked.

"It's not over."

"They were Spetsnaz, and they lost," Pete said. "Bender's funeral was three days ago, and Alicia was reprimanded but given the Bureau's Medal for Meritorious Service—their second highest."

"General Kanayev retired, and his son-in-law committed suicide," Otto said. "Case closed, and you're getting a new leg."

"Thanks to you," McGarvey said.

Mary had been watching him. "But it's not closed, is it?" she said.

"Hammond."

"No chain of evidence actually connecting him with anything," Otto said. "I'll find it."

Pete was exasperated. "For Christ's sake, darling, give it up," she said. "We won, they lost. Period, end of statement."

"We lost Serifos. ETII"—the Greek national intelligence service—"convinced the government to seize the lighthouse and ban us from ever returning."

"We'll get another island," Pete said. "Anyway, they paid us the fair market value."

"Small potatoes," Otto said quietly. "All that shit is superfluous. The main thing is the leak here in the States. The White House, the Pentagon, somewhere."

"They won't stop until I find them," McGarvey said.

"We find them," Pete said. "All of us."